A *LESS THAN ZERO* ROCKSTAR ROMANCE
ENDLESS
KAYLENE WINTER

I0757701

A *LESS THAN ZERO* ROCKSTAR ROMANCE

ENDLESS

KAYLENE WINTER

Sensitivity Statement

READERS,

THE LESS THAN ZERO series dives into the highs and lows of rock-star life, inspired by the raw and real experiences of many in the music world. Across these stories, some characters face challenging themes, including abuse, sexual assault, mental health, fertility, and struggles with addiction. These topics are not universal to every character but are woven into the journeys of a few, which impact the entirety of the series.

At its heart, though, this series is about love—how it grows, heals, and transforms. Each couple's story ultimately leads to a well-deserved happily ever after, filled with passion, hope, and redemption. The band's journey supporting each other as "band brothers" also is a predominant theme throughout.

Please take a moment to reflect on your comfort with these themes before reading, and know that these stories are told with care and respect, sensitivity readers have vetted each one. Thank you for joining me on this emotional journey through love, life, and music.

With all my love,

Kaylene

Prologue

I BURROW INTO MY delicious rocker's side and breathe in his manly scent, a mix of leather and grapefruit body wash. I reach up to carefully brush a long, chocolate-brown wave from Tyson's full lips while he sleeps deeply.

His long, silky hair cascades over the pillow; his square jaw is covered with the beginnings of a beard because he hasn't shaved in a few days. It makes my sweet rocker look slightly dangerous.

Gazing at the three small scars nearly hidden in his thick, dark eyebrows, I still can't fathom how tough his childhood was and how anyone could hurt such a beautiful soul.

My breath hitches. I try to memorize everything about him, to soak in every detail of my gorgeous man because I know I'm about to hurt him.

Which *destroys* me.

When I trace my finger over a smattering of his rough stubble, he sighs in his sleep and pulls me in even closer. I hold him tightly too. Rest my head on his lithe but defined chest. Grip his hip, careful not to rouse him.

I wish I could gaze into the pools of his deep-blue eyes one more time.

If only I didn't have to leave him.

But, I do. I'm moving to Bellingham to embark upon my new normal. Living with a roommate in a dorm so I can work toward my college degree in social services.

Ty's leaving too. His band departs for their first tour in a few hours. He'll be traveling cross-country in a small van for six months. It'll be grueling enough for him to spend long hours in such cramped quarters without the added weight of heartbreak.

The least I can do is let him get some sleep now.

So I lay for as long as I can against my love and listen to his heartbeat. My mind is a hamster wheel. Second-guessing. Third-guessing. Then—resolved.

I've been asked by possibly the most influential person in his life to do something for Ty. As much as I don't want to, they convinced me breaking things off now is the right thing for Ty's future.

But it doesn't make it any less devastating.

When my tears wet his chest, I know it's time to go or I'll wake him. He'll try to talk me out of what needs to be done.

So, while my heart seizes in agony at the thought of never seeing him again, it's time for me to go.

Even if I'm not sure how I'll survive.

I have to set him completely free, without any ties to me, so he can embrace his shot at fame.

Maybe someday Ty will understand why I left him.

Maybe someday he'll forgive me.

Chapter One

Five Months Previous

C'MON!" ALEX PLEADS WITH me. "We're going to be late!"

"I can't help it if I need extra time, you look amazing in a paper sack," I whine to my best friend since diaper-hood.

My family moved neighborhoods from where she lives in Ballard to Wallingford when I was eight. It didn't matter. Alex and I still spend time together most weekends and nearly every day during the summer. Our houses are close enough that we retain our sisterly bond, which is still so tight we can finish each other's sentences.

With only a few weeks to go until graduation from our respective high schools, we obsess over music and boys, sometimes not in that order.

Which means on a Saturday night, as per usual, we get ready at my house before we go out for the evening.

"You look gorgeous, you always do." Alex surveys my outfit, her hands on her hips.

Tall and thin with supermodel beauty, my BFF looks fantastic in her simple getup of a black, V-neck fitted T-shirt, baggy boyfriend jeans with a beat-up brown belt, hoop earrings, a distressed, black motorcycle jacket, and black Frye boots. Her blonde hair is styled with fringy bangs, effortlessly tussled as though she's spent hours on it, when really all she does is run her fingers through it a few times.

I sigh, studying my image in the full-length mirror. As a short and slightly voluptuous girl, I try to accentuate my curvy assets. Tonight, I wear a casual outfit of skinny black jeans with shredded knees, my favorite flat black- suede knee-high boots, and a vintage Van Halen T-shirt with the sides and back cut out in a crisscross pattern, which gives a glimpse, but not full view, of my D-cup boobs.

"Well, this is as good as it's going to get." I shake out my long, thick blonde hair streaked in beachy waves, and turn to check out how my butt looks.

I love my curves, and thanks to the Kardashians normalizing a bit of tits and ass, I can hold my own even if I can't be bothered to paint on a perfect Instagram contour.

"Thank God, the Uber is here." Alex swooshes out of the room and bounds down the stairs, with me following close behind.

We've been waiting all week for tonight's show at The Mission, an iconic Seattle all-ages venue, which launched the grunge era over two decades ago. My parents met there at a Limelight show, so they're surprisingly cool about my acute love of live music. The club, which is worn and old, still features an awesome lineup of up-and-coming bands.

Alex and I love nothing more than experiencing live music up close and personal.

Tonight, we're finally seeing Less Than Zero, a throw-back rock band that makes actual real music and doesn't rely on auto-tune or fancy production. Their music is lit, driven by screaming guitar riffs, anthemic lyrics, and groovy beats.

Alex and I are obsessed with their YouTube channel and Instagram account because the band members post crazy video snippets. It doesn't hurt that all the guys are tasty, tasty snacks.

"Are you staying over tonight, Alex?" my dad calls out as we dart past him in the living room.

"No, Mr. Pearson." Alex stops to address him. "Mom and I have plans early tomorrow morning."

Alex's mom and dad are divorced. She lives with her hilarious mother who has a successful online pie business. If Andrea LeRoux's sense of humor isn't reason enough to hang out at her house, we *live* to be guinea pigs for her kitchen experiments, which always end up delicious. Her dad, Allen, is a developer who's remarried and lives on Bainbridge Island, a suburb across Puget Sound.

"Alex, how many times do I need to tell you to call me Mike?" Dad chastises my bestie good-naturedly. "Are you off to The Mission, then?"

"Yep!" I bop over to give him a kiss on the forehead. "I'll be home by midnight."

"How are you getting home?" He lowers his reading glasses and fixes me with a stern gaze.

"Jeez, Dad. Stop interrogating me like a lawyer. You know I'll take an Uber." I roll my eyes. For God's sake, I'm a dedicated 4.3 GPA student, it's annoying when he doesn't think I can figure out a ride home.

"I'm glad you're finally getting out of the house, peanut. I love it when you're more social." Dad hugs me. "I'm all for education, but it's good you're not buried in books for a change."

"Is Mom home tonight?" I ignore his annoying comment. My mom, Olivia, travels a lot for her job as a pharmaceutical sales manager. She's flying in tonight from a conference in Miami.

"Yep, I'm going to pick her up in an hour." Dad smiles cheekily.

They're still so in love, I hope to find that for myself someday.

Maybe when I'm old. At least thirty.

Chapter Two

Half-hour Later

WHEN WE FINALLY MAKE it through the long line into the divey, dark club, Less Than Zero's melodic, guitar-driven, ass-kicking rock is already in full force. We push our way to the front of the stage so we can see the band in action and, of course, dance. Our bodies can't resist moving to the music. LTZ is so on point. By the time they launch into their third song, I feel electrified. The energy in the crowd is intense, as if we all know we're witnessing something special.

If the guys in the band looked hot in the videos we've obsessed over—LTZ in person? Holy. Fucking. *Moly*.

Drummer, Jace Deveraux, plays shirtless. He's lean with taut muscles, intense, piercing green bedroom eyes, and sexy dirty-blond hair that brushes past his shoulders. He thrashes hard yet keeps the most complicated groovy rhythm while his mouth moves in time to the beat.

Zane Rocks, a pretty boy with an infectious grin, dark-brown eyes, and a mop of jet-black, unruly hair, plays lead guitar. He bounces all over the stage but manages to make eye contact with everyone in the crowd, drawing them in. Effortlessly channeling classic icons like Carter Pope, Slash, and Eddie Van Halen, his natural skill translates into his own unique sound.

Bassist Connor McLoughlin is the hottest ginger I've ever seen, his curly reddish-brown hair hangs well past his jaw. He stares into the crowd with light, golden-brown eyes that are brooding. Almost dangerous. Ropy, thick muscles bulge underneath his vintage Alice in Chains T-shirt. He's cool AF, popping and thumping in perfect rhythm with Jace's percussion.

As hot as the other LTZ guys are, lead singer Tyson Rainier is the most magnificent-looking guy I've ever seen in real life. His chiseled, square-jawed face, with just a hint of stubble, makes him look like a young, rogue biker. Long, brown hair hangs in loose waves. He swings it wildly, scanning the crowd through sapphire-blue eyes rimmed with dark, long lashes.

His lithe yet muscular body rocks tight skinny jeans and a frayed, fitted white V-neck. He stomps around the stage like a throwback grunge rocker in duct-taped, forest-green Doc Martens. Ty's voice is mesmerizing—a mix of soaring range, complicated lyrical phrasing, wolf-like growls, and passionate, emotional delivery.

He figuratively and literally masters the stage and audience.

I'm hypnotized. There's no way not to stare. He's passion personified. My body is consumed with what feels like an intense, gravitational pull.

While I'm gaping at him, the beat changes to a slow, sultry low groove. At that moment, he looks down from the stage directly into my eyes.

It's like a lightning bolt straight to my core.

My heart thumps so fast, I'm afraid it's going to explode. Then I glance around and see beautiful women everywhere having the same reaction as I'm having to this magnificent rock god.

Immediately, I feel foolish. He didn't single me out, specifically. I'm nothing special. He just has that effect on his fans, which is why LTZ is destined for something bigger than a local club like The Mission.

Throughout the rest of the show, I purposefully avoid looking at the sexy singer. Making eye contact is too much like looking directly into the sun. Smiling to myself at the ludicrous thought I could ever have a chance in hell with someone like Tyson Rainier, I immerse myself in the music. Alex and I sway, dance, and cheer at LTZ's awesomeness.

Hands down, they're the coolest band I've ever seen.

After their second encore, Alex and I are still sweaty by the time we push through the crowd to find our friends, who are live-streaming commentary about the show. Alex adds to her own IG story, and I flash her some rock horns when she turns the camera phone toward me.

We can't stop squeeing about the band and how incredible they are. Although I don't say anything to anyone else, I can't shake the feeling that something about the lead singer strikes a chord deep inside me.

"I think he looked right at you." Alex nudges me and waggles her eyebrows. I should have known she could read my mind.

"*Uh-huh*. There's no chance," I guffaw, "the lights were shining in his eyes, he couldn't see anyone in the crowd."

"No, I'm serious. He kept trying to catch your attention," she asserts. "You didn't see it? He was singing to *you*. My Gawd, you *have* to talk to him!"

"I can't do that." I wrap my arms around myself protectively. "I'd die of embarrassment. I'd just be standing there looking completely *basic*."

The thought of it makes me cringe and want to go home.

"Holy crap." Alex's eyes grow wide with excitement. "Well, you better think fast because I'm pretty sure he's heading this way."

I barely have the chance to turn around when a big hand clasps my shoulder and a distinctive, deep, husky voice asks, "Hey, um. Sorry to interrupt, but haven't I seen you before?"

Looking up into the deepest blue eyes I've ever seen, electricity crackles throughout my body. I manage to speak, if not eloquently, "Um—Umm. I just was watching your show." I stare at his exquisite face, not able to help it. After a beat too long, I finally look down at my shoulder where his hand rests. "You're *amazing*, I mean—the band was amazing— I mean— I *loved* it!" I stutter, wanting to disappear through the floor at my flirting ineptitude.

"Oh, uh, cool. Thanks." Ty's cheeks visibly redden. He looks at his boots almost bashfully. This takes me by surprise, I hadn't expected any of the LTZ guys to be modest. Or nice. Or shy. They're all so, well, overwhelmingly hot.

Brushing off the compliment, Ty looks at me intensely. "No, I mean it. I feel like we've met somewhere and it's driving me crazy trying to figure it out."

I can't find my words. With little dating experience, having this powerful reaction to a guy is new. Exciting. Scary. But then this is not just any guy—he's a fucking rock god, so maybe it's to be expected. "Oh- kay, but *no*, I think I'd remember you."

Realizing this comes out somewhat snarky, I change my tone, trying to be sexy and confident. Unfortunately, instead, I sound like a total nerd fangirl. "I mean, I'd for sure remember meeting *you*."

God, I'm an idiot.

I blush literally everywhere.

The crowd swarms around us when they notice the singer of LTZ is among the masses. Ty doesn't appear to be aware of his effect at all. His focus is solely on me. He moves in closer. His fingers lightly stroke down my arm, almost like he's afraid to touch me but can't help it. "I'm not super good at this, um. Well, maybe I made up an excuse to say hello. So, *hello*. I'm Ty."

Not good at it? How could this possibly be? Everyone wants a piece of him, as evidenced by the crowd of people pushing toward us.

Beautiful girls of every size, shape, and color surround us, batting their eyelashes. Poking him. Prodding him. Trying to catch his attention. Clearly wondering how to divert his attention from me.

"I'm Zoey," I mumble as I get lost into his gaze. My mind empties of all coherent thought.

That's when the world around us falls away and there's only me and him in the room. We stare at each other, both of us with goofy grins on our faces. The silence between us is embarrassingly long. I don't know how to flirt with him. Apparently, he's in the same boat.

"That's a pretty name for the prettiest girl here," he finally speaks before breaking eye contact to glance down at his phone.

My bullshit detector immediately activates.

"*Really?* That's your line?" I cock my hip and wrinkle my nose in dismay. "I almost fell for it. *This* is actually how you meet girls after a show. Ty, I'm not a thirsty groupie, I actually genuinely loved your music."

A look of pure mortification passes across his face before his expression changes into intrigue. His hand continues running up and down my arm slowly. "Hmmm, well, I admit—that did sound super cheesy." He looks back down at his phone but smiles up at me through his mane of brown waves, scrunching his nose slightly.

My arm is tingling, hyperaware of his touch. Can he feel the energy between us too? I study him and challenge, "I was hoping you wouldn't be a pick-up-line guy."

His blue eyes snap up from his phone, piercing mine again intensely. "I'm *not* a pick-up-line guy," he insists.

A text lights up his phone. He reads it quickly before shoving the device back into his pocket.

"I've gotta go help load out, *Zo*-ey." His deep voice draws my name out, which sends sparks to my girlparts.

"I didn't mean—" I call out to Ty's back. He's already stalking back toward the stage where the rest of the band is packing up their gear. Feeling deflated, I trace my arm absently, immediately missing the warmth and zing of his hand rubbing it.

"OMG are you *SERIOUS*?" Alex whisper-squeals, interrupting my trance. "He's the most gorgeous man I've ever seen in real life. Although... No. The drummer is delicious, more my type."

"Alex, I just royally fucked that up." I pout dramatically. "I'm such a tool, I basically put the hottest guy I've ever talked to on blast. No wonder he bailed. I totally just missed my chance."

"*Shut* the fuck up. Did you see the way he looked at you? He'll be back, trust me. Let's just chill and hang out for a bit. Look nonchalant, cool. As your dad would say, 'Be Fonzie.'" She laughs.

I try to be Fonzie. Unsuccessfully. I watch the band load out, hoping to catch a glimpse of the gorgeous singer and make amends. Alex chats with our friends while I wait around impatiently and pray Ty will come back.

I'm so short it's hard to see the loading dock, even when I continuously stand on my tiptoes to assess the situation. After a while, there doesn't appear to be any sign of LTZ, their gear, or Ty.

He doesn't come back for me.

Dejectedly, because my curfew approaches, I pull out my phone, open my Uber app, tap in the address of The Mission and order a car. It's time for me to say my good-byes. "Alex, besties, I'm calling it. I'm heading home."

Because the club is in the heart of downtown Seattle, a car arrives in under two minutes. I'm a wannabe Cinderella, and the hourglass has run out for any chance at talking to Ty ever again.

I take one last, sad look around the club before dashing out the side exit to find my car. When it pulls up, I jump in and am about to close the door when it suddenly flings back open.

"Hey, wait, did you forget about me?" Ty is nearly out of breath when he pokes his head into the car. "Can I catch a ride?"

"Tyson, uh, uh I-I— I'm going home. I have a curfew." I mentally thwack my hand against my head. I don't want this rock god to know I'm still some dumb high school kid for another month.

He frowns. "Uhh, *shit*. I thought I would be a great idea to ride home with you so we could talk."

I have no idea what sort of dazed, shocked expression I'm wearing, but I can't speak.

"Okay, well maybe you'll give me your number and we can hang out sometime." Ty's hair flops over his eyes. "That's not a line. It's just what I hope will happen."

My smile stretches from ear to ear, and it feels like a thousand butterflies have been released from the top of my head. Holy shit, this is like a movie. A once-in-a-lifetime chance to change my destiny.

Determined not to blow it, I scoot over and pat the seat. Ty slides in next to me, pressing his long, lean thigh against mine in the tiny back seat of the car.

He turns toward me and grins, just a hint of white teeth peeks through his full lips. I lean toward him, my smile widens even more. The car speeds off and I can't help but get lost in the depths of those piercing—sad—blue eyes.

Crap, this guy's gonna break my heart.

But, I push the thought aside. Beam at him like a fool, and hear myself saying, "Pretty good comeback, rocker-boy."

Chapter Three

That Same Night

"DUDE, ARE YOU READY?" Zane slings his arm around me, gauging my nervousness. He knows I didn't fall into this lead-singer gig willingly. He always makes sure I feel comfortable before we play. Tonight, after all, is a huge night for all of us.

"I'm *so* ready." I shake out my hair after finishing my standard pre-show vocal warm-ups. "This is so fucking *awesome*, have you seen the crowd?"

For once, I'm as exhilarated and giddy to go onstage as my bandmates. I don't have an ounce of my usual pre-show jitters. Crammed into the small closet next to the stage that The Mission designates its "green room," this is our biggest night as a band. Something in my gut tells me this show will change my life.

Connor, our big, burly bass player finishes changing a string that busted right before we're meant to start and is now tuning his bass. "Sorry, guys." He looks up from his instrument, his eyebrows still furrowed in concentration at the task he's completed. "It's fixed."

Jace, who's filming us with his camera phone, speaks directly to our Facebook Live audience. "And that, folks, is how you miss your set time for only the biggest show of your life!" He has a sneaky way of capturing us all on his social media videos, while remaining relatively anonymous himself.

"Fuck off, Deveraux," growls Connor as he pushes the camera out of his way.

"Okay, *okay*!" I hold up my hand to get everyone's attention. "Knock it off. Tonight's gonna kick ass. We've worked hard and now, after two years of playing every coffee shop, house party, and dive bar in Seattle, we're finally playing a sold-out, headlining gig at The Mission in front of five hundred people. We've got this!"

"Fuck yeah!" Zane bops up and down excitedly. Holds his fist out toward the group of us and shouts, "Fist pump!"

Obligingly, we all hold out our fists and knock knuckles before Connor stalks out and heads up the stairs to the stage. Jace follows behind him. Finally, Zane laughs and salutes me as he bounds to his place onstage. When Connor and Jace are in place, they give Zane a nod.

Legs spread wide, our brilliant guitarist strikes a chord before shredding into the mind-blowing intro to our new song *Catatonic*.

I become emotional while waiting for my cue. It truly feels—for the first time in my life—like I'm where I belong when I watch my band-brothers start the show. The crowd is going mental. I can hear them screaming my name, which still freaks me out a bit, but I'm learning to deal.

All I want in the world is out there on the stage. Within my grasp. Tonight is my ticket out. My way to turn my life around from being the shy, nerdy loser I was not that long ago.

Singing, playing guitar, and songwriting are permanently in my blood, but I know my specific role: to represent a rock-star fantasy to our followers. As the lead singer of LTZ, my job is to present a captivating stage presence and interact with fans.

None of this comes easy to me. But, I have no choice. Music and my band are all I have in this world. My only hope of breaking free from my fucked-up home life is if LTZ makes it big.

It's taken a long time, but I've come to terms with the reality of the music business: good business decisions matter almost as much as talent if you want to make it.

I *have* to succeed.

Taking a deep breath when I hear Zane play my cue, I'm determined. To secure a future for myself. To secure a future for my band. Tonight is when I fully up my game and embrace my destiny. I'm the fucking lead singer of Less Than Zero. I'm going to blow the faces off our fans, whether they're seeing us live in the club or watching our live-stream.

When I take the stage, I feel the crowd humming with anticipation. This buoys my confidence. I'm energized. Alive. Giving everything I have, I wail and thrash around the stage, belt my heart out and feed off the energy of hundreds of fans who sing our songs with me.

It's mind-blowing.

I'm so pumped with adrenaline, I make it my goal to own each and every person in the audience.

Halfway into the third song, like a powerful magnet, my eyes snap to a pint-sized beauty in the second row. She has a mane of the most beautiful long, sun-kissed hair that cascades in waves and frames the milky, smooth skin on her angelic face. Her huge hazel eyes are kind and confident, her full lips beg to be kissed. She wears some sort of cut-out Van Halen shirt and black skinny pants. The luscious curves on her stunning body make me salivate. She's not posing or pouting, she doesn't try hard at all.

She's the most jaw-dropping woman I've ever laid eyes on.

But, it's more than that. Observing her swaying, almost hypnotized by our music, sends a bolt of lightning into my heart. She's lost to the beat and her glossy, pink lips mouth the words.

Every fiber of my being wants to jump off the stage and kiss her senseless. For now, all I can do is try to catch her eye. Make a connection. So I sing directly to her with every ounce of emotion I possess, hoping to get her to look at me, even if just for a second.

As if she reads my mind, her gaze locks with mine and it's all over.

Adorably, she blushes and glances to her right and left as though she can't believe I've noticed her. I keep my eye on her for the rest of the show, hoping for more of a connection. It feels like I hit the jackpot every time I catch her peering at me from under her lashes. Even if it's just for brief moments before she quickly averts her eyes or shyly shares secret smiles with her tall friend.

We play for two exhilarating hours, ending with two encores. After we finally leave the stage, watching from behind the curtain, I keep my eye on my wild-haired blonde crush.

She and her friend skip toward the front of the club as the crowd dissipates. They talk animatedly with a group of people who are filming them with their phones. Her mass of hair cascades around her face when she gestures with an exaggerated rock horn sign and rolls her eyes at the camera.

I'm fully smitten. A sensation I've never experienced quite like this. Wanting her makes me feel brave enough to maybe talk to her.

She's so incredibly beautiful, like a butterfly made of all the colors in the world. Yet she's not showy. Her demeanor is, well. . . settled. Grounded. She seems genuine and comfortable in her skin, unlike the women who usually throw themselves at me.

Unlike *me*, truth be told.

My heart races when she keeps glancing back toward the stage where the band is starting to pack up our gear and sign autographs. For the first time in my entire complicated life, things are simple.

This woman is meant for me.

No matter what my insecurities are, I won't risk not seeing her again.

"Ty, you remember Fiona." Zane interrupts my thoughts. He has his arm around the dark-haired, pixie-like daughter of Gus Reynolds, the owner of The Mission. "Fiona Reynolds, you remember Tyson Rainier."

"Hey," I say absently to the Zane's childhood friend. I'm not really paying attention since I'm so intently watching the blonde beauty from afar.

Fiona struggles halfheartedly to unwind herself from Zane. "Nice to see you again, Tyson. Will I settle up with you?"

"You're breaking my heart, Fee." Zane reaches for her hand to pull her to the office. "You'll settle up with me!"

Jace shakes his head, his tattooed arm lazily draped around Cassie, a pretty redhead who always wears low-cut tops and too much makeup. She looks at him adoringly, but he arches his eyebrow disinterestedly and stares out into the crowd where I've been fixated. "Who's that girl you were singing to?"

"Um, I dunno. I want to go talk to her before she leaves." I try to sound nonchalant. Confident.

Connor lurks behind us, huge, muscled and menacing, his penetrating glare is directed at me. "My dude, for the love of God, please be chill."

"It's a lost cause, Connor." Jace untangles himself from Cassie. "But if Ty's gonna make a move on a pretty girl, I'm not standing in his way."

"Fuck you." I flip him off. "I'm not *that* bad."

"Uh, *yeah* you are," Connor deadpans. Jace's sister Jen, who Connor's dated for years guffaws at his comment.

As we've gained bigger audiences in Seattle, women and men pursue us relentlessly, which makes me uncomfortable. Not because they're interested, that part is flattering—even if I'm straight. More like, as my bandmates all know, I have less-than-zero game when it comes to romance.

Hence, the backstory of how they originally chose our band name. A joke on me, which is true. And *funny*.

The truth is I have my own private reasons for living by my strict principles that are not necessarily befitting a rising rock star. One of which is I don't hit on random women. *Ever*.

Until now, it seems.

Tonight, fueled on endorphins from our life-changing show, I'm determined to embrace my fate. There's something about the little blonde beauty. Almost like we're both meant to meet in this place at this time.

My heart thunders in my chest when I approach her and the friend. Their eyes go wide with surprise as I near. Once I'm close enough, it takes all my willpower to resist burying my nose in the crook of my butterfly's neck to breathe in her delicious scent of flowers and oranges.

Of course—just like Jace called it—when I attempt to talk to her, I sound like a cheesy asshole. I manage to get her name, but then fizzle at the small talk part of things. Sometimes I hate how socially awkward I am.

Thank God Connor sees me struggling, and texts me at exactly the right time. Loading band gear gives me an excuse to abort the mission with Zoey to calm my nerves and regroup.

The last thing I want to do is fuck things up with her completely before we even get started.

Chapter Four

Half-hour Later

I NEARLY MISS ZOEY altogether. Flustered, I charge into the Uber like a bull in a china shop, determined not to miss my shot and find myself heading to an unknown destination with a beautiful stranger.

As we near her house, my confidence and adrenaline evaporate. I have no idea what the fuck I'm doing or what I've gotten myself into.

Covering up my self-loathing by grinning and feigning confidence, I can't help but wonder if she still thinks I'm a typical arrogant dickhead musician trying to get into her pants for the night. My behavior certainly would give that impression, truth be told.

Fuck. I vowed never to act this way. To *be* this way.

"I've never brought a guy my parents haven't met home at midnight." Zoey's sweet voice jolts me out of my thoughts.

Wait. *Uh...parents?*

"Uh, um, well, I hadn't thought that far. I sort of panicked when I saw you were leaving without me getting your deets." I can't control my own word vomit.

"You panicked?" Her eyebrows rise high on her forehead.

I nod. "Yeah, I kind of panicked!"

"Um, okay?" She looks at me with a weird expression.

The seconds tick by awkwardly.

"Zoey, can I get your number?" I blurt out suddenly, thrusting my phone at her.

"Um. Okay." She types in her number quickly and hands it back to me, watching me read it.

"Why 'Z' not Zoey?" I tap *dial* and she picks up.

"You're clearly gonna be a huge rock star, it won't be good for your stud reputation to have a bunch of girl's names in your contacts. Better to be stealth." She sinks back in the seat and saves my number into her own contacts.

It bums me out. Zoey truly thinks I'm a player when she's literally the only woman I've ever pursued. "I'm not that way, I don't ever ask for numbers. I can promise you that."

She just blinks in disbelief, her long lashes flutter against her gorgeous hazel eyes. I'm overwhelmed by how drawn I am to her. "God, your eyes are amazing."

"Wow, thank you. Yours are too." The sides of her lips quirk up.

We stare at each other awkwardly again. I'm fucking this up so bad. I have to keep the conversation going, but have no clue. Finally I come up with something, though it's shallow and stupid. "What's your Instagram? My band's really into social." I hand my phone back to her.

She grasps it in her tiny, perfect hand tipped with nails painted shiny black. Pulls up her Instagram and clicks follow. "Why are you here with me, Ty? You could have anyone you wanted, you're—"

"Into you. Big time. I'm pretty sure you've ruined me for anyone else," I cut her off with another cheesy—but truthful—line.

God I'm so bad at this.

I take my phone back and glance at her Instagram account, which has a fresh post of the video I saw her friend record. The one with the rock horns.

"Zoey *Pearson*, huh? Cute video." I smile and before I can think too much, reach over to gently tuck a piece of wild blonde hair behind her ear. "How old are you anyway, Zoey *Pearson*?"

"Seventeen," she sighs, sucking on her lower lip, which sends electric currents straight to my groin. "I'll be eighteen in two weeks. How old are you?"

"Twenty-one," I sigh and inwardly groan. Damn. She's too young. I should have known when she mentioned her parents. We sit in silence for a minute.

"Hmm, that skeptical look on your face says everything," she sort of questions, one eyebrow raised. "You thought I was older."

Thinking about my own past, I decide to be honest. "Yeah. I mean, you're a teenager and I'm...not. I won't take advantage of you, Zoey. We can only be friends. I'm not a creeper."

Fuck. Just my luck.

"You want to be *friends?*" Zoey's sweet, melodic voice teases. "You're not a creeper, Ty. My eighteenth birthday's in two weeks. I'm going to college in a couple of months." She smiles. Tentatively reaches down and traces the top of my hand. "Besides, the age of consent in Washington State is sixteen, so even though going on a date wouldn't be illegal, my parents will be cool. I'm a homebody. They'd love for me to get out more and I'd really like to hang out with you. Would you genuinely want to hang out with me?"

"I really would." Staring at where she's tracing, I turn my hand over and marvel at how little she is compared to me, her fingers only reach the first digit of mine.

Clasping our fingers together, I hold her hand tightly as I sink back into the seat, grinning like an idiot. As scared as I was earlier, in an instant the thing between us is easy and comfortable, yet crackling with electricity. Zoey calms me. I feel like I've known her for a long time, not just for an hour. "Hopefully once you get to know me, you won't find me too boring."

"Oh my God, are you kidding me? You're already the least boring person I've ever met. I can't even believe you're here with me right now. LTZ has thousands of fans because your music is so badass. Exceedingly badass." She looks at me with one eyebrow raised again, so adorable. "But, in case I wasn't clear at the club, I'm not a band groupie type, so if this is some sort of conquest game you're playing, I'm not your girl."

Watching her as she animatedly speaks, I see myself through her eyes and I like being that man for her. Plus, the groupie comment is music to my ears.

"Zoey, I'm going to confess something to you." I take a deep breath. "I know I was just on stage, but it's probably pretty apparent that I'm, well, socially awkward when I'm not singing and playing music."

"No way. C'mon, you had so many women waiting for you after the show, you could've had anyone." Zoey cocks her head. Studies me intently.

"I sang to you the entire show, and you barely even looked at me. You were dancing to my music, and God— look at you—I had to meet you, even if I was petrified," I explain as honestly as I can, hoping I don't sound pathetic while she considers what I'm saying. "Music is the one thing I can do really well. I'm shit at talking to pretty girls."

My mind feels like a rapid-fire machine gun of competing thoughts as I look at her, my eyes searching hers. Does she feel what I feel? Now that I know she's interested in me romantically, should I kiss her or abort the mission? God, she smells amazing.

I squeeze my eyes closed and take a deep breath. My life depends on being in the recording studio all summer and touring during the fall and winter to build up our fan base.

It's the worst timing ever to start something up with Zoey. A friggin' high school girl who's three years younger than me.

Despite what my head is saying, the unexplained deep gut feeling that I can see into her soul and she can see into mine is so overwhelming and powerful, the next thing I know my lips are firmly pressed against hers.

She hums against my mouth and kisses me back.

Holy shit, does she kiss me back. Our tongues touch tentatively. I bury my hands in her mane of hair and hold her face, my thumbs stroking her cheeks. She opens her mouth further and we explore, stroke, and taste each other.

Kissing her is everything and like nothing I've ever experienced. She mewls like a kitten stretching against me, gripping my biceps and then melting fully into my side. I delicately taste all around her lips, our mouths open hungrily, tongues colliding again, dancing and swirling until time disappears.

A kiss for the ages.

When the Uber arrives at her house, we reluctantly pull apart, panting. Her eyes open slowly in a passionate haze. Every one of my body parts is charged, my heart pounds, my jeans are tight with arousal.

Her lips are swollen from our passion. With my shit background, not in a million years would I have believed in love at first sight. In this moment not only do I believe, but I know I will do anything for her. Anything she ever asks of me.

Please, don't let this girl break my heart.

Chapter Five

A Few Minutes Later

NOT IN A MILLION years would I have believed in love at first sight, but when Ty kisses me in the Uber, I know it's not only possible...but it's happening to me right now.

He's *everything*. It's hard to fathom but undeniable. I've always felt like my soul is older than my physical age, which is why I know without any question that Ty's been made just for me. It's an easy decision to invite him inside to meet my parents.

"Mom, Dad?" I tentatively call out as I lead Ty through the front door.

"Maybe they're in bed?" Ty whispers, looking around our house, his expression wary.

"In the kitchen, Zoey. Are you hungry?" Mom peeks her blonde head around the corner. Her eyes widen when she sees I have a guest.

"Mom, I want you to meet my new friend, Tyson Rainier. We saw his band Less Than Zero tonight." I pull Ty by his big hand into the kitchen, noticing he looks like a deer in headlights.

I can understand why. My parents are both professionals and look kind of intimidating. Dad is a high-powered corporate lawyer and my mom's sales position makes her kind of intense. She's still wearing a black business suit at midnight, after flying across country from a pharma conference.

Despite appearances, they're actually very cool. Avid supporters of the Seattle arts community and voracious music lovers. If anything, I'm the uncool member of the family.

"Hello, Tyson, I didn't expect Zoey to bring a guy home with her." Dad raises an eyebrow in an attempt to be intimidating while at the same time sticking out his hand to Ty. "But, we are big fans of music."

Inwardly, I laugh. Just like I told Ty, unlike most dads, he's probably pumped I've brought a long-haired rocker home to invade our kitchen at midnight.

"It's nice to meet you, Mr. Pearson. Mrs. Pearson." Ty is courteous and polite, if not almost painfully shy.

He ends up staying and visiting for about an hour. All of us are shocked to find out that Carter Pope, the famous guitar player from the legendary Seattle band, Limelight is not only Ty's bandmate, Zane Rocks's father, but a patron of LTZ. Limelight has always been Dad's favorite band. They were playing the night he met Mom at The Mission. The connection gives Ty legitimacy.

Or *something.*

"So, Carter Pope, huh?" I beam up at Ty while we wait for his Uber outside. My parents went to bed once they were sure Ty was on his way home.

"Yeah, I guess he's kinda like my pseudo-dad." Ty shifts his weight from foot to foot before flashing a smile in my direction.

"That's cool." I kick my toe at the ground. "So, are you still scared off by a seventeen-year-old high-schooler who lives with her parents?"

Ty reaches down, takes my hand, and raises it up to his lips. "No, you have such a wonderful family. It's nice."

"I guess." I shrug.

"Zoey, seriously. Thank you for introducing me." The look he gives me eradicates my initial concern that I'm his one-night-and-done conquest. "I've never met anyone's parents before."

Gazing at me like I'm a precious jewel, he bends down and softly kisses my lips. I nearly get lost in our kisses again, but the Uber pulls up to the front of the house.

"You're the most beautiful butterfly, Zoey." Ty's forehead touches mine. His incredible blue eyes peer into my soul.

I press a finger to my lips where his lips have just been. My heart soars at his words. "I hope you meant it about hanging out, Ty. But, I'll understand—"

"What are you doing tomorrow?" Ty tucks a flyaway hair behind my ear and strokes my neck with his rough-padded fingers.

I go for bold in my reply. "Hopefully kissing you some more."

Ty cups my cheek. "Good, because that's what I was hoping for."

And that's how it starts between us.

Chapter Six

The Next Two Weeks

FOR THE NEXT TWO weeks, because I'm technically underage, Ty irritatingly insists on "doing the right thing" by me. Which, unfortunately, means he only visits me at home when my parents are around. He seems to enjoy hanging out with us when he doesn't have band obligations or shifts at the popular bistro where he works as a line cook.

It's nothing like real dates, though. Mainly, we eat dinner with my family and watch TV in the living room. Sometimes we hold hands. Every now and then we sneak in a PG-rated kiss, but only when my parents leave us alone. Which isn't often.

Holy fucking moly, I adore him. Luckily, so do my folks, which is a good thing because their opinion matters to me.

It's just...I can't wait for my birthday. I want alone time with Ty. I want to make out with him. I want him to touch me—and I want to touch him. He's gorgeous and the desire I feel is overwhelming. I've never really masturbated much but I get so wet and tingly just thinking about him, it's become my only relief.

Call it instinct, but there's something huge happening between us. I might be young, but I'm not a silly teenager. I'm head over heels in love with him and I think he feels the same way.

Ty is the best of all worlds. Genuinely sweet, polite, and gracious. And, despite what he says about his stage persona being different than real life, he's is one hundred percent rock god *all* of the time. A commanding presence softened by his underlying innocence and wonder.

Maybe because he hasn't grown up with much, Ty has a drive to succeed unlike anything I've ever known. It's inspiring. On the other hand, he's humble and grateful for every opportunity that comes his way. This combination of attributes gives Ty an inexplicable aura that makes him completely irresistible.

When my eighteenth birthday finally arrives, I'm beyond ready for us to take our relationship to the next level. After dinner with my parents, Ty and I set off on our first real date in my new Toyota RAV, a generous gift from my folks.

Neither of us have much money, so we share a pint of Molly Moon's Salted Caramel ice cream on the top of the hill at Gasworks Park. He thought it would be romantic to watch the sunset together for our first solo date.

He's right. It's perfect.

"Did you have a happy birthday, butterfly?" Ty wipes a drip of cream from my lip with the rough pad of his finger and sucks it.

"The best ever." I tip my head up for a kiss, eager to feel his soft lips on mine. "I'm never taking my necklace off."

At the restaurant, Ty presented me with my beautiful rose gold filagree butterfly. It's dainty and precious. I'm never taking it off.

Ty lazily explores my mouth, raking his fingers through my hair. Lost in our kisses, I swoon when his big palm cups my cheek, a move which has become one of my favorites. When I open my eyes, he looks at me with so much adoration. "So, now that you're officially an adult, will you officially be my girlfriend?"

Looking into his blue eyes, I notice he seems to be nervously waiting for my response. I'm practically stunned stupid. Does he really have any doubt?

Like a true geek, I word-vomit my reply. "OMG, Ty! Yes! I'd love to officially be your girlfriend."

"You make me so happy, I wasn't sure what you'd say. What your parents *will* say." Ty kisses my nose and touches his forehead to mine.

"You make me happier." I poke his flat, muscled stomach playfully, longing to caress his whole sexy body but still feeling too shy and unsure to initiate. "They like you a lot. They won't have a problem with us being a couple as I don't change my college plans."

"Your folks are so cool. So supportive." Ty feathers kisses along my hairline. "I can't believe you got a brand-new car."

I shrug. I know I'm privileged. Ty doesn't have his own vehicle, he either drives the band's van or takes the bus to come see me. "I'm their only daughter. I guess they want me to be safe when I'm at college."

Ty threads his fingers through mine and squeezes. "You know I'd never ask you to change your plans. You *should* get your college degree."

"Yeah, I know. I just haven't figured out what I want to be like you have." Ty knows what he wants: LTZ. His next nine months with the band are completely planned out.

I'll figure my future career out later.

For now, I want to enjoy life as Ty's girlfriend. Because *nothing* is better than having Ty as a boyfriend.

It's hard for me to think about college when Ty makes me feel worshipped in the present. Now that we're a couple, I can't imagine my life without him. Neither of us are into playing relationship games. We know what we want—to spend every waking minute together.

Everything else pales in comparison...

Unfortunately, my new romance is leaving Alex out more often than not. She supports my relationship with Ty, but part of me feels terrible about breaking our summer plans.

I don't want her to miss out. It'll be so much easier if my worlds collide, so I decide to play matchmaker. "Does Jace have a girlfriend?"

"Kind of?" Ty looks up to the sky as though he's trying to find the right words. "Um. He's notoriously tight-lipped about his personal life but he seems to regularly hook up with this girl Cassie."

"Oh." I'm a bit dejected.

"Should I be worried?" Ty nips at my earlobe, causing zaps of energy to ignite from my nipples to my pussy.

I manage to keep my composure because even though I want to straddle him and feel him get hard, we're in public. "Of course not. I'm thinking about Alex. We're supposed to spend our summer together too." I burrow my face in the crease of his neck and breathe in his grapefruity scent. "I'm being a bad friend because I only want to be with you."

"Well, let's include her as much as possible. I don't know if Jace is an option, but I want you to be happy, butterfly." Ty squeezes me tight against him. "Let's make this summer epic with all of our friends."

He means it, I can tell.

How in the world did I snag the most perfect guy? I'm ruined for anyone else.

Chapter Seven

Two Weeks Later

As IF THE PAST couple of weeks haven't been the best of my life, today Ty helped my parents surprise Alex and me with an LTZ acoustic show at our joint graduation party.

I'm on cloud nine, but today's also surreal. Like I'm floating above my backyard observing myself living a manifested fairy-tale hanging with my best friend, family, and gorgeous, thoughtful rocker boyfriend.

My life is *perfect*.

"So, are you psyched to go off to college?" Alex nudges me as we groove to the gorgeous rockers, who seem perfectly at ease in this setting.

Ty's eyes never stray far from mine, I'm in so deep with this man. "No, but at the same time I want to get through it as quickly as possible. I'm going to miss him so much." I make a kissy face at Ty.

"Is it that serious?" Alex pokes me, forcing my attention on her. "You've been MIA lately."

She's right, of course. "I'm *sorry*. I've never had a real boyfriend until now. I can't get enough of him."

"Which leaves me high and dry." She masks a flash of hurt with a smile. "God, wouldn't it be perfect if Jace wanted to date me? All our evil masterminded plans would be in place. Tragically, he won't even look at me. I'm not sure why."

"I'm sorry, I hate being such a bad friend. I asked Ty about Jace." I scrunch up my nose. "He just does hookups, I guess."

"Well, that's okay. I'm not looking for anything serious. If we're both going to lose our v-cards before you leave for college, I need to make a move or move on." Alex taps her finger to her lips.

"Why don't you talk to him about social media and your new travel influencer plan, he's a total geek for that stuff." I point my finger at the sky like I have the most brilliant idea in the universe.

"*Dude.*" Alex nods. "Perfect plan."

She wastes no time. After the performance, within minutes, Alex and Jace are deep in conversation about all things social media. Connor and Zane chat with my parents. Ty seems to have vanished, but when I turn around he's behind me.

"Hey." Ty smiles down at me. "Happy graduation."

"I can't believe you surprised me with a show. You guys *killed* it. I could listen to you sing all day long—" Ty interrupts my stream of consciousness by leaning in and brushing his lips against mine. So softly it barely registers as a kiss, though I can feel it through my entire body, all the way to my pink-tipped toes.

Pressing my lips more firmly against his, I push us one step further by sucking on his lower lip until he groans. Threading his fingers through my hair, Ty tilts my head where he wants me and he begins a warm, lazy exploration of my mouth.

Oh, what a kiss. We go deep then backoff. Lost in a haze of desire, we caress each other's necks, cheeks, backs, and arms while our tongues slide together in a slow rhythm. A moment of realization hits both of us at the same time. The most soul-searing moment of our young relationship is being carried out in front of parents, friends, family, and Ty's band.

Reluctantly, we step apart but he keeps a tight grip on my hand. I look nervously around to see the band gaping at us. My mom and dad try to avert their eyes and busy themselves. Alex's expression is priceless, complete with cocked eyebrow.

Deciding I don't care who sees us, I shrug and turn back to Ty. Wow." I beam at him. The world always seems to disappear around us. Nothing is more important than making Ty's life as wonderful as he makes mine. "What brought that on?"

"I can't help it. You're my beautiful butterfly, and you make me so happy." Ty's expression nearly makes me weep. He not only reciprocates my feelings, but also makes me feel truly alive.

With graduation in the rear-view mirror, Ty and I continue to fill our summer with each other when we can. It's tough because of our jobs. He's still at the bistro and I'm working part-time at Dad's law office.

Additionally, Ty has LTZ obligations like rehearsals and occasional gigs. We're saving our paychecks—his for his tour expenses and mine for college spending money—so when we're able to hang out, we can't afford fancy dates.

It doesn't matter. I gleefully plan our social calendar, coming up with fun, cheap ways to be together. When we have a full day, we explore the Pacific Northwest in my new car, taking long drives to the ocean or mountains.

Other days we play tourist in our city. Wander around Pike Place Market. Explore the exhibits at MoPOP. Watch a stunning summer sunset on Alki beach. He's even brought me to a few concerts at The Vera Project, where LTZ played their first shows.

Some of my favorite moments are when we're alone in my room. In between make-out sessions, he loves to serenade me with his guitar while I work on the arduous task of decluttering eighteen years of my life as I pack up my room for college.

When we're not together, I flip through hundreds of pictures of us on my phone. My heart melts each time Ty texts a sweet message or poem. At night, we FaceTime each other to sleep.

No matter what we do, our relationship is effortless. We fit together like a puzzle, except for one thing.

After the sweltering kiss at my graduation party, I hoped we'd be more physical with each other. Despite my feeble and inexperienced efforts to nudge things further, Ty hasn't even come close to touching my boobs. Or my pussy. Even with our clothes on. I'm sexually *frustrated*.

Two months in and I'm no closer to losing my virginity than I was when we met.

On some level, it makes me feel insecure. As much as I love being enveloped in his big, strong arms, I don't understand why we're waiting. Especially because we really can't keep our hands off each other. His fingers thread with mine wherever we go. Our kisses are scorching. We're always touching each other. Caressing. Touching.

The thing is, I know he's attracted to me. Whenever we're pressed together, I feel his cock harden against me. Then he just...*stops*. Claims he wants *me* to be sure when I know, without any doubt, I want him to be my first. *My only*.

I'm scared to tell him that, though.

I *love* him.

Deep in my soul, I know there will *never* be anyone else for me.

But, he's going to be a famous rockstar. Is he trying to protect me from getting my heart broken? Does he feel the same way about me or when he leaves on tour, will that be the end of us?

Chapter Eight

Three Weeks Later

"When did you start playing?" Zoey reaches out to brush the hair out of my eyes. I'm sitting on her bed, strumming my guitar before we leave for a barbeque at Carter's house. Each of her soft touches feels like balm for my wounded soul.

Proof that I deserve to be loved.

I look into her beautiful hazel eyes and hesitate to answer. I've avoided sharing too much about my personal life with her so far. Mainly because she's so sweet and caring and has such a wonderful family.

Mine...isn't.

I don't want to scare her off. Our backgrounds couldn't be more different.

"One of my mom's boyfriends taught me a few chords when I was about twelve. That was that. I loved playing." I strum a few notes of a song I'm composing.

"Will I ever meet your mom?" Zoey looks at me solemnly. "Are you afraid she won't like me?"

"God, no, butterfly!" I set the guitar down and pull her toward me, taking her hand in mine. "Not everyone is as lucky as you are to have such great parents. I don't ever want you to meet my mom. She's an addict. Sex, drinking, drugs, you name it."

Shit, that slipped out before I could help myself.

Zoey's eyes fill with tears. "*What?* Where's your dad?"

Ugh. Considering Zoey's upbringing, her reaction is expected. Her parents have welcomed me with open arms, which is wonderful—and confusing. I'm ashamed to explain my family secrets. Although she truly cares for me, I've never confided about my life to anyone. As we get to know each other, I feel safe with her but that doesn't mean it's easy for me to open up about my secrets.

With Zoey, though, I think I'd like to try.

"Um. God, I don't ever talk about this." I take a deep breath. "Okay. My mom's name is Jada. She got pregnant with me super young. Maybe fifteen or sixteen. I don't know who my father is. My mom doesn't either. She jokes all the time that there are multiple possibilities."

"*Oh.*" Zoey grips my hand in hers and squeezes, trying to hide her shock.

"Please don't feel sorry for me, Zoey." I tense up, realizing how fucked up what I just said sounded. She's truly the first person who knows me as the man I am now, not the loser I once was. I reconsider what I should tell her. I definitely don't want to ruin things by revealing too much about my fucked-up situation.

"Ty, you know *everything* about me," Zoey encourages, still stroking my hair. "I don't feel sorry for you, I want to *know* you. All of you. Sometimes it feels like you hold things back to protect me. You don't need to do that."

She's a fucking mind reader. Instantly, I relax again. God, Zoey is my miracle. She gets me like no one ever has. This is a safe space. I lie back on Zoey's bed, close my eyes, and sigh. Zoey presses herself against me, snuggling into my side, stroking the three small scars on my eyebrow.

It's getting really hard not to want to ravage my sweet girl when I feel the swell of her ample breasts pressed against my chest. She's a virgin though, and I have very little experience. I'm terrified of being a disappointment. Her first time should be something special.

With *someone* special.

I don't know if I'm worthy.

Pushing my sexual frustration and insecurities aside, I try to remember she sees me differently than I see myself. To be the man she thinks I am, I have to take a chance and truly let her in. Somehow, the very last thing I ever expected to confess tumbles from my lips. "Well, first off, my last name isn't really 'Rainier.'"

She's stunned. "*What?*"

"Well, I mean it is *now*." I arch my eyebrow. "I've never told this to another person, not Carter, not the band."

"Okay..." Zoey thumbs my cheek, encouraging me to continue.

"My mom's last name is Rogers, and so was mine until I was eighteen. I met Zane in high school. When he asked me my name I said, 'Rainier.' By the time I turned eighteen, I didn't want to be a liar, so I had it legally changed."

"Why? I mean, Tyson Rainier is a great name, but Rogers isn't so bad." Zoey seems intrigued. "Why lie to him in the first place?"

"I guess I just wanted to be someone different. *Anyone* but me. My first thought was of Mt. Rainier. It's so majestic. So beautiful. *Powerful.* I just blurted it out when Zane asked my name. Since that moment it's who I aspire to be. In some ways, changing my name helped make me believe..." I look out Zoey's window at the summer sun, still high in the sky.

"...You were manifesting the man you wanted to be." Zoey squeezes my fingers with hers tightly.

"Yeah. I guess so." My cheeks get hot and, feeling unsure, I lower my eyes to gauge Zoey's reaction.

"And no one knows? How is this possible?" Zoey smooths my hair again. I love how she always does that. The time I have with her is the best part of any day. It's impossible for me to imagine my life before she was in it.

I don't want to.

"You're the only person who needs to know." I gaze into her hazel eyes.

"Wow. I'm blown away. My lips are sealed." Zoey makes a zipping motion with her fingers to her lips. "I'm so touched that you would trust me with this."

"I do trust you, butterfly." She makes me feel worthy and loved. Things I've never felt before.

"So, you were telling me about your mom?" Zoey prompts after a few minutes of silence.

"Right. Well, at one point she was very beautiful. Fun. Kind. When I was little, she was a good mother, I think. We'd go to the zoo or the beach." I smile, recalling my limited memories of long ago before things turned so dark. "To support us, she bartended at some fancy, high-end bar. At night I'd go to work with her, and she'd let me sit in a booth to color or do my homework."

Zoey is rapt with attention. I've never had anyone so acutely interested in me. My mind explodes at the possibilities of a life with Zoey by my side. All because I had the courage to put myself out there with this goddess of a woman.

I love her.

I fucking love her.

"I really don't know what happened. It was so gradual or maybe I was too young to have perspective. To me, it seemed like anything good about my mom evaporated right in front of me." Ordinarily, I don't allow myself to think too hard about my upbringing. It's too traumatizing. Every ounce of energy for the past decade has been funneled into getting myself out.

"There were always a lot of men around, because she was so pretty. Her relationships, if you could call them that, made her unpredictable. Irrational," I continue, still baffled at the realization that I'm recounting such a terrible time in my life when I've just realized I'm in love with Zoey. "It was confusing. She'd either be yelling and screaming at me to leave her alone or making me sleep in her bed and beg me for hugs. Eventually, she ignored me altogether unless she needed something."

To her credit, Zoey doesn't interrupt me. She just listens. Soothes me with her caresses.

"I'm pretty sure her erratic behavior got her fired from the cushy bartending job. We had nothing and it went further downhill from there. She'd leave me alone for days at a time and I'd try to fend for myself. When she was home, she was drunk or high, maybe both, and often didn't get out of bed for days at a time." I can't help but wince at the horrific memories. "When we were evicted from our old apartment, the two of us lived in her car until my grandparents helped her rent the apartment we live in now on Beacon Hill."

Zoey massages my temple lovingly. "Where are your grandparents now?"

"Dead. A car accident. I never met them, actually. Luckily, they left money with a trust lawyer to cover rent until I turned eighteen." I repeat the story my mom told me. I'm not exactly sure whether it's true or not. Jada is a pathological liar.

Zoey squeezes me tight. "That's so heartbreaking. But you turned eighteen a few years ago. Who pays rent now?"

"Ah, babe." I close my eyes. "I do. I have to, or we'll be evicted."

Zoey rests her hand on my chest while I comb my fingers through her mane of golden hair for a few minutes while that bit of information sinks in.

"You've been under too much pressure for someone so young," she whispers against my T-shirt.

"Well, now at least it's in my control." I'm fully spilling my guts now, so I figure that I might as well put it all out there. "When my mom didn't get the fat inheritance she expected, she took the bartending job at the seedy dive bar where she works now. She's still has a pathetic rotation of assholes men in her life except now they're even shadier."

Zoey keeps her head pressed to my chest as she listens. It feels good to unburden myself of secrets I've kept for so long.

It feels good to trust someone.

"I always knew her 'boyfriends' were using her. More likely paying her. Some of them were nice to me. Some yelled. Some ignored me altogether." I take a deep breath. "Some were psychotic. One guy punched me so hard, I went to the hospital. My mom wasn't much better...I still have these scars on my eyebrow." I reach up to touch the ridges that are a constant reminder of the abuse I endured.

"I can't believe you have to live like that." Zoey props her head up on her elbow. "Can't you make her go to rehab?"

I shake my head. "It doesn't work like that with an addict, babe. She'll promise then not go. She'll scream, cry, and threaten. She's tried to sell my guitar for drugs, which is why everything that means anything to me is at Carter's." The thought angers me. "Zoey . . . I mean, I'm done. I've done everything I can. She's a shell of a woman, she looks like death warmed over. She gives zero shits about me. When we leave on tour, I'm getting out for good, I *have* to. Nobody in the band knows any of this. Can you keep it on the down-low from the guys, and well . . . everyone?"

Zoey tenderly strokes the small scars on my eyebrow again, studying me. "Absolutely. I'll never betray your trust, Ty. I won't lie to you, though. It makes me really mad at your mom. I couldn't survive it."

"I've learned to be self-sufficient. Writing stories and poetry about how I wished my life could be has become my therapy. When I was twelve, I found some odd jobs around the neighborhood and saved to buy my beat-up Strat on Craig's List." I smile at the thought of my instrument. "Music saved me, and that guitar is still my favorite."

"What I'd give to see you at age twelve." Zoey looks at me with such admiration, I can't believe she's real.

It gives me courage to continue. "My teen years were solitary, but I didn't really mind. I didn't play sports and was no academic. I was a geek who locked myself in my room and learned classic rock songs. Copied my favorite '90s grunge bands' style from YouTube videos. My guitar became an extension of me, and I became proficient, even if I had no one to play for but myself.

"I just can't see that, you're so hot. And so together." Zoey studies me like she's trying to picture it. "And *cool*!"

"Yeah, I'm *soooo* cool. Well here's where you're going to dump my ass." I laugh.

"Nope. You're stuck with me Tyson Rainier—er—Rogers." Zoey smacks me.

"*Well*...There's a picture at Carter's that could make you change your mind. When I hit puberty, I was a mess; my clothes were dirty, I smelled rotten, and my hair was an absolute unruly nightmare." I still see that kid in the mirror.

"I'll believe it when I see it." Zoey traces my lips with her pink-tipped, manicured nail. I suck it into my mouth and waggle my eyebrows at her, causing her to giggle adorably.

Releasing her finger, I stroke her shoulder as I finish my sad tale. "Seriously, I was a real outsider. I couldn't relate to my classmates who, like you, had parents who loved them and money. I had no way to go to prom, buy clothes or participate in extracurricular activities. I didn't have any friends until Zane. What was I going to do? Invite someone over and risk getting reported to social services when they saw my mom passed out wasted on the couch? Or worse, some naked dude walking through the living room?"

Fuck. I never want to go back to that time. I became an expert at disappearing in plain sight. I was so painfully intro-verted and insecure. No one noticed me. My survival often depended on it. Now that I've spoken about it for the first time in my life, I'm feeling almost disassociated from myself. I'm not sure what motivated me to keep going to school. It would've been so much easier to drop out and give up.

I'd like to say it was because I wanted to get my diploma but, truthfully, it was more about being hungry—breakfast and lunch was provided through the school meal program.

"Ty, I know talking about this is hard. Especially with me, who had everything you didn't. Thank you for trusting me. For opening up. It makes me feel closer to you." Zoey's earnestness snaps me out of my thoughts. "And protective. I won't *ever* let anyone hurt you again."

I nearly burst out in tears. Instead, I press my lips to hers, feeling closer to her than anyone in my entire life. "It *is* hard. But I'm glad I told you. I certainly never dreamed that I'd be here now, the lead singer in an ass-kicking band with the hottest girlfriend in the world."

"Ooooh, tell me the story of how you guys got together!" Zoey claps her hands.

"Yeah. It's a much better story. As I said, my name—and life—changed when I met Zane in tenth grade. He didn't have any friends either, mainly because he transferred from out of state. At that point, I kept my guitar safe at school so I played during my study hall break and at lunch. He heard me singing one of my songs under the bleachers one day. The next afternoon, he joined me. The rest is history, we became fast friends and brothers."

It's impossible to keep a smile off my face when I speak of my "adopted" family, Zane and Carter. "Zane and I bonded quickly over our love of music. I was also blown away when I learned who his dad was. It's common knowledge, but Carter had severe addiction issues. He lost Zane in a custody battle, but they eventually reconciled after Carter got clean."

"That must have been strange for Zane to adjust to." To her credit, Zoey barely reacts when I mention Carter's struggles.

"I guess. Zane's mom is a famous ballerina, Lianne Rocks. They're very close. He's had some angst in his childhood too, but she's, apparently, very cool." I've never met her, but Zane worships the ground she walks on. "She moved him away from Carter during his bad years. That's why his legal last name is 'Rocks' not 'Pope.'"

"Wow. It still blows me away that Carter Pope is Zane's dad." Zoey shakes her head. "I can't imagine having a famous parent."

"Truthfully, I don't think about him like that. I'm grateful to be in Carter's orbit. He's always been so incredibly generous. When I first met him, I'd outgrown most of my clothes. He let me pick out a new wardrobe from branded swag that was just sitting around in boxes. I started spending all my free time at their house. It's where I did my laundry, took showers, and Carter taught me how to shave."

Zoey presses against me. "I love that you had him on your side."

With Zoey so close, my dick's so hard it's painful, but I make sure not to press against her so she's uncomfortable. "Carter's the closest thing to a father I'll ever know, but I'm always careful not to take advantage. When he took me to get a haircut at a real barber, I saw him slip the guy some cash and was so upset he didn't let me pay. I never wanted him to think our relationship was about handouts. It's why I decided to just grow my hair long. After that, he respected my boundaries."

Zoey leans closer. Her breasts are once again pressed against my chest. My cock throbs. Her lips hover over mine. She rakes her fingers through my hair. "I *love* your hair. So much."

I'm not stupid. I'm pretty sure Zoey wants to do more with me than kiss. So do I. It's just that somehow I know sex with her will change my life. I want her to know I'm committed to her fully before anything happens that we can't take back.

Now's not the time, so I sit up. "I can't wait for you to meet him, you'll love him."

I'm excited for Carter to meet Zoey too. He's going to be so happy for me.

"Your father figure is worshipped by guitar players around the world." Zoey laughs. "And my dad."

I can't help but chuckle. "The thing is, he's never made a big deal about it. He's a humble man because of his demons. He also never asks too many questions about my home situation, which I'm grateful for."

Because it's humiliating.

"How you grew up wasn't your fault." Zoey sits too, reaches for my hands and winds her fingers through mine. "God, I'm so grateful for my parents, I'm never going to be mean to them again."

"You should be. Your parents encourage you just like Carter encourages both Zane and me to take our music seriously." I hold Zoey's hands tightly, loving our connection. Loving that I can talk to her about anything.

Zoey rubs her thumbs over my knuckles. "It's so remarkable how far you've come."

"I've had help. Carter's always raging about the lack of resources for music-minded kids in public schools," I explain. "After he saw Zane and I play at our high school talent show, it inspired him to give back. He rallied the other guys from Limelight and created an endowment for a music program at my high school. It supplied instruments and music lessons for underprivileged kids like me. That's how I was able to afford vocal and guitar lessons."

"Wow. That's so cool." Zoey's eyes widen with wonder. "I never knew that sort of thing existed. Maybe that's something I could do one day."

The thought touches me. "You'd be amazing, butterfly. It's so important. For me it was a real turning point."

"How?" Her interest in me doesn't waiver. Incredible.

"When I sang flat out for the first time, it was a huge surprise for me, Carter and Zane that my voice had power and range. I assumed I'd be able to hide behind my guitar, but Zane is an actual virtuoso. He's even *better* than Carter," I muse. "By the time we graduated they basically forced me into the lead singer position."

"Well I, for one, am grateful to both of them." Her adoring look is addictive. I want to keep talking so she'll keep looking at me this way.

"Zane and I started writing together. Soon, we had dozens and dozens of songs and lyrics. A couple years later, we finalized the band lineup with Jace and Connor." I think back to our first meeting at Vera. "We all just clicked, the four musketeers united in our quest to make it!"

"There's no doubt you're going to make it, Ty. You've worked so hard." Zoey still rubs my hands with hers.

"LTZ is *everything* to me." I look her in the eyes. "It's my ticket out."

"I have every faith in you, Ty." Zoey leans in for a kiss. Touching my lips to hers feels heavenly. When my tongue meets hers we're lost to each other as we always are.

Zoey is *also* becoming everything to me.

I need her like I need air.

It feels like fate has led me to her. Not only do I have my band, but now I have a confident, affectionate, supportive girlfriend to spend my time with.

A beautiful butterfly who smells heavenly and looks at me like I'm the sun.

A girl who I love. Will *always* love.

Zoey is part of the new life I've created with my tight-knit band family and Carter. A *big* part.

My missing part.

"Oh crap! Do we need to leave?" Zoey pulls away from me suddenly, looking at her phone. "It's already 6:45."

"*Shit*, yes! We're going to be late." I get up quickly, stopping to caress the side of her face. "Thank you for listening to me."

"I adore you. Sometimes I have to pinch myself when I realize you're my *actual* boyfriend." Zoey kisses my forehead before she gets up and darts over to her closet.

"Oh, I'm your boyfriend all right. Okay, missy. Let's get outta here so you can finally meet Carter." I can't control my excitement. I start for the door.

Zoey rests her hands on her hips saucily. "Ah—*no*. I need fifteen minutes to change and put some makeup on. *Out*, you. Go hang out with Mike and Olivia."

Gazing at her stunning face, which needs no embellishment whatsoever, I happily do as I'm told and wait for her downstairs.

Tonight is the night everyone's gonna know exactly how much Zoey means to me.

How Zoey's going to be part of my future.

For once in my life, I'm going to have it all.

Chapter Nine

An Hour Later

WE ARRIVE AT CARTER'S sprawling house on Lake Washington in Madrona, one of the wealthiest neighborhoods in Seattle. I look up at the beautiful, immaculate craftsman mansion and suddenly feel tense.

Ty holds up his hand when he parks my car, making sure I stay seated until he opens the passenger door. I step out, take his arm and sneak a kiss because I want him to know I notice all the little things that he does to make me feel cherished every day.

"I'm nervous." I can't help but clutch vise-like to Ty's hand as we walk up to the house.

Truthfully, I'm also a shy introvert who isn't great at meeting new people. I purposely dressed to blend in by wearing a simple pair of cut-offs, a gray flowy top, and flip-flops. My stomach is churning with excitement at the thought of meeting Carter Pope, but part of me wishes we were back in my room making out.

"Don't be nervous, butterfly." Ty cups my head to hold me against him. "I've got you."

Ty uses his own key to unlock the ornate, old-growth wood door into the house. Carter's house is surprisingly traditional. Tan walls with thick crown molding stained a deep cherry red adorn each room. Throughout the house, beautifully gleaming light hardwood floors are covered with sumptuous rugs, the walls adorned with gold and platinum records and photos of Limelight throughout their career.

I hear laughter coming from the backyard, and Ty leads me through a sunken living room with a grand piano, stone fireplace, and a wall of windows that overlook Lake Washington.

"Dude, you're here!" Zane appears behind us descending from a back stairwell. He leads a stunning curvy girl with glossy black hair by the hand.

"Hey, Zane. Hi, Fee." Ty stops, draping his arm around my shoulder. "This is Zoey."

"Hey." I smile nervously.

"Ahhh, Fee. This is the girl who's stolen our guy's heart." Zane chuckles gleefully, pulling me into a bear hug.

"Zoey, Fiona Reynolds is the daughter of Gus Reynolds, who owns The Mission." Ty rolls his eyes at Zane.

"Oh, that's cool!" I practically gush. "Nice to meet you."

"You too." Fiona is polite, but is clearly disinterested.

"Well you guys are late, the food's probably ready. Let's go eat!" Zane bounds over to the sliding glass door and motions for all of us to follow him.

We step outside holding hands. Ty's bandmates, Carter, and a guy I don't recognize are gathered around a fire pit in the middle of a beautifully manicured lawn. The yard is surrounded by a stunning garden filled with shrubs, trees, and flowers of every color.

After Ty introduces me around, we fill our plates with barbequed corn on the cob, salmon, and potato salad and then join the others around the fire pit.

Carter and the guys are all so nice and welcoming, my nervousness subsides immediately. The guys talk relentlessly about band business. I sit quietly, soaking it in. Once everyone is finished, Fiona gets up and collects the paper plates. Wanting to be useful, I decide to help her.

"So, you're Ty's girlfriend?" Fiona asks as we bring the trash into the house.

"Yes, we've been together for a couple of months." I smile. "Are you Zane's girlfriend?"

"Uh, it's not like that for us." She rolls her eyes. "He's leaving on tour. I know how it is out there. I'm not about to get my heart broken."

"Oh." I look at her wide-eyed.

"Don't worry, I'm pretty sure Ty's a saint. So is Connor." She smiles at me kindly as we make our way back outside. "Zane and Jace? Meh."

"Musicians aren't meant to keep it in their pants on tour." Jace snorts. "We're too young to be tied down."

"I got into a lot of trouble not keeping it in my pants," Carter retorts while warming his hands over the fire.

"There's a visual." I surprise myself when I say what I was thinking out loud.

Everyone erupts in laughter, making me feel like I fit right in, even though I didn't actually mean to be funny. Still laughing, Ty pulls me onto his lap possessively and bands one arm around my waist. I lean back against him and he nuzzles my ear.

Pinch me now. I can't believe I'm at Carter fucking Pope's house, sitting on my boyfriend's lap in front of the entire LTZ band.

Life can't get much better than this.

"Zoey, Ty tells us you're going off to college in a couple months." Carter eases back down in his chair.

I'm shocked that he knows anything about me. "Yes, I'm going to Western this September."

"Ah, that's great. It's important to get a college degree," Gus Reynolds chimes in. "I'm hoping Fiona will finally agree with me."

Fiona fixes him with a pointed look that only a daughter can give her father. "I have a degree and I like helping you run the club, *Dad*."

"Speaking of which, we need to go." Gus has a gleam in his eye. "Carter, do you want to come with us and risk these guys destroying your house?"

"Ha! These boys are wusses. They don't party. I left Ty and Zane here last winter when we were in Europe. I think the worst thing that happened was a pizza stain on my new rug." Carter gets up to follow Gus. "Anyway. I'm going to pass, but I'll walk you to the door."

With Gus, Fiona, and Carter gone, there's a bunch of empty chairs. I feel conspicuous still sitting on Ty's lap. Nervously, I shift to move into my own seat.

"Don't get up, Zoey. We're all pretty stoked Ty's finally brought a beautiful girl around." Zane's leg bounces energetically.

Ty wraps his arm tighter around my middle and leans his head against mine. I decide to go with the flow and relax against my boyfriend. I've waited my whole life for a moment like this, might as well enjoy it.

"If you're with Ty, you'll be seeing a lot of us." Jace looks up from his phone. "We're so busy preparing for the studio and our tour, we're all practically living here."

"We're all curious, Saint Ty never hangs out with chicks." Connor takes a long pull from his beer. He seems older than the rest of the band.

"Guys, quit with the Saint Ty shit." Ty strokes my stomach. "Can't you lay off for a night?"

"I hadn't realized my charm and beauty made you switch teams, babe," I gently tease.

The entire band bursts out in laughter again, including Ty. It's a great feeling, to fit right in by just being my nerdy dad-jokey self.

"Remember when Carter actually thought we were gay?" Zane laughs. "Zoey, listen to this. In high school, Carter was always going on and on about us protecting ourselves and avoiding skanky girls, yada, yada, yada. We never brought anyone around because we were so obsessed with music. One day, Carter sat us down and interrogated us about our love lives, and it morphed into how being gay was okay and how he'd support us no matter what—"

"Zane, God. Please don't." Ty covers his face with one big palm, his cheeks reddening with embarrassment.

Zane ignores him. "We'd just lost our virginity in the band room at school."

"Together? Dude!" Connor's mouth lolls open.

"No, not together. Well kinda. Two chicks were hitting on us after the school talent show. We brought them back to the band room to make out. We were on opposite sides but when I looked over at Ty, his girl had nearly impaled herself on his monster dick before he threw her off him to fumble for a condom," Zane relays the story gleefully. "I was, like, yeah! Green light! We both did them right there in the same room, it was awesome."

"Not awesome." Ty frowns.

"Monster dick?" Jace winces. "God, please erase that visual."

"Yeah, I told Carter that even if I was gay, I'd be keeping my pristine ass far away from that thing." Zane is laughing so hard he nearly falls off his lawn chair. "It's huuuug-gggee! Right, Zoey?"

My face is flaming red. The entire band assumes we're sleeping together, but I haven't gotten anywhere close to seeing Ty's dick. Plus, now all I can picture is some girl impaling herself on my boyfriend, which pisses me off. I feel enraged. Confused.

Jealous.

"I have no problem with a little slagging, but have a little respect, guys." Ty grips my waist and gently eases me off his lap so he can get up. "Zoey is my girlfriend, our love life isn't any of y'all's business."

"Oh dude! I'm so sorry." Zane jumps up and runs over to Ty, looking remorseful. "I didn't mean anything."

"It's fine, just please shut the fuck up." Ty grimaces but holds out his hand to me. "Z, do you want me to show you the practice space?"

"Sure." I feel so uncomfortable, but I appreciate Ty wanting to diffuse the conversation. Admittedly, after Zane's story, I'm even more anxious to see Ty's "monster" dick because, though I've felt it brush up against me, I have nothing to compare it to. I'm also bummed because I was beginning to wonder if the reason Ty hasn't tried anything sexually with me is because he's still a virgin too. Now I know for sure...he does *have* sexual experience.

Why he won't go there with me?

Does he not want me that way?

He and I need to talk about this. My mom made me promise to wait for the person who would love and cherish me. I'm sure that guy is Ty. I'm sure I want him to be my first. The thing is, I'm desperately in love with him...and I'm beginning to question whether he feels the same.

I need to know. It's time.

Oblivious to my inner dialogue, Ty leads me back through the living room and down a hallway lined with Carter's personal photos. I stop to take a look.

"That's Zane when he was a baby. His mom, Lianne, is holding him." Ty points to a picture of a waiflike beauty with long, dark-red hair, porcelain skin, and doe eyes holding tiny Zane dressed in a baby version of Grunge wear, flannel, cutoffs, long underwear, tiny Doc Martins, and a gray skull cap.

The next picture is Carter and Limelight on their tour bus, with baby Zane dressed in a similar outfit, playing with some toys. The rest of the pictures are early band shots of Limelight. A ton of Carter and Zane through the years when he was little, both of them sporting various rocker hairstyles. In a still, from one of the band's most famous videos at the iconic club RKCNDY, you can see Zane's stroller in the background.

Ty tries to move me quickly past the so-called geek picture of Ty and Zane. After our intense conversation earlier, I can't help but touch it, fascinated. They're about sixteen or seventeen, with crazy hair and sullen looks. Both of them hold guitars. Ty is definitely not a geek, his pent-up charisma seems ready to explode out of a mussed-up, angsty-teen boy.

"God, I hate he has that brutal picture hanging up." Ty buries his face in my neck. "It's mortifying."

"I love it." I continue to trace Ty's face in the picture.

"I'm sorry about all that talk about dicks out there." Ty wraps his arm around my shoulders. "And, I'm sorry you found out about the virginity thing that way."

"It was before me." I peer up at him. Decide to throw out a fishing line. "We've never talked about it, but I didn't think you were a virgin. I figured there were lots of women before me."

"God, it's sure not my proudest moment." He squeezes his eyes shut. "Once it started happening, I really just wanted to get it over with."

"Did they scare you off?" Carter saunters in beside us, interrupting our conversation before I get the answers I want.

Ty tilts his head toward him. "Nah, they were just trying to get a rise out of Zoey, so I brought her inside."

"Ah, well. Musicians. We're at best, heathens." Carter shrugs.

"I love these pictures." My voice is barely a whisper. I'm nervous around Carter, more so now that he's up close and personal.

"Me too. Zane has always been the light of my life, my little dude. He was the mascot of Limelight when we had our first gold record." Carter looks at me pointedly. "But I got caught up in booze, blow, smack, and any mind-altering substance I could get my hands on. I fucked around on Zane's mom. It's not an easy road for the girlfriend of a rock musician. Lianne ditched me and took my son away for many years, which I deserved."

"It's so wonderful you've reconnected with Zane." I tentatively touch his arm. "I know how important my dad is to me, and Ty tells me you're like a father to him."

"Shit, I don't know about that." Carter laughs sharply. "When Zane brought Tyson home, I was just glad that he had a friend to spend time with while I figured my own crap out."

"It worked out pretty well." The reverential way Ty looks at Carter warms my heart.

Carter's laid-back coolness cracks a bit. "Ty has the most inner determination of anyone I've ever known. It has been an honor to help in some small way."

"Well you're lucky to have each other's back." I untangle myself from Ty's embrace. "But now I need to use your bathroom."

"Right over there." Ty points to a room next to us. "We'll be in the rehearsal space, come find us when you're done." He gestures to another door across the hall.

"Okay." I slip into a beautiful coffee-colored tiled bathroom. Needing a few moments to collect myself, I breathe deeply and stare at myself in the mirror.

Our sex talk will have to wait, but maybe it's for the best. Until today, Ty's home life was something he'd been reluctant to share with me. Now—especially after seeing Ty with Carter—the full impact of how he grew up hits me hard.

Ty's unstable childhood with an absent, addicted mother is mind-boggling for me to comprehend. I live such a privileged life, coming from a normal household in a nice neighborhood with parents who are still in love and happily married.

Yet, that old cliché about people being attracted to a person from the opposite side of the track holds true for us. I don't have much experience to draw on, but in all the ways that matter we seem to be a perfect match despite our different backgrounds.

I'm not going to worry about his past. Ty is perfect, and he is mine.

I can't believe my luck at having found my person at such a young age. I need to trust in my gut, and my gut tells me Ty feels the same way about me as I do about him.

Maybe he just needs a bigger nudge.

Chapter Ten

A Few Minutes Later

CONSIDERING HOW EMBARRASSED I am about Zane outing how we lost our virginity, it's good to have a few minutes without Zoey to get my head straight. We haven't really talked about sex yet. It's not something I'm used to discussing, even though I want her desperately.

All I know is Zoey means more to me than a quick, meaningless fuck. My heart has forever longed for what I've found with her. I don't want to mess it up. Mess *her* up.

Carter snaps me out of my thoughts by picking up one of his guitars and strumming. *Fuck*. I know I'm going to get an earful.

"So, she's pretty great, right?" I jut out my chin, daring him to say otherwise.

Carter doesn't even look up from fiddling with his amp. "She seems nice."

"She's not just nice, she's perfect. I think she's the one for me." I sit on an amp opposite from him. "My *only* worry is she's too young."

"Wow, Ty. That's big." Carter's tone is noncommittal despite his words.

"Yeah," I press on so he understands how serious I am. "But I need this band to make it. I don't have anything else to fall back on, I've got to get away from my mom."

"I know. LTZ has my full support." Carter stands and clasps my shoulder. "So do you."

I try not to get choked up. Though he's said it before, hearing it never gets old. "Thanks, Carter. It means a lot."

"How does Zoey being the 'one' fit into those plans?" He squints, curious.

"I *love* her. I haven't told her yet but I've never had feelings like this. She's just so beautiful. And kind. And sweet." It's hard to put into words why she's come to mean so much to me in such a short time.

"So, why make it about love? Why not enjoy the summer with her and not take it so seriously?" Carter taps a finger on his chin, studying me intently.

"How do you not make it about love? This *is* serious for me." I take a pause, then continue. "I know she's going to college at Western in the fall and we'll be on tour. It doesn't matter. I want us to stay together. All the other guys are going to be partying and fucking around. I'm just not into it. Part of me wishes there were a way for the band to be successful without having to be out on the road. Don't you think being home more would've made a difference with Lianne?" I realize I'm anxious and need some fatherly advice from the only man who can give it to me.

Carter stares at me, dumbfounded. Ty, I'm going to give it to you straight. Get her out of your system and let her go when you leave. It will suck, you'll be sad, but you are way too young to be thinking about forever with any girl, especially one who just graduated high school."

"I don't *want* to get her out of my *system.*" I'm angry. This reaction is not what I expected.

"C'mon, you've never really *dated*, let alone had a serious girlfriend." Carter is incredulous. Confused.

"No. But, I haven't been completely immune to the women that throw themselves at me either, Carter." I scowl petulantly.

He throws his hands up. "Thank *God*, you're far too young to settle down."

"Really?" I snark. "You were with Zane's mom at my age, weren't you?"

"Yes! It was the *worst* fucking mistake of—" Carter stops mid-sentence. His face drains of all color. "*No*, it wasn't a mistake. Zane was *never* a mistake."

"You *loved* Lianne." I try to get him to understand. "Maybe if you'd—"

"I did," he interrupts. "And, take it from me, having a girlfriend and a kid and living this life just doesn't go together."

Carter shakes his head. "Trust me, if you go down that path, it will inevitably blow up."

"Carter, I've had to make my own decisions and support myself for a long time now. I didn't have anyone who ever gave two fucks about me until I met Zane and you. But Zoey is a whole new level, I *know* I want to be with her." I dig my heels in. "My life and what I want from it is different than yours, that's what I'm trying to say."

He raises his eyebrows, unconvinced. "You're only twenty-one, you don't know a lot."

"Well, neither do you," I snap. "I sure don't feel twenty-one. I'm not going to *ever* fuck a bunch of girls who are strangers. I'm not my mom. I'm also not like the sleazeball guys who fuck my mom. I'll never be like that. I'd die first."

"What does Zoey want?" Carter backs off a bit after my outburst. "Didn't she just turn eighteen? I mean c'mon. You said it yourself, she's young. Do you think she feels the same way?"

Uncertainty kicks in a bit. "I hope so. If she stays with me, I'll do whatever it takes to be a good man for her, because that's the kind of guy she deserves."

"Look, I'm not trying to fight with you, Ty." Carter picks up his guitar and strums a few notes. "Just promise me you'll not do anything stupid. Or permanent. Use *condoms*."

I sigh without answering and play a counter-melody. Zoey slips into the room and stands against the wall, watching us with a look of awe on her face. We play and sing a few covers, Led Zeppelin, Soundgarden, Oasis, and finally a couple of Beatles

When we finish and I set my guitar back on its stand. Zoey gleefully bounces over to me and throws herself into my arms. "You guys are so talented, I'm so lucky to just be able to hear you play like this. Thank you, Carter, for letting me be here today."

"You're welcome, sweetheart. Anytime." Carter smiles at her kindly. He sets his own guitar on its stand. "You take care of him, yeah?"

"I'll do my best," Zoey sounds as though she's taking a solemn oath.

"I'm gonna call it a night." Carter makes a move toward the door. "Ty, remember I'm off tomorrow for those festival shows. When I get back it'll be time to focus in the studio."

"I can't wait, hope everything goes well." I salute him as he leaves.

Carter salutes back and departs. "Yep."

I grab my guitar and started strumming again, thinking about the conversation I've just had with Carter. Summer is going by quickly. It's time to make sure Zoey and I are on the same page for what comes next.

"So, are you going to visit me when I'm on tour, butterfly?" I catch her eye while plucking through the notes of a tune that's been formulating for the past few days.

"If I can, I'd love to." Zoey sits on an amp across from me.

"I'll pay for your ticket." I try to keep eye contact with her to gauge her interest. "I'll check the tour schedule when it gets finalized."

"I'd like that, but I'm going to have to see how my classes and school obligations shake out, Ty." She stares off into the distance, avoiding my gaze. "Plus, you might change your mind about us once you're on the road."

"I'm not going to change my mind about you or us, Zoey." I place my guitar on its stand again and cross the room. Gently lift the butterfly on her necklace from her throat and rub it with my thumb.

"I hope not." She sucks in a breath as I place the little charm carefully against her throat.

Bending down, I touch my forehead to hers. Her hazel eyes find mine and her pink lips part. She studies me with a mixture of excitement and anxiety. My cock instantly hardens, I want her so much.

I lift her chin, and Zoey captures my mouth while gripping my shirt tightly in her fists. She sips from my lips as her tongue searches for mine. Exploring her pouty mouth is pure bliss.

Zoey's hands moved downward to rest on my hips. I wrap my arms around her head and shoulders, pulling her flush against me as we devour each other. One hand moves across the front of my board shorts tentatively, cupping my erection. Instantly, I twist my hips away.

"*Oh*! I'm sorry. I didn't mean..." Zoey's eyes fill with tears. "Oh God, I was right. You don't want me like that."

"No! Z, *no*. I want you so much." I take her back into my arms, not caring that my dick is as hard as it's ever been and that she can most certainly feel it against her belly.

"Are you sure? This isn't just a summer thing for you?" Zoey's voice quivers.

"It's so much more than that." I search her eyes with mine. "So much *bigger*."

"You'll be on the road. I heard Carter. Aren't you afraid of being tied down?" She looks down at my chest, breaking eye contact.

Tipping her chin up with my finger, I catch her gaze again, hoping she can see how much she means to me. "After everything I told you today, do you *really* think I want to be with someone else?"

"I hope not." Zoey runs her hands up and down my arms nervously. "But, you always pull away from me when we start to do more than kiss. If you feel this way about me, I wish I knew why you were so anxious to get the job done with the band room girl and don't seem to want me?"

"Shit. Z. Don't think like that. It's the opposite. I want to be with you more than anyone in the world." If she only knew that I've rubbed one or two out every day since I'd met her.

Or maybe not.

"You've never even tried to touch my boobs. Or my..." Zoey's anguish seeps into her voice.

"I don't know how to handle this," I confess, gesturing between us. "The only sex I've ever had was meaningless and empty. It's meant nothing to me. This is so much more. So much bigger."

Zoey buries her face in my shoulder. "All your band-mates assume I've seen your dick. I felt so stupid out there because I *want* to. So badly. I mean, we've not even talked about it and I just tried to touch you..."

"...you deserve for your first time to be special, butterfly. Not in the band practice room, trust me on this." I hold her to me, stroking her soft hair.

Zoey pulls away. "Carter said he doesn't think it's a good idea for us to be serious. Are you sure that's not why?"

"Of course not. Carter has his own baggage that doesn't apply to me. To *us*. I may only be twenty-one, but I'm a grown man. You must have heard me say I'm not going to fuck around like he did. I rarely drink, I don't mess with drugs. I'm serious about my music. My career." I scratch my head and take a deep breath. "Most of all, I'm serious about *you*."

"I'm serious about you too Ty, but you're going to meet so many beautiful women and have so many experiences without me." Zoey sighs dramatically. "Carter is just looking out for you."

"I have worries too, you know. You're hot. You're fun. You're the smartest person I've ever met. When you're at college you'll have your pick of any dude you want. Someone who you'll have a lot more in common with than a wannabe rock musician. Maybe you'd be better off..." I feel sick at thinking of her with someone other than me.

She grabs my hand. "No. Don't say it. You're an intelligent, ambitious guy. And, you're the one I want."

"Ahh, fuck. Okay. I'm just going to say it. I've never had anyone look at me the way you do. You're *everything*. I *love* you, Zoey." I can't stop my feelings from spilling out of my mouth. "I'm so fucking in love with you, I can barely think of anything else. I'm trying so hard to do the right thing. You're so much younger than me. I don't want to push you into having sex before you're ready. But, *fuck*. The thoughts I have about you. What I want to do with you. *To* you. I can't help it. I want to bury myself in your body, butterfly. I've never felt this way about anyone. *Ever.*"

"Oh, God. *Ohmygod*, Ty. I love you too. I'm having all of the same emotions and feelings. I've never loved anyone so much, and I know I'll never feel like this about anyone else. *Ever.*" Zoey squeezes my hand. "I want to do all of those things with you. To you. And have you do them to me."

I sit next to her on the amp. My free hand strokes through her hair and I nuzzle her neck before our lips meet, smashing together furiously. Sucking her lower lip into my mouth, I savor her. Then place soft kisses all over her entire face, eyelids, cheeks, and temple before revisiting her supple lips to taste her again.

Zoey caresses my neck, her lips swollen from our passion. "Ty, you've got to know that you're the only one I'm ever going to want to be with."

"Oh, butterfly." I suck her earlobe. Her words are the most precious I've ever heard spoken to me.

"We're both leaving in a few weeks and we won't see each other for months." Zoey once again tentatively caresses the bulge in my shorts. I gulp, watching her hand stroke me as I stiffen even more. "We don't have many days left to be together like this. I want to do everything with you. I don't want to wait anymore."

"Look how you affect me." I drag my hand through my hair, watching my cock grow bigger under her touch. I'm barely able to hold it together. It's possible I'll come in my shorts if I'm not careful.

"I mean it. Please don't make me wait," Zoey pleads. "I love you so much, Ty. I've never wanted anything more."

"Oh, Z. Me too." I cup her hand over my erection. "I want you to be sure about us having sex. I don't want you to regret anything."

"Don't be ridiculous, Ty." She kisses me, keeping her grip firm on my cock. "My only regret would be if we waste any more time."

"I'm not sure what I'm doing, Z. I mean, you're a virgin. What if I don't know how to make it good for you?" My mind whirls, I'm overcome with so many emotions.

"I'm fairly certain we'll be able to figure it out, together," she assures me. "I *know* it will be good, there's no way it won't be."

I can't help but breathe a sigh of relief, realizing that traditional gender roles seem to be reversed in our situation. "Do you really love me?"

"So much! From the moment I met you," she gushes.

"Me too." I help reposition her so that she's straddling me. Grip her ass and pull her core flush against my hard cock. Her delicious heat surrounds me.

"*Ohhh.*" Zoey braces herself with her hands on my shoulders. Her eyes clamp shut as she grinds her pussy against my erection. She unabashedly seeks pleasure from my body, which I long to give her.

I brush my fingers lightly up under her top before pushing it up to expose her stomach and ample cleavage. My mouth finds hers and our tongues dance again. Tracing the undersides of her white, cotton bra with my fingertips, I continue exploring, cupping and stroking her breasts.

"Jesus, Z." My dick swells against the seam of her cutoffs when she circles her hips against me. I lick and suck the soft swell of creamy cleavage spilling over the top of her bra. My thumbs strum her nipples, hardening them to bullets poking through the fabric.

I *have* to taste them. I can't wait.

"Ty, please," Zoey begs.

Her beautiful eyes are half-mast with desire when I click open the front clasp and expose her luscious tits tipped with dusky-pink nipples. Fascinated, I pinch each bud gently, alternating between pulling and stroking them to watch how she responds.

Her little whimpers let me know that I'm doing something right. Groaning, I suck each delicious nipple into my mouth one after the other and swirl my tongue all around each taut peak. Lost in my worship of her perfect breasts, I don't hear the door open.

"Oh shit, sorry," Connor shouts and immediately retreats. "I thought you took Zoey home."

Wrapping my arms around my love, I make sure she's flush against me so her breasts aren't exposed. I hold up one hand with my finger pointed to the ceiling. "We need a minute."

"Uh, aye." Connor keeps his eyes to the ground but holds the door ajar about an inch. "Everyone is coming to jam, dude, so get yourselves sorted."

"Oh, God." Zoey is mortified. She refastens her bra and pulls her top down. "Did he see my boobs?"

"No, I kept you covered." I smooth her hair down. My boner deflated when Connor interrupted us, so I focus on getting Zoey pulled together. Within a minute we're decent. "I knew this was a terrible place for us to do this, Z. I'm sorry."

Zoey blushes. "As embarrassing as being caught was, I loved what you were doing. For the record, it felt amazing."

"You almost made me come in my pants, which I'd have never lived down." I laugh at the absurdity of the moment.

"*Really?*" She stares at me in wonder.

"Really. I was two seconds away." I kiss her forehead. "It's under control now. Barely."

"Well, maybe I should go before they come back in." Zoey tries to move off my lap.

"No, stay while we jam." I grip her hips to keep her from moving. "*Please.*"

"Are you sure?" Zoey's surprised. "I'll have to see if it's okay with my parents."

"Text them. It'll be fun," I assure her. "Feel free to see if Alex wants to come over, I'm sure a few more of our friends will show up."

"Wow! That's so cool." Zoey picks up her phone and texts furiously.

"Hey." I encircle her wrist.

Zoey's big, hazel eyes look up from her phone to me.

"You're so beautiful and sexy." I kiss her softly. "That was my first time...uh, exploring like that... uh. I hope we'll do it again. *Soon.*"

"We'll need to make sure we're alone, though." Zoey winks. "I swear, Connor's a cock-blocker."

Just as we disengage from each other, Zane and Jace bound through the door with Connor trailing behind. Alex joins not long after and Zoey seems so happy to have her best friend included. Later Fiona returns with a couple guys who are joining our tour as roadies.

We work through a few new songs and play through our set, but it's hard for me to keep my eyes off Zoey.

The feeling must be mutual because we can't stop shooting each other shit-eating grins as we jam well into the night.

All I know is, with Zoey by my side and my band on the rise, life has never been better.

Chapter Eleven

A Couple of Weeks Later

FOR SOMEONE AS VIBRANT and wonderful as Ty, the sparse, sad, and damp-smelling place he calls "home" is depressing. Ty keeps his room neat, but there isn't much to it. It consists of a twin bed with a plain, blue comforter and tan sheets, a small plastic end table, a guitar stand, and stacks and stacks of notebooks lining the walls.

"What are those?" I point to the piles.

Ty glances quickly and looks away. "Nothing. Poems, song ideas, random shit.".

I pick one up to read it, but he gently takes it away. "Please don't. These were written during some troubling times, Z."

"Maybe you should record them." I put my arms around him, hoping I'm a comfort.

"I don't know." Ty's smile doesn't quite reach his eyes. "There's so much darkness inside these books. Probably not hit material."

"I love you so much, babe. There's no more darkness in your future." I stroke his back and try to be reassuring. All I want to do was absorb any of the pain he's ever been through.

A noise in the front room startles us. Ty looks panic-stricken.

"Is your mom home?" I ask tentatively.

"God, I hope not." Ty pops his head out to check. "Nope, it was the window. It slammed shut."

"Good. Do we have time to take up where we left off in the practice room?" I waggle my eyebrows. We haven't been alone much since Carter's almost two weeks ago. Since then, all I've thought about is his lips on my nipples.

Other places I want him to taste.

"*Zoey.*" Ty gives me a pointed look as he gathers his notebooks. "Not *here*. Besides, we don't have time. I can't be late for the studio."

I get it. He has other things on his mind. It's exciting times for LTZ. The rest of the guys are in the recording studio setting up for sessions with Carter and their producer tomorrow. My heart fills with pride. "It's all happening, babe!"

Ty takes my hand and brings it to his lips for a kiss. "I know! I just found out Carter's management company is going to take us on."

"Wow!" I follow him out of his room to the front door. "And now the tour is completely booked. I can't believe you're opening for Limelight in New York."

"Well, if all goes well in the studio, hopefully we can all quit our day jobs after this tour." Ty locks the apartment behind us. "Thanks to Jace, our social numbers are close to a hundred thousand now. Zane wanted to do this without help, but I'm all for a little nepotism from Carter. We'll be able to launch nationally without signing our lives away to a record label."

"I'll miss you while you're so busy but I'm behind you all the way, Ty." I vow to be the most supportive band girlfriend in history.

"I want you to be there as much as possible. The summer is slipping by, I'm not giving up any more time with you, butterfly." Ty smooches my forehead before we get into my RAV4.

A few days later, Alex and I are at the recording studio. After she came to the jam session at Carter's house, she feels a lot more comfortable hanging out with me and the band. During their recording sessions, we get lost in our own private world of giggles and gossip.

I guess we're lucky the guys seem to genuinely enjoy both of us. Supplying them with Alex's mom's pies, Dick's burgers, and Slurpees doesn't hurt. Either way, we're in heaven. I feel grateful to witness LTZ create innovative, hard-rocking anthems that are sure to become part of Seattle's storied rock history.

"He's so fucking sexy, look at his arms." Alex ogles Jace, who keeps his eyes decidedly averted from my BFF.

We're sitting in an overstuffed couch in the lounge off the control room, which gives us a bird's eye view of the Viking drummer laying down tracks for *Rise*. The other three guys are in another studio making changes to the chorus of a different song.

I nudge her with my elbow. "Have you at least got him to kiss you yet?"

"He isn't interested. He treats me like I'm a child. Do you hear him call me 'Beanie' because apparently, I'm skinny like a string bean? *Mortifying*." Alex slumps. "Have you made it past second yet?"

"I wish. Ty's taken on double shifts at the bistro to save up money for the past two weeks. When I actually see him, we're lucky to even sneak a kiss in without my parents hovering." I pout. "I think they have spidey sense that things are moving fast with us and they're trying to thwart it."

"Well, duh." Alex rolls her eyes. "You guys are so completely whacked over each other, I'm sure they think you've already gone there."

"How's the Instagram coming along, Beanie?" Jace tromps toward the door to the alley. Apparently, he finished playing and we didn't even notice.

"Good," she calls out after him.

"Sweet." He holds a hand up in acknowledgement, but disappears outside.

"*See?* I hate it." Alex wrinkles her nose. "I'm not sure why I keep crushing on him, he so clearly has put me in the 'little sister' category."

"At least he's helping you build up your social," I encourage. "Plus, he's easy on the eyes."

"And, he's super witty." Alex's eyes dilate with lust. "His commentary on the studio time is so funny, he could have been a professional comedian."

I purse my lips. "I'm not a fan of his annoying 'spycam' posts of me and Ty making out. The fans are going to hate me so much."

As the band's social media guru, Jace records every moment. I didn't realize how seriously he took the marketing stuff and how instrumental his work has been to propel the band forward. Religious about algorithms, tracking post engagement and views, Jace is the wizard behind LTZ's PR and social strategy.

I enjoy spending time with the other two guys too, especially Zane. The process he and Ty use to write songs is fascinating. They fight like cats and dogs over lyrics and guitar lines, but always come to agreement in the end. The result is magic.

He's also super affectionate, always hugging me. Not in a sexual way, more like a brother. It makes me feel accepted into the LTZ family.

Connor is quiet and introspective and harder to get to know, especially because I've been extremely bashful around him since he walked in on us. He's a sweetheart, though. Great Irish accent. Devoted to his girlfriend and family. He seems to have an endless number of brothers who get themselves into situations that require Connor to come to the rescue. My observation is the big, gruff ginger is a bad boy on the surface with a marshmallow heart.

I'm seeing a new side of Ty. He's hyper-focused on making sure his vocals come out perfect on the first take so he's not responsible for wasting expensive studio time. His pre-recording routine is strict: hot tea with lemon, vocal warm-up exercises and visualization. All of which he learned in vocal training. It works, he nails every take.

My heart swoons when I listen to the playbacks of Ty's raw vocal tracks. Now that I know him so well, I can hear every nuance in his voice. His burly yet soulful yowls are a combination of rough sensuality tinged with sorrow. His lyrics, while sometimes playful, are poignant and expose the raw vulnerability he tries to keep hidden.

Like one of his Seattle idols, Chris Cornell, Ty's natural voice is deep, almost baritone, but he has no problem reaching higher pitches with his incredible, multi-octave range.

In other words, he's exceptional.

LTZ's going to be huge and I can't wait to be there for the ride.

Chapter Twelve

A Few Days Later

A WEEK INTO LTZ's recording session, Ty and I finally catch a break to an entire day alone. A tech company paid big dollars to book out the studio for twenty-four hours at the last minute, so we find ourselves with a full day to ourselves with no work and nothing to do.

It's our *chance*.

Ty arrives at my house after my parents leave for work. We race up to my room. Shut and lock my door.

Stripping his worn jeans and black T-shirt off in two seconds flat, Ty stands before me in his sexy, black boxer briefs. Eagerly, I step into his tight embrace.

"God, Z. You're so incredibly beautiful, I can't believe you're mine." Ty pulls me close to him and runs his hands up and down my back while kissing me so passionately, I don't remember my name.

Slowly, he slides one hand across my side, over the soft swell of my stomach and cups my pussy over my yoga pants. Flicks his finger over my clit. Gripping his soft hair at the nape with one hand to make sure our mouths don't lose contact, I yank down my waistband. Ty helps me shimmy them down and off.

Our tongues dance together as he slips his fingers into my wetness under my panties. Moaning, I surge against his fingers, seeking more contact. Each touch triggers jolts of desire throughout my core.

Things have ramped up slightly between us after that night in the band room, but up until this moment, we've never been this free. Feeling the rough pads of his fingers directly on my clit is a revelation. I squeal. Squirm. Mewl. It feels so good, I can't even comprehend.

I wish we'd been doing this every minute of every day for the past four months.

Smiling against my mouth, Ty sucks on my bottom lip then licks and kisses along my jaw to my neck and under my ear. "You like that, Z?"

"*Oh!*" is all I manage to eke out. Holy hell, when he inserts his finger inside me every muscle in my pussy clenches around it. Every molecule in my body feels like a live wire. My belly knots in arousal, and I can't stand up a minute longer.

We sink side-by-side onto my bed, his finger still pushing in and out of me, spreading my wetness everywhere. I kiss his neck, caress his face, and reach down to grip his thick, hard cock straining in his boxer briefs.

Ty and I may be fumbling novices, but our passion is real as we explore each other and work our bodies into a frenzy.

Panting, our lips part from our soulful kisses for just a moment. He traces my face with the fingertips of the hand that isn't still busy giving me the greatest pleasure I've ever known. I flutter my fingers over his knuckles. Turn his hand over and trace each finger with mine.

"I love you," I whisper over and over.

Ty whispers back, "I love you too."

Ty withdraws his finger, sucks it clean and together we pull my white tank top off. My nipples are puckered and almost painfully tight with arousal. Staring in wonder at my breasts, Ty cups them in each hand, running his thumbs over my diamond-hard peaks.

Electricity shoots straight down to my pussy.

"Holy fuck, Zoey, you're so—soo—*fuuuuck*." Ty looks at me with such devotion, so much unconditional love, I hope he knows without any doubt that I feel the same way.

Bending over me, he worships each breast in succession, kissing and swirling his tongue all around my flesh, sucking my nipples into his mouth. The sensation of his wet tongue and his gentle suction nearly send me over the edge. Whimpering with untethered desire, I clutch at his shoulders and grind my core against his thigh, desperately seeking pressure where I need it.

Ty's hard cock presses against me as he continues his adoration of my body, exploring my arms, belly, back, and thighs thoroughly, as if he's cataloging every inch.

Shifting us so that I'm straddling him, Ty positions me against his cock so that it nestles tightly between my pussy lips through our underwear. Instinctively, I thrust against him, bracing myself on his chest. He guides my hips back and forth and side to side, building our pleasure to an absolute boiling point.

When he cups my ass and pulls me even tighter against his shaft, I pulse and cream, soaking my panties. I'm so wet that it trickles down my inner thighs.

Growling with desire, he pulls my face to his and we kiss fiercely. His free hand keeps a grip on my hip to move me faster back and forth against his hard length. The stimulation is overwhelming. I'm building to something I'm not sure I understand, but I know it's going to be incredible.

"Zoey, God. You feel so amazing, you're so fucking beautiful." Ty thrusts up against me. He'd be inside me if it weren't for our underwear.

"Ty, please let me see you. Ohmygod, this feels so good." My full sexuality is unleashed. Desire for my guy is the only thing that matters to me now.

"Yes, *yes*." Ty releases his grip on my hips. Run his hands along my thighs, encouraging me to take what I want.

Eagerly, I scoot down his thighs and pull down his boxer briefs to reveal his cock. Like a present, it protrudes up from a thatch of dark hair flush against his flat stomach. It's the first I've seen in real life, and even I know it's utterly magnificent.

Awestruck, I tentatively grasp him with one hand, which doesn't begin to fit around his thickness. Not sure what to do next, I stroke him slowly, feeling slightly petrified about how he'll ever fit inside my virgin walls.

I'm fascinated, though. His cock is beautiful perfection. Smooth, velvety skin stretches over his iron-hard length. Ty's hand closes over mine and together we stroke up and down his shaft. I watch our hands work together in awe, grateful he's showing me how he likes being touched. I want to please him so badly, I lean down and lick, then suck on the bulbous head.

"Jesus, butterfly." He bolts up and I comically flop to the side of him. "Putting your mouth on me, *fuck*— It feels too good. I'm already hanging on here by a thread."

"Do you have a condom?" I don't want to stop. Sex with Ty is going to be epic. Huge or not, I'm so excited, so aroused, I just want him inside me.

Fucking me.

"I don't, Z. We need to take things slowly." Ty rolls toward me, takes me in his arms and reaches down and traced circles around my clit through my panties. "It's probably going to kill me not to be inside you though."

"But—" I protest, pouting because all I can think about is we've wasted all summer when we could have been—should have been—making love. Our bodies were made for this.

Ty laughs softly. "Hear me out. As much as it pains me to say this, it'll be better if we wait. I've been tested for tour, so know I'm clean. Maybe you can go on the pill or something?

I want to be inside you with nothing between us. Does that freak you out?"

"No, of course not. I started the pill a month ago, Mom brought me in." I stroke his hair.

"What?" Ty's eyes widen in horror.

I scoff. "C'mon. She saw the kiss at the graduation party, she's not stupid."

"Your parents are going to fucking kill me." Ty buries his face in my hair, then peeks up, smiling. We kiss again. Our lips are like magnets.

"They know I love you. I told mom you were the right guy for me," I assure him between kisses.

"I *am* the right guy for you. I'm the *only* guy for you." Ty tickles my ear with his tongue.

I giggle then sigh with contentment when Ty rolls on top of me, caging my torso with his arms. Bending down, he lavishes my nipples with his tongue as he moves my panties aside with the pad of his finger, tenderly tracing circles directly on my clit.

Over the past couple of weeks, he's made me come a couple of times through our clothes, but I've never known what it's like to be directly stimulated like this. I've never been wetter. My hips involuntarily thrust against Ty's hand when he rubs my little nub more furiously. He's the first person to touch me so intimately. It's intense.

It's pure fucking ecstasy.

"Ohmygod, Ty," I whisper as my arms fling up above my head, unable to do anything but give in to the pleasure.

Ty props himself up on one elbow, his expression wondrous. He watches his finger move against me inside my panties as I undulate like a wild woman against him. When he slowly inserts another finger inside my tight channel, he twists his hand so the heel of his palm applies direct pressure against my clit. The combination is overwhelming, my head thrashes on my pillow.

"I love figuring out your body, butterfly." Ty flicks his eyes up to mine. "I want to make sure I know everything that makes you feel good."

I can't speak because nothing prepares me for the intoxicating dual sensation of him pumping his finger in and out of my wet channel while pressing against my pussy. I whimper with pleasure and clench around him like a vise.

Ty carefully works his fingers even deeper inside me, watching my every reaction as he tests out different rhythms and strokes. He loves me so much. Without a shadow of a doubt, I know I've entrusted my heart to the right man.

"Z, you're so, so tight." Ty's hard length twitches against my thigh. "I don't want to hurt you. We're going to need to get you ready, for um—"

I bite my lip and nod, still unable to talk because of the intensity of the pleasure encompassing my body but understanding completely what he means. He's so huge, no matter how wet and ready I am, we need to take the time to stretch me out.

"Does this feel good, baby?" Ty adds another finger and circles my clit with his thumb. Everything he does is a revelation. I'm flooded with sensation. My body overwhelmed with the staggering strength of what he's building for me.

Everything starts to go hazy. I wail when a full-body jolt floods me in waves. My entire body seizes and my pussy convulses around Ty's fingers. Orgasms from Ty's direct touch are intense and amazing.

"Oh, you are so, so beautiful, butterfly, watching you come—" Ty sucks his fingers that taste of me. He shakes his head and smiles. "Z, I'm already addicted to making your pretty eyes flutter like that. Can we make love for the first time on my birthday? It will be my present. That way, we can remember our first time together. Forever."

I pant and clench through what seems like a million aftershocks, overwhelmed by what just happened. When I'm finally coherent, there's a lump in my throat. Ty is so thoughtful. Romantic. Sensitive.

Mine.

"You make me feel *soooo* good. I'd love to be your birthday present." I'm splayed out next to him, overcome with emotion. All my greedy thoughts from before this magical moment vanish. We love each other. We have all the time in the world. There's no reason to rush when we'll be giving each other this kind of pleasure for the rest of our lives.

"Oh, I'm not nearly done, yet." Ty's big palms span my hips and he shifts over me, a glint in his eye.

His lips kiss down my body. His tongue traces a line down my breasts and ribcage before heading lower. I'm incapable of speaking, only moaning. His dark hair falls forward, blocking his face and brushing my skin. He moves lower as my muscles tighten and flex, every nerve ending on high alert.

When Ty kisses my belly button and slightly rounded belly, I try to move away, knowing I haven't shaved down below.

He won't have it. "No, Zoey, everything about you is sexy, please don't ever hide yourself from me." Ty looks up from under his hair at me.

I reluctantly move my hand away. Ty beams. His hands smooth over my thighs, gently moving them apart. Bending down, he licks and swirls his tongue around my sweet spot, causing my eyes to roll back into my head.

Holy mother of God, I thought what he did to me before was as good as it could get. But, *this*. I didn't know anything could feel this phenomenal. My whole body shakes as he relentlessly kisses and licks my pussy and fucks me with his tongue. Propped on my elbows, I can't help but watch Ty devour me.

It's intense. Overwhelming.

I cry out and flop back against the pillows when I detonate into a puddle of bliss. Then he sucks my clit hard into his mouth and pulses his tongue and logic and reason disappear. My body was made for this. To come. And come. And come. I'm flailing. Clenching. Screaming.

At some point I realize that Ty is slowly lapping at me with long, soothing licks. Easing me through spasms that are slowly subsiding. He smiles when he sees I'm coherent again.

"It's official. I'm addicted to watching you come." He moves up to snuggle me tightly into his side. His cock presses against my hip, wet at the tip.

Feeling him against me is intoxicating. I never want this afternoon to end. "That's good news because I'm *hooked* on you making me come."

"So, I did okay?" He nuzzles the hollow of my neck.

"You were worried?" I skim my hand all over his back. "You didn't need to be, that was uh-may-zing. I'm not sure I'll be able to take any more awesomeness than that."

"Can I admit something to you?" Ty feathers kisses along my jawline before catching my gaze.

I mentally brace myself. "Oh God, what?"

"I watched a couple porns to learn what to do because I've never...uh, done that before. I wanted to make it good for you." He grins like he just got an A+ in pussy-licking, which, come to think of it, he did.

"That's too funny. I read about a million blogs about blowjob techniques because I've never given one." I reached down to stroke his cock the way he showed me earlier. "I want you to teach me how to drive you out of your mind. I think we should be doing this all the time."

Ty's expression is slightly haunted just for a second before he smiles. "Touch me. Suck me. Whatever you want. I'll like it."

Eager to please him, though still slightly intimidated by my inexperience, I roll my thumb over his cock head while I stroke him up and down with my free hand. Ty rakes his fingers through my hair as he bucks languidly into my fist. His breath comes out in faint moans. His eyebrows knot and release. Spellbound, I stroke faster and harder, using my thumb to rub the ridge under his crown like I read about.

I must do something right because Ty's mouth lolls open and his breathing becomes more rapid. Feeling powerful to have such an effect on my man, I keep pumping while kissing and sucking on his flat, brown nipples. When I'm feeling bolder, I lick my way down his stomach until his cock is right in front of my lips.

I grip him at the root and take his shaft in my mouth as far as I can, mimicking my research by licking and suctioning him, swirling my tongue around his little opening. He caresses my hair and our eyes lock when he thrusts in between my lips. I hollow my cheeks, creating a tight circle of pressure around his cock.

That's all it takes. Ty's eyebrows arch, his hips jerk forward and his mouth open in a silent scream. He abruptly withdraws from my mouth just in time to spurt streams of thick come all over his sexy stomach. His whole body trembles.

Afterward, we lay together, marveling.

"I would have swallowed." I rest my chin on his chest, wondrously tracing a finger through the fluid on his belly.

His deep voice sounds almost drugged. "Next time, I'll take you up on that."

"So, I was an okay student?" I feel a bit shy about my skills.

"You're an A+ everything." Ty grips my hair. "I'm going to put that blowjob in my memory bank for the long, cold nights on the road without you."

"Ty!" I swat at him.

His lips find mine, our tongues wind together. "We taste good." He smacks his lips.

I'll admit, kissing Ty after our mouths have brought each other such immense pleasure feels wicked. Addictive.

"We do." I giggle. "You've ruined me for anyone else."

"Thank God." Ty snuggles me against him.

We doze off wrapped in each other's arms. Around noon we wake up for more sexy time, and laze nakedly in my bed for a while watching a show on Netflix. Too soon we have to get dressed, clean my sheets and freshen up before my folks get home from work and Ty has to go back to the studio. Throughout our tasks we sneak glances at each other, our smiles so big we can barely contain ourselves.

Life as we both know it has changed forever. He and I are going to be doing this the rest of our lives.

I'm all in with Ty.

I'm sure he's all in with me too.

Chapter Thirteen

Ten Days Later

AFTER OUR MAGICAL SEXUAL awakening, Ty and I can't keep our hands, lips, and body parts away from each other. I'm sure we make everyone around us sick of our PDAs. I'm also sure we piss people off when we disappear.

But neither of us care.

It's become almost an obsession to steal alone time to learn what our bodies are capable of. My house is tough. The car is easier, but cramped. Then, like a miracle, Ty's mom left a note telling him she'd moved to Spokane with a new boyfriend. As shitty of a mother as Jada is, it's like he and I have our own place.

All it takes is the *look*, and I literally soak my panties in anticipation of exploring Ty's lithe, strong body or of him finding a new erogenous spot on mine. No toys. No gimmicks. Just us. We experiment freely to learn everything that gives each other pleasure. The only thing we haven't done is vaginal sex, which we're saving for Ty's birthday.

In just a little over a week, I'll have officially given Ty all of my firsts.

I can't wait. I know how special it'll be. It will bond us forever.

LTZ is winding up their studio sessions, moving into the phase of mastering and mixing the songs. As one of the producers, Carter spends more and more time at the studio with the guys weighing in and helping refine the sound. He's used his fame and connections to help LTZ sign a distribution-only deal with his label, which is huge.

LTZ's album will be made widely available throughout the world on all digital platforms and in physical stores, but the record label will only take a ten percent administration fee rather than the traditional ninety percent. All the band members—even Zane—are thrilled, but Ty remains stoic, or "cautiously optimistic" as he calls it.

I think it's because he doesn't want to get his hopes up just to have them dashed. Now that his time to shine is getting closer, he's nervous about the unknown. Plus, we've become each other's most important person—and six months apart seems like six years. We're going to miss each other like crazy.

Which is why I'm at the studio and in his bed every chance I get. I won't miss even a second of being with my sweet rocker.

Tonight, I'm waiting for Ty while the guys are packing up their instruments. Carter saunters into the front office where I'm waiting, wearing his signature outfit of an LTZ T-shirt, cargo shorts, flip-flops and Mariners baseball hat worn backward over his shaggy, long, graying hair.

"Mind if I talk to you for a minute?" Carter casually leans against the reception desk.

"Of course." After a couple of months of being around him, I've gotten over being starstruck. He's kind of like an eccentric uncle at this point.

"Zoey, you know Ty needs to focus all of his energy on the band if they're going to make it." He fiddles with a candy dish but studies me intently. "What are your plans when they leave?"

"Of course he does, and I'm behind him all the way. Don't you remember? I'm leaving for WWU the same day the guys go on tour." I'm confused why he's asking me something he already knows. "LTZ will be up there for a show. I won't see him until then."

He continues to look at me intensely. "Hmm. Right. And, you've had a good summer together?"

Still not sure of the reason for this discussion, I figure—as a father figure to Ty—he needs me to reassure him about my feelings for his protégée. "The best. Ty's so special, I'm so lucky to have found him. And the band? They're great and so are the guys. I'm so excited for them, they really deserve to have the world hear their music."

"Yeah, I think so too." Carter turns and points out one of Limelight's platinum records on the wall. "Did anyone ever tell you about Zane's mom?"

"Um, you did. A little. At your house the night of the bar-beque." Now I'm really confused. Officially, this is the most Carter has ever spoken to me on my own.

Carter's face visibly softens when he speaks of her. "She and I were a lot like the two of you. Passionate, unable to keep our hands off each other."

I laugh nervously, worried that somehow I've embarrassed myself. Maybe he's seen something he shouldn't have.

God.

"We were together just a short time before she got preg-nant, but madly in love. Excited and petrified about the baby. Both of us were only nineteen when Zane was born. I was on the road with Limelight for months at a time..." From the faraway expression in his eyes, I can tell Carter is going deep into story-telling mode.

I've learned he's a bit of a talker.

"...Lianne was a rising ballerina, having a baby so young was rough on her with me being away. Her career would have suffered if Gus and his wife, Faye, hadn't helped out. Since I was focused on gold records and touring, I was oblivious. Not to mention all of the perks that were thrown in my face. Women. Drugs. Alcohol. I checked out of our relationship, I guess. Cheated on her. A lot." Carter's eyes cloud, he's so lost in his tale about the beginnings of Limelight.

He continues, "Lianne was devastated by my betrayals and drug abuse. She stuck by me for a while until I did something stupid. Unforgivable. She was fed up, understandably. When Zane was about six, they moved to Denver to get away from me. It should have been my rock bottom, but addiction took over my life in a huge way. I fucked up for so many years and missed out on most of Zane's childhood. Moral of the story, Zoey? She and I were just too young."

Then he drops the bomb. "Just like you and Ty are *too young*."

Carter's impassioned tone makes it clear that somehow he believes his story somehow directly applies to me and Ty's situation, which is ridiculous and untrue. "I'm sorry, Carter. That's terrible. You have to understand that Ty and I are not even remotely the same. We love each other and are going to support each other while we start this next phase of our lives."

"Zoey, I know. I also know you guys *think* you're in love. Hell, the way the two of you carry on, I guess you are." Carter levels his gaze at me. "The thing is, I've brought in all my connections to set LTZ up for success. None of it matters if they don't commit and focus on everything they need to do to get to the next level. And the level after that. And so on. They have a better opportunity than my band ever did because they'll retain full ownership of their music. But if they don't make an impact out of the gate, the opportunity will be blown."

Acid roils in my belly. "Okay, I get all that, but I still don't understand what you're trying to say to me, Carter."

"Every one of those guys has worked hard in their own way. They're going to achieve a level of success that is really hard to come by in the digital age." Carter slaps his palm on the doorframe.

Fear prickles down my spine. "I know, Ty's told me all of this."

"Look, Zoey, I think you're a great girl." Carter moves over to where I'm sitting and takes the chair next to me. "I've never seen Ty happier, which is why this is such a shitty conversation to have. I'm begging you. He needs to be free and clear of this relationship. You guys are too young to be tied down."

"I'll never stand in his way, Carter." My lungs feel like they've turned to ice. I can barely catch my breath. "We're better together. I *do* love him and will support him in whatever the band needs, just like he'll support me while I'm in college."

"Sweetheart, I know you think that. Part of me wishes I didn't have to spell this out so harshly. You're strong and smart and—pardon me for saying this—are a baby. Ty might be your first love, but you'll probably have many. Go to school. He'll go on tour. Give it some space. Then, when you reconnect in a few months or years, if there's still something between you, I'll eat my words." I realize Carter is not asking, he's telling me what he expects me to do—break it off with Ty.

My confusion and irritation morph into full panic.

"A few years? Neither of us want to be with anyone else, Carter. *Ever.* Sometimes you meet your person when you're young. Our situation is so different than yours. Don't you get it? It will hurt him even worse if we break up. It will *crush* him. Why would you ask me to do this?" Tears pool in my eyes then spill uncontrollably down my cheeks at the thought of doing anything to hurt my precious Ty.

"Ah, darlin', don't cry. I'm not trying to hurt you. Or Ty. I'm trying to be a voice of reason. To help you both." Carter reaches out to touch me, but I recoil so he stops. "Take some sage advice from someone who's been through it. I hurt my first love because of the life I led touring and playing music. The road is hard. It's lonely. Temptations are too great. You're apart for so many months, doubt creeps in and you're both so young..."

"So you're saying Ty is going to cheat on me just because we happen to be young?" I rage. "You must not know him well because that's not who he is. I don't believe he'd be anything like you were."

"No. What I'm trying to tell you is, despite what you believe, staying with him *will* hurt him. I *do* know him, darlin.' He's not interested in fame or being a rock star, but he *needs* this. LTZ is his ticket out of a terrible situation. Did you know all he can talk about is how much he's going to miss you? How he wants to fly you out to see them. Limit how many shows they play so he can go visit you?"

"So what?" I wipe my tears furiously. "It's all I think about too. Because we're going to miss each other, Carter."

"You're making my point, sweetheart. Young love feels like you'll die without each other. For a dude like Ty, his relationship with you is becoming a bigger priority than the band. It worries me." Carter gently touches my shoulder.

"Stop calling me cutesy nicknames, Carter. And stop saying I'm *so* young. I'll never do anything to hurt Ty. To let him down." I yank my arm away.

"Not on purpose, Zoey. But...mark my words, by the time LTZ arrives in Bellingham and he sees you, I have no doubt he'll rationalize why he needs to quit the band to stay with you. Which would fucking suck for everyone else." Carter smacks his palm on the wall again. Passionately. Authoritatively. "Mostly, it would suck for him. He'd give it all up for you and then what? He'll be a line cook? Do you really want to chain him to you like that?"

"Wow. So, you actually want me to dump him. To deliberately eviscerate him." I suspected this conversation was heading in this direction, but not to this degree. I'm dumbfounded. Resistant. Furious. "No. I won't do that to Ty. I love him. We've made promises to each other. *No.*"

"God, Zoey. It's not that dramatic." Carter backs off a bit. "It doesn't have to be forever. Just until he gets his priorities in order. Think of it like a hall pass. We need him to at least follow through on this tour. Everyone is concerned—"

"What do you mean, everyone?" I'm mortified.

"The other guys are worried. They think he's too into you. Everyone likes you, don't get me wrong. But they're worried that Ty is becoming too dependent on you," Carter implores. "This is a once-in-a-lifetime shot."

My entire body feels like it's seizing in agony. "So, what you're saying is I need to break it off completely with Ty. Do you hear yourself? It's such bullshit. He trusts me. He trusts you. What you're asking me to do is *horrible*."

"Jesus Christ, Zoey. I'm just saying give him the freedom to live the dream he's had for almost six years before he met you a four months ago. It's all he's been working toward since I've known him, and I don't want him to throw it away." Carter sighs and shakes his head, clearly frustrated with my righteous indignation. "Or don't. I want him to have his shot, get financially stable, and be able to make real choices. I also want the best for my son, Connor, and Jace. I hoped you would feel the same way."

"You underestimate him." I point at Carter, shaking with sorrow. "He would never give up the band or this shot for me."

"I know him better than you, and you're wrong." He shrugs. "But let's say you aren't. When you're thousands of miles away from him studying for exams, will you be able to handle seeing hundreds of social media posts taken by beautiful women at VIP parties? They'll hang all over him. Try to kiss him. Maul him. Flash him their tits. Will you still trust him unconditionally? Even if you do, groupies will do and say anything to get into Ty's pants. He's twenty-one years old, for Christ's sake. You can't expect him to not to fuck up at some point." Carter squints at me. "And, let's say he's faithful. Fan girls who see you with Ty are already picking you apart. It's about to get a million times worse. Will you be able to deal?"

I'm crying harder now, unable to speak through my sobs.

Gently, Carter places his hand on my shoulder again. "Zoey, you're beautiful, smart, and a truly awesome young woman. The kind of girl everyone wishes could be their first love. God knows I'm not the guy who should give advice. My delivery sucks, I know it. Just think about what I've said. You know the old saying, 'If you love something set it free...'"

"If I do this, Carter, it's permanent. I'd never be able to face him, you, or the band again. It will break his heart into so many pieces. He's given me his trust and you're asking me to shatter it. He'd never be able to forgive me." My heart feels like someone is squeezing it with their fist. "I won't be able to live with myself if I hurt him."

I won't be able to live without him.

"Zoey." Carter's voice softens. He awkwardly tries to comfort me by squeezing my shoulder. Ty and I are a lot alike—if we didn't have music, we'd have nothing. We *came* from nothing, unlike you. I don't think you understand. He won't be a good man, a *whole* man, unless he makes something of himself on his own. Something he can feel proud of. Don't misunderstand me, I sincerely believe that if you are meant to be, you will find your way back to each other someday. I really do."

Before I can reply, Ty and the guys came out the side door of the studio. He sees my tear-streaked face and rushes over, pulling me to him. "Butterfly, what's the matter?"

"Nothing. I asked Carter for some advice of how to handle you being on the road for so long, and I'm just a big baby," I try to reassure him. Quickly paste on a fake smile and wipe my eyes.

"Think about what I said, if it resonates, it resonates." Carter squints at me before dashing to catch up to Zane, Connor, and Jace, who made a hasty exit when they saw me crying.

Ty uses his thumbs to wipe my tears, concern etched in his face. "What did he say, babe? Tell me the truth. Why are you so sad?"

"He said being apart would be hard and gave me some tips for getting through it. No big deal." I cover my despair with lies. The first I've ever told him.

I'm overwhelmed. I want to tell him what Carter said, but I can't risk destroying their relationship. After all, he only has Ty's best interest in mind. I must be convincing. Ty seems to take me at my word.

Hand in hand we depart for his apartment where we get lost in each other for a couple of hours before he takes me home.

It's the first time since I've met him things feel weird. And, it's all my fault.

Chapter Fourteen

A Few Days Later

CARTER'S WORDS HAUNT ME on a nonstop loop.

I'm so confused. On one hand, I can see why he believes Ty should be free. It makes logical sense, but we are real people with real feelings. My heart knows what it knows—there is no one else but Ty for me.

But am I too young? Carter has a fair point about college. There's so much of life that I haven't experienced. Am I being selfish in holding on to Ty? I could never live with myself if I stood in his way.

I don't talk about it with my parents, because I'm afraid they'll agree with Carter. I also stuff all my feelings down when I'm with Ty because I don't want him to worry or know that there's something wrong when our time together—regardless of what I decide—is running out.

Deciding it's a game-day decision relieves the pressure, so I concentrate on making Ty's birthday, our last day before tour and college, special. Together, we've saved up enough money to book a nice hotel room and have a fancy dinner at the Metropolitan Grill.

I dress up in a stretchy, low-cut, black-lace dress that hits just above my knees with knock-me-down-and-fuck-me black heels that crisscross around my ankles. No panties. I curl my hair and, using a YouTube tutorial, create a smoky, rocker-chick makeup look.

Ty looks scrumptious in dark-black moto jeans and a gray-striped shirt with his favorite black boots. We sit snuggled together on the same side of the booth at the restaurant. Despite my whirling dervish of a mind, I'm able to relax at the restaurant with Ty, who is sneakily working his finger up my thigh to where my panties would have been.

"Whoa." His eyes go wide when he finds me bare and wet for him. He flicks my clit, causing me to squirm.

"I can't wait to get back to the room, I'm ready. I want this so much." I kiss him as he continues to tease me.

"Yes, you are." He grins, removing his hand when the waiter approaches.

After we order, I present him with his birthday gift, a custom-made black, braided-leather bracelet with a sterling-silver, heavy-duty clasp, and the initials "T" and "Z" engraved on the side touching his wrist.

His eyes mist, he's so clearly touched by the gesture. "I love it, Z. I'll never take this off."

We can't keep our hands off each other. Kissing. Touching. Foreplay for where the night will take us. By the time our food arrives, we have little interest in eating. We're both anxious to get to the main event, so we pay and leave in a hurry.

In the hotel elevator, Ty presses me against the wall and wedges his knee in between my legs, allowing me to grind my pussy against his thigh while he sucks on my earlobe. As our floor approaches, he cups my face in his hands. A shadow passes across his gaze. "I don't want to go, Z. I don't want to be without you. I'm not cut out for this."

"Ty, the guys are relying on you. I don't want to be without you either, but it's only for a short time. We'll FaceTime every night and see each other as often as possible." I squeeze his hands against my cheeks, I want him to believe it, so Carter won't be right. "You were *born* to do this, babe."

His face crumples in pain. "Zoey. I'm serious. I've given it a lot of thought. I won't be able to concentrate on anything when I'm gone. I need *us*. I need *you*."

Oh, God. No.

"Ty, I love you so much and need you too. But you won't have this type of lightning in a bottle again. Pursue your dreams. That's what's most important right now. I have to concentrate on school," I plead.

"I'll never love anyone but you, butterfly. I hope you know that." Ty strokes my face. "*Nothing* means more to me than you. Even the band. I used to think it was my only way out of my situation, but now I'm not so sure. I could move to Bellingham..."

His words caused my heart to plummet to the bottom of the elevator shaft.

Carter's right.

"Oh *Ty*." I lean into him, hold him tightly.

My heart breaks into a zillion pieces. If he can't be strong for himself, I need to find the fortitude to love him enough to set him free.

I need him so much though. I still want Ty to be my first. It might be selfish, but I'm going through with tonight. It's my only chance to lose my virginity to the only man I'll ever love. He'll hate me at first, then I'll be long forgotten once he's famous and can have anyone he wants.

I'll never love anyone like this again. I feel it deep in my bones. I also know if I see or hear about him with other women, it'll kill me. This has to be a clean—and permanent—break. Carter's idea that I should let him sow some wild oats and resume like nothing happened is...impossible.

We reach our room. Ty's hands rest on my hips. He nuzzles the back of my neck as I swipe the card key and open the door. Once we're inside, I turn and look into his trusting, blue eyes and kiss him like it's one of the last kisses we'll ever have.

Because it is.

Ty hooks his fingers in the bottom of my dress, and lifts it up over my head, leaving me practically bare in my bra and butterfly necklace. Drawing me close, his hands roam all over my body, as if he's imprinting himself.

When I reach back and unclasp my bra, my breasts spill out and Ty immediately cups them, thumbing my nipples into hard points. We devour each other hungrily, moving toward the bed. When the backs of my knees hit the mattress, he swoops down the comforter and helps me lay back on the sheets.

"I love you so much, Zoey." Ty's words bore into my soul. His deep voice breaks with emotion. "I've been waiting for this day for *so* long."

Trying to focus on anything but my despair is proving difficult until I watch Ty undress. We're so comfortable being naked together, his earnest smile when his clothes hit the floor makes me relax instantly. Just because he hasn't "put it in" doesn't mean anything. Sex with Ty is natural. Like breathing.

Except now I want him more than I've ever wanted anything in this world. Slowly, I stroke my clit because I know watching me touch myself makes him go mental. Tonight may be our last night together, but we have hours in front of us. I want to do everything to make him happy while I still can.

Snarling, he pulls down his boxer briefs to reveal his hard cock flush against his abs, already wet at the tip. I scoot closer to him, still flicking myself. Ty pushes my legs open and, leaning over me, swipes his tongue against my fingers through my wetness. Engulfs my pussy with his mouth and works two fingers inside my already soaked channel.

Licking then sucking, swirling then blowing, Ty's mouth explores every part of my pussy so deliciously while he fingerfucks me into oblivion. As I get close, my thoughts begin to whirl. Knowing that tonight will be the last time we'll make love like this is confusing. It feels like our bodies were created for the purpose of connecting together.

Which is devastating. Every part of my body is fully aroused. Primed and ready to receive him. My heart is connected to his more than I can comprehend, let alone express. I have to squeeze my eyes shut against the tears that threaten to spill.

I'm so close. My fingers dig into his scalp. I moan his name over and over as his tongue relentlessly circles my clit and his fingers curl against my G-spot. All of a sudden, I'm overcome, arching and bucking against his lips so hard I nearly black out.

"That's it, butterfly. You're so beautiful when you let go." Ty crawls up my body so we're lying side-by-side. He holds and kisses me until I'm cognizant.

I stroke his face, overwhelmed with emotion and desire. "I love you, Ty. I'm ready. We've waited for so long. I want you inside me."

Ty gazes deeply into my eyes and gently pulls my leg over his hip. "I love you too, baby. I can't wait a second longer."

Fisting his cock, Ty swirls the thick crown through my creamy folds and taps it against my still-pulsing clit. Positioning himself at my entrance, he rocks inside me shallowly a few centimeters at a time. Caresses my body with his free hand. His eyes locked with mine to make sure I'm okay with every move. How he maintains control, I don't know. His breathing is short and static, as if it takes every ounce of willpower not to thrust in.

"Zoey, thank you for the most amazing birthday. I love you endlessly." Ty's lips touch mine, his eyes dreamy.

He repositions himself so he's hovering over me, but carefully keeps his full weight suspended. Holding himself up on one elbow, Ty grips his cock and more firmly thrusts into me, still careful with his pace. My walls adjust to his girth and length as he works himself inside.

Despite all the almost-sex we've had over the past weeks, nothing prepares me for the overwhelming connection I feel to Ty now that he's actually inside my body. The sheen in his eyes makes it clear that he feels it as deeply as I do.

"Ty, I love you so much, I don't deserve you," I whisper while gripping his ass to pull him all the way into me, wincing at the pressure before relaxing into it.

The sensation of being filled by the man I love so unconditionally is indescribable. I'm now complete. This is what destiny feels like. The look of awe that passes between us when we're finally fully joined can—and will—never be replicated.

Nothing else matters. Together, we are miraculous, glorious, and perfect.

How can you walk away from this man?

"Oh, butterfly," Ty rasps. "This feels like my first time too. You're magical. We're magical."

I crush my mouth to his, lost in the beauty of our incredible connection. Ty wraps his arm around me, cradling my head, stroking my face. We rock together. I can't help but whimper and clench around his cock while he moves in and out of me.

Ty's extraordinary expression of devotion imprints on my soul. He never looks away. Even as the intensity of pleasure become nearly too much, his focus is concentrated on me.

Our pace amplifies gradually. His hips roll into me faster and faster when he can't help but lose himself in his own bliss. I revel in my beautiful man's exquisite look of nirvana and uncensored gasps and moans. He deserves every ounce of pleasure I can provide him.

Reaching between us, he rubs my clit in furious but gentle circles with the rough pad of his index finger, just the way he's learned I like it. "*Please*. Come with me, baby."

I'm already there.

Sparks ignite from my scalp to my pussy and I shatter. He emits a deep, guttural cry and slams his hips into me, letting go with a roar. I feel his cock thicken and pulse and he shoots stream after stream of hot release until he's spent and I'm overflowing.

When we finally come down to earth, Ty smooths my hair and peppers me with the lightest, sweetest kisses. Too soon he softens and slips out leaving me empty, lonely, and overwhelmed. Tears leak from the corners of my eyes. It takes every ounce of willpower I have to keep from flat-out bawling. Instead, I shake uncontrollably from the emotion of it all.

Misunderstanding my reaction, Ty's face scrunches up with worry. "Oh, Z, did I hurt you? Are you okay? Was that too much?"

"I'm fine, you didn't hurt me at all." I bury my head in his neck, his hair soft against my cheeks. "You're perfect. *That* was perfect."

Ty beams with pride. He gets up and ducks into the bathroom, returning with a warm washcloth, which he uses to sweetly clean me up. Afterward, we cling to each other, kissing until my lips feel bruised.

I've never known love like this. I'll never know love like this again. Devastation permeates my entire being at the thought that tonight will be the only time we'll ever be this close again. My heart is crushed. I never want to be with anyone other than Ty, but I have to be selfless.

Ty turns me so we can spoon. We continue to cuddle, kiss, grope and explore until Ty's cock grows hard against my hip. "I want you again, babe. I'll never, ever get enough of you."

"Yes. Again, *please*—Ty," I beg, never wanting this night to end.

"We don't have to if you're too sore. Are you sure?" Ty strokes my face with his knuckles, kissing the nape of my neck.

"I'm sure. You feel too good. I need you, I *want* you." I reach back to stroke his steel-hard shaft.

Kissing behind my ear, Ty runs his hand along my calf and under my leg, pulling it up and over his hip. Gripping my thigh, Ty enters me shallowly from behind then tugs me back against him with his free hand so he's buried all the way in. He's so crazily deep, his slow, deliberate thrusts make me feel incredibly full. At this angle, his cock head rubs against the spot deep inside me that he usually manipulates with his fingers, triggering the most intense sensation.

My eyes squinch shut when Ty releases my leg and brings my fingers to my still-sensitive clit. Together, we circle it lazily, just like we've done on so many stolen afternoons this summer.

Except now, he's buried inside me and all of these erotic sensations mesh and reverberate throughout my entire being. We move in perfect harmony. I scream through my climax, which is a rolling explosion so pleasurable my muscles contract around Ty's cock, taking him over with me.

My heart breaks a little more when he moans how much he loves me and how we're going to be together forever as he floods me for the second time tonight. Neither of us move until, eventually, he can't help but slip from my body, leaving a trail of our combined release down the backs of my thighs.

"You're my heart, butterfly," Ty mutters sleepily. Not long after, his arm slackens, and his breathing slows to a steady tempo against my neck.

I turn toward him. For the next few hours I watch my amazing, perfect boyfriend sleep, knowing that I have no choice but to break things off in the cruelest way. God, how I wish we could have a conversation about it, but I'm too in love with him. He'll talk me out of it and I can't be the reason Ty doesn't follow his dream.

He'll only resent me later.

Besides, I have to face facts. Carter knows him better than I do. He's also been in Ty's shoes. I may not like it, but Ty can't be tied down to a girl who hasn't even started college yet. He's destined for greatness and I don't even know what my major's going to be.

Resigned, I sneak out of bed, willing myself to be quiet despite the tears streaming in rivulets down my face. Not to mention the sobs I can barely keep contained.

I can still feel Ty inside me. I'll *always* feel Ty inside me, I realize.

Nothing will ever compare to the look of astonishment and wonder on his gorgeous face when he took my virginity. I'll replay the memory forever, but for now, I have to shove it aside.

Dressing quickly in the sweats I packed, I throw my evening clothes into my bag, grab my purse, and scribble out a stupid, lame note because there are no appropriate words for what I'm about to do:

"Someone told me recently, if you love someone, let them go. I love you more than anything, my precious Ty, please always believe this. It breaks my heart, but I have to let you fly on your own.
Forever, your butterfly"

Placing it on the nightstand, I tiptoe across the floor and slip out the door. In the foyer of the hotel, I wait for an Uber to take me home. I pull up Ty's number and hesitate but hit "block." Next, I delete my social media accounts and archive all our pictures one by one.

Ugly crying all the way home, I pray Ty won't hate me forever. That he'll understand and forgive me one day. Especially once Carter explains *why* he asked me to do this. I just want him to be happy. Have the best life. Even if that's without me.

Because I love him more than anything in the world.

He deserves to share his gift with the world without anyone and anything holding him back.

I'll survive. I just don't quite know how.

Chapter Fifteen

The Next Day

I WAKE UP WITH a feeling of profound joy and a morning woody. I can't wait to worship Zoey's body again. And again. And again.

Except, she's not next to me. She must be in the bathroom. I patiently check my texts. Nothing. It's too early. I admire my bracelet while I wait for her to come back to bed and think about getting lost in each other one more time before we both have to leave.

When I don't hear any movement after a few minutes, I get up to check on her. *Fuck.* Her overnight bag is gone. Panicking, I quickly dress and gather my stuff because if she's already gone home, I better hurry so I don't miss saying goodbye to her in person.

As I'm leaving, I see the note on the nightstand. Relieved, I pick it up. My relief turns to agony when I realize she's gone. Zoey broke up with me.

"What the actual *fuck*!" My hand is shaking as I read the words again. Who in motherfucking hell told her to let me go?

I crumple the paper and throw it across the room in disgust. Angrily, I dial Zoey's number. A *beep beep beep* blares in my ear, letting me know the call hasn't gone through. I try again four times before it registers: Zoey blocked my number. I click on her Instagram account to DM her, but it's been deleted.

My heart thunders in my ears. The walls close in. I can't breathe. I feel like I'm having a heart attack. I burst into tears when I realize Zoey's disappearance isn't spontaneous. She planned it.

My mind whirls trying to figure out what happened.

What I did wrong.

I plop down on the edge of the bed and mentally review every promise we made to each other since we met. Her leaving me doesn't make sense. I can't understand why she'd leave without saying goodbye? Worse, why would she ghost me like this?

The pain is unbearable. The knot in my throat is so big I can't swallow. Frantically, I shove the rest of my stuff in my bag and leave the hotel so fast I don't remember to check out.

I have to see her.

In the Uber on the way to Zoey's house, I can't decide if I'm furious or sad or scared, or all three. Ever since the day in the studio when I found her crying, she's been a bit distant and distracted. She claimed it was nerves about leaving for school. I didn't question it because I was also frazzled trying to get the last-minute details of the LTZ tour ironed out.

It never occurred to me that something was wrong with us. Not even once. Clearly, I missed something.

The Uber pulls up to her house. Before it comes to a full stop, I leap out and run up the porch to her front door where I bang on it, frantically screaming her name. One of the neighbors emerges bellowing, "Stop yelling! They left about an hour ago."

"*Fuck!*" I punch the door, bruising my knuckles. After noticing the neighbor's shock, I calm down. The last thing I need is to get arrested when I'm due at the rehearsal space in two hours. We're leaving in four. I slump down on her front porch and try to call her again.

Beep. Beep. Beep.

Taking deep breaths to calm myself, I call another Uber and return to my apartment to shove what little I have in the world into a duffle. The rest I'm leaving behind forever because I'm never coming back here. Mom hasn't been home in weeks. No one will even notice I'm gone.

By the time I arrive at our rehearsal space to help load the van, I'm beyond devastated. When I see the guys and Carter looking hopeful and excited, I can't help it. I break down and sob uncontrollably.

My band brothers are truly shocked that Zoey left but rally around me and emphatically assure me she'll be back. Carter, on the other hand, mumbles something along the lines of, "If it was meant to be..."

It's a weird thing to say, but I sadly nod in agreement despite the sinking feeling I've just lost the love of my life. I don't want to believe Zoey dumped me. Not on the day that's supposed to be the start of LTZ's world domination.

"Give her a couple of weeks, man." Zane throws an arm over my shoulder. "She loves you, I'm sure she'll come around. When we do the show in Bellingham, you can see her then."

"We'll find her, Ty. Just keep it together for a couple of weeks." Carter gives me a quick side hug, but something in his expression doesn't make me feel any better.

For the past two weeks I've clung to hope, though I've acted like a crazy stalker sending Zoey hundreds of messages on every chat and text app I can think of. I beg her to call me. Profess my love for her. Angrily demand to know why she left me.

I know I'm acting unhinged, but I can't help it.

Mustering enough energy to play the first few shows is excruciating. Something inside me musters through. My love life isn't the fans' fault, so I try my best. The only thing that keeps me going is rubbing the "T" and "Z" on my bracelet, scrolling through our pictures on my phone, and counting down the days to the Bellingham show when I can find her and talk things out.

When we finally pull into the venue parking lot in Bellingham, I'm surprised to find Carter waiting for us. While the rest of the guys load in, he offers to drive me to Zoey's dorm on campus. The ride is tense, but I'm a bundle of nerves so it's no surprise. He hugs me before he drops me off.

Gathering the remaining dregs of courage, I find the front desk and ask if I can talk to Zoey Pearson. I didn't realize they wouldn't tell me where she lived, but it makes sense. Safety and all that. With no choice, I write her a note, keeping it simple and sweet. I include my number with the information for the gig and let her know she's on the guest list. Add in how much I want to see her for good measure.

I hand it to the girl at the front desk. When she sees Zoey's name, she looks up at me quizzically. "Um, are you in that band?"

"Yeah, I'm Ty. I'm in Less Than Zero. Zoey is—*was*—my girlfriend. Do you know her?" It's the first glimmer of hope I've had in two weeks.

"Um, well, *yeah.*" She studies me intently, probably taking pity on me since I look bedraggled and desperate. "Look, I'm not supposed to give out any information about residents but Zoey was my roommate. I didn't really get to know her but she said she had a bad breakup with someone in your band. From the time she moved in, she was really sad. She never got out of bed. I was really scared and told the RA. About a week ago, her parents picked her up and she dropped out of school."

"Oh my God, *Zoey*! Where did she go? I'm trying to find her. If she's hurting, I need to get to her, but she's blocked my number." I'm frantic, pounding my palm on the counter.

The girl regards me warily. "*Um*...you should try her folks. They packed up her room and took her home, I *think*. I don't think she'll be back."

Horrified at what I've just learned, I call Carter. He arrives minutes later and we head back to the club. After I let the band know what I've found out about Zoey, every bit of my spirit evaporates. Any positivity I've managed to hang onto has been based on my belief we'd reconnect here. That we'd fix things between us.

I manage to get through the gig, but I suck and so the show sucks for all of us. With my heart shattered into a million bits, I know I can't drag my band brothers down with me. When I try to quit, both Carter and Zane convince me to tough it out.

They assure me my heart will heal. That I'll feel better soon and enjoy the success we're having.

What they don't realize is nothing matters without Zoey by my side.

Chapter Sixteen

The Same Time Frame

NOTHING PREPARED ME FOR the crippling depression I suffered after leaving Ty.

The drive up to Bellingham for school was agony. I didn't tell my parents what happened, only that Ty and I were through. They assumed he broke up with me, not the other way around. I didn't have the energy to correct them.

Not wanting them to worry, I went through the motions. Moved into the dorm. Registered for class. Met my roommate. Check. Check. Check. When the first day of classes arrived, I couldn't go. School seemed pointless after what I'd done.

Ty left me hundreds of texts and voice messages. After seeing and hearing his anguish and then anger, I knew I'd never be able to face him again. I also worried if we spoke, he'd drop everything to get to me, which would ruin his career and the band's success.

Since I couldn't let that happen, I resigned myself to disappear from his life forever. It was hard to feel hope when I tossed my beautiful relationship in the dumpster like it was trash. I was ashamed. Heartbroken. Paralyzed. Regretful.

Frozen.

It got so bad, I couldn't function, let alone attend classes. My roommate called my parents, who were very supportive. They withdrew me from school a few days before LTZ came to town.

Rather than going home or to a therapist, mom took me to Hawaii, where we stayed in my grandparents' timeshare for an entire month. Vaguely, in between insane bouts of crying and sleeping, I remember floating in the warm ocean, trying to find my equilibrium.

A few weeks later, Alex reached out from Europe and mentioned Jace contacted her. Ty was still frantic to connect with me. It *killed* me that he was hurting. I nearly caved and called him back because I wanted nothing more than to hear his voice. To beg him to let me back into his life. Being without him felt like both my arms and legs had been cut off.

It still does.

Except, by this time, LTZ's song *Rise* had done just that—risen up the charts at breakneck speed. No one with a pulse could escape LTZ's meteoric ascent to the top of the music world. Photos and videos of Ty and the guys were everywhere. He looked fine. Happy.

That's when I knew I'd done the right thing. Carter had been right all along. My precious rocker deserved to be free of all ties to embrace his new life. *Including me.*

Rise seemed to follow me wherever I went, triggering not-so-distant memories of the guys working through the song at band practice. Ty's hands all over my body in between recording sessions. And, of course, the night before I left when he took my virginity.

It was all too much.

For my own sanity, I transferred to a small college in the middle of Texas, far away from Seattle. A place that played only country music and didn't seem to know about LTZ.

I didn't know a soul, nor did I really attempt to make any friends or keep up with Alex anymore. Burying myself in academics kept me from facing the truth of what I had done to Ty. It kept me focused and busy. In some ways, I suppose, by depriving myself of the usual college fun and activities, I was also punishing myself.

As time passed and LTZ achieved more and more success, I turned further inward, though I secretly kept up with the band and their accomplishments. I needed to know he was okay.

Over the next couple years, seeing him tour the world and play bigger and bigger shows, it seemed like he'd moved past us—me.

As much as it hurt, I was also relieved.

All I ever wanted was for Ty to have his dream.

Now he does.
Soon, I'll be just a distant memory.

Chapter Seventeen

A Month Later

Getting over Zoey is futile.

My band brothers do what they can. Jace got in touch with Alex, but she didn't reply. He pinged her on social media and got the silent treatment. Within hours, my last remaining outside connection to Zoey is removed when all of her pictures are deleted from Alex's feed.

I'm not willing to give up. I try her parents, going so far as to activate a new private Facebook account to message them because I don't have either of their mobile numbers. I leave messages at Zoey's dad's law firm. I send letters.

Nothing works. I can't believe it's over. Zoey's gone. Disappeared. It's like the past summer didn't even happen. Like I meant nothing to her.

I've been abandoned. Again.

Carter and Zane try to intervene, eventually convincing me to give her some space. The way Carter sees it, we'll be back in Seattle in a few months. By then she might have a change of heart.

Since I clearly have no choice, I compromise by restricting myself to sending her one message every day. I'm careful not to say anything that sounds angry or accusatory. Something must have spooked her.

Above all, no matter why she left, I still love Zoey. I want her to feel safe.

As I navigate my heartbreak, the tour and playing music is what keeps me sane. Things with LTZ have taken off so quickly, it's hard to catch my breath. Our first single, *Rise*, was released the day we left on tour. None of us had any idea that it would catch fire and explode across the US, then Europe and now the rest of the world.

It's been number-one on multiple charts for months.

LTZ is famous.

Life is becoming more and more complicated by the hour.

Days bleed into nights back into days as the months are filled with live shows, festivals, television appearances, interviews, fan events, appearances, and meetings all around the globe. It's a relentless pace to move the LTZ machine forward.

Time goes by at warp speed. My schedule is so packed I can barely remember my own name. I send messages to Zoey less regularly. It's not like she answers me. What does it matter?

Besides, I'm so busy and exhausted all the time, the intensity of my heartbreak has dulled into an ever-present ache that I've learned to live with. I thought I found someone who loved me. To have it ripped away is like a wound that will never heal.

I'm also angry. At times it really feels like something inside me has snapped and I'm in danger of lashing out at anyone who crosses my path. I don't want to fuck things up for LTZ, so aside from when I'm on stage, I live a very solitary life.

If anyone thought to ask me, they'd know I'm barely keeping it together. Most of the time I can barely muster interest in this tour, the fans or even my bandmates. I'm more comfortable alone with my thoughts, so I isolate myself whenever possible on the tour bus, my hotel room, or my dressing room.

The only half-decent thing to come out of this nightmare is how easy it is for me to channel my pent-up love, hurt, rejection and anger into new music. While Zane and Jace fuck groupies, I write dozens of songs about heartbreak and hope. When Connor gets drunk with the crew, I'm laying down tracks in the back of the bus.

I don't blame them for reveling in the new life fame affords us. I don't care about any of it. My job, as I see it, is to show up for band obligations. That's it. The thought of hooking up with another woman makes me physically ill. Just like how

Connor is faithful to his girlfriend, Jen, I'm determined to be faithful to Zoey.

I know it sounds crazy.

Something deep inside me knows there's more to what happened. I don't want to fuck things up until I can at least talk to her.

Ironically, rather than my reclusiveness and lack of interest in fan interaction hurting the band's reputation, it supercharges my personal fame and lore. LTZ's popularity grows every day. None of us can go anywhere without getting mobbed by well-meaning fans who want autographs or selfies.

It's the strangest feeling when people think they know you and you don't even know yourself. I internally cringe when people touch me or take pictures without asking. Shy away when someone shouts my name. Feel like a zoo animal every time a fan giggles, whispers and points when I walk by.

The attention is annoying and scary, but as invasive and strange as my new life is, I know I have a job to do. I smile and play nice.

If nothing else, I owe it to my bandmates.

They haven't let me completely fall completely apart, so I'll play the game as much as possible.

Even if it's all a lie.

Chapter Eighteen

Two Years Later

I HAVEN'T BEEN IN Seattle for two years.

My heart and head are in a completely different place. I'm still brokenhearted, but mostly angry. I always knew something was weird about how Zoey left me. When Carter confessed what he did at the studio, I cut him out of my life, which was hard to do considering he's around the band all the time.

What can I say? I felt manipulated and betrayed. By two of the only people in the world I thought had my back.

I'm furious at Zoey, but also confused. How she reacted was so extreme. It still doesn't make any sense. I can't believe she didn't deem me worthy enough to have a discussion about our future before she decided ghosting me was the answer. I didn't rate a phone call. A message. A chance to talk through Carter's interference.

To save my own sanity and finally move on, I've decided to get closure and put Zoey in my rearview mirror. My suffering has gone on for far too long. It's time for me to join my bandmates and embrace the success LTZ is having. I want to live a little. Being sad is exhausting.

I have good reason to celebrate, with royalties from our incredible success lining my pocket, I just purchased a gorgeous house on a secluded street in West Seattle overlooking the city and Puget Sound. In cash. I'll never have to worry about where I live again.

Even better, I bought my first car—a black Porsche 911 Carrera. I'm on a mission in my badass ride. It's time to give Zoey a piece of my mind. Maybe, even, a little taste of what she's missing. My first stop is her house.

Her dad, Mike, answers the door.

"Ty, what a surprise! Come on in." He certainly seems shocked to see me unannounced but welcomes me warmly and shows me into the living room.

His kindness takes the vinegar out of my reason for this visit. We make small talk for a few minutes before I get to the point. We both know why I'm here.

"Mr. Pearson, I'd like to speak with Zoey. I haven't seen or talked to her in almost two years and I want her to tell me why she left me." I slump in the same chair I'd spent so much time in two summers before.

He sits across from me, clearly uncertain of what to say. "Um. Well. Um...Ty."

"I'll tell you what happened." My voice cracks with emotion. "Carter told her to break up with me for my own good. He was wrong. I've tried to contact her, I've left hundreds of messages..."

"Yeah. I know. She told us what happened with Carter." Mike leans forward when he sees me start to shake. "Tyson, are you okay?"

"No, I've never been okay. I don't understand why Zoey won't have the decency to... I love her and want to—" I sigh without finishing, wincing from embarrassment. Being here is a terrible idea. Her dad isn't the right person to have this conversation with. But it's as close as I've been to Zoey in two years.

In this moment, I also realize how ludicrous my behavior has been for too long. I'm a grown man. A successful man. A *coveted* man. What the hell am I doing pining over a girl who clearly isn't into me?

"Zoey's finally doing better but it's been a long road. She's convinced what she did was the best thing for you. And LTZ. Nowadays, her studies take up all her time. She finished her undergraduate degree, if you can believe it. Now we're waiting to see what law school she'll attend." He smiles with unabashed pride. "She's hyper-focused on her studies, determined to cram seven years of school into four."

Oh, I believe it. I once knew what it was like to have Zoey's attention concentrated on me. It's not something you can ever forget.

It's the loss of her attention that's unbearable.

"Do you think she'd at least talk to me?" I toss it out there, careful not to sound creepy. "Would you be willing to help me?"

Mike scrunches up his face in thought before answering. "It's been a couple of years. How about I pass your number to Zoey. I need to leave it up to her."

"Okay, I respect that, Mr. Pearson." It's not what I want to hear, of course. I realize I'm absentmindedly rubbing our initials on my bracelet I still can't bear to take off. "It nearly killed me when she left without even saying goodbye. You have to know, I wanted to marry her. Someday."

Mike sighs heavily, reminding me of Carter. "Ahhh, Ty. I know the two of you had an intense romance. She was only eighteen. She handled it...well, like an eighteen-year-old. At the end of the day, she didn't want you to resent her for derailing *your* dreams."

The revelation stings on such a deep level. "If that's true, why couldn't we talk now? It doesn't make sense."

"She's focused on her own future. *Finally.*" Mike shakes his head. "I know it doesn't feel like it, but maybe things are happening like this for a reason. Zoey cares so much about you. She didn't want you to be chained to her when you needed to focus on the band. Carter warned her..."

"Oh *God.* She was never a *chain.*" My voice hitches with despair. "*Never.* She was my *life.*"

"Hey, hey. Listen. She's sincerely happy for your success, we all are." He pats my hand soothingly. "Carter may not have gone about it in the right way, but there was wisdom in his advice. At this stage in your lives, you're both better off working on yourselves separately. It will give you a chance to become who you're supposed to be. Live life. Make mistakes. Stay positive. You never know what the future holds."

My entire body crumples with disappointment. I know this is truly the end.

Mike leans back, assuming a fatherly stance. "Ty, remember she's still only twenty. Younger than you were when you left on tour. You're in a much different head space. With a new house. New car. Fame. Success. She'll be in law school this fall. Take it from me, it's intense and requires full dedication without distraction. In many ways, your roles are reversed now."

"She never told me she wanted to be a lawyer." I feel utterly crushed. I don't even know her anymore.

"Zoey's only now discovering what's possible for herself. You're already achieving your dreams. Even an old guy like me hears your songs on the radio every other minute." He leans back over to pat my hand. "Look, give me your number and I'll tell her you stopped by."

Although I give him my number, something about the conversation feels like the final nail in our coffin. Instinctively, I know it's over. Really and truly over.

With a belly full of acid, I say my goodbyes and leave.

I wake up still ruminating on my conversation with Mike Pearson a few days ago. Acid roils in my belly, for some reason. My hair follicles feel like little electrical sockets.

When I pick up my phone, I see a notification from a number I don't recognize. My heart pounds when I hit play and hear Zoey's beautiful, sweet voice.

Hi Ty, it's Zoey. My dad gave me your number. I don't know what to say to you except I'm sorry I hurt you so badly. I'll never forgive myself for causing you any pain. It's been a long time since you've reached out, I thought maybe you'd moved on. Hopefully forgiven me. Maybe even forgotten about me.

The thing is, it hurts too much for me to talk to you when I know we can't be together. I'm finally feeling somewhat normal. I want you to feel that way too. The band's doing great. You look like you're taking to fame well. I wish you all the best and for you to continue your amazing success. There's no one who deserves it more than you.

God. I don't even know what to say. I guess I'm about to start law school and it's going to be intense. I just can't risk any other setbacks right now. I don't want you to hold yourself back for me anymore. It kills me that you're not living your best life, which is all I've ever wanted for you. I think its best if you let me go.

Hearing her speak for the first time in two years is jarring. She sounds so disengaged and aloof, until the last bit when her voice breaks with emotion. I listen to the message a few times and decide I have to harden my heart against her if I'm going to survive.

"*Fuck* this. I'm done," I bitterly mutter to myself before throwing the phone across the room.

She can fuck off. I'll do whatever it takes to forget her.

I'm not wasting one more minute on Zoey Pearson.

Chapter Nineteen

Many Months Later

"WHO'S Z?" OUR MANAGER, Katherine leans back in her chair. Jace, Zane, Connor and I are in her New York office playing the new album titled "*Z*" for her and our new PR team, Andrew Nolan and Sienna King.

Sienna, a tall woman with black hair tilts her head knowingly when I wince. She doesn't miss much. "Ty, if she's a real person, we need to know. Getting her on board with the promotion plan for the album could be epic."

"No." I shake my head. "She's not real."

I don't want them to find out about her. Not even a little bit.

Despite my best instincts, I kept Zoey's message for a long while. Probably listened to it—easily—a couple hundred times. I couldn't bear to get rid of the recording. Until I knew I had to for my own sanity.

Still, when I hit 'delete,' I cried for an hour. But, I did what she asked. I let her go.

For the next couple months, I poured all my heartbreak into a new batch of songs and honed the tracks I'd written while on our last tour.

At first my goal *was* to hurt Zoey as much as she hurt me. I *wanted* the whole world to know how much I loved her and how badly she fucked me over. It somehow gave me comfort knowing, wherever she was, she'd hear my songs and be forced to think about me and what she'd done.

Once the songs were written, however, I felt less angry. Less vindictive.

"She's not real." I reiterate, holding my ground until the publicists leave for another meeting.

"We need to deal with this." Jace lowers his reading glasses to address all of us. "LTZ is heading for a significant pop culture moment with this album. You heard them, Ty, everyone's curious. If we let our fans find out who Zoey is, they're gonna rake her over the coals."

He's right. Songs like *Shine*, *Butterfly*, and *Down* chronicle my anguish, anger, and acceptance about my love and loss of Zoey. It's a journey of my heartbreak from heavy to beautiful to melancholy to ethereal, but it's all out there on the table.

I bury my face in my hands. "Maybe we shouldn't release it."

"Fuck that." Zane shakes his head angrily. "We're putting it out there. Carter produced it and considering everyone's reaction to the music, this is lightning in a bottle."

I can't help but sigh. The past few months have been agonizing. Letting go of Zoey. Writing and then recording the songs. All while reconciling with Carter. It was wrong of him to impose his own history on my relationship with Zoey, ultimately destroying us, but he's been so remorseful. He's the closest thing to family I have so...

Who knows. Maybe he did me a favor.

"I'm just saying, these songs aren't hard-driving, cheerful power rock that got us here." I glance around at my bandmates. "These new tracks are dark. More personal. Maybe it's too far a departure of our style."

"I disagree. You unleashed every ounce of emotion into your vocals. Zane's haunting guitar riffs soar. Jace and Connor's rhythm section create a thumping, pulsing heartbeat that ebbs and flows to perfection." Katherine almost looks giddy. "I agree with Zane. These songs are going to catapult LTZ to the top."

Her reaction isn't unexpected. When the five of us sat down in Carter's living room to listen to the final masters for the first time, we knew we had magic. An elusive unicorn album that every band strives for, but few achieve.

"Look, all I was trying to say, is we need to do some clean up before we hand things over to Andrew and Sienna." Jace always has a way of bringing us back to the matter at hand. "Unless, you feel differently. It's up to you, Ty."

I regard him seriously. Despite my initial intention to hurt her, Zoey doesn't deserve to have her world turned upside down. Not when she's in law school. It isn't fair. "What do we need to do?"

Jace recommends taking drastic steps to protect her true identity and takes it upon himself to make sure our socials are scrubbed of all traces of Zoey Pearson.

Within a day, she's erased from LTZ's history.

***

"You want me to do *what?*" I'm still getting used to Andrew and Sienna trying to coax me out of my shell.

They want to dirty up my image. Whatever that means. "Go to the party. Do a few lines. Be a fucking rockstar," Andrew scolds.

"Ah, Okay. Right." Embracing the rockstar life is kinda fun. I'm famous. Financially secure. I have no one to answer to. Why the fuck not?

The thing is, I like having a PR firm. We relied on Jace to keep up our social media for too long. He was burnt out and getting grumpy, it was time to pass the torch.

Especially because, as predicted, critics and fans have gone wild for *Z*. Nearly every song is charting and *Down*, *Rise*, *Butterfly* and *Kick It* are holding fast in the top ten. If I thought we were hardworking before, I knew nothing.

We're ten times as busy—worldwide tour, festivals, interviews, television appearances, Grammys. Everything is magnified by the level of our newfound success.

I missed out on so much during our first tour, I feel little justified in finally letting loose. Andrew and Sienna make sure we're on the guest list at every who's who party, celebrity event, or red-carpet opportunity. These days, I'm generally up for anything.

My band brothers joke I'm in a "sex, drugs and booze" phase. Fuck yeah, I am. It's my way of making up for lost time. Why wouldn't I hang out with celebrities and athletes, eat at the best restaurants, vacation in elite locations, fly in private jets, and indulge in whatever experiences come my way?

And why wouldn't I fuck my way around the world?

I have an endless pool of gorgeous women to pick from. I don't give a shit who blows me or does blow with me. The PR team takes care of the NDA and I get my dick sucked. In the dressing room. Backstage. On the bus. In an alley.

Easy. There's always someone willing to accommodate. I don't discriminate. Models. Actresses. Musicians. Fans. As long as they don't look like Zoey.

According to the press, I'm no longer a brooding, reclusive asshole. I've graduated to being the out-of-control asshole who treats women like shit and breaks hearts wherever I go.

They're right.

Crazily, fans eat it up.

So do dozens of companies who pay me small fortunes to endorse their products.

Officially, I've moved the fuck on. Zoey's in my rear view mirror.

Finally.

Life's never been better.

Chapter Twenty

Three Years Later

"HELLO?" I RASP INTO the phone. I'm completely winded after running five miles at my new faster pace.

Sienna's grating voice makes me wince. "She said yes."

Fuck. I hate being on a worldwide "clean up my image" tour. "Okay. What happens now?"

Sienna laughs. "You are officially in a 'relationship' with the beautiful and kindhearted Ronni Miller. I'll send you a list of appearances when I coordinate with her PR."

I look out at the city from my workout room. Wondering how in the hell I've been talked into a fake relationship with a sitcom actress named Veronica "Ronni" Miller. I've met her a few times. She's been at a few shows. I like her well enough. She's pretty.

It still seems stupid, but I'll do what the publicity team says. "Okay. Fine. Gotta go."

I'm not interested in talking to Sienna any more than I have to. She's a reminder of my old life. I stopped drinking and doing drugs nearly a year ago. I changed my diet, workout like a madman, meet with my therapist. Stuff like that. I've focused my energy into music again.

We're a few weeks into our latest tour supporting our latest album. We're keeping better control over our schedule to allow more downtime, which is why I find myself with a day off in Amsterdam.

These days, instead of partying, I write songs for artists outside of LTZ in many different genres. Sometimes I dip my toe into producing. Many of the tracks I've worked on have charted. I'm now pulling in significant royalties for my non-LTZ songwriting and publishing portfolio.

Working with other artists keeps me inspired. Focused. The new wave of creativity also helped influence my writing for the band. Rather than Zane and I taking the lead, the four of us collaborate more often. The proof is in the results. LTZ remains the biggest band in the world.

It's comforting to know I'll never have to worry about my finances again. No matter what happens, I'm secure beyond my wildest dreams.

And yet, I've never felt more alone in my life.

I'm not turning back though. I've come too far. Risked too much.

I may never know how close I was to losing everything, but I did know my LTZ bandmates were getting tired of me.

I was getting tired of myself, truth be told. Deep down, I knew something inside me was broken. Something that had nothing to do with Zoey. Getting high was the only thing that allowed me to cope.

Things were heading toward an intervention. At first, Jace offered to get sober with me and proposed a plan. I almost took him up on it. Unfortunately, right before our European tour for *Z*, he showed me Zoey's reactivated Instagram account.

It was only one picture, but it shook me to the core. Her wild, blonde hair, cocked brow, sexy librarian glasses perched on her nose and those striking hazel eyes. My heart stopped.

I might have been able to handle seeing her if it wasn't for the handsome guy hugging her from behind. My biggest fear came true. She met someone in law school, fell in love and made it Instagram official.

Oh, I wasn't over her. Not by a mile. Seeing her with another dude hurt so fucking bad, I slipped back into my same old bullshit.

No. That's not even true. I *amped* up my bullshit. I didn't give one fuck about myself. The only thing that dulled my pain was ingesting copious amounts of cocaine. Pills. Booze. I didn't have the willpower to stop and I hated myself for it.

Hated that I'd turned into my own mother.

A few months later, after a days-long bender to end all benders. I woke up feeling like death warmed over. But, I wasn't alone. A familiar woman was passed out next to me in my hotel room, which was utterly destroyed. Used condoms, empty whisky bottles and drug paraphernalia littered the floor.

As I looked around at the mess, I took stock of my reality.

There were too many nights I couldn't remember. Too many drugs. Too much depravity. I wasn't proud of myself. My reputation was utter and total shit. Videos of my escapades were all over social media. Photos of me in various states of nudity, intoxication and sexual activity were made into memes and gifs.

Music was *everything* that mattered to me yet my lifestyle overshadowed everything I'd worked so hard for.

Revulsion coursed through my veins. I'd hit rock bottom. It jolted me into action.

No matter how mortifying. Humiliating. Excruciating.

I knew I had to make a change that day

So I did.

Zane and Carter helped me. They arranged for the three of us to spend a week at a spa in France where I detoxed, found a therapist and started my journey to get healthy.

Now that I'm clean and committed to a new way of living, I might be unsettled.

But, at least I'm at peace.

Chapter Twenty-One

A Year Later

I GAZE OUT AT the Pacific Ocean from Ronni Miller's house in Malibu. It's time for us to put an end to the charade, though it's been an interesting few months.

"Where should we do it?" Ronni hands me a glass of lemonade and sits on the couch next to me.

I take a sip and gaze at the woman who the world thinks I'm in love with. She's gorgeous, long, chestnut hair, creamy skin, big tits, full, lush lips that are made for kissing. The only problem is, she's someone else's girlfriend. "You pick, this is your town."

"It's yours now too. Congratulations on your new house." She holds her glass up to mine. We clink.

"I'm glad we're ending this. It's always been weird." I lean back. Ronni's become a great friend during our ruse. "You need to focus on your real relationship."

She laughs. "I'll never forget our first meeting after we decided to do this. You had no idea about how this PR stuff worked."

It's true. I actually tried to kiss her, thinking that the PR set up was more like a real set up. Her boyfriend wasn't amused. Luckily, he took it easy on me. I'm still not sure how he's put up with this stupidity for so long.

Fake dating is common in the world of celebrity, so I've learned. PR teams pair people up all the time for various reasons. In Ronni's case, she's America's sweetheart. Her sit-com's ending, so she needed to dirty up her image. I was the man for the job because, coincidentally, I needed to clean up my image to redeem myself. We share the same PR firm, so...

Presto! The perfect match.

The world believes we're dating exclusively and are deeply in love. In real life we rarely see each other. Our PR teams coordinate schedules to make sure we're at other's respective red-carpet events and other Hollywood functions. We hold hands. Hug. Never kiss, but we are good at faking affection.

Too good. What's shocked both of us is social media, bloggers and the world have gone batshit crazy at the thought of the two of us as a couple. We knew we'd make headlines, but never imagined it would mushroom the way it has. Hell, we even have a moniker, "Tonni."

Paparazzi follow us wherever we go—even more than before, just trying to get photos of the two of us. Rumors of weddings and babies and cheating follow us everywhere. It's out of control. Too much. Ronni's boyfriend is losing patience, and I don't blame him.

"Thank you for helping me. I think I've redeemed myself in the LTZ world. Jace managed to scrub the internet of the worst of my shit. I hope it's worked out well for you too."

Ronni looks off into the distance. "Well, it is what it is. I was happy to help you out. Who knows, maybe someone will cast me as a stripper. Or a band groupie."

We both laugh at the inside joke. She's great. Truly a good human.

"I've got to be in the desert in the morning. As you know, Jace and Zane are there already." I look back out at the water. The sun is beginning to set. "Connor and I will head over in the morning."

Ronni types into her phone and looks up. "Dan Tana's?"

"Mr. Chow." Ronni's boyfriend calls from the other room.

We both nod. Ronni makes the arrangement.

The breakup goes pretty much as we planned. Plenty of paparazzi are waiting as we get out of the car. Ronni and I fake a dramatic ending to our fake love affair. We don't tell Sienna or Andrew. We knew they'd be pissed, and they are.

By the time I take the stage at Coachella the next evening, all hell has broken loose. Old paparazzi pictures resurface confirming I'm a bad guy who can't be trusted. Tyson Rainier is back to being a ruthless heartbreaker, this time hurting Ronni Miller, who can do no wrong.

Which is true, she's great and feels terrible that I'm bearing the brunt in the court of public opinion. It's fine, I guess. I have no choice but to let it play out.

But *fuck*.

It's a lesson finally learned, though. No matter how many times Jace tries to get it through my thick skull, I'm constantly underestimating how much celebrity media is manufactured and controlled. Or how hungry the press is to build up celebrities only to knock us down.

I've played into it for years. It makes me sick.

Hopefully, a new scandal will hit within a couple of weeks and I can, once again, become yesterday's news.

If nothing else, it makes me determined to live my life authentically from now on.

Chapter Twenty-Two

One Year Later

GRADUATING LAW SCHOOL SUMMA cum laude last year meant I had my choice of law firms across the country. When Joe Finney personally recruited me to join the top firm in Seattle, Finney Cooper, I decided to move back to my hometown.

My parents are thrilled but, truthfully, the decision was made easier because Alex also moved back home. She's spent the past eight years globe-trotting as a travel influencer. With millions of Instagram followers, sponsors sometimes pay her more for one post than I make in a year as a second-year associate.

Funny how life works. Now she's planning on opening her own animal rescue with the money she's saved up. My BFF's success at doing something she loves is inspiring.

Which is why, after a particularly grueling week at work, I'm calculating the billable hours I need to make partner in eight years instead of ten. I'm also creating a target list of potential clients to recruit into Finney Cooper, knowing that rainmaking can speed up my partnership track even faster.

When my office phone rings, I'm so lost in what I'm doing, I pick it up without thinking. "Zoey Pearson."

"Well aren't you the elusive one?" A gravelly, slow-paced voice sends a bolt of apprehension through my entire being.

I clench the stress ball that's always on my desk so hard I nearly break it. "Um...Is this...*Carter*?"

"Hello, Zoey." Carter chuckles. "It's been a long time."

I swallow hard. I have no idea why Carter Pope would be calling me after all this time. "Yeah. It has."

"I was wondering if I could take you to lunch." He clears his throat. "I hear you're the kind of lawyer I need for a project I have in mind."

Despite everything, I've never gone down the rabbit hole and blamed Carter for wrecking my relationship with Ty. I was pissed. I knew it wasn't personal. He wanted the best for a guy he considered a second son.

No, I blame myself. If I'd just talked to Ty about everything back then instead of essentially ghosting him, who knows what would have happened. I can admit it. I'm at fault for the heartache I've endured over these past eight years.

"Well. Um. I'm just a junior associate. I should probably connect you with one of the partners if it's something complicated." The timing seems too good to be true, considering I was literally just making my plan to make partner. Aside from the LTZ guys—who are clearly out of contention—clients don't get bigger than Carter fucking Pope.

Carter breathes out a heavy sigh. "I understand. You're probably still pretty mad at me after all these years."

"No. Of course not. Everyone's moved on." My heart races when he references our last conversation. The last thing I want to do is dredge up old shit. On the other hand, landing such a big fish for the firm will catapult my career above all of the other associates. "Tell me where and when to meet you."

He gives me the details to meet him the next afternoon. I'm scared shitless.

I've tried so hard to put my past behind me.

Can I afford to bring Carter into my present?

I enter a small coffee shop close to Carter's home in the Madrona neighborhood. I'm wearing black jeans, a white, fitted T-shirt, and a black-and-purple brocade jacket. I always try to push the boundaries of business attire at my firm, today my outfit feels more than appropriate.

Carter is already there in his uniform of jeans, LTZ T-shirt, and a baseball cap. He looks exactly the same as the last time I saw him. Well, older. Still very handsome.

"Zoey, you look lovely." He grasps my hands. "You're so grown up."

"Thank you, Carter. I was surprised to hear from you after all these years." I kiss his cheek.

"I was afraid you wouldn't come. Figured it was fifty/fifty." He rests his chin on one hand and looks at me pensively.

"Well, how could I say no when you want to set up a non-profit to fund music programs in schools? Helping kids in underserved communities is my jam." I smile. "Tell me more about what you're thinking."

He squeezes my hand. "Tell me about what you've been up to first."

The years flash before me.

Carter in the studio. My last night with Ty and subsequent mental breakdown and recovery. Closing the LTZ chapter and preparing to start law school only to have Ty reach out again. I couldn't face him back then. I just wasn't capable.

Little did I know what was to come. There was no way to prepare for the insane success of LTZ's album, *Z*. Ty's raw vocals about how I ruined his life were pure anguish. *Down*, the most cutting song, became the worldwide break-up rock anthem.

By my second semester of law school, everyone in the entire world was trying to find out who I was, which sent me into a panic. Alex was still in contact with Jace and assured me the band—including Ty—took great measures to keep my identity secret.

I'm still not sure how, considering LTZ was *everywhere*. I certainly couldn't get away from it no matter how hard I tried. Every song gutted me because while I knew I handled our breakup horrifically, when I listened to the lyrics...damn. I destroyed my sweet Ty in ways I'll never be able to fathom.

Now the most famous Seattle rock band, Ty, Zane, Connor and Jace are the most coveted men in the world. I stalked them—him—online. I told myself it was to make sure he was okay...

I noticed something. He still wore the bracelet I gave him for his birthday on our last night together. I still wore my butterfly necklace too.

I never took it off.

Would never take it off.

It's all I have left.

I don't say any of this to Carter, though. I've mostly been studying. Now lawyering."

"Ah. Right." He leans back. Squints. Studies me.

I'm not stupid. He's still in Ty's life. He clearly thought Ty was better off without me. Fortunately, I've learned how to compartmentalize my emotions. It's been necessary to deal with...everything. I'm here for a reason and chit-chatting about my life with Carter is not it.

Protecting my heart has become like a second job. A *crucial* job. Otherwise I'd still be living in despair. Otherwise I wouldn't be able to comprehend the evolution of Ty's quiet yet enigmatic energy when we were together to his arrogant swagger of today.

It's working for him, I guess. He's considered the sexiest man alive. One day he's smoldering in a plaid tux on the red carpet, the next he's shirtless, wearing leather pants at some nightclub.

I suppress a shudder when my mind flashes to those horrible sex videos of him with other women...

At this point, I don't recognize Ty as the humble, gorgeous man who so sweetly took my virginity. He's not the same guy. Instead, he's become a cliché rock monster who dates beautiful models and actresses like Ronni Miller.

My life is drastically different. I've only been on a few dates in the past eight years. I let my guard down once to hook up with a nice guy I met in law school. He wanted more, but I couldn't go there.

Because no one will ever compare to what I had with Ty. I knew it then and I know it now. I threw away my chance. Now, he's traded up.

I'm where I belong. He's where he belongs. Carter called it years ago, and he was right.

Speaking of which, Carter's still scrutinizing me. At least, that's what it feels like.

"Why don't we discuss this non-profit project you need help with." I try to steer our conversation back to the reason I'm here.

"Sure." He glances down at a notepad on the table and opens it. "I read your bio. It seems like you have an interest in helping underserved communities. Especially children."

I can't help but raise an eyebrow. He did some homework. "Yeah, well too many kids get left behind when they have talent in areas that have been eliminated from school curriculum."

Honoring Ty and kids like him is my passion. Maybe even my redemption. While not the sexiest type of law, specializing in corporate work means I can make good money and spend my days giving back to the world. Like non-profits.

Carter and I chat for over an hour, discussing his idea for his arts program. He asks if I will set up and represent the company personally. As a young associate, I can't make the call because we have a protocol at the firm, but bringing Carter on as a client is a done deal.

Partnership track, here I come.

Even better, Carter doesn't bring up Ty. Or LTZ for that matter. When I leave to go back to the office, I feel strangely at peace. I'm never going to be ready to face Ty again, but spending time with Carter was pleasant.

Maybe—just maybe—I can put the past behind me and move all the way on.

Finally.

Chapter Twenty-Three

Two Months Later

For the first time in a long time, as my thirtieth birthday approaches, I feel positive about everything in my life.

Over the past eight years, LTZ has sold over 125 million records with six number-one singles, eleven more top-ten singles, twelve Grammy nominations and seven Grammy wins. We've headlined world tours four times, have nearly five billion views on YouTube, accumulated 140 Million TikTok, Instagram and Twitter followers and now all of us have enough money in the bank to never stress again.

I'm so far ahead of where things started: living in a shit-hole apartment with my mentally unstable mom and getting dumped by the only girl I'll ever love via a note on the nightstand.

Shockingly, I've survived my own bout of mental illness and addiction. In a couple of months, I'll be a sage old man of nearly thirty, with an incredible perspective I owe mostly to my therapist, Lisa Kinkaid, a woman Carter introduced me to a few years ago at our retreat and the medicine that regulates me.

Or, maybe time has healed my wounds. Who knows? All I know is I wake up feeling good every day. I've put in the time and I've worked through all of it. My mother. My substance abuse and promiscuity. Zoey. I feel like a grown-up in control of my life for the first time ever.

I'm a man, not a scared little boy craving acceptance.

As a band, we've decided to give LTZ a one-year hiatus at the end of this year to recharge our batteries. My plan is to focus on doing something lasting. Something bigger than me. It's time for me to give back. Inspired by what Carter did for me, I've spent my free time on the road working out a strategy.

Now it's time to execute.

Today, I'm dressed to the nines in a sweet black-and-gray pinstriped Hugo Boss suit, my hair is pulled back into a knot, my Prada sunglasses are hooked on my pocket and I'm entering one of the modern buildings in the middle of the downtown area Seattle affectionately called "Amazonia."

I feel confident and excited as I take the elevator up the twenty-third floor where I'm meeting Carter. He greets me in the gleaming, pristine lobby of a big corporate law firm responsible for putting together the paperwork for my new non-profit.

"Welcome home, man!" Carter pulls me into a hug.

I robustly slap him on the back. "Thank you. God, what a grind that last leg was. Thanks for getting this stuff started. I'm excited to finish up everything and help some kids."

"No problem. Happy to help." Carter grips my biceps as we pull apart from our hug.

He's been such a rock for me over the past couple of years. I don't know that I could have stayed sober without his example. "I feel like I'm about ninety years old in a thirty-year-old body. I never want to see another tour bus again."

"I get it. Trust me." Carter squints at me like he's trying to read my mind. "Ah, Ty. It's so good to see you looking so well." He nods. "Hopefully, I'll finally be able to make things right."

"I have no clue what you're talking about, old man." I hug him again. "I'm so psyched you're going to help me out with this. I owe everything to you."

"Yeah, well—Let's get in there, they're all waiting." He blows off my sentiment and gestures to a conference room behind the reception desk. It's a large room with floor-length windows overlooking the Space Needle and Lake Union.

Today's the day I'm formalizing my plan to establish music programs in every public school in Washington state before expanding my vision nationwide. I can hardly believe my dream is going to become a reality.

It's my idea, but without the backing of a great team and Carter finding this law firm, it wouldn't be happening. In the coming weeks I'm facing a mountain of complicated paperwork but it will be worth it when kids who don't excel at academics—kids like me— have arts programs to fall back on.

I'm pumped when I open the door to the conference room.

Immediately a short man with a commanding presence stands before us. "Welcome, Carter. Hello, Mr. Rainier. I'm a big fan. My name is Joe Finney, the founder of Finney Cooper. My team has a detailed presentation about the things we've put into place for your foundation. Come with me so I can introduce you to one of our star associates."

I turn to where he's pointing and all of the air leaves the room.

I have tunnel vision.

Because every cell in my body recognizes every cell of hers.

She doesn't notice me yet because she's fussing with the projector. She wears a snug, dark-navy suit that accentuates the curve of her ass paired with a white, fitted blouse with a blue-floral pattern—no, they're actually abstract skulls. *Wow*. Her blonde hair is as wild and beachy as ever but tugged back into a messy bun. Her lips are tinged dark pink. Blue, polka-dot-rimmed reading glasses are perched on her nose.

My heart beats so furiously I hear it in my ears. I stare at her and it seems like time stands still.

She still has the same effect on me after all these years. Fuck. Fuckity *fuck*.

"*Zoey*."

At the sound of my voice, she turns from the projector and we lock eyes for the first time in eight years. The color drains from her face. Her eyes are wide as saucers.

"*Ty?*" she questions, though she knows it's me.

Zoey blinks rapidly, almost in confusion until she quickly recovers. Steadies herself by palming the conference table.

"How nice to see you." Her voice is strong. Confident. *Detached.* "I didn't realize you were part of Carter's project."

All I can think is...

What the actual fuck?

Chapter Twenty-Four

The Same Day

CONFUSION CLOUDS MY BRAIN. My heart thunders in my chest. Tears threaten to spill. My body aches. I've been kidding myself for years.

I'll never be over this man.

I'm going to throw up.

No, *seriously*. I'm going to throw up.

Ty sits across the room. His piercing blue eyes stare at me. Haunted. Like he's seen a ghost. He's even more gorgeous than I remember, wearing a friggin' business suit with his long hair pulled back so you can see his sharp jawbone covered in stubble.

I look away.

What the hell kind of dream am I having?

I glance back at him. He's still focused on me, clearly uncomfortable. Shocked, maybe.

I know the feeling.

Shit. Does he think I set this up?

Carter, on the other hand, wears a cheek-splitting grin. He glances between me and Ty like he's expecting something. I dunno, gratitude?

As if.

It takes every ounce of fortitude I have not to lose it in front of my boss when all I want to do is run and hide. Speaking of which, Joe clears his throat and fixes me with a look that says, "get on with it."

I've got to get my shit together.

Carter is my first big client, which is why I set up this meeting with Joe, the head of my firm. I've spent hours preparing and fine-tuning my presentation about Finney Cooper and the services we're going to provide.

Taking a deep breath, I paste on a smile. "Welcome, Carter. Ty. Setting up a nonprofit organization can be an exciting and fulfilling journey. Today, I'm going to walk you through the steps involved and how Joe and I will make sure everything is done correctly."

I look up at Joe, who nods approvingly.

"The first step is to define your mission and purpose. Carter, when we met over coffee, you mentioned setting up an arts organization for underserved communities. This is a broad goal, and my job is to help you more clearly articulate your organization's mission because it will guide all your activities and the legal paperwork as well." I pull up a slide on how to craft a mission statement.

"You met for *coffee*?" Ty's voice is wobbly. When I look over at him, he's got a hold of Carter's arm.

Carter beams and pats Ty's hand. "Yes. Zoey and I met a couple months ago when you guys were still out on tour. I told you I'd find the perfect lawyer."

Ty looks at me, confused. I decide to push forward. "Carter, have you chosen a name for your organization? If so, I'll run a check to make sure it's not in use by another company..."

"Stop." Ty holds up his hand. "Mr. Finney, Zoey, I need to step out for a minute." He gets up and bolts for the door. "I'll be back."

Then he's gone.

My already frazzled nerves threaten to electrocute me. This was supposed to be my first ever law firm victory. A kick-off meeting where my plans would be presented as a formal welcome to our new client. Everyone at the firm has been so supportive. They're excited to have a famous rockstar on our roster.

Never in a million years did I expect to see Ty today. The question is, *why* is he here?

What the hell was Carter thinking?

Chapter Twenty-Five

A Few Minutes Later

I HAVEN'T LAID EYES on Zoey Pearson in eight years.

Every fiber of my being is on high alert, but Carter just smiles like he gave me the greatest present in the world. When Zoey saw me in the room, it was clear she was as surprised as I was.

What the fuck is he up to?

When Zoey starts her presentation, I can hear her speaking. It's like a fog. Nothing registers.

Truthfully, I'm absolutely blown away that we're in the same room. She's absolutely stunning. So grown up. Still a sexy rocker chick with wild hair—but wearing clothes that remind me of a naughty librarian.

A few minutes pass before I realize she's directing her presentation to Carter, not to me. I'm confused when she asks him—and not me—what the name of the foundation is. All I wanted from Carter was a recommendation for a good law firm. My expectation for this meeting was the introduction, not a presentation to an existing client.

That's when it dawns on me: Carter *fucking* Pope hired Zoey to be my lawyer.

I make some excuse and leave the room just to catch my breath. This obviously isn't going to work. I can't hire her to be my lawyer...no way. Decision made, I go back in to break the news.

"Look, I think there is a misunderstanding, this is my project, not Carter's." I'm irritated at the entire situation I find myself in, and let it show.

Zoey's hazel eyes widen, she's clearly perplexed. "*What?* Um...I didn't know—um. Okay. Carter maybe you can..."

"Mr. Rainier, we have a lot of experience—" Joe Finney authoritatively cuts Zoey off, which pisses me off. By the look on her face, it guts her.

"I'm sure you do, but, um—" I glare at Carter, willing him to speak. "Shit. This is awkward."

Carter reclines far back in a conference chair, amused at the confusion. "Mr. Finney, may I speak with Ty and Zoey for a few minutes alone? They're actually old friends who haven't seen each other in a while. I fear I've sprung this meeting on them both without warning."

"Of course, take your time." Joe is hesitant but when Zoey nods her assent he steps out of the room, leaving the three of us.

"Carter, you're such a meddling grandma. My *job* is at stake here." Zoey scowls, her displeasure is intense. "You said this was *your* project."

Her tone stabs me in the heart. Even after all these years she wants nothing to do with me.

Well, fuck this.

"It's good to see you, too. *Zoey*." I ignore her outburst, keeping my voice calm though I'm a raging river inside.

Zoey looks through her sexy glasses at me with shock.

Carter rolls his chair closer to her. "Zoey, please accept my apology at springing this on you, but I wasn't sure if you'd agree to meet with Ty." He clutches her hand. "I made a mistake many years ago. My delivery sucked ass, though my advice was pretty solid. My God, sweetheart, you could give seminars on how to disappear. Luckily, I found you and I'm here to sort you both out."

"You only had Ty's best interest in mind, Carter." Zoey flops down in a conference chair, still grasping his hand. Tears brim in her eyes. "I did what you asked. I also told you that night I'd never be able to face him again."

Anger sears through me. "Carter told me everything. He never meant forever, that was all you, *butterfly*." I spit out her nickname, which is also the name of one of my biggest hit songs.

Time feels like it stands still. She *crumples* and curls into herself, but not before I see the tears streaming down her cheeks. "I *never* wanted to leave you, Ty. It was excruciating for me to stay away, but look at you. You achieved your dream, which was all I ever wanted for you. I hope it was the right thing for me to do."

Although her dad told me she'd been a mess, seeing her cry makes my heart clench. Despite everything, all I want to do is take her in my arms and never let her go.

"Fuck, Zoey." I sit down next to her. "This is a lot. I never, in a million years, expected to see you today, or really ever again."

She glances at me, her face etched with sorrow. Her voice is not much more than a whisper. "Me either."

"Tyson. Zoey went to law school to work with people who help underprivileged kids, especially in the arts. Why do you think that is? She's the perfect person to help you with the foundation. It's time to heal and move on. *Both* of you. I hope you can forgive an old, stupid fuck-up like me and do something amazing together." Carter gets up from his chair, claps me on the back and opens the door. "I'm out, I'll leave you two to talk."

The door closing behind him seems inordinately loud.

"Zoey." I smile at her. There's no use in denying it. The electricity in the air is palpable. Like no time has passed.

"Ty." She smiles back, though her eyes are still watery.

We hold each other's gaze for a few seconds before she nervously looks down and begins to fiddle with the projector cord.

"So, you did it. You're a lawyer." I try to break the ice by referencing her last voicemail to me. Strangely, I'm as nervous as I felt the first time I summoned the guts to talk to her at The Mission.

She visibly relaxes. "Yeah, and you did it too. You're a famous musician."

"Yeah, I suppose that's true." I can't keep the grin off my face. "Still a geek, though."

Zoey rolls her eyes. "Yeah, right. From what I've heard, you're quite the playboy now."

Ouch...and, WTF?

"I won't apologize, Zoey. You dumped me pretty spectacularly. And put the nail in the coffin over and over again." I shake my head. I'm so conflicted. Mortified because maybe she's seen something I'm not proud of. Petulant because who is she to have an opinion about anything I do?

Her voice hitches and warbles. "God. No, you *shouldn't* apologize, I have no right to say that. All I ever wanted was for you to live your best life."

"Look, it's been so many years." I take pity on her and on myself. Why go backward, maybe we have an opportunity for closure. Or even friendship.

She clasps her hands together in one big fist on the table. "I was *so* young and naïve. It's no excuse, but I'm *so* sorry I made everything so *fucking* dramatic." She fidgets nervously. "It seems so *stupid* now. You deserved so much better after all we meant to each other. *What you meant to me.* I hope you can forgive me someday."

Every ounce of tension in my body releases when I hear the words I've longed to hear for nearly a decade. "Zoey," I speak softly as I reach over to gently touch the top of her hand. My bracelet grazes her skin. "Neither of us need to be forgiven. We were *both* young and did the best we could. Hopefully, we've evolved into more mature and rational people by now."

"I hope so. But, I honestly don't know what to say to you, Ty." She looks down at where my hand touches hers. "I never thought this day would come."

"Fucking Carter." I roll my eyes. "Whatever his reasoning, I'm glad to see you again. Do you think we could talk, *really* talk about what happened someday? At the very least for closure? Today's not the right time. Not with all of your coworkers around."

Zoey blinks up at me pensively as if considering whether I mean it. "I'd like that. I mean, I've owed you an explanation for years. I'm pretty sure about where you stand after your songs *eviscerated* me." The corners of her lips curve up in a hint of a smile. A glimpse into the saucy girl I once knew makes me unspeakably happy.

"God. I never expected the songs would become so big. I wrote them after you left me that message. Until then, I'd never given up hope." I look out the window overlooking downtown Seattle, remembering. I glance back at her. "You know what? It doesn't matter. You were such an important part of my life."

"Yeah?" She shifts in her seat. I catch a sparkle from the chain around her neck. It's the butterfly necklace. She still wears it.

Holy shit.

I don't let on that I see, though. "*Yeah*. C'mon, it'll be okay. Let's put this stuff in the rearview mirror. We'll finally move on so things don't have to be awkward between us or our friends."

Once again, zings of electricity zap between us. I nearly move my hand but I'm still so irresistibly drawn to her. Maybe even stronger than before. It's like the magnets that brought us together in the first place have strengthened over time.

Which is terrifying, but also exciting. *Hopeful.*

"I know Alex and Jace have hung out over the years." Zoey cocks her brow.

"Mmm-hmm." I don't know how much she knows so...

She chews nervously on the end of her ballpoint pen, glancing between me and our hands.

"Can we leave that discussion for another day?" I lean back in my seat, breaking our physical contact. "Today is about my foundation, which I'm really proud of."

"Oh! Of course." Zoey's body jerks back as if she's been pushed. She quickly cloaks her shock with a mask of polished professionalism, though she rambles a bit in her delivery. "You *should* be proud. Um, I should call Joe back in. Or are you going to go with another firm now that I'm involved? I'm happy to turn this over to someone else if you're not comfortable with me."

I shake my head. "Of course not, if Carter chose you and this firm then I'm good. I want you to stay. It gives us a legitimate reason to, well, reconnect as older and wiser adults I guess."

"Of course. In a professional sense. Ethically I'm your lawyer." Zoey's mask slips firmly back in place.

"Right. Okay. In a professional sense." I nod my affirmation.

Truth be told, Zoey's need to clarify our relationship feels like rejection. Which stings. Maybe I'm too sensitive. After all, today surprised us both.

It's just...now that I've found my elusive butterfly, there's no way to deny I want her.

But, does she want you?

Shit. I finally feel stable in all aspects of my life. It's probably a terrible idea risking my heart and sanity for Zoey.

Fuck it.

This witty, stunningly gorgeous, smart woman is meant to be mine. I know it as surely now as I did when I met her.

Carter came through. Working with her is going to be the best of both worlds. I'll have her in my life professionally—for now. It'll give me time to slowly win her over.

Sooner rather than later.

We've already wasted too much time.

Chapter Twenty-Six

Five Months Later

REGRET.

I can't help but feel utter and total regret at losing eight years with Ty because of my own stupidity and stubbornness. It's a cycle I can't break.

Probably because the Rainier Arts Foundation dominates most of my day, every day.

Working with Ty is an absolute joy. His intelligence and insight about how he wants his non-profit to run is intoxicating. Not only do I respect the hell out of him, but I'm proud to be part of the team that will make his dream become a reality.

As we've set up his foundation over the past few months, we've settled into a friendly yet professional rhythm. It's crazy to think Ty and I have now been platonic business associates longer than we were a couple. Which is weird.

I'm also confused as hell. I find reasons to call or text him under the pretense I need information for the legal documents I'm preparing. He calls and texts me a lot too. Invariably our conversations stretch into other subjects. It's the best part of my day. I crave it. Want more of it.

There's nothing romantic in any of our interactions, which is how it should be. I have ethical obligations, after all. I try to convince myself I'm happy enough being friends. Then, my heart explodes when Ty does something sweet. Like remembering my birthday and stopping by the office with two cupcakes, one bearing a "2" candle and the other with a "6."

As for me, I'm try not to read anything into any of this, but I'm in grave, grave danger.

He still wears the bracelet I gave him for his birthday. The leather might be faded and worn, but he's kept his promise never to take it off. Not to mention, Ty's sexy, deep voice still gives me goosebumps every time we speak. His goofy, dorky sense of humor is so endearing. His sweet demeanor is the same as it always was...everything about Tyson Rainier melts my heart.

So, no. I can't deny I want us to be something more. Part of me sometimes even believes he wants more too.

And then he doesn't respond to me for days. Or, in a way that seems reserved and cautious. He can be cold. Distant. Almost like he's protecting himself.

From *me*. Which is crushing. But understandable.

Our past still blankets us like a thick fog.

Though I'm not proud of it, I'm spending hours poring over everything I can find about him on Google, social media, YouTube. Anywhere. While I can't find any of the sordid videos and pictures I saw when I was in law school, it doesn't mean there aren't plenty of smokin' pictures of Ty for me to fantasize about.

I'm partially disgusted with myself. I've become some kind of stalker fangirl I always swore I wouldn't be. I can't help myself.

A few of my favorite images are from a *Rolling Stone* article where he's shirtless and his jeans ride so low you can see his happy trail. He's looking directly into the camera with those piercing, blue eyes. In a Breitling watch ad, Ty's gorgeous but unshaven, smirking face is shot in extreme close-up, a $20,000 watch encircles the wrist he rests his chin on.

The hottest one, in my opinion, is *People* magazine's Sexiest Man Alive Issue. Ty sits cross-legged in front of a swimming pool in frayed, holey jeans. He leans back on his arms with his head thrown back in laughter. It's an image that captures him perfectly.

God, my heart literally yearns for him. The cycle continues. I'm riddled with fresh bouts of remorse because this amazing, complicated, wonderful man was mine and I threw him away.

Too soon, all of the paperwork is filed, the organization infrastructure is finalized, executive staff are vetted and hired, board members appointed, and everything is in place. My one final task is to help him onboard the rest of the staff. Then my formation work will be done.

LTZ's publicity team is now on the job. They're overseeing the public announcement of the Rainier Arts Foundation at a private event on his birthday in September.

My official reasons to talk to Ty are nearly over, which is so depressing I can't bear to think about it a minute longer.

Lost in my malaise, I nearly jump out of my seat when Joe Finney knocks on my door.

"Zoey, we need to have a chat." Joe's hands are behind his back as he stands in front of me.

My heart beats wildly. I haven't been able to concentrate for many days now, so I brace myself for a reprimand. "Sure, Joe." I try to sound confident. "What can I do for you?"

"Congratulations on bringing in the Rainier Arts Foundation. An amazing client. I appreciate it and wanted to personally thank you." Joe sets an expensive bottle of Veuve Clicquot champagne on my desk and heads back out the door. "Oh, and now that the foundation is set up, I'll be the primary point of contact. There's other client work I'd like you to focus on."

Keeping a calm and what I hope is a gracious exterior, my insides feel like they're being incinerated. I have no interest in my other client work. The foundation is what I look forward to. Not only does it mean day-to-day interaction with Ty, I love being an integral part of his foundation. It makes me feel like I'm making a difference in people's lives.

I'm beyond devastated that it's being ripped away.

Before Ty came back into my life, my perspective was different. I'd been singularly focused on the partner track here at Finney Cooper. Now I'm not so sure. I've been working nonstop and seeking validation from professors and now bosses for eight years.

Ugh.

Ty is stoked about his foundation. When was the last time I was truly excited about my future? Not just going through the motions to achieve corporate goals. I wonder if it's time to make a drastic change.

I don't have a social life other than a handful of embarrassing online dates. My student loans are paid off. The rent on my apartment is reasonable, I have no other big expenses. Maybe, if I'm careful with money, I could take a year off. Finally go somewhere exotic with Alex.

The only person I want to talk about this with is Ty. And now I have no professional reason to be in contact. In the blink of an eye, it's now inappropriate for me to call or text. Not that he's reached out in quite a few days. Other than a short response to one of my questions about the foundation.

Maybe he's already distancing himself from me. Maybe he said something to Joe. Maybe it's his turn to break my heart the way I broke his. All I know is losing him will probably send me into a deep depression.

Again.

It's been a week and I haven't heard from him.

I'm struggling to muster interest in my new workload because I've fully resigned myself that I'll never hear from Ty again.

My assistant, Becca, knocks and brings me a package. It's a beautiful custom-made VIP invitation for me and a guest to the Rainier Arts Foundation launch party at the Space Needle Loupe. LTZ is playing a special acoustic set for an exclusive broadcast on Sirius.

Only one hundred people will be there. Becca confirms that Joe wasn't invited, which makes me feel smug, considering he ripped me away from my passion-project to finish and take credit for it himself.

Then it hits me. *Holy shit, I'm invited.*

My body immediately buzzes with adrenaline and stress. It's one thing to see Ty, but at such an intimate affair there'll be no way to avoid the LTZ guys.

I can't go. It'll be too awkward.

Besides, I have nothing to wear. My wardrobe has two modes: business attire or sweats. I won't be able to dress fashionably enough to compete with the women Ty's used to. He was practically engaged to Ronni Miller, for God's sake.

I'm coming up with every excuse not to go when my phone pings with a text from Ty.

Ty:

Hi Z, did you get the invite?

Me:

Y

Ty:

You should be there.

Me:

I'll Try

Ty:

Not good enough

You should be at the party

Me:

I'll try

Ty:

Come on. You're part of my team.

Me:

Not anymore, Joe reassigned me to other projects

Ty:

WTF

My phone lights up. "What the fuck? He can't do that."

"He can, and he did," I sigh.

"Who am I going to work with?" Ty growls.

"Well, it's his firm and you'll be in good hands with anyone. I'm just an associate," I rationalize, even though it sucks.

"You're the one who did all the work, Zoey," Ty fumes. "I'm going to have a word with him, I want you back on the project."

"No! I'm still just starting out as a lawyer. This is how it's done. I may not be happy about it, but I can't afford to burn any bridges this early in my career. Please don't say anything," I plead. Despite my recent misgivings, I don't want Ty to do something that'll interfere with my job.

"Ah, *bay*—Zoey. Fine, I won't do anything to get you in trouble, I promise. But I'm not happy about it. Not at all." Ty is pissed.

I pause for a moment; did he almost call me "babe?" I throw out a fishing line. "If it means anything, I'm crushed."

"Of course it means something. I was looking forward to seeing you more often when we go on hiatus." Ty's voice remains even.

"I was looking forward to it too." I'm overcome with emotion. My voice catches. "I'm so grateful we're back in touch and that things between us seem to be okay."

Ty's voice is tight. "Zoey, for many years I wasn't okay, but I am now. I *really* am."

"I mean, of course you are. You've got everything you ever wanted." I swallow, feeling foolish. "I didn't mean to imply anything—"

He sucks in a breath. "Uh...don't worry about it."

"I just wanted to say that working on the foundation has been inspirational." My voice comes out weirdly high-pitched, almost like a fangirl and not like the woman who once saw him naked. A lot.

"Thank you," Ty says quietly.

I feel so out of my depth. I have no idea what he's thinking, so I take a deep breath. Decide to say my piece.

After all, this might be the last time I talk to him if I don't attend the event. "The truth is, I'm nervous to see you play live. Spending this much time with you on the foundation brings up a lot of memories from when we were together." I squeeze my eyes shut. "I'm just so sorry about how I handled things. Even if I think you're meant to be where you are right now, I could have done better."

Babbling is definitely my greatest superpower. *God.* There's utter silence on Ty's end. "Are you there?"

He rasps, "Yeah."

"I'm also not sure if I can face the guys after everything..."

"Wow, um—" Ty coughs. "That's a lot to process. I admit, spending time with you *is* confusing. But, seriously, don't worry about the guys, they understand what happened. They might have been sick of me because I was a mess, but they never hated you. They still talk about the Dick's burgers and pies you and Alex brought to the studio."

"They do? *Really?*" I'm genuinely surprised.

"Yeah." Ty hesitates for a few seconds. "Does it really matter though? The bottom line is, *I'd* like you to be there. Without your help, I wouldn't be achieving this new dream."

Not exactly why I want to be invited, but I don't have any right to expect more. "Okay. Thank you. I'm happy that I've played a small part." I swallow my pride and ask the question I really need the answer to. "So...what if your fans realize it's me?"

"Uh... Oh. *Right.* I guess I've performed the songs on the album so many times." Ty sucks in a breath. I hear him breathe in and breathe out a few times. Almost like he's calming himself down. "Shit, Zoey. I didn't even consider you might be outed." The silence stretches out for a minute or two, but I can feel the energy between us through the phone line. I'm pretty sure he can hear the thump-thump of my heart. "I never thought I'd have to face you singing those songs. Shit."

"Well, you hated me. You *deserved* to hate me." My voice cracks. I can't stop the tears from rolling down my cheeks.

Then I hear T choke back a sob. "You have no idea, do you? It's the opposite. I *loved* you. I fucking *loved* you, Zoey. You were my *heart*. You were my *everything*."

My heart feels like it has been wrenched from my chest. "I loved you too, Ty. So much. I hope you know that. It's also why I'm questioning whether it's smart for me to be there. It feels like we're opening a can of worms. I mean, after you announce the foundation, we don't have any reason to see each other. I don't know if I could..." I close my eyes tight, squeezing tears out as I say the words. Grateful that we aren't having this conversation face-to-face, because I couldn't handle it.

"Zoey, of course we have a reason to see each other." Ty's voice is soft. Soothing.

"We do?" We're in such different places. We're such different *people* now.

"We do." I hear a commotion in the background and Ty's emotions are back in check. "Look, I'm in the studio in LA until the day of the party but promise me you'll be there. Bring Alex, she's still friends with Jace so it will be fun. We'll *make* it fun. Let's stop taking all of this so damn seriously, for God's sake, we were babies. It's in the past."

I'm not convinced, but if he wants me to be there I'll go. "Okay, you're right. I'll talk to Alex."

"Great. Zoey, look, I'm sorry to cut this short but I'm late for a meeting and gotta jet." Ty's all business now. "I'll see you next week, okay?"

"Yes. I'll see you next week." Truthfully, even though my emotions are all over the map, I haven't felt this happy in many years.

Though I have doubts and fears, Ty invited me personally.

He's who matters to me. He's *always* been who matters to me.

So no. I can't miss it. I *won't* miss it. I've worked hard on the foundation, and I deserve to be there for the big announcement.

And maybe, just maybe, Ty will finally be back in my life.

Chapter Twenty-Seven

The Next Week

WE'VE FINISHED OUR SOUNDCHECK on the makeshift stage at the top of the Space Needle.

Me and the guys are hanging out waiting for the party to start. I have to admit, it's a pretty badass place for a music event. You can see through the glass floor all the way down to the mangled architectural mess of MoPOP and the cool-as-fuck Chihuly Glass Museum.

The only problem is my heart's beating so hard I can practically see it thumping under my black T-shirt. Zoey should be here soon. Being around her makes me feel things I've pushed deep down inside of myself. The spark is there, but I'm petrified of putting myself out there.

More petrified not to.

At least I have music to hide behind, though it's been a while since we've played acoustically. Almost a decade since the show we surprised Zoey with for her high-school graduation party. Last week we rehearsed a ton to make sure our arrangements are perfect for a live streaming event, so I'm not nervous about the show.

In our makeshift backstage area, Zane's sitting on a stool tuning his guitar, oblivious to my fidgety self. Jace's trying to be covert, but he keeps glancing at the elevator platform. Waiting. Connor's outside looking out over the crystal-blue waters of Puget Sound. We're all biding our time until showtime at sunset, which isn't for another hour.

"Shit, happy birthday, Ty!" Zane's head snaps up from his guitar. A smattering of the crew mumble birthday wishes.

"Thanks, I'm more excited about the kids we're going to help than turning thirty." I nod at them.

"Or, you're super excited by a certain blonde lawyer." Jace cocks his head. "I'd tell you to be careful, but I can see you're going down the well again no matter what I say."

"Ah, well, there's a lot of baggage but it's been good getting to know her as a professional, for the past few months. She's remarkable at her job. And now that we're friends again, hopefully we can put the past behind us." I try not to be defensive, but Jace's snarky comment irks me. I'm far from the boy who anguished over Zoey for years, I've grown up. Worked on myself. I've earned the right to make my own decisions.

"Carter's an idiot, he's the last person who should have ever given Zoey advice." Zane shrugs. "I know it. *He* knows it. You know it."

"Zoey didn't know it though. He was a famous rock star. She was only eighteen." I repeat the words I tell myself whenever I still feel angry about how she left me.

Jace shoots me a crooked grin. "Sounds like you've made peace with it."

"Well, what am I supposed to do, man?" My irritation at my band brother dissipates immediately. "She's even more amazing now than she was then. I want everyone to be nice to her, she's nervous about hearing the songs live and being outed. She has her career to consider."

"I don't blame her, those lyrics put her on full blast." Zane mimics an explosion with his hands. "Good thing we made everyone lock up their camera phones."

The distinct ping of the elevator causes the three of us to stop our banter and watch it open. Alex steps out first, wearing a simple T-shirt, Levi's, and black Frye boots. She narrows her eyes when she spots me, then blushes when she sees Jace.

Behind her, Zoey looks like an angel. She wears her hair in a long, thick side braid with wild flyaway pieces framing her beautiful face, a light-purple sundress and silver sandals. Every fiber in my body ignites. The exact reaction I had when I first saw her at The Mission.

I'm about to say hello when Andrew and Sienna pull me into an interview, which takes forever. By the time I'm finished, we have to do our pre-show rituals and get on stage.

Anxious to see where Zoey is, I crane my neck to try and find her in the small crowd. Jace and Connor's family are there. Carter, of course. Fiona too. The rest are super fans who won tickets on Sirius, various LTZ staff from the management office and the Sirius execs.

I don't see Zoey. *Shit.*

We huddle and pump each other up as we always do, but I'm distracted. Somehow, I have to find Zoey before I can begin the set. I frantically scan the audience until I *finally* locate her. She stands with Alex in the back by the bar. They're talking animatedly to each other, oblivious to the world around them.

Some things never change.

The sun begins its descent over the Olympic Mountains. As the golden light gives way to a brilliant pink and purple hue, the Sirius host announces us and we all take the stage.

We're only playing six songs, leaving out our biggest hit, *Down*, despite threats of bodily harm from the Sirius suits. I refuse to sing about my visceral heartbreak in front of Zoey tonight. We're not on solid footing and I don't want her to head back down the glass elevator and out of my life forever. It's my event. My birthday. I simply pulled rank.

After we're announced, I don't say anything or engage in any banter, I close my eyes, feel the music and belt out our earliest releases *Rise* and *Gemini*, then jump into *Long Road* and *Kick It*.

I'm at my most comfortable in front of an audience. Playing like this is second nature. The audience loves it, if the reaction in the room is to be believed, Fueled by positivity, I find the courage to search for Zoey. It doesn't take long, she's still in the back next to Alex, staring at me with such adoration, my entire body ignites.

I stop and let Zane play a solo which morphs into the first chords of *Shine*. The audience cheers and whoops wildly. When we finish, it's already time to wrap things up. "These next two songs were written during a time when I was utterly heartbroken. I lost the love of my life. I lost myself. I've never publicly discussed who she is. We, uh, lost touch for many years and I didn't want LTZ's fans to hurt her." I look over at Zane, who nods.

I flick my eyes to my guitar, which I continue strumming for a few seconds before glancing back at her through the audience. "I want to thank everyone for coming here to celebrate the announcement of the Rainier Arts Foundation." I pump my fist into the air. The crowd cheers wildly. Alex leans her head on Zoey's shoulder.

"I'm feeling, well, psyched because my love and I recently reconnected." I flick my eyes on each of my bandmates and then back at her. "I'm grateful for her. Wherever she is, I hope she thinks of me fondly as I do of her."

"Now, before you folks out in Sirius land start giving her shit on our social media, know that without her, my foundation wouldn't exist. Without her, these songs wouldn't exist." The room buzzes. A slow smattering of applause starts and grows louder.

Zane riffs on the opening notes of *Butterfly*. I manage to catch Zoey's gaze and hold it. I practically *will* her to look at me so I can sing this song to her. I *need* to sing to her. And

I do. Our eyes are locked throughout. When the song ends, she wipes a tear from the corner of her eye as the crowd loses their mind.

"Okay, okay, shhhhh." I wave my hands to quiet the audience. "I know you're only expecting six songs tonight, but as a special thank you for supporting my foundation, we're debuting a new song tonight for you and for our Sirius fans."

Connor and Jace leave the stage. Zane hands me my Breedlove acoustic and follows them. This one is all me.

I pluck the strings and take a minute. When I'm ready, I glance up to see Alex with her arm protectively around Zoey. They lean together, watch me intently.

I swallow hard because I'm about to make a declaration that will either change my life for the good or destroy me forever. "This song is called *Heart* and it's for the woman who has mine."

With my eyes squeezed shut, I get so lost in the song that it takes me a minute to come back to Earth when it ends. The audience is wild and begin to squeeze us in, so I lose my visual on Zoey. Luckily, our security is ready. They organize everyone so I can greet the fans and make the necessary small talk with the station executives.

All I really want to do was get to Zoey. Initially I panic when I can't see her until I spot her and Alex outside on the outer observation deck.

She didn't leave.

I stare at them for a few minutes until Jace grabs my arm and spins me around. "For fuck's sake, you've been waiting for eight years, will you stop dicking around and go get your girl?"

I don't need to be told twice.

I push through the crowd to get to her, leaving Sergey, my security guard, at the door to give us some privacy. I approach Zoey tentatively. Alex waves me over, squeezing my forearm when I reach them. She kisses Zoey on the head and disappears back inside, leaving us alone.

I sit on the bench next to where Zoey's standing and pat the seat. Wordlessly, she sits next to me and fidgets with her sparkly bracelet before shyly looking up at me. Searching her eyes, I reach across and stroke her hair the way I used to do so long ago. "Are you okay? Did I go too far?"

"It was wonderful, you didn't have to say those nice things." Zoey blinks at me, capturing my hand and cupping it to her face.

I lean in closer. "I meant everything."

"The song." She swallows hard. "Was that really for me?"

"*Zoey.*" I tilt my head and look down at my beautiful girl. Trace her face with the knuckles of my freehand down her neck to where the butterfly necklace rests against her neck. "It's *always* only been you."

"I don't know what's happening." She twists away and wraps her arms around herself as if she's cold.

I feel bold. Confident. It's now or never and I don't want to spend another day without her. "*Yes*, you do."

I bend down to kiss her sweet lips. Moaning, she reaches up and laces her fingers through my hair and pulls my head closer. Our kiss deepens into something desperate and needy. I suck on her tongue gently before I tug her against me. Her breasts are pressed against me, which is sweet torture.

We're in public, so I try to regain control and rest my forehead on her shoulder. Breathing heavily, I keep her tight against my side, unwilling to lose our connection.

Zoey kisses my eyelids, then my nose and mouth. I released the clasp so her hair falls all around her shoulders and down her back. I cup her breasts. My thumbs sneak over her nipples as our tongues tease and taste.

Moaning, Zoey grips my hair tightly, which stings so beautifully. Our passion is for each other is unchanged after eight long years. Making out with Zoey is my idea of heaven. If only I could make everyone else inside at the party disappear, it would be a perfect end to a perfect night.

Zoey is my home.

"What are you smiling about?" She leans her head on my shoulder, looking up at me, her hands still caress and rake through my hair.

I kiss her temple, breathing in her delicious flowery, citrusy scent. "I'm being cautiously optimistic."

"We've gone from zero to ten pretty fast, I'm a little overwhelmed." Zoey leans back but holds onto my index finger with hers. We wiggle them together.

I coax her back against me and she burrows into my side. "Zoey, we've been separated for years, but we can't deny what is still between us."

"Do you believe that?" She tucks my hair behind my ear, absently, like the way she used to.

"I really do. I haven't been able to think about anything else since I first saw you again. But, I'm not sure what you want, do you think we can put the past in the past?" I trace her lips with my finger.

Instead of answering, she searches my eyes as if to make sure I'm telling her the truth. And then, as if she has the answer, presses her lips to mine and kisses me like she's never going to stop.

Forehead to forehead we grin like fools at each other. Smooching. Holding hands. Cuddling.

The moon is high in the sky and its light dances on Puget Sound below us.

I know with all certainty that this birthday will turn out better than the last one I spent with her.

Chapter Twenty-Eight

Fifteen Minutes Later

MY HEART BURSTS INTO a million fireworks when Ty holds tightly to my hand and navigates us through the crowd like an expert.

I can't help but notice every yummy thing about him. Ty's once unruly chocolate waves are soft and shiny, still flowing just past his shoulders. His piercing, blue eyes embody the confidence of someone who's commanded 200,000 people at a festival. He's much more muscular now, the definition of his chest and biceps under his plain black T-shirt is swoon worthy. Not to mention the impressive package easily discernable under faded black jeans held up by a studded, black leather belt.

The contrast between the shy, introverted young man I knew and the poised, articulate, self-assured celebrity he is today is bewildering. People clammer to get his attention.

Ty is kind. Patient. Accommodating. He poses with everyone who asks. Signs autographs, talks music and even gracefully fends off a couple of ladies who get too handsy. His skills are impeccable. Everyone feels singled out and special though I can tell it's a carefully crafted façade.

Throughout these interactions, Ty holds my hand tightly and strokes my palm with his thumb. I play with his bracelet to keep me somewhat grounded. This entire night feels like a dream. A good dream, but surreal.

I'd come to this show hoping we could stay professional friends. Am I leaving with a boyfriend? I can't believe he premiered another song he wrote for me live on air in front of all these people—it's such a big gesture. The conversation we just had. The kissing. I'm so confused.

Does he really want us to be a couple again? And if so, does anyone here know I'm *Z*?

I need a quick moment to myself. I drop Ty's hand and excuse myself to find the restroom, and run into Zane and Connor on the way.

"Hey, Zoey!" Zane pulls me into a hug.

I hug him back and break our connection. "Hi, Zane."

"So, you're a lawyer now I hear." He leans back against the wall.

"Yep." I nod at Connor, who looms silently. "Hey, Connor, good to see you."

He nods. "Aye."

I feel awkward and out of place. "Well, I'm just trying to find the bathroom."

"Zoey." I'm surprised to hear Connor gruff tone directed at me. "I haven't seen Ty happy in a long time. *Um*. Feck. Never mind. It's none of my business."

Zane intervenes, "Look, we were *there*, Zoey. It was bad for so many years. Ty's our brother. We have his back."

"I'm not sure what's happening with us, but whatever it is, we're older and hopefully wiser now and it needs to stay between us." I understand their concern, but I can't allow anyone to intrude in our relationship, whatever that is. The consequences were too high last time.

"Guys, you all saw me through some rough times, but Zoey's right, this is between us." Ty surprises me from behind. He places both hands on my shoulders and draws me back against him before wrapping his arms around me. "We're going to figure this out *together* without any more interference."

Connor flips Ty off with a grin. "Fair enough."

"*Dude*—" Zane drolls apologetically.

Ty moves beside me, keeping me tucked against him. "You're cool, my brother. We're gonna head out."

"Wait!" A beautiful dark-haired woman approaches, shooting me a scathing look which is replaced with a smile the instant Ty turns his head to acknowledge her.

"What's up, Sienna? We're leaving." Ty's arm around me tightens possessively.

She strokes his other bicep familiarly, causing my hackles to rise. "Aren't you going to introduce me?"

"Oh. Of course, this is *the* magnificent Zoey Pearson." Ty kisses the top of my head.

"Hi," I say quietly while studying her unabashedly.

"Ahh, how fun. The famous '*Z*.'" Sienna looks me up and down. "So great to finally meet the girl that, um...he's been *sooo* secretive about you for all of these years..."

"That's enough, Sienna. As I said, we're heading out. I'll talk to you later." Ty ignores her superior attitude and tugs me away from the shark-like woman.

"Who's that?" I pray he doesn't say a former girlfriend with all my heart.

He rolls his eyes. "Just Sienna, one of our publicists. She and her business partner, Andrew, do all of our PR."

"Oh." I have no idea what I'm allowed to ask at this point.

"Ignore her." Ty bends down and gives me a scorching kiss to end all kisses. "Let's get out of here."

Hand in hand, we make our way to the glass elevator through the area reserved for the band. We nearly run into Alex and Jace, who are huddled together in a corner. They spring apart when they see us approach.

Ty and I give each other knowing side looks and say goodbye. A minute later, we're alone in the glass elevator deescalating down the side of the Space Needle. Ty squeezes my fingers between his, but gazes out the window as the ground rushes up to meet us.

A couple of burly bodyguards, including Sergey, wait for us at the bottom. I'm astonished at the huge crowd waiting to get a glimpse of Ty or anyone in the band. I can't get over how different the Ty I knew so intimately years ago is from rockstar Ty. I had some idea from lurking on LTZ's socials and our work on the foundation, but it's different when you're in the inner circle.

He's a *real* celebrity.

"I was hoping you might come back to my house to hang out, and well, talk some more?" Ty keeps a tight grip on my hand as security shuffles us to the waiting car.

The air whooshes out of my body. "Uh...I'm not sure, I'm still processing all of this. I want to, but—"

"Yeah, it's okay if you're not ready." Ty's face falls but his voice is kind. "I can bring you home."

I bite my lip. "No, I'm ready, I *think*. Ty. I've never stopped—" I stop myself from saying it. It would make me too vulnerable.

"Me either." He lights up again. Bends down and kisses me.

"It's a lot to take in." I gesture between us, truly floored at the turn of events. I don't know what to think. What to hope for.

"I've never been able to play it cool with you, butterfly." Ty drapes his arms around my shoulders protectively, the way he always used to.

Instinctively, I wrap my arms around his waist. "I came to this show thinking I'd be happy if we could be friends. Now there's been kissing. And *songs*. Your house..."

"Zoey, I'm not trying to force anything on you. I'd take you somewhere public, but there'd be no privacy. We had precautions in place up at the event to make sure no one took our picture, but if we go somewhere, our pictures will get posted everywhere." I didn't realize all the things that went into keeping Ty—and me—safe. "I want to keep you to myself until you feel comfortable about what's going on between us."

He assuages some of my anxiety. Going home with him, though. Are we going to fuck tonight? Will he expect it? "Umm. Okay?"

"Z, seriously. There's no pressure. Let's just hang out, catch up, and maybe make out a bit?" His innocent grin gets me every time. He's intoxicating. It feels like we're right back to the days when we were first exploring our sexuality and couldn't wait to find some alone time.

I want this. I want *him*. "Okay," I agree definitively.

My smile cannot be contained. It feels like my dreams are coming true.

"Okay." He looks as giddy as me.

Chapter Twenty-Nine

Ten Minutes Later

WE'RE USHERED INTO BACKSEAT of the waiting car but can't leave because there are thousands of fans surrounding the Space Needle. Luckily, Sirius sends more security. We see Zane appear behind the barricades to wave at the fans. For a quick moment, it distracts them from our car, which allows Sergey to whisk us away and speed through downtown over the West Seattle bridge to Ty's house.

I'm in awe when we drive through an automatic modern steel gate onto a long, wooded driveway surrounded by tall shrubbery. Around the corner, a sprawling three-story glass-and-wood structure appears among the beautiful foliage of the Pacific Northwest. Behind the house is an expansive view of Puget Sound and the city skyline.

"Wow, this is stunning. Look at that view," I marvel.

"Right before I visited your dad, I bought this house. It didn't look quite like this and there was no gate, no security. I never thought about setting up a holding company for it so my name was on the public records." Ty leads me through the front door. "We were gone for months and months at a time. Fans camped out here. A few broke in and stayed inside. It got a bit scary." I follow him through the entryway. "A few years ago I sublet a condo downtown in between tours while I remodeled and amped up my security game. The band's lawyers moved the deed out of my name into a trust, so now it's harder to figure out that I own it."

"You've come a long way from that run-down apartment, Tyson Rainier." I beam as I take in the open-plan living/dining/kitchen backed by a wall of glass overlooking the entire city skyline, including the landmark we spent the evening in. "Wow, just wow!"

"I guess so." Ty flicks his eyes to mine. "Are you thirsty? I don't drink anymore, but I probably have some wine somewhere."

I sit on a stool at the expansive granite waterfall island in his pristine chef's kitchen. "No, I'd rather have some tea if you don't mind."

"What's a singer without tea?" He puts the electric kettle on just as my stomach growls embarrassingly loud. "You're hungry. I'll cook something for us."

"No, I'm fine." My stomach protests with another growl. Ty arches a brow.

"Let me put my line cook skills to the test, I can make us grilled cheese sandwiches." Ty opens the double-sized fridge and takes out some fancy cheese. Pulls a loaf of bread out of a drawer.

Ty's acting like everything between us is normal. Like no time has passed. Like what happened to us never happened. I'm not sure how I'm supposed to act.

"My belly can't say no to your cooking." I nervously cover up my anxiousness with enthusiasm.

"I'll just be a few minutes. Why don't you go sit down and make yourself comfortable. My couch is fucking amazing and the view is something I never get tired of." Ty nods toward the living room and turns his attention back to the sandwiches.

I do as he asks, taking in the dark hardwood floors, plush, oversized gray couch, and the gold and platinum records decorating the walls. Sinking back against the cushions, I look out at the city. He's right, this is a multimillion dollar view.

The smell of melting cheese has my mouth watering. My heartbeat's in overdrive. I can't stop fidgeting. I'm now on the edge of the cushion watching Ty bustle around the kitchen. Is this really happening? Am I really alone with Ty at his house?

Surreal.

"Here you go." Ty snaps me out of my trance and hands me a tea and grilled cheese. He goes back to the kitchen to retrieve his own tea and sandwich and plops down next to me. Blows on his own cup. "So, you're *here*."

"I am." I blow on my tea too, looking up at him over the cup.

His cheeks redden adorably. "Zoey, I'm *so* fucking nervous."

"Me too." I release a breath I didn't realize I'd been holding.

He searches my eyes. "Should we talk?"

"I guess we should." I nod, grateful that we're finally going to clear the air.

He picks up his sandwich. "Eat first?"

"Yum." I pick up my plate and nibble at the sandwich, licking the dripping cheese from my lips.

Ty stares at my tongue flicking against my lips. His mouth curves into a grin then expands into a full-blown smile. I can't help but let out a burst of anxious laughter. He follows with his own guffaw. For a few minutes we laugh at the absurdity of where we find ourselves. Which breaks the tension completely.

When our chuckling subsides, Ty's expression changes. Like he's hungry for something more than a sandwich. I swallow and lick my lips again. His eyes follow my tongue, almost enraptured. The sexual tension crackles between us.

I put down the sandwich on the coffee table. Ty sets his empty plate down next to mine and sinks back against the cushions. His arm skims the top of the couch. Resting his head on one hand, he reaches over to trace my lips with his finger then caresses my cheek with his whole palm.

"You're still the sweetest and most beautiful woman in the world, Zoey. I'm not proud of how I behaved over the years, I haven't been a good man. Or, an honorable man. I'm not sure what to say to you, other than you were right to leave me back then." Ty's head bobs solemnly. "I would've been such a disappointment."

I'm floored. He's been blaming himself? "Oh, Ty, that's not true. You made it against all of the odds. How I handled things will always be the biggest regret of my life." I shake my head sadly and look away. "I'm so, *so* sorry."

"Zoey." Ty tips his finger under my chin to make me look at him.

"Do you think we could have made it?" I ask the question I've asked myself every day for eight years.

Ty studies me, holding my gaze. "I try not to think about it. My therapist told me there's no point in wasting energy on something that you can't change."

"You're in therapy?" The surprises keep coming.

"Yeah." He seems uncomfortable for a second then re-covers. "On and off for a few years. The guys and Carter encouraged me to go. I think it helped me deal with, well, what happened with us. But, also my upbringing. My mom. The abuse."

Ty scoots closer to me. Instinctively, I lean against him. Just like I used to when we'd cuddle and talk for hours. "So much lost time, it's so stupid." I can't help it when a tear escapes.

"Ahhhh, *babe*, no tears. This is a happy night. Should we maybe fill in some of the gaps?" Ty wipes my cheek with his thumb.

"Not much on my side, I studied hard and now I'm working hard." I shrug. It's the simple, boring truth.

Ty cocks his head. "I know that, but you had someone?" Ty winces, but he's asking me a question. "I mean, it's none of my business."

"Do you want it to be your business, Ty?" I trace a line on his shoulder, feeling comfort and safety in his embrace.

He whispers, "I'd like to know."

"I've dated, but not much. There was someone I was seeing in law school, but I broke it off. He wasn't for me. I don't really put myself out there..." Going out with other people is pointless. They're not Ty.

"Why?" Ty seems genuinely curious.

"Umm. Well, the world was trying to figure out who I was, and I didn't want anyone to find out I was the girl who...uh, hurt you..." I remember when I was on edge all of the time. "I appreciated none of you ever outing me."

He grips my wrist. "*No*, why is there no one else?"

I shoot him a pointed look and look away. There's no way to answer without just coming out and saying there will never be anyone else. It's probably too soon for that type of admission.

I continue to trace my finger on his shoulder while staring at the hole in the knee of his jeans. We sit quietly for a while.

Ty's deep, melodic voice breaks the silence. "I'm sometimes a little regretful I put it all out there. After your voice mail, I hoped you'd hear it and maybe call me and yell at me, or just, I don't know. *Anything*. Being without you was agony."

"From what I saw, you had plenty of women to cheer you up." I close my eyes so I don't have to see his reaction. I can't not say anything though. I know about all the women he's been with.

Ty strokes my hair. "I tried to forget you. I couldn't."

"You didn't take it off." I rub my thumb under the bracelet, feeling the worn grooves of our initials.

"I told you I never would." Ty's fingers trace up to my neck where he touches the butterfly resting against my collarbone. "You didn't either."

I bury my head in his shoulder, overwhelmed. When I regain a bit of courage, I look into the deep-blue pools of his eyes. "How can I ever compete, Ty? You can have any woman in the world, you're famous and so fucking gorgeous. I can barely remember to pluck my eyebrows!"

"I'm the same guy, Z. A lot of people think they know me, but I'm still the same socially awkward guy who thinks you're the most beautiful woman in the world." Ty kisses the side of my head. "And I love your eyebrows."

I scrunch up my nose. "What's it like going out with models and actresses?"

"Terrible. Most are *literally* the worst." Ty laughs.

I take his hand and rub the calluses on his fingertips the way I used to. "It was hard to see all of the pictures of you... I couldn't even be mad, I didn't have the right."

"I understand. When I saw a picture of you with your law school boyfriend on Instagram, I lost my mind." Ty clasps his big hand with my tiny one.

I'm stunned. I had no idea he lurked on my socials too, not that there was much to see. "I'm sorry."

"Ah, Z, I don't want you to feel bad. I'm sorry too. I gave up trying after your voicemail. You seemed so sure that you didn't want me in your life. I didn't realize how badly you were hurting." Ty kisses my hand. "I wouldn't have stayed away."

I trace my finger along his arm. "Thanks for including me tonight. It was special. You're an amazing songwriter. Musician. You absolutely deserve all of the success."

Ty watches me stroking his arm with a furrowed brow. "I wish you had talked to me back then. We always shared everything, you were the only one I've ever let all the way in."

"I've beaten myself up about this a million times," I try to explain. "I don't know, Carter convinced me that you needed to be free and that we would find each other again if it was meant to be. I just knew I couldn't face you."

"It was a dick move, and I've told him so." Ty winds a tendril of hair around his finger. "He had no right to use his influence on you. But he's my family and I've forgiven him."

I nod. "I'm glad. I truly think he was trying to protect you. *I'm* the one who took it too far."

"I've never experienced pain so bad as when you left. I questioned everything we meant to each other for so many years." Ty closes his eyes and takes a deep, confessional breath. "I wrote those songs to hurt you as much as you hurt me."

"Oh." His revelation cuts a little deep, especially hearing him actually say the words. Although, I'd known it all along.

"It felt like you threw me away," Ty continues, but pulls away. "I didn't understand it. After we had sex that night? You gifting your virginity to me? Zoey, I would have never left you. *Ever.* I went from being the happiest guy on the planet one night to being destroyed by the next morning. It was like you died, you just disappeared. I thought I meant more to you than that."

"Oh Ty." The flood of tears that's been looming all night finally escapes. "You meant *everything* to me. I did it to make sure you were free to follow your dream. I didn't want to hold you back. That's why I did what I did. I hope you can forgive me someday, and we can at least be friends."

He shakes his head. "I don't want to be *friends.*"

"What?" I'm shocked. He's been so affectionate. We've kissed.

Ty looks me in the eye. "I want you *back.*"

"You do?" I want to make sure I've heard him correctly.

I subtly pinch myself.

Because I'll never recover if I find out this night is just a dream.

Chapter Thirty

A Few Minutes Later

THIS ISN'T A DREAM.

Well, maybe it is because everything I've dreamed about over the past eight years seems to be coming true.

"I knew it from the minute I walked into that meeting and saw you again." Ty reaches over and caresses my face. Thumbs my tears away. "No, I've always known, even through all the bullshit."

"Ty, I want you back too." Overcome, I sob uncontrollably and try to pull away because I'm mortified at the depth of my emotion. I've kept it contained and in check for so many years just to survive.

Ty doesn't let me go, instead he envelopes me into his body. "Butterfly, I think our timing is finally right. I *want* our timing to be right. We deserve happiness."

"I hope so. I still love you, Ty. I've never stopped," I confess through my tears. He keeps me tight against his body, rubbing my back as I tearfully release years of devastation in the span of minutes.

"I love you so much, Zoey, please stop crying." Ty gently cups my face in his hands, and kisses my tears away. We slide down on the plush couch until we're lying side-by-side, facing each other.

I comb my hands through his silky hair and pull him to me, kissing him roughly. My lips explore his and we run our hands all over each other's bodies, which we both still remember so well.

Ty reaches down and pulls the skirt of my dress up, causing it to bunch around my legs. Our tongues tangle passionately, and I whimper when he strokes my inner thighs with his palms, causing my dress to move up farther around my waist to reveal my panties. Groaning, he wraps his arms around my lower back, pulling me so close I can feel his rock-hard shaft burrowing into my core through his jeans.

"I want you." My voice is yearning, sexual.

"You have me," Ty whispers.

"If we do this, we won't have to sneak around to avoid our parents and the guys." I giggle and writhe against his cock.

Ty grips my hips to hold me in place against his hardness. His finger moves my panties to the side and dips into my folds. "*When* we do this, I'm going to keep you in my bed all weekend and do everything I've fantasized about."

"Head on a stake? Poison? Death by fiery dragon?" I tease in between feathering kisses along his jawbone.

Ty takes a long suckle on my earlobe and inch by tortuous inch inserts his long finger inside me and growls, "Nah, I'm finally going to be able to *fuck* you in all the ways I've ever imagined."

His *words* make my newly waxed pussy soak his finger with arousal. "Yes. *Please*, Ty. I want that so bad."

"Whatever my girl needs." Ty adds a second finger and wiggles them deep, hooking them against my G-spot when he clues in. "Oh *fuck*! Your pussy is bare!"

His intimate touch makes me blind with rapture. Ty's lips descend on mine and I melt into as he rubs me deliciously, nearly to the brink. He remembers everything about my body. Knows what makes me hum. Sensing I'm close, he rolls me over and pulls me up to straddle him so I'm still riding his fingers.

I reach down to free his cock, but he encircles my wrist and positions it at the small of my back. Thrusts up against my core while pumping in and out of me. The friction between us is insane.

His thumb strokes my clit in quick little circles. My hips move frantically of their own volition against him, soaking his jeans. Bringing me just to the edge, Ty repositions me again by flipping me on my back. He pulls his fingers from my channel and sucks them into his mouth.

"I need your panties off," he growls wolfishly and yanks them down.

Closing my eyes, I give in to the sensation of Ty's hot tongue and lips slowly licking, tasting and kissing down my ribs, then stomach, and over my slight belly swell. Writhing with pleasure and anticipation I buck toward him when his palms press my thighs apart. His hot breath is so close to my pussy, I arch toward his mouth, wanting more. He obliges by lifting my legs over his shoulders, parting my lips with his thumbs and dipping his tongue in for a taste.

"Oh, oh, oh my God Ty, yes!" My legs squeeze against his ears as he relentlessly sips, nibbles, and sucks every inch of me, deliberately avoiding my clit, until I'm begging for release. "Please, Ty. *Please*!"

Ty smiles up at me through the hair that's fallen over his eyes and sucks my sweet spot hard between his lips then rapidly strokes his tongue over and over and over my clit until all the shooting stars in the universe explode behind my eyes, and my body convulses in waves of utter bliss. The cries of ecstasy I can hear somewhere in the distance are from me, I realize.

"God, you're so fucking beautiful when you come." Ty stares up at me with so much adoration as I return to Earth, his head resting against my inner thigh.

"You still know my body so well." I clutch his hand to bring him up for a kiss. I love tasting myself on Ty, I'm never going to miss an opportunity.

"I missed your body, you're my goddess." Ty nuzzles my neck, and we lay in each other's arms, lazily making out while my aftershocks subside.

"Please, Ty, I need you so much." I tug off his T-shirt when our kisses once again become heated.

My hands skim down his sides and reach for his buckle. Together, we pull his jeans down over his hips. His exquisite cock juts out hard against his cut abs, long and thick. Tracing the v of his stomach leading to my prize, I grip him firmly at the base, noticing he's also well-groomed down below. Ty kicks off his boots, then stands to wriggle out of his jeans.

"Let's take this dress off, butterfly." He gently coaxes me to my feet, reaches around and unzips it all the way down. My dress floats to the floor, pooling around my sandals, which I promptly step out of. I'm not wearing a bra, so Ty's eyes widen when he sees my bare breasts exposed. My hard, pink nipples stand at attention.

"Ahhh, fuck. Zoey. I missed this. God, I missed you," Ty hisses, cupping my breast and rubbing his thumb all around my puckered peak. Bending down, he sucks my nipple into his mouth, grazing it slightly with his teeth.

Sensation shoots straight between my legs and I whimper, gripping his hair and holding him to my breast. I beg, "I've wanted you for so long, Ty."

Wordlessly, Ty picks me up and carries me across the living room down the hall through a large double door into his luxurious master bedroom. Striding to his king-size, modern canopy bed, Ty backs himself to the fluffiest white comforter

I've ever seen and sits, making sure I'm straddling him. I smooth his hair and our lips meet passionately.

"I'm clean, Zoey. I haven't been with anyone in a very long time, and I've been tested more than once." Ty thumbs my puckered nipples. His long, heavy cock is stiff in between his belly and mine. "Do you trust me?"

"Of course, I trust you. I'm clean too, and I'm still on the pill." I grip his thick girth in my hand and stroke him the way he taught me.

"Fuuuuuck." Ty watches me slowly and places his hand over mine to help. "I never want there to be anyone or anything between us again."

I swipe my thumb over his crown. "Me either."

Ty and I scoot back a little farther on the bed, so his back rests against the headboard and I'm still straddling him. I cant my hips so his bare cock nestles in between my slick, sensitive folds. Reaching down between us, Ty grips himself and flicks his cock head against my opening to drive me out of my mind. I'm already so wet and ready for him, but he's not been inside me in nearly a decade.

Suspecting my slight hesitation, Ty is careful to go slow as he guides the fat tip inside. Inch by inch he works himself into me, until we gradually become fully joined. Looking down, marveling at the wonder of his thickness disappearing into me, I feel complete for the first time in forever.

Ty presses against the small of my back, giving me exquisite pressure on my pubic bone. He waits for me to relax then thrusts his hips up. My tits jiggle in front of his lips as his thumb sneaks between us, circling my clit. When he sucks a nipple between his lips and nips it, I gush around his cock, allowing him to go deeper. All of the sensations send my hips into a frenzy.

I can't help it. I ride him hard. Fast. Deep. Eight years ago, we made love. Tonight, I'm fucking him in a way that's almost desperate and feral. He's giving it to me the same way. I can't get enough.

Will never get enough.

As our bodies move faster and more urgently together, Ty shifts his angle. My eyes roll back in my head when his cock hits my magic spot as he continues briskly circling my clit. Every nerve ending in my body ignites. My climax is so intense, I clench forcefully around him like a vise, causing him to go over with me.

"Ahhh, baby. Oh, my fucking *God*. Zoey." Ty's eyes squeeze shut and his face goes slack when he explodes his hot flood of release inside me.

Overcome with exhaustion and the emotion of the day, I slump across his chest, feeling him still pulsing and throbbing inside me. He clutches my hips and places sweet kisses all over my face while rocking me slowly back and forth against him, triggering several small mini-orgasms around his softening cock.

We stayed joined for a while, not willing to lose our connection. I wrap my arms around him and breathe in the mixture of his grapefruit and leather scent and our love. I'm in heaven and can hardly believe what just happened.

"I *love* you, Zoey," Ty whispers against my hair. "I want to wake up with you here. Please don't leave me again."

His words pierce my soul.

I'm only beginning to realize the damage I caused to my sweet Ty. I know I was young and inexperienced with relationships, but it's hard to forgive myself.

If this is our second chance, then I'm going to do whatever it takes to make it up to him.

"I love you too, Ty. Nothing—*or no one*—will *ever* make me leave you again."

Chapter Thirty-One

The Next Morning

THE INCREDIBLE FEELING OF Zoey laving the head of my dick with her tongue is a much better way of waking up than our last sleepover.

Stretching like a cat, I flex my legs and fling one arm over my head and stroke her hair with my freehand, just watching. Though I didn't let her do this much when we were younger, I have to admit...my cock between her lips is something to behold. She sucks me to the back of her throat then licks and teases me to utter insanity. Too soon my balls are tingling, and my hips buck reflexively, driving my shaft past her gag reflex. She chokes and I pull out, not wanting to hurt her.

"Come up here, butterfly, your blowjob is phenomenal, but I'd rather be inside you." I guide her up to my side and kiss her deeply.

"I got you a birthday present. In all of the...intensity of last night, I forgot to give it to you. I was going to go get it, but didn't want to leave the bed until you woke up. So, I thought you might like a blowie." She smirks and traces my nipple with her finger.

"*You* are my birthday present." I cradle her head in my arms. "The best one I've ever had. A blowie is the icing on the cake." I kiss down the side of her neck and suck on the spot behind her ear, remembering how hot it used to make her.

It still does.

Zoey moans and writhes against my hard cock still nestled between us. I roll on top of her, careful to keep my full weight from crushing her. She reaches around, grips my ass and opens herself up to me. Like a homing missile, my cock nudges through her slickness, seeking its destination.

"You're so wet for me, Z." I surge against her warm heat and push inside. She takes me much easier this morning.

"Ahhh. *Yesssss*." Zoey runs her hands up and down my back. "Perpetually. Have you seen yourself?"

I palm under her thigh and run my hand down the back of her leg to push her knee up higher. "*Fuuuuuckkk*," I groan when I surge deeper.

God, I'm finally home.

Our bodies grind and slap together. We don't speak, just pant and moan and cry out. The sounds of our lovemaking fill the room with our own music. Zoey reaches between us to rub her clit with two fingers. I watch her take control of her own pleasure and it makes me lose my friggin' mind.

"I can't hold back much longer," I buck into her wildly.

Just like last night, she gasps and contracts around me so tightly when she comes, I have no choice but to let go and empty inside her.

"You're a sex god," Zoey pants after I recover enough to pull out and flop to her side.

"Hardly." Laughing, I jump up and dash into the bathroom to grab a towel to clean us up. I turn to go back to her but find she's followed me into the master bathroom.

Zoey gazes around in awe. "The shower is like a friggin' car wash for ten people!" She gleefully steps into the walk-in, charcoal-tiled shower with eight body jets and two large rain showers and whirls around naked and glorious. "Take a shower with me, I promise to wash your back."

Needing no other incentive, I turn on each nozzle one at a time, hungrily ogling her gorgeous body. She giggles joyfully each time a new jet ignites. I join her under the cascading waterfalls, and squeeze a dollop of my grapefruit bodywash to explore her nakedness, under the guise of washing her clean. I never want to stop touching her. Ever.

Goosebumps break out all over her arms as I run my hands over her body, despite the warm temperature of the water. Her nipples tighten when I flick them with my fingers. I crouch so my face is level with her bare pussy. Holding her steady by her hips, I take a big lick across her seam.

"This is my new favorite room in your house," Zoey squeals, clinging to my head to hold me against her.

Looking up at her with a gleam in my eye, I suck her clit between my lips before I have another idea. Taking a seat on the expansive, tiled shower bench, I turn Zoey around to sit on my lap facing away from me. My hard cock presses against her back. Reaching up behind her head, Zoey clasps her arms around my neck, causing her plump tits to jut out.

"Z, you're so gorgeous." I kiss her neck and run my hands over her breasts, down her stomach, then spread her legs over each of my thighs, exposing her completely. I pump two fingers in and out of her as I thrust my cock up between her pussy lips.

She gasps, clutching my hair. "Yes, oh God, Ty."

The mirror above the vanity reflects our naked bodies writhing together and my fingers inside her. She catches my gaze in the glass and we watch ourselves in the reflection.

"Watch us, Z. We fit together perfectly." I grip my cock, pumping it first, then I impale her.

The visual in the mirror is easily the most erotic thing I've ever seen. Zoey's legs are wide open, draped over mine, as I thrust up into her. I pinch her taut, pink nipple and rub her clit as I suck and lick my beautiful girl's neck.

Together, we watch ourselves fucking as the showerheads spray in all directions. Our noisy moans are amplified in the cavernous bathroom. Zoey's close. She undulates her hips frantically, so I wrap one arm around her small waist to keep her in place and press her pelvic wall against my cock with the other.

Her tits bounce as I ram up into her like a wild man until she screams out my name when we catapult into blissful oblivion. I come so hard my head hits the back of the wall. Zoey collapses back against me, spent. I wind both arms around her to keep her from sliding off me.

"Are you okay?" She reaches up and rubs the back of my head.

I catch her earlobe with my teeth. "Ohhh *yeahhh*. That was intense, sooooo good. No damage done."

Zoey tilts her head back against my neck and sighs. "I must say, that's a well-placed vanity mirror, sir."

"I can't get enough of you." I press my lips to hers and give her a long, deep kiss until I slip out of her body. "God, I love you."

"I love you too." Zoey shifts so her feet touch the floor. "You're so wild now. I love all of your rock-star sex tricks." Zoey steps out of the shower, looking for a towel.

"What do you mean?" My voice is shaky. What she said hits a nerve.

"It's okay, Ty, I know you were with a lot of girls over the years," Zoey playfully nudges me with her shoulder then turns away to grab a towel and wrap it around herself. "You've taken your sexy factor to an entirely different level since we were together."

She isn't wrong, but the wind whooshes out of my sails after our incredible night and morning, which for me is easily the most mind-blowing sexual connection I've ever had. For the past couple of weeks, knowing I would be taking my shot by singing *Heart* to her, all I've hoped for is the two of us expressing our love, devotion, and recommitment to each other.

I hoped we'd pick up where we left off. Put the past behind us. Which is why it cuts me deep when she jokingly references my sordid history.

That's on you.

Desperate to get things back on track, I tug her to my wet, naked body and caress her cheeks with my palms. "It's only *you*, Zoey. There's no one else. There's never been anyone else."

"I'm not saying anything bad, Ty. Only that sex with you is different now, more intense." She looks confused.

Recalling every faceless, nameless woman who I've used to forget Zoey is impossible. It makes me sick. I'm not going to apologize for things I've done when we were apart, but I'm not proud of my behavior either.

I release her, grab a towel and dry off. "Yeah, well. If you're fishing for information, it's a crappy way to do it."

"No. No, I didn't mean it like that. You don't owe me anything...please don't be mad." Zoey ducks under my chin to make eye contact.

I refuse to look at her. I don't know what to say. The lump in my throat is thick because I'm pissed at my-self—and Zoey. I tried to be truly vulnerable in front of the only woman I'll ever love and her first thought—after she came all over my cock—was me fucking women other than her.

"Those times make me feel thoroughly fucking ashamed, Zoey." I finish drying off.

She covers her mouth in horror. "Oh God, no, I didn't mean—"

"Don't you understand? I used women for years to forget you. It was disgusting behavior." I stab my finger at her. "I don't appreciate you bringing it up."

Zoey's eyes pool with tears. "You're not disgusting, you're the most considerate, thoughtful, wonderful man I've ever known."

"I don't fucking feel that way." I wrap the towel around my waist, recognizing the irony of her compliment to how I'm reacting right now.

She covers her breasts with her hands. "Ty, what we just did, how we are together is *beautiful.*"

"That's what I thought too." I shake my head. I'm not handling this correctly, but I'm not sure how to turn things around.

She stares at me. Her face is ashen. "I was so rude to joke about something that isn't my business. I didn't mean to make you feel bad." Zoey looks like she's about to cry again. "I can't bear to hurt you again. I'll leave if you want me to."

"I never want you to leave." I force myself to keep eye contact. "I can't *change* what happened. But...it happened."

She blinks at me and lets out a big breath of resignation. "I know."

"Look. I take responsibility. But it was a long time ago. You're so precious to me. I don't want you to ever feel like there has ever been anyone but you when we fuck." I try to explain my outburst.

Zoey takes my hand. "Ty, if we're going to try this again, we need to stop apologizing about what happened in our past and work on trusting each other *now*. Everything we've been through has brought us back to each other, right?" She squeezes my hand, willing me to believe her.

I *do* believe her. I take her in my arms. Yeah. I'm sorry for freaking out. Sometimes I..." I cling to her for dear life. I'm uncertain why I reacted so vehemently. I feel nothing but remorse.

"Shhhh. Ty, it's okay." Zoey leads me back into the bedroom. We lie down on the bed and hold each other a while.

My mind races. I thought I'd dealt with all my shit in therapy. I thought it would be easy to jump right back in with Zoey and ignore why we split up in the first place. She's right. We have to focus on our future.

My heart beats out of my chest. I'm scared shitless.

If I can't figure my shit out, I'm in danger of fucking things up with Zoey.

Am I really going to sabotage myself after I finally have her back?

Chapter Thirty-Two

An Hour Later

EXHAUSTED FROM A NIGHT of incredible sex and the emotions of my freak-out this morning, Zoey dozes off in my arms. I can't stop thinking about how I reacted. It scares me how much I love this woman. How much I've *always* loved her. Despite everything.

Am I setting myself up for heartbreak again? Once the thrill of finding each other again wears off, will Zoey realize I'm not everything she's built up in her mind?

Will she leave me again?

My mind eventually quiets but as I start to drift off, my stomach growls loudly. Zoey stretches and snuggles against me. "I'm hungry too."

"I don't have much in the house but let's see what I can scrounge up." I get up and grab some board shorts and toss Zoey one of my T-shirts.

We sleepily pad into the kitchen to eat. I prepare a fine meal of cold cereal for both of us and wait for the kettle to boil for tea while Zoey folds up our discarded clothes from last night.

I watch her reach in her purse and retrieve a medium-size box wrapped in black-and-white paper with a red bow.

"This is for you. Happy birthday." She holds the gift out to me, her wary smile not quite reaching her eyes. I take it from her and open it. Inside is a fountain pen and a notebook with a handmade covered in red and orange butterflies. "I figured you can buy anything you want, but maybe you'd appreciate a handmade journal. I remember the stacks you used to keep in your room. Who knows, maybe you can write some new songs."

I'm touched by her incredible thoughtfulness. She really knows me on such a deep level. Everyone I've met since LTZ hit it big...doesn't.

"It's perfect." I trace the butterflies with my finger then fold her into my arms. "I'd love to write new songs about us if you aren't too freaked out about earlier."

Zoey looks up at me with such adoration. She's stunning with no makeup and damp hair curling around her face. "I'm sorry for bringing up that stuff. It's my issue. I guess I let my fear that I don't measure up to what you're used to make me feel insecure." She strokes my cheeks with her thumbs. "What we did last night and this morning, how incredibly bonded we are when we make love is once in a lifetime. I know there's no one else for either of us. How could anything feel so right?"

"I've never had anything that remotely comes close. I've never brought any woman to this house. Well, other than the cleaning service, my publicists, and our management team." I kiss her and stare deeply into her eyes. Will her to understand. "Our connection...the intensity is beyond anything I even remembered."

"It was so hot, watching you inside me. If I wasn't so sore from your big dick, I'd be climbing you like a tree right now." Zoey winks. She's always had a knack for breaking a tense mood with humor. I'm glad she hasn't changed.

"Well there's plenty of other things we can do while you recover." I waggle my eyebrows at her and scoop her into my arms.

I have visions of feasting on her delicious pussy when my front door swings open. Surprised, I scramble to shield my pants-less girl from whoever dares enter my home without knocking.

"Wakey wakey, you didn't answer my text. It's time to hit the gym." My trainer Eric waltzes into my foyer, stopping when he sees me holding Zoey. "Tyson Rainier, I never thought I'd see the day when I caught you with a woman in your house. Who is this lovely young lady?"

"Eric, meet Zoey. Zoey meet Eric. Now, get the fuck out. I'll get changed and meet you outside." I set Zoey down and stand in front of her.

Eric is stunned silent. He turns around and screams, "Holy shit, are you *Z*?"

"Out!" I point to the door but can't help but smile. He hunches his shoulders and shuts the door.

I turn back toward Zoey who's clearly bewildered. "You're have a training session today?"

"Yeah, I'm on a strict routine to make sure I'm in shape for a movie premiere in New York and our Christmas show in LA. It's our last show before the band takes a year-long break." I tuck her hair behind her ear.

Zoey tugs at my T-shirt. "You never mentioned going on a break."

Shit. I forgot she didn't know my schedule, I mean, how could she? I take her hand and lead her back into my bedroom so I can get changed. "Yeah, we're taking a year off starting around the new year. We're all exhausted." I grab my workout gear from the drawer.

"Wow. That's a long time." She watches as I pull on my gym clothes.

I sit on the bed to put on my socks and shoes. "Yeah, being on the road isn't as glamourous as it might seem, it's strenuous. And I want to live a little. Work on the foundation. Recharge."

"No, I get that. It just occurred to me we're at such different stages in our career. After Joe took me off your foundation, I contacted a headhunter. I'm starting to get a few bites." Zoey flops on the bed. "I'm hoping to find a new job where I have more autonomy. I also want to make more money."

I try not to let the panic that's seeping into my system show and remain casual. "That's cool. Will you stay in Seattle?"

She stares at the ceiling, lost in thought. "It depends on whether I can telecommute."

"Oh...right. Okay, well, I've got to hit the gym." I reach over and stroke her thigh.

Zoey sits up, her expression almost carefully neutral. "I guess I'll call a Lyft."

"No! Stay. I won't be long. We can go to your house and grab some clothes from your place when I get back." My smile feels weird.

Probably because, after our declarations of love, I'm stunned she'd even contemplate leaving Seattle. I'm fast-forwarding our relationship to marriage and babies at full speed in my mind. It'll kill me if she's not on the same page.

"It might be easier if I go home now and you come to get me later." Zoey's expression is still unreadable.

I cross my arms across my chest. "I told you, I plan on keeping you here all weekend."

"I don't want to interfere with your schedule, Ty. You already had other plans." She fidgets with the sheets a bit.

It didn't occur to me she'd feel like an intrusion. Of all things. "You're not interfering, I just forgot about Eric's workout."

"I—I just don't want you to have to be on a timeline for me." Zoey looks really uncomfortable. "If you have something else to do . . . I'm just trying to be practical."

A horrific thought occurs to me. Maybe she doesn't want to be here with me. "I'm *not* on a fucking timeline for you,

I'll be gone an hour or two tops." My voice is cutting. Snide. I don't want her to go home because part of me believes she'll never come back. "Why is this a thing?"

"I'm not sure I'll feel comfortable here without you." Zoey crinkles her brow.

Jesus. I'm not going down this path with her again. "Fuck, Zoey. Fine. You're a grown woman. I'm late. If you don't feel *comfortable* here, go."

"Ty—" I hear her call after me as I storm out the bedroom and slam the door behind me.

I'm pissed at myself for acting out at her.

I'm also terrified of being hurt.

Especially, if all she's going to do is leave.

Chapter Thirty-Three

A Few Minutes Later

I STARE AT THE door after Ty slams it, in utter shock.

Twelve hours ago, I was nervously getting ready to go to his show, and the thought that Ty and I would potentially be back together romantically was a mere fantasy.

Last night, he serenaded me with a new song declaring his love. My lips are tender from our passionate kisses. His hands explored every inch of my body. His fingers, lips, and cock made me come more times than I can count.

This morning, we started off the same way only to have our reunion derail after two dreadful misunderstandings. I don't know how to handle it. We'd never had even a hint of a disagreement when we were together before.

Crushed, I pad out to the living room to gather my clothes so I can go home and lick my wounds. Instead of celebrating my reunion with the love of my life, now I'm not sure what just happened. I'm devastated.

Glancing down at the plates of grilled cheese we left on the coffee table last night, I can't help but reflect upon the past few months. Ever since that day in the conference room, I've been on edge, desperately wanting Ty to love me again. To forgive me.

I had so much hope. It *seemed* like Ty had come to terms with what happened so long ago. He's the one who took the lead in getting us to where we are now. First by reinstating our friendship. Then by reassuring me we could forget the past. Finally, by making his intentions known about us getting back together.

I jumped right in. I mean, I want it too. So much.

But, have we moved too fast?

We talked a bit last night, but despite his assurances, I don't think Ty has fully reconciled our history. His angry reaction to me going home seemed so out of character. Does he really think I'd leave him again when I've apologized profusely so many times for being young and immature?

Clearly, Ty's past also weighs on me. Our sex was *insane*. So far from inexperienced explorations when we were learning each other's bodies. My skill certainly hasn't progressed the way his has. But Ty? He was putting me in positions and touching me in ways that I'd never known were possible.

Instead of staying in a moment that should have been a celebration of our reconciliation, I made a useless and thoughtless comment. I *never* meant to cut Ty to the core, but my flippancy comes from somewhere. Maybe I haven't reconciled Ty's history either.

I *want* it to work with him. I want to rewind a few hours to when we made such heartfelt declarations of love and devotion.

Why does it have to be so hard?

It crushes me to think the easy trust and utter devotion we shared eight years ago has been destroyed forever.

I need some advice so I text *SOS* to Alex.

"Red alert." I pace the floor when she calls a few minutes later.

There's some commotion in the background, but Alex, as always, is there for me. "Okay, start at the top,"

After explaining what's happened since I saw her, Alex sighs heavily. "Okay, Zoey I'm going to give you some tough love. Two things, and this is not meant to shame you in any way, but what in the fuck did you expect when you brought up other women after you had what sounds like the hottest sex I've ever heard of?"

"I didn't mean it like that," I say defensively, but can't help but slump down in the couch. Ugh.

"*No.* Stop it," Alex groans. "I love you, Z, but I am so fucking sick of the drama."

I'm stunned. "What are you talking about?"

She sucks in a breath and lets me have it. "It's like you both bring it on yourself, this angst. Make all the excuses you want, but that man has never thought of anyone else but you. He has wanted you, and only you, since he was twenty-one years old."

"But Carter—"

"No!" Alex's voice slices through the phone line. "Look, I get it, but it was *you* who didn't even talk to him, give him a chance. Maybe it would have worked, maybe it wouldn't have, but you'll never know, will you?"

My heart falls to the floor. She's right. Instinctively, I've always known what I did was wrong. I need to take account-ability somehow. "*Ohmygod.*"

"Zoey, you need to think long and hard about what you want." Alex's voice is gentler now. She knows how heartbro-ken I've been for years. But, she's also been around Jace and the band during her travels with a perspective I don't share. "Do not play with this man's heart again. You're a grown woman, a fucking amazing lawyer, and the smartest person I know—but if you want him—fight for him, show him you won't leave him again."

Still, I can't erase what he said before he left. "He doesn't want me here, Alex. He told me to leave."

"Of *course* he wants you there. It's all he's *ever* wanted. "Alex snorts her disagreement.

If what she says is true, have I misjudged what happened today? "I'm so scared, I don't know what I'm doing, Alex. I'm completely over my head."

"No one does." I can almost see her throw her hands in the air at my obtuseness. "Just stop getting in your own way."

How I wish I could. "How do I get all of these women out of my head without making him feel bad? I'm scared that he's built me up into something I'm not, and when he finds out he'll realize he's wasted so much time pining over a girl who only knows how to bury my nose in books"

"I've never heard you talk this way, snap the fuck out of it. Ty has never stopped loving you for exactly who you are. He fucked around to forget you." Alex sounds exasperated. "But you dumped him. You're not allowed to judge him, you need to support him. And if it means anything, Jace says that it wasn't remotely as bad as the press made it seem."

I take in what she's saying, but her reference to LTZ's drummer makes me pause. "C'mon spill. Are you, um, with Jace?"

Alex doesn't let me off the hook. "We're not talking about me. Now, *buckaroo*, you're going to give it your all and see where the chips fall. Because whether you end up together or you don't, make sure that you have given everything you have to him. Then you will never have any more regrets.

She's right. This time I don't want to have any regrets. "Okay. I will, I love him so much, Alex. I knew there was a reason you were my best friend." I breathe out a nervous sigh. "I'm petrified, but I'll do it."

"Duh! Get your shit together, I'm hanging up." The call ends abruptly.

Exhausted from the emotional torrent of the past couple hours and the lack of sleep from our activities last night, I crawl back into Ty's bed, pull up the covers, and read on my Kindle app for a while. Though he said he'd be back soon, Ty still isn't home two hours later. I tap out a text.

I'm so sorry for everything, Ty. I'm here waiting for you whenever you get back.

An hour goes by with no reply.

Zoey: I'm worried about you, are you coming home?

Nothing. A half-hour later I try again, now anxious and worried.

Ty, I'm freaking out that something has happened to you. Please, if you get this, just let me know you're ok

Nothing.

Now I'm panicked. Acid roils in my belly. After another fifteen minutes go by I start pacing around Ty's house. If something happens to him before I make it right, I'll never get over it. After taking a few deep breaths to try and calm down, I will myself to keep only positive thoughts in my head.

Just as I'm about to text him again, a message from Ty comes through.

I'm ok you should go

I don't want to go, I miss you. Where did you go?

Ty:

> I had to take care of a few things, I'm at Jace's house.

Me:

> I'll wait.

Ty:

> It's ok, Z. Just go.

His dismissive text makes me angry. Hurt. Rejected. I've been here all day for this? I pick up my dress, sandals and underpants to get dressed, but I'm shaking so bad I can't manage it.

To settle myself, I let out big breath and try to regulate my breathing like I've seen Ty do. Within a few minutes it works and I'm able to think more clearly.

I can hear Alex's voice telling me to fight for him. To show him I won't leave him again. Grown-up relationships take work. Communication. I need to hear him out. He might be testing me but it doesn't matter. I'm going to be an adult and face our past and hopefully put it behind us.

For now, I'm not going anywhere, if for nothing else but to prove it to Ty. Moving to the living room, I snuggle under a blanket and turn on Bravo. A marathon of *Southern Charm* is in progress, which is a perfect distraction.

I text Ty again.

Me:

> I'm not leaving

Then I wait.

Chapter Thirty-Four

The Same Time Frame

SATURDAY WORKOUTS ARE ALWAYS grueling. Usually I'm able to shut my mind off and focus on what I'm doing.

Not today, though. My mind whirls. I'm second-guessing all things Zoey. Every word, every kiss, and every conversation. When Eric finishes punishing me on the treadmill and weight bench, I stick around for two more hours and punish myself.

I can't fucking believe I had Zoey back and pushed her away in the span of a few hours. There's something seriously wrong with me. My therapist, Lisa Kinkaid, is out of town and I can't face going home to my empty house.

I need to talk to someone to make sure I have perspective. Carter's out, for obvious reasons. Zane has other things he's dealing with. Connor isn't in town. Which leaves Jace. He's the perfect touchstone. For a long time now, he's the only person who gives it to me straight without walking on eggshells.

He buzzes me up at his downtown high-rise condo. When he opens the door, shirtless and rumpled, it's clear I've interrupted something. I can hear a woman's voice in his bedroom. She's probably on the phone.

"I'm sorry to intrude, my brother, I'll leave." I gesture to the voice.

"Nah, it's cool. What's up?" He goes to the Sub-Zero fridge and grabs a water, offering me one too.

"I'm fucked." I gratefully take the water and drink it down in one gulp.

Jace waggles his eyebrows. "But did you get fucked?"

I hang my head. "Uh, well. Yeah. But this morning we fought, and I told her to leave. *Goddammit.* I'm fucking still in love with her and I told her to leave."

"Hmm." He regards me strangely and flicks his eyes to his bedroom door.

I nod to the door. "Who's here?"

"No one," Jace says out loud then mouths, *"Alex."*

I'm floored. All of us suspected they've hooked up before, but this is a whole new level. "Holy shit!"

Jace shrugs. "After all this time and all the drama, I'm not surprised you fought. Your past shit had to boil up at some point, better earlier than later."

"I guess. I told her to leave because she's probably taking a job in some other city." I open his pull-out garbage and throw my bottle in the recycling.

"Well, we're taking a year off, you could just go with her." Jace leans against the wall and scrubs his chin with his hand.

I hadn't even thought of that, but still. "I didn't hear an invite."

"Fucking hell, Ty. Stop being such a dramatic baby-man." Jace wrinkles his face in disgust. "You guys are your own worst fucking enemies."

My phone vibrates. I glance at the phone and hold it up. "I guess she didn't leave, she's still at my place."

He shakes his head. "Then why the fuck are you here, you dickwad?"

"I've wanted this for so long." I wince.

"Duh. You've got to stop with all of this, dude." Jace walks toward the door and gestures for me to follow. "Sort your shit out with her and live happily ever after or move the fuck on."

I run my hands through my hair in frustration. "I'm just not sure."

"Um, Ty. Brother to brother, I'm kicking you out for your own good." Jace opens the door and gestures at me to get out. "She's at your place. Go talk to her. I'm not sure why she still wants you when you act ridiculous like this, but she clearly does so will you go and make up with her and put us all out of your misery for once and for all?"

"Fine." I step outside the door and turn around. "But—"

Jace slams the door on me, his grin wide.

Chapter Thirty-Five

Twenty Minutes Later

THE SOUND OF THE deadlock and the front door opening wakes me up. I hear Ty's footsteps stop by the entryway and resume when he crosses the room over to where I'm curled up on the couch.

He sits next to me, still in his gym clothes and clasps his hands together, resting his elbows on his knees. He stares at the ground. Sighing heavily, he finally looks up, his eyes tired. "Why are you still here, Zoey?"

"I told you I wasn't leaving, and I didn't leave." I rub the sleep out of my eyes.

"I can't do this." He gestures between us. "I don't think this thing between us is going to work."

His words stab me deep in my heart. "What do you mean?"

"Call it self-preservation. In the light of today, I can't go through this with you again. Because when you leave—and you will eventually, I won't survive it this time." Ty looks back down.

I push myself upright. "But I'm *not* leaving. I told you that. Even when you told me to go, I stayed."

"Ah, but you *will* leave. Either my past will come back and fuck you up or you'll take a new job far away from me," Ty snarls before stalking back to the kitchen. He opens the fridge and takes out a small bottle of orange juice.

"That is not fair, Ty." I'm pissed. Last night meant every-thing to me. Today he ditched me all day only to come back and reject me outright. I follow him into the kitchen. "In your past while you saw the world, hobnobbed with the rich and famous, romanced a bunch of women, and became successful in your career, I was buried in books. And, I was all *alone.*"

He throws his hands up. "It's not like you gave me a fucking choice."

Our past coming to a head is long overdue. Inevitable.

As I feared, last night was so sexually charged we glossed over some deep resentment in order to get naked. Now that we've released the tension, so to speak, I guess there's room for our true feelings to spill out.

We're at a critical juncture. If we're going to have a chance, Ty deserves to express himself without my bag-gage. I want to be his safe place.

"I've apologized, Ty. I'll never forgive myself for not talking to you before I left that morning or for ignoring you afterward." I'm calmer. More centered. "You didn't deserve what happened and I was too immature to understand the consequences of my actions. You don't need to answer to me for anything you did while we were broken up. Truly, you don't."

Ty's anger is now tinged with sadness. "I know I shouldn't have to. *Fuck*! This is too much."

"So, we finally find our way back to each other, and you want to give up after one day because it's hard to work through eight years of emotions?" I take a step toward him.

"No, I don't want to give up." Ty's face is ashen. "I feel like I'm on a rollercoaster. I don't want to talk about this stuff, I just want us to be happy."

"We have to talk, babe." I tentatively reach for his hand. "If we don't, you'll never believe in us again."

Ty takes my index finger in his. "I fucking love you so much, Zoey. Even after everything, you're still my favorite person. I'm scared shitless you're going to leave again. When you said you may not stay in Seattle, it freaked me out."

"I fucking love you too, Ty." I squeeze our fingers together as the lightbulb goes off. "Oh God, is *that* what triggered this? Me talking about taking a new job?"

Ty shrugs. "I don't know. Everything. I guess I thought I'd sweep you off your feet and we'd be together and the past would be where it belongs. Behind us."

"I want that." I sigh, because life is so much more complicated now. "I also want you to understand why I finished undergrad and law school in five flippin' years, immediately took a job as an associate in a super-competitive law firm, and have been grinding so hard. I want to find my dream job when I'm young."

He squints at me, confused. "But, you told me you wanted to make partner."

"Yeah, and after helping you with the foundation, I've set my sights higher." I hold his gaze, willing him to put himself in my shoes. I know if our relationship stands a chance my career needs to have equal consideration.

Ty's expression softens. "Okay, do you care to fill me in?"

"Of course. I've decided I'd rather be an executive at a non-profit and get out of law-firm life altogether." I can't help but beam. "My headhunter is looking for opportunities around the country because before you and I...well, it didn't matter where I'd be."

Ty's entire demeanor shifts. "*Wow*. That's really cool."

"I'm passionate about my work, Ty." I relax because he's truly listening to me. "But it's *you* I want most." I swallow my emotions down. "If you decide you can't be with me, fine. If you want to take back everything you said last night, fine. If you never want to make love to me again, fine. But know this—just because I want my own career that means something to me doesn't mean I'm leaving *you*. Get that through your thick skull." I grasp his hand tightly over the island.

Ty sighs and leans forward, dropping his head on our clasped hands. "*Fuck*."

"I'm not the same person, Ty. I've grown up too." I caress the back of his head. "You're it for me. I won't let you or anyone ever talk me out of choosing you first again."

He looks back up, his gorgeous face finally calm. "I didn't think you'd be here when I got back."

I move another half step toward him. "But here I am."

Ty stands to his full height, his square jaw is now dusted with a five o'clock shadow. His blue eyes bore into mine. "I fucked up, Zoey. My plan was to ease us both into this. Maybe go out for dinner, try to start completely over. But when I saw you after the show, I got caught up in all of it. I've dreamed of being back together for so long. The next thing I know we're fucking and it's so amazing we're fucking some more. It feels like we're connected on such a deep level..."

"We *are*, we always have been." I can't stop myself from walking around the island and hugging him.

"I'm acting so crazy. I need to just get myself under control, Z." Ty draws me close and whispers in my hair, "Today sucked. Well, aside from your birthday gift. And the blowjob. And the shower sex. All of those things were epic."

I step back but keep my hand on his hip so we don't lose contact. "It's okay. This is just a hiccup."

Ty cuddles me under his arm and strokes my back. "Tell me the truth. Do you really want to be with me?"

"*Yes*, it's what I want more than anything." I peek up at him. "I fucked up too. I let my insecurities about how I'll measure up to all those models and actresses get the best of me. I didn't mean to hurt you. I promise that I won't throw the past in your face again."

Ty cradles my face in his palm. "For the record, you have *nothing* to be insecure about. You've always been the only girl I've ever wanted. I meant what I said. I lost myself in the cliché rock-star life to try to forget you. It never worked. That probably doesn't make you feel any better, but it's why I don't drink anymore and why I haven't been with anyone in almost two years."

"Two years?" I'm shocked and also skeptical. "That can't be right. What about Ronni Miller?"

Ty kisses my head softly. "Smoke and mirrors. We share a publicist, Sienna, who you met last night. After I went to therapy and got sober, she set us up as a fake romance to clean up my image and dirty up hers."

"Wait, so she *wasn't* your girlfriend?" I'm skeptical. I've never heard of anything so preposterous.

"Nope. She actually has a boyfriend you know, but it's not public yet. We were just friendly partners in crime for this publicity game. I needed someone popular and family-friendly to date. For events and stuff." Ty tries to explain something that sounds stupid. Because, it *is* stupid.

"Wow. So, I've been jealous of her for no reason?" I cock my head. "There are pictures of you kissing and everything, you looked so in love!"

"Ronni taught me her acting tricks." Ty steps back and grips my shoulders. "Eventually, we got sick of the lie, so we went rogue and broke up without clearing it through Sienna. It blew up in our faces. Well, my face mostly. I got labeled the asshole. As for Ronni, she's great. I actually think you'd like her."

"Huh. We'll see." I'm not so sure.

"Would it make a difference if you knew she was the one who encouraged me to get back with you, butterfly?" Ty runs his hands down my arms and takes my hands in his.

I rub my thumb over his knuckles, entwining our fingers together before nestling back against his chest. "Well, I'm glad she did."

I'm exhausted. It's been such a heavy day, I want to move on. He winds his arms around me and we embrace tightly for a minute.

"Ty, even now that you're so famous, I don't think you realize how sexy, confident, and commanding you are. Years ago, you made my first time so special and were careful with me for so many weeks leading up to it. But last night? How you took full control of everything? You played my body like a Zane Rocks guitar solo." I gaze up at him, still stunned that we've seemingly overcome our past to be together again.

He arches back and raises one eyebrow. "Sexy, huh?"

"Beyond." I lick my lips.

"You waited." He leans close so our lips are almost touching.

"I'll always wait for you." I press my forehead to his. "I won't give you up again."

Ty kisses me softly. "Z, it would be smart for us to slow this down, but—"

"We have too much time to make up for." I finish.

We make our way into the master suite, where we slip off our clothes and take an R-rated shower together. We're both a little worked up when we dry each other off and fall into his cushy bed. Ty nestles in between my legs and enters me slowly.

We rock together, his hands holding mine above my head as we stare into each other's eyes in wonder. Afterward, tangled in each other's arms, it feels like we're rewriting our story.

As long as we can focus on the future and not the past, this time, I'm hoping for a happily-ever-after ending.

Chapter Thirty-Six

A Few Weeks Later

THE JOY OF HAVING Zoey back in my life is indescribable.

Being away from her sucks so badly, I'm not sure what to do with myself.

I've been in LA for the past few days because LTZ is contributing a few songs to the soundtrack of an action movie called *Phantom Uprising*. We're finishing the tracks at a studio here.

Sure, we FaceTime every few hours to check in. It's not the same as being together. I miss her desperately, but my schedule is packed until New Years Eve. Slowing the LTZ machine down to prepare for a year off requires, apparently, a lot of meetings.

It's not like Zoey has time to pine for me. Her schedule at the law firm is ridiculous.

It's a good thing we're both committed to our relationship and developing it on our own terms. In between our schedules, we've managed to enjoy a lot of quality time. Aside from spending every night possible together, we've hung out with her parents a few times and resumed our long drives outside the city in little towns like La Conner and Langley, where I won't be recognized as easily.

Zoey is still getting used to my fame. Luckily, Seattle is a chill town. No one usually bothers us aside from wanting an autograph or selfie. Still, it's been an adjustment because she loved me before I was famous and these little intrusions get annoying sometimes. As a public figure, it's not like I can blow them off.

In many ways, I'm more worried about her getting recognized. I'm proud when my beautiful butterfly is on my arm, and I can't wait to share her with the entire world, but I'd like to keep her identity on the down low for as long as possible. When people find out Zoey's "Z," she'll be in the spotlight too.

I'm not thinking about any of that now. It's nine p.m. on Friday night. I'm leaning against my sick new amethyst-black McLaren 720s Performance Spider with a dozen red roses in hand, waiting to pick her up outside baggage claim at LAX.

Sergey is going to kill me for being so ostentatious and attracting attention.

Zoey emerges from the glass doors wheeling out a shiny, purple carry-on case with her laptop bag nestled on top, looking ravishing in black wedge sandals, tight, black capri leggings, and a low-cut black tunic shirt that's cinched at her tiny waist. I catch a glimpse of a black lacy bra when she leans over to zip up her laptop case.

My cock fills immediately. Waiting for her to spot me, I lick my lips in anticipation of kissing her senseless. Six days is too long to be apart. Adorably flustered, she looks back and forth for me. When her eyes meet mine, her smile is radiant as she wheels her bag over to my car.

"*Ohmyfuckinggod.*" Her hazel eyes bulge when she takes in my wheels. "*Ohmyfuckinggod,*" she squeals seeing the roses, launching herself into me and kissing me full on the lips.

Stealing kiss after kiss, she burrows herself in my arms. I notice a few people paying too close attention to us and holding up their phones, which means it's time to get out of LAX. Stat.

"Your chariot awaits." I push the button on my fob and the doors rise straight up like batwings, the coolest thing ever.

Zoey inspects the purplish-black paint and the black interior. "This car is completely over the top."

"It's LA, baby, I've got to give you the full A-list experience." I manage to fit her suitcase and laptop in the tiny space behind the seats and help her into the passenger seat. "You look like you belong in this car."

"Can I drive it?" She arches her eyebrow. "I promise I won't crash it."

"Sure, we're going to take a drive to Orange County on PCH tomorrow, I've booked us in the Ritz in Laguna Beach."

I speed off after spying a few paparazzi heading in our direction.

"Ty, you didn't need to do that, I'm happy just spending time with you and hopefully seeing even more of you soon." She winks at me, puts her hand over mine on the gear shift, and squeezes.

"I'm wining and dining you first, babe. Get used to it." I smirk.

Showing her the prowess of my fine automobile all the way from the airport to West Hollywood, I squeal up to the valet on Santa Monica Boulevard in front of Dan Tana's, one of Hollywood's oldest establishments, figuring Zoey will appreciate the ironic atmosphere of a "seen and be seen" location. Handing the valet a hundred bucks, I grab her hand when the telltale flashes of the paparazzi cameras flicker like fireworks around us.

"Ty, who's your date?"

"Tyson Rainier look over here."

"Who's the girl, Ty?"

"Is that your girlfriend, Ty?"

Zoey doesn't let go of my hand but is clearly taken aback by the crazy level of attention on me. I'm used to it in LA and other big-media cities, but curse myself silently for making such a rookie mistake. I'm an idiot. Usually Sergey is with me and I avoid paparazzi havens. I should have factored in the possibility of us getting ambushed.

Luckily, once inside, we're treated just like every other celebrity who frequents the Italian staple. The host ushers us to a red-leather booth tucked into the back of the restaurant. Strategically, I sit with my back to the room, allowing Zoey to take the seat where she can survey our surroundings.

"That was intense." Her eyes wide, she reaches across the table and hooks my index finger in hers. "Is it always that way for you these days?"

"Depends on where we go. I wanted to take you here because it's so iconic. Even after all these years, I sometimes forget being out in public has its disadvantages." I don't want to overwhelm her with the reality of my public appearances quite yet. Better to ease her in.

"I'm sorry, I don't mean to interrupt, but can I get you to sign this?" A teenage boy holds out a piece of paper to me, which I quickly scribble on, so he'll go away. He asks a few questions, which I try to politely answer. Soon enough he returns to his family.

Zoey beams at me. "Are you always so sweet to your fans?"

"I guess so." I shrug. "I wouldn't be here without them."

She smiles and goes back to studying the menu. "So, what are we eating?"

"The lasagna is my favorite." God, it's so comforting to be with someone who's known me before I had fame. She loves me for who I was. Who I've always been. I can only hope she'll adjust to the celebrity shit of who I am now.

"That sounds great." She shuts her menu and glances around the room, quietly giving me a comical play-by-play of various other celebrities who are scattered at tables around the room. Her observations are spot on, causing both of us to laugh over and over.

A bellyful of lasagna, four autographs, and a repeat paparazzi performance later, we're finally speeding through the Hollywood Hills to my rambler house, which is modest by LA standards, but has a nice pool and a great view of the city.

"I can't believe you own two homes, Ty." Zoey flits about the house, taking in the décor—more cottagey than my modern Seattle abode, mainly because I never bothered to remodel.

"I got it only because we're here so much for industry stuff." I put on the kettle for tea. "It gives me more privacy than a hotel, and it's weird to say but having real estate is good business."

"You're dreamy." Zoey moves toward me and stands on her tippy-toes to caress my hair and bat her eyes at me flirtatiously. "I love grown up Ty talking about real estate, he's very, very sexy."

I reach around her waist to grab her ass and yank her flush against me. "What am I going to do with you?"

"I can think of quite a few things I'd like you to do to me." Zoey jumps into my arms, hooking her legs around my waist and winding her arms around my neck. "First, I want to ride my cowboy!"

Growling, I thrust my hardening cock against her heat. The tea forgotten, I carry her to my bedroom where the floor-to-ceiling windows look out onto the pool and the valley below.

Zoey hops down and slowly pulls her tunic off, wiggling her cute, curvy butt as she steps out of her shoes and strips off her leggings. Skipping to the window in just her black bra and tiny black thong, she places her hands on the window and looks over her shoulder at me, smiling through her long, wild blonde hair.

I stalk over to her like a panther, stripping off my T-shirt on the way. Placing my hands over hers on the window, I can't resist tracing the sensitive spot between her neck and ear with my tongue. My cock is hard as a steel pole against her ass. She gyrates, pushing against my boner as I suckle behind her ear. I trace my fingertips up her arms to her shoulder and back down again, reaching around to cup her breasts and thumb her pebbled nipples through the lace of her bra.

Zoey lays back against my shoulder and continues to shim-my her ass against my swollen cock. Using my thumbs, I push the cups of her bra lower, exposing her fully in the mirrored image of the window. Leaving no inch of her gorgeous tits untouched, I enjoy the view in the reflection on the glass.

That's when I happen to notice movement down by the pool house. Immediately, I curse myself again for giving Sergey the night off.

Gazing down suspiciously, I'm relieved and yet mortified to see Connor and Zane standing by the pool watching us with beers in hand and big, gummy smiles. When Zane realizes I've caught them, he raises his hand over his head with a big thumbs up, and both of them whoop.

Fucking Zane.

"Shit, shit, shit! I totally forgot those fucks were staying in the pool house." I turn Zoey around quickly to shield her and move us away from the window.

"Do they always stay here?" Zoey snickers. "I know I should be embarrassed at Connor seeing my boobs again, but, strangely, I'm not."

"Not usually, and after tonight never again. And, missy? I don't want anyone seeing your goods but me." I hit the button to shut the blackout curtains, flipping the assholes off as the blinds close. Laughing hysterically, they both flip me off too, throwing in a couple of lewd gestures before they disappear from sight.

"It's awesome you guys are still so close." Zoey is still unbothered. She removes her bra and tosses it at me, then sits on the edge of the bed.

I catch it in one hand. "Yeah. They've stuck by me when I didn't deserve it."

"Having great friends is something you *definitely* deserve, Ty." Zoey lures me toward her so I'm standing between her legs. Undoing my belt, then my jeans, she slides them down my hips, exposing my cock, which is flush against my stomach. "Mmm, let's do something about this."

Licking her lips, Zoey reaches down and cups my balls with one hand, grips my base with the other and takes me into her warm mouth. Hollowing out her cheeks, her eyes close as she languidly sucks, licks, and tastes me while feathering strokes over my sac. Lost in the amazing sensation of the wetness and suction combined with the visual of my cock between her glossy pink lips, tingles at the base of my spine ignite almost immediately.

As if sensing this, Zoey looks up at me, smiling around my shaft. Holy fuck, she's so hot. Doubling down, she flattens her tongue to take me down her throat as far as she can and hums against my crown. The sensation causes my hips to buck on their own volition.

I grip both sides of her face and rhythmically pump in and out of her mouth, marveling at the erotic spectacle. She ups the ante by stroking my perineum and increasing the suction around my cock. Unable to stop myself, my hips lurched into her as I come hard down her throat, shouting her name.

"Mmm, you rarely let me do that all the way." Zoey swallows and laps at me until I'm clean.

"That was unbelievable." I move to her side and collapse next to her on the bed, snuggling her against me while I recover. I fully intend on feasting on my girl when I can breathe again.

"I love you." Zoey lays against my chest, looking up at me, smoothing my hair away from my face. "I want to make you feel good all of the time."

I stroke her back with the tips of my fingers, looking down at her. "I love you, too."

"I like being here in our little cocoon where it's just us, I can't get close enough to you." She hugs me tightly.

I fight the tears that well up. "Me too, it's my favorite place to be. You're my favorite person."

"You're mine too," Zoey whispers against my neck and nips at my earlobe.

It's time to make my girl lose her mind. I lightly kiss all around her face while stroking her wild hair. Deepening the kiss, our tongues dance together, the taste of my release still strong.

Rolling her on her back, I savor my way down her body, paying special attention to her perfect, plump breasts, her tiny waist, and her stomach with the luscious swell. Zoey squirms with arousal, trying to press her thighs together to get some friction. I pull down her black thong and fling it to the ground, moving to a kneeling position on the floor between her thighs.

She opens her legs for me, running her fingers through my hair. "You smell delicious." I spread her legs wider, exposing her soaking core and bend down to lap up her honey.

Her quiet whimpers of bliss nearly do me in. Using my thumbs, I open her pussy lips and alternate fucking her with my tongue and skimming all around her clit. Zoey lays back on the bed on her elbows watching me, her nipples hard as diamonds as her breath hitches with every swipe of my tongue.

She almost absentmindedly rolls both of her nipples with her shiny, red-painted fingers, and her thighs shudder around my ears. Picking up the pace on her distended nub,

I lick back and forth hard and fast, which I know will get her there. It always does.

Zoey cries out when she comes with a full-body shudder. I suck on her clit soothingly, enjoying her tangy nectar as her tremors subside. Knowing I have the power to make this beautiful creature feel so good makes me want to take things up a notch.

She sighs contentedly when I climb up on the bed, kneel on the soft mattress between her thighs, and rotate her hips to match mine. Grasping her calves, I press her legs together, bend them, and kiss her red-tipped toes before placing her knees over my shoulders on either side of my head.

Her breath hitches when I drag two fingers through her soaking slit and plunge them inside her, even though I know she's more than ready for me. My cock is so hard it's painful, so I quickly replace my fingers and sink fully into her with a loud groan. Zoey reaches for my hand and sucks my fingers coated with her essence into her mouth.

"Holy mother of God, you're killing me." I moan as I swivel my hips to find the perfect rhythm.

The sounds we make as our bodies slap together is the best music in the world. The smell of our sex permeates the bedroom. I place one foot on the ground, so Zoey's leg can rest over mine and use the additional leverage and angle to drive into her wildly.

We transition from lovemaking to downright fucking in under a second. I know there's no holding back. I barely touch her clit with my thumb when Zoey screams out my name and convulses around me again. Shouting as I empty inside her, I pulse my release for what seems like hours.

Satiated, Zoey slumps back, relaxed as a noodle, and I carefully tuck her under the covers. When she falls asleep against me, nestled in my arms, I stroke her hair and think about how lucky we are to have a second chance.

It would be easy to remain angry at all the circumstances and people that have kept us apart for so long.

Why though? All that's in the past.

Everything is right again because we're together.

Chapter Thirty-Seven

The Next Morning

MY EYES OPEN WHEN I hear loud laughter and general commotion outside the bedroom door. Before investigating, I take a moment to myself, burrowing under the silky sheets and inhaling the smell of me and Ty.

Smiling at the memory of the past twelve hours, I can't help but adore how sweet and kind Ty is to everyone around him, including me.

From my suitcase, I pull out some leggings and a T-shirt and pad out of Ty's bedroom to locate the source of the noise. Connor and Zane are sitting on stools at the kitchen island slagging Ty while he stands with his arms crossed, gloriously shirtless, his wavy hair a rumpled mess around his shoulders. He's glaring at them good-naturedly.

Zane bops over to me and envelopes me in a big hug. "Hey, Zoey."

"Connor, Zane, you better erase the image of my boobs from your mind." I cover his eyes with my hand.

He waggles his eyebrows at me from under my palm. "Aww, not possible, they're spectacular."

"It *better* fucking be possible," Ty growls.

Connor leans back on his stool, his ripped arms crossed above his head. "So, are you guys back together?"

"We are, and this time it's for good." I nestle into Ty's side. He kisses the top of my head.

"Finally!" Zane shouts, fist in the air. "Now you won't be such a pain in all of our asses."

Ty knocks his fist down. "Don't be so sure."

Connor points at Ty. "Don't forget to call Jace, he's fucking pissed about the paparazzi stuff."

"What paparazzi stuff?" I look over at Ty.

Connor taps his phone and holds up the TMZ page where, sure enough, there are several pictures of Ty and me in front of Dan Tana's. Ty looked absolutely gorgeous, he's clearly become accustomed to having his photo taken and knows his angles. On the other hand, my two expressions range from scared rabbit to triple-chinned yokel.

"I'll call him later," Ty promises. "We have plans today."

"Just be careful, bring Sergey with you," Zane cautions.

Ty nods. "He's meeting us in Laguna."

"Well, if he can prevent ugly pictures being taken of me, I'm all for it." I scrunch up my nose. "I'd like to avoid my name getting out there, I'm afraid I'll get backlash at the firm."

Zane stands and gestures to Ty. "Well, we're pretty recognizable now. You need to get used to it quickly if you're going to be with him."

"Knock it off, dude. Don't you have somewhere to be?" Ty shoos the guys back to the pool house.

After they leave, I don't have a chance to ask about it because the sexy shower is too distracting. When we're dried off, I put on cutoffs, a black tank top, and my wedge sandals. As always, Ty wears jeans that are barely held together by the threads, a vintage Soundgarden T-shirt, a baseball cap, and flip-flops.

We spend the day driving Ty's not-too-incognito fuckmobile down the coast, leisurely stopping in some of the beach towns to browse the kiosks, hold hands, and enjoy the sun. Zane is right about Ty's popularity. We can't go anywhere without camera phones following us.

Ty is acutely aware of his surroundings, having lived this way for so many years. He's refined escape from aggressive fans into a fine art. When someone recognizes him and asks for a selfie, he graciously handles it like a pro. If they get demanding, he expertly deflects. Although he takes it in stride because he's so used to it, for me it feels intrusive and a bit terrifying. After the first few incidents, it's really hard not to show my discomfort.

At some point during the day, Jace sends Ty a stern text with links to half a dozen photos that Ty's been tagged in. Apparently, the LTZ universe is all abuzz about Tyson Rainier's mystery woman, but according to most of the comments the fans are not impressed with me in the slightest.

Talk about ego-crusher.

I can't believe Alex actually sought out fame on Instagram. My introverted self doesn't know how to handle it. It occurs to me that it's now only a matter of time before I'm outed as "Z," the bitch that broke Ty's heart.

By the time we arrive at The Ritz at Laguna Beach, it's nearly seven in the evening. I'm sick, sore, and tired of people. Sergey, who met us in the lobby, escorts us to our room. As quiet and unassuming as he is, his mere presence serves as a reminder of Ty's need for security.

Our room turns out to be the penthouse suite, with over-the-top sweeping views of the purple, red, and orange hues of the sun setting over the Pacific Ocean. It's so gorgeous, my crankiness wanes immediately.

"I hope you don't mind if we have dinner in the suite, I want you all to myself tonight." Ty slides his hand around my back, holding me at the curve above my ass.

I picked up the room service menu. "That's perfect, I'm starving."

"No, no. I've got it all arranged." Ty takes the menu from me and leads me out to the expansive private patio overlooking the water. Outside is a beautiful table set for two on white linen complete with roses, and soft guitar music playing in the background.

I'm blown away. "Wow, when did you do all this?"

"Don't you worry about it." Ty leans against the patio rail, so fucking handsome with his scruffy, unshaven face and long hair completely windblown from our drive.

I sit and beckon him to join. "Come sit down with me."

Ty immediately obliges, sitting in the wrought-iron, padded patio chair next to me. We clasp hands and look out at the sea as the sun disappears over the horizon. Then we move to the table and indulge in a delicious, romantic dinner. Being here with Ty in such a romantic setting quiets my mind.

Will this be my life now?

After a while, the breeze turns chilly and we move inside to recline on the plush, gold sofa in the living room to watch a movie.

"I'm sad you're leaving tomorrow night." Ty squeezes my hand, which rests on his stomach as I lay against him. "I love having you with me all the time."

I blink up at him. "I love being with you too."

"Can you stay longer?" Ty traces my eyebrow with his finger. "I mean, no pressure."

My heart sinks. "I wish, but I can't."

"Okay." He nods then stares out into the room.

My mind spins again. "People are going to find out it's me, Ty."

"Yeah, probably." He looks at me quizzically.

"Is that what you want?" I have to ask, considering we've been out in public all day and now there are likely hundreds of pictures of us posted everywhere.

"Well, yeah. Of course. Although, Jace wants to get ahead of it first." Ty lets out a breath that he's, apparently, been holding.

"Even if it freaks me out?" I sit up to face him. "I've deliberately kept myself out of the public eye for years, I don't even post on socials."

Ty wrinkles his brow and rounds his shoulders, almost sulking. "So you *don't* want people to find out about us."

"You don't get to do that." I don't want to reassure him when it's me that needs the reassurance. "You're not that insecure boy anymore, you know that's not the case."

Ty doesn't say anything, so I continue. "Just because you wanted to be a famous rock star doesn't mean that I want everyone to know my name. You already took that option away from me with the album."

"And we took every precaution to protect you. I can't help that we're well-known, Zoey," Ty grumbles. "That's part of the gig."

"Well, it's not part of *my* gig. I'm in the middle of a job search while balancing a very competitive position at my firm." I get up and stride over to the window, needing some space. "Your fans already hate me. They think I'm heinous. It's all in the comments."

Ty stretches out on the sofa, crosses his legs, and shuts his eyes. It looks like he's practicing breathing exercises, but he remains silent. After a few minutes, his eyes open slowly, and he finds me gaping at him. "No, Z, they want to be you, so they try to tear you down. It's part of the fame game."

I frown. "*I'm* not famous. They don't even know me!"

"Look, I didn't think it through. I just wanted us to have a fun day out like we used to do back in Seattle." Ty pats the space on the sofa beside him and beckons for me to come back.

It's hard for me to be mad at his sentiment, but at the same time we're just getting to know each other again. Figuring out how our lives can mesh. It occurs to me that he's used to having every detail of his life catered to. Maybe he's forgotten how it is for people who aren't in the spotlight.

"I'm worried," I confess, my arms akimbo. "My reputation and integrity are vitally important in my profession. A careless photo or slimy article can take on a life of its own and destroy my career. I could get cancelled."

"That's why we have publicists." Ty holds his hands up. "They take care of that for us, and they'll take care of that for you."

I call bullshit. "Uh, isn't their job to get you *in* the media?"

"Well, yeah. True." Ty rolls his eyes. "But they do crisis management too, that's why you don't see any of the old embarrassing drunk footage of me around anymore."

My stomach clenches. "Did you take me to all these public places because you want me to be outed, Ty?" I sit on the edge of the sofa next to him. "Because once I'm outed, we can't take it back."

"I mean, I didn't *not* want people to find out we are together. I already basically announced it on Sirius." Ty strokes my back in a feeble attempt to calm me down. "Sienna thought it would be fine."

Shrugging him off, I chew on my thumbnail. "Wait a minute. You talked about this with *Sienna?*"

"More like cleared my plans." Ty is so nonchalant. But, of course, this is what he's used to. On the other hand, all of this is utterly scary to me.

"I'm feeling very vulnerable and out of my league." I pick at my thumbnail. "I need to understand what say I have in all of this. Did Sienna consider my feelings? What price I might have to pay?"

"Butterfly, shhh. Come here. I'd pay *any* price to be with you." Ty pulls me to him in an attempt to get our romantic weekend back on track.

"Ohmygod! Stop it." I know he's sincere, but I don't want to get diverted from an important conversation with a cheesy line.

Ty recoils, exasperated. "Stop what?"

"When you say that you'll pay any price to be with me, it sounds so selfless. If you read between the lines, what you're really insinuating is that I should *also* pay any price to be with you. Even if that means the world finally identifies and annihilates me. Even if it means harming my own career." I pound my fist into my palm. "Do I have that right?"

"Zoey, when did you get so argumentative?" Ty squints at me. "Did they teach you that in law school? We're on the same side. I don't know what you want me to say. I'm famous, my picture gets taken so much I don't even notice anymore. Scandalous things have been written about me for years now, it rolls right off my back."

"So, I guess it should roll off of mine too." My sarcasm is real.

"Jesus, there's only been a few pictures, you're making such a big deal out of this." Ty huffs and pulls out his phone. "If it makes you happy, I'll interrupt our romantic weekend to text Sienna. We can spend our last night before you have to go home getting a media plan together."

Something feels really off. Life was so much easier when we were younger. Being back with Ty is a dream come true, but now I worry that Ty's fame and notoriety will suck me dry and overshadow all that's good between us.

"Come back here." Ty motions.

"No." I shake my head. "You're not taking my feelings about this seriously, and I need to think about how I'm going to fit into your life without losing my own identity."

"Wow." Ty deflates and looks like I've kicked his puppy. "I had an entire romantic night planned for you, and now it's all messed up."

I get up, go into the bedroom, and shut the door. "Sorry, not sorry."

Sprawled out on the king-size bed, I fling my arm over my eyes. Something about this whole situation is bugging me, but I can't put my finger on it. It's not like I have a bunch of job interviews lined up. I've only had a few nibbles from the headhunter. None of the positions are even close to interesting.

All I know is that I simply can't afford to be part of any scandal until I figure out where I'll be working. Even then, depending on the non-profit, I'll probably have some sort of code of ethics to abide by.

Then it hits me and utter panic sets in.

I already have a code of ethics to abide by.

Tearing out of the bedroom, I find Ty out on the balcony looking completely out of sorts. I can't worry about him at the moment because I have real problems.

I grab his arm. "Ty, I need to go back to Seattle."

"What?" Ty's eyebrows nearly jump off his face. "Why?"

"You're the firm's client and we're sleeping together." I'm freaking the fuck out.

"Zoey, you're the love of my life, we're more than sleeping together," Ty roars. "What's going on right now? Since we got here you've been acting so irrational!"

Frantically, I type into my phone, ignoring Ty for the moment. When I find what I'm looking for, I expand the words on the screen and hold it up for Ty to read.

"A lawyer shall not have sexual relations with a client unless a consensual sexual relationship existed between them when the client-lawyer relationship commenced," he reads from my screen.

"I'm in so much trouble." I sink down on one of the patio chairs.

"I don't understand." Ty sits next to me, looking completely confused. "We had sex years before you were a lawyer."

I point at the phone. "You have to read the words exactly how they're written."

"I'm no good at this legal stuff, Zoey. Just spit it out." Ty looks at me, bewildered.

My mind feels like it's going to implode. "Bottom line is that I'm violating ethical rules. We didn't have a consensual sexual relationship when the firm took your case."

"You're not even helping the foundation anymore." Ty throws his hands up. "This is so fucking stupid."

"And yet, I could get fired," I whisper.

We sit in silence as that little tidbit sinks in.

"Fuck." Ty pulls me into his arms.

I fight the tears that threaten to spill. "You need to take me to the airport, I have to go home."

"Z, it's late. There's nothing we can do about it tonight. Stay, we'll book on you on the first flight out and we'll go from there." Ty kisses my head and I tunnel into his arms, seeking comfort.

Unfortunately, I have a sinking feeling that I'm about to lose everything.

Again.

Chapter Thirty-Eight

The Next Morning

Lying in a beautiful hotel suite with Zoey should have been absolute heaven.

With LTZ's hiatus looming, my plan was to convince her to move in with me, get married and quit her job so we could spend an entire year together with no schedule and no commitments. Just me and her.

Man, I'm stupid.

Jace warned me the LTZ fans would figure out she was Z. They haven't yet, but it's imminent. He's convinced the backlash against her will be brutal. He's been on my case since the Space Needle to work on a strategy so we can soften her introduction to the fans.

I impulsively ignored his warnings and now Zoey is paying a price.

She hasn't taken the paparazzi and fan stuff very well, and for good reason. I've irresponsibly ditched my security team in a misguided effort to have some privacy with her, which has backfired spectacularly.

How could I have forgotten how it felt years ago when I first became famous? I hated being ambushed. The whispering behind my back. The pointing. Everyone trying to touch me. Now it's my normal and I'm used to it but, as Zoey pointed out, it's not hers.

Mentally admonishing myself won't help, I simply have to do whatever it takes to protect her. Which, unfortunately, means she has to go home early.

Part of me wonders if there's more to it. All I want to do is help her, but I can't if she doesn't open up to me. Maybe that's my anxiety talking.

I watch her quietly snore beside me, finally resting. I don't want to wake her up because she tossed and turned all night, stressed because of some ethical rule I don't understand. I can't lose her again, but it definitely feels like she's slipping away. Right when we're finding our groove again. I don't know how to handle it.

I'm close to losing my shit. I might need to have another session with Lisa.

"When do we need to leave?" Zoey yawns and rubs her sleepy eyes.

I want to show her how much she means to me, that she can trust in our relationship. Plus, I can't keep my hands off her for another minute. I stroke her head and kiss her deeply. "We have some time before we need to leave for the airport."

"I'd better get packed." She sits up and the sheet floats to the bed, revealing her flawless, curvy body clothed in only a tiny tank top and panties. My dick is like granite.

I trace her shoulder blade with the tip of my finger. "Why do I get the feeling you're going to say goodbye to me today?"

"*Ty.*" Zoey shakes her head sadly.

The silence stretches out between us.

"You're perfect." I pull off her tank top, nearly losing my mind at the sight of her tits spilling out. I want to devour her. Touch her everywhere. Imprint her with my love, fate be damned.

"Please—" She pulls away for a minute, pleading. It's hard to tell if she wants me to stop or to keep going.

"Zoey, I've always been yours, and only yours." I cup her cheeks before taking off my boxer briefs to free my erection. "Please, let me make love to you."

She nods, bites her lip and reaches for me.

I kneel between her legs. Zoey grips my hips and watches while I rub my cock through her wet folds then guide myself into her. Reaching under us, I cup her ass and pull her up to me. She wraps her arms around my neck as I rock her back and forth on me so I can surge deeper. Our bodies were meant to be joined like this, we fit each other perfectly.

I hope she knows this too.

Zoey rakes her fingers through my hair as I thrust up inside her, the sounds of our desire fill the room. Zoey's tits jiggle tantalizingly with each thrust, and I can't help but lean down and taste her nipples, suckling one after the other into my mouth. Her sexy breaths of pleasure when my cock rubs against her magic spot do me in.

Zoey screams my name, shattering. I blow right after her with a loud roar.

"Don't go home, stay with me." I nuzzle her neck then look at her intently. "We're a couple now, let's figure this out together."

She tenses. "I can't lose my job. Risk my license. I sacrificed years of my life. Don't ask me to do that."

I don't know what to say, my heart seizes. I've been so overwhelmingly happy having her back in my life, but how can I ask her to give up her career? Our relationship can't only be about her fitting into *my* life, I have to fit into hers. I'm desperate to find a solution.

"I'll fire the firm." I reach for my phone. "Then there's no conflict."

"No! Ty, whether you fire the firm or stay, I'm facing the same ethical issue. It would be worse if you leave, it will bring all of the attention on me." Zoey gestures frantically. "I don't *want* this to be a thing. It's killing me, but I have no choice but to deal with it. Alone."

Ah, there it was. My mind screamed at me.

You're not good enough for her, she's found the perfect excuse to leave you again.

"You do have a choice. You're just not choosing me. You'll *never* choose me." The words tumble out of my lips before I could take them back.

She's stricken. "*Ty*, that's not true. That's not fair, you're not listening to me."

"You know what? Nothing about our relationship is fair. Do you know what is true? You call the shots, I just follow you around like a lovestruck puppy hoping you'll keep me." I can't control my emotions, and right now I'm scared. Furious. "I'm *never* going to be enough for you. All I do is try to do things that will make you feel the same way I do. For nothing."

"No! Babe! Stop! That isn't true!" Zoey clings to me. But I hold up my hand to stop her from saying anything else.

The sheets nearly rip when I shoot out of bed and angrily throw my things in my duffle bag. I stalk to the living room, leaving her sitting in bed with her mouth hanging open.

A few minutes later she emerges, dressed in leggings and a T-shirt, wheeling her suitcase. We silently exit the room and ride down the elevator in silence. When the door opens, I stride through the lobby, leaving Zoey in my wake. I hand the valet ticket to the attendant and wait, staring straight ahead behind my mirrored sunglasses.

When my McLaren pulls up, I pull out a couple of hundreds and shove them into Zoey's purse.

"Take a cab," I growl before jumping in my car and speeding away.

I don't look back.

This time it's going to be me leaving *her* in the dust.

Even if it makes me the biggest asshole on the planet.

Chapter Thirty-Nine

Three Hours Later

STRANGELY, I CAN'T EVEN cry. I'm just numb.

On the flight home I put on my noise-canceling headphones so I didn't have to talk to anyone. At first, I didn't blame Ty for being angry. After all, I was the queen of self-sabotage when it came to our relationship. It didn't excuse his behavior though. I didn't deserve to be treated like a disposable groupie.

Not by a long shot.

I find myself in an impossible situation, though. I've been living in a fantasy world for weeks, believing that Ty and I could have our happy ever after without any issues. For the most part, other than the day after the launch party, things between us have been wonderful. Easy. Drama-free. As far as I was concerned, it was only a matter of time before we moved in together. Maybe even got married.

The humiliating scene at the hotel changes my perspective. Something deeper's going on with him, I think. His reaction doesn't make sense.

Doesn't matter, though I'm alone. Again.

Of course, I'd told him I needed to handle my situation alone, so I guess I got what I asked for.

The thing is, alone is better than being disrespected.

Alone is also better than being continuously vilified for something that happened years ago.

It's not right for him to use my past against me. Or to justify his cruel and dismissive behavior. If he can't let it go, how will anyone else? I can't live my life apologizing for something that happened when I was eighteen.

If Ty can't forgive me, we don't have a future. And goddammit, if he forgave Carter why am I still bearing the brunt of his anger?

Truth be told, as sad as I feel, I'm also livid. And weary. It's been overwhelming to bear the burden of our split on my own. I *never* wanted to break up with Ty, but I certainly didn't expect to be the subject of a dozen songs about it. Songs that are part of pop culture now.

Unlike most breakups and heartbreaks, Ty's side of our story has been shared, no exaggeration, with the entire world. It stands to reason that the world will always be behind him.

Which is evidenced by how rabid LTZ fans are. I'd been lulled into a state of complacency. In Seattle, no one really bugged him, and we certainly didn't have a fleet of paparazzi following us around. It was easy for me to forget Ty was famous. I got lost in him and us again and pretended that things were exactly the same as before.

But, holy shit, the reality of his fame smacked me in the face when we were out and about in LA.

Truth be told, it really bugged me to learn Jace warned Ty about the potential consequences of being out in public—and he ignored the warning. Call it self-preservation, but I didn't want to face the judgment of LTZ fans without a plan in place. They've been waiting for years to find out my identity to tear me down.

Years ago, I would have believed that I deserved it.

Now? *Not so much.*

Ty had to have known that if we were in public, holding hands, cuddling and kissing, hundreds of people would be taking his picture. I *didn't* know, so I was taken by complete surprise. It was irresponsible, and maybe even unsafe. Don't get me wrong, nothing makes me prouder than to be on Ty's arm. I just deserve an equal say in my life.

Luckily, the trolls don't know my identity yet. Their cruel comments about my physical appearance and worthiness to be with still Ty hurt.

Whenever I feel out of my element, I need to think things through. Reset. Analyze. Problem-solve. Ty *knows* this about me. I've always been this way. That's the only reason I needed to come home early.

Anyway, I can't believe we're over.

I need my mom.

She picks up on the first ring. "Are you already back in town? I thought you got in later tonight."

The tears I couldn't muster on the plane flood out of me at the sound of her voice. "I came home early. Ty and I broke up."

"Oh, Zoey, are you okay?" Mom's voice instantly goes into soothe mode.

I sniff loudly. "I don't know. He's so angry with me."

"Sweetie, everyone argues, it's to be expected. Tell me."

As I explain what happened and how Ty reacted, I'm so glad I called. She never lectures me or makes me feel bad. She also doesn't place judgment on Ty. My mom is the best at helping me figure things out. I'm so lucky to have her.

She's able to pinpoint a few things I hadn't considered. "Zoey, from what you told me, Ty had a challenging childhood. I'm sure he's struggling with abandonment issues, maybe even more. In any relationship, communication is the most important element and if you plan on being with him long-term, it will be up to the two of you to work on these issues together."

"That's what I'm most afraid of. I'll never love anyone the way I love him. I know I messed up when I ghosted him all of those years ago, but I've apologized so many times and promised I'd never do that to him again. And I won't. At the same time, when I have my own fears about how things are going, I don't want to walk on eggshells worried that he's going to storm off. He's already done it twice. It's not sustainable for any relationship." I flop down on my bed, exhausted.

"That's true," Mom agrees. "What will you do about the ethics situation?"

"It won't matter if I get a new job. But, Mom, all of the photos, autographs, and selfies? It was overwhelming. It wasn't until we were at the hotel when I realized that if Joe finds out I'll have serious issues at the firm. I freaked out. My homing instinct ignited, and I just wanted to be here to calm down and come up with a plan."

Mom drops a bomb. "If it's any consolation, Ty came over when you were working late a couple of weeks ago to talk to me and your dad."

"Why?" I'm beyond shocked. He said nothing about it.

"He loves you. He's a good man, but he's not perfect." My mom 's gentle voice soothes me a bit. "And neither are you, sweetheart."

"God, don't I know that." Tears leak down my cheeks. "What if I just tanked my career and Ty and I are through? I'm so confused. I'm not sure what to do."

"Zoey, you've always been such a serious, careful girl. Now, you're a serious, careful young woman. Your dad and I always encouraged you to come out of your shell. We've worried about your solitary tendencies for years." Mom pauses thoughtfully. "Only you can decide what makes you happy and how you want to interact in this world. All I ask—as your mother—is that you don't make decisions out of fear. Don't always plan for the worst, or you'll draw the worst to you. Tonight, allow yourself to dream about your perfect life and all the people surrounding you. Think about how you'd feel in this perfect life. I guarantee, you'll know what to do."

"You sound like a self-help book." I'm able to muster up a smile.

She laughs. "Moms always know best, remember that."

———

A couple days later, I sit at my desk well past office hours. I still haven't heard from Ty, and I haven't reached out to him either. I'm back to being numb, bordering on depressed.

Staring out my window at the Space Needle, I wait for Joe, who requested a meeting. I know it's do or die time. Even if Ty and I aren't together anymore, my ethics professor advised me to let HR know about my relationship with Ty. I emailed them that morning and the meeting request from Joe followed within minutes. All day the wait has made me feel nauseated in anticipation of the conversation I'm about to be having any second now.

My mind is swirling around on a loop. When I get this way, Ty teases me about the hamster wheel in my head. Where is he now? Does he even care? My career is about to tank because of our relationship that doesn't even exist anymore.

I glance at the clock and realize Joe is over half hour late. Figuring, or maybe hoping, he's forgotten our meeting, I decide to pack up and go home to my empty condo. Nothing says "party" more than eating a pint of Haagen-Dazs Peanut Butter and Chocolate for dinner in front of Bravo after you lose your job because of your famous boyfriend who isn't your boyfriend anymore.

I power down my PC and notice Joe standing at my office door. "Zoey? Good, I'm not too late. Do you still have a minute?"

"Sure, Joe." I inwardly sigh, smooth the slacks on my black pantsuit, and sit back down at my desk. He takes the seat across from me, leaving my door open.

"We need to discuss Tyson Rainier." He lowers his reading glasses to look me in the eye.

Inwardly I sigh. "Okay."

"Zoey, I learned that you've been seeing Mr. Rainier. As a client of the firm, there are ethical concerns." He taps his fingers on my desk.

"Yes, which is why I disclosed my relationship to HR. Ty and I have been lovers since I was eighteen years old. Many years before I brought his foundation business to the firm." I hold his gaze, refusing to apologize for my sexual history or my relationship with Ty. It's none of his fucking business.

Well, maybe it is, but I have to stand my ground.

"Ehh. Umm," Joe sputters, visibly shocked at my unexpected crassness.

I try to ease the situation. "You might remember from that first meeting that Ty and I lost touch for a few years, but we started dating again."

"Zoey, you have to understand, this firm takes its ethical responsibilities—"

I cut him off. "I didn't do anything to deliberately compromise this firm."

"I didn't say that." He fixes his gaze on me.

"Look, I need to take some time." When the words come out of my mouth, they feel right. "I know that I don't have enough seniority for a sabbatical. I'm happy to formalize my resignation in writing."

He's visibly shocked. "Zoey, wait. We don't want to lose you."

"I'm not making this decision irrationally. I appreciate all that you have done for me. I just..." I look out the window without finishing.

"Want to do something else?" Joe finishes for me.

I nod. "I don't know. But I need a change."

Joe taps his finger to his nose. "Zoey, forgive me for asking, it isn't my business but are you sure he's the man for you? It seems like he has a pretty troubled history."

"He's always been the only man for me, Joe." I furrow my brow. "You don't know him, and you shouldn't believe everything you read."

"Wait a minute—" His eyes open wide. "You're *Z*!"

"Umm." My downturned eyes say it all.

"Oh, *wow*." Joe is stunned. "Wow."

"Yes, Joe. I'm the one he wrote all those songs about." It's so weird my boss is the first one to figure it out. "I won't go into everything, but there are two sides to the story and his version has become our truth. Until he showed up last June, we'd lost touch. He's a public figure, which means I'm going to be outed. It's inevitable. It's best if I leave to protect the firm."

"Um. Um. Well, um—Huh." He looks completely befuddled. If that's your decision, I won't stand in your way."

"Thanks, Joe. Seriously. For everything." I stand and reach over my desk to shake his hand.

"You can always come back if it doesn't work out, Zoey. I mean it." He clasps my hand in both of his. "You're an exceptional talent."

"I appreciate it." I feel a weight lift off my shoulders. "I've boxed up my personal stuff, but I'm happy to help with a transition if you need me to."

"That won't be necessary, Zoey." Joe turns to leave. "Good luck to you."

Afterward, I sit behind my desk, stunned that I've actually quit my job. I have no back-up plan and no true prospects, just about a year's salary in my bank account to keep me going until I land on my feet.

It's already 8:25 p.m., and my heart sinks when I see I've missed a dozen texts and calls from Ty.

6:41 pm Tyson – missed call.

6:42 pm Tyson:

Hey can we talk?

6:58 pm Tyson – missed call.

6:59 pm Tyson – missed call.

6:59 pm Tyson:

Z, please pick up.

7:13 pm Tyson:

I'm back in Seattle, I need to see you Z.

7:38 pm Tyson: missed call.

7:39 pm Tyson:

Z, please just let me know your ok.

7:45 pm Tyson: missed call.

7:50 pm Tyson: missed call.

7:59 pm Tyson: missed call.

8:05 pm Tyson:

I'm coming to you.

Frantically I dial Ty's number, hoping to intercept him before he comes here to find me. The call goes to Ty's voicemail, and I leave a message explaining I've been in a meeting and to call me.

Grabbing my purse and box of stuff, I rush out, desperate to talk to him. If for no other reason than to end things more civilly this time.

At the elevator, I'm rustling through my purse to find my car keys when the door opens and I take a step forward.

In my rush to get to the parking garage, I smash straight into a wall of my rock god.

Chapter Forty

A Min Later

"Z, BABY." I'M SO relieved to see my beautiful girl, I instinctively pull her into a bear hug before realizing she has a big box of her things in her hands. She looks tired and stressed but relieved to see it's me and not some rando.

She pulls away quickly. "Hi."

"Sorry, I don't want to cause trouble for you at your job." I look around, mentally chastising myself for being inconsiderate. *Again.*

"Former job." She kicks the rug with her Fluevog boot. "I quit today."

"What?" I'm blown away, leave it to Zoey to thwart my grand gesture again.

She hits the elevator button with her elbow and looks up to watch its descent. "Yep, I chose you."

"*Zoey.*" My heart melts into a puddle on the floor. "Let me take that."

She says nothing when I take the box, just keeps her eyes fixed to the floor indicator. When the elevator arrives, she steps in and presses the button for the parking garage.

I follow her. "Can we talk?"

"Okay." She nods slightly.

"I wrapped up my vocals and came back as soon as I could." I know I sound so lame.

"Look, I know I didn't handle things well in LA." Zoey shuts her eyes and takes a deep breath. "But I was really worried about being outed. You leaving me in the dust like that wasn't cool. It really hurt me."

"I was wrong." I shake my head in shame. "I'm so sorry."

"Getting back together is a big adjustment for *both* of us." She stares straight ahead. "After what just happened, I'm not sure if it's the right thing."

"For me it is." I slump against the elevator wall, clasping her box to my chest. I've got to get a hold of my emotions if things are going to work with us.

The doors open and I follow Zoey out to the garage. She opens the trunk and I set the box inside. She tosses me the keys and we both get into her RAV, I'll pick up my car tomorrow.

Silently, I ease out into the shitty Seattle traffic and inch toward West Seattle. We sit in silence because the air is so heavy with tension.

After twenty minutes, when we only manage to travel a few blocks, the pressure gets to me. "I have an idea. After how badly I fucked up you'll probably reject it outright. Will you hear me out anyway?"

"I have absolutely *no* idea what you're going to say next." She tilts her head.

It's a serious question. One I've been contemplating since before the Sirius show. I haven't been sure when to bring it up, but it seems like I have nothing to lose. "Run my foundation as the CEO. Carter and I are the trustees, and we haven't hired for that position yet. It should be you."

Zoey eyes widen, her mouth falls open, shocked. "Holy fucking moly, Ty. I don't have the background or capability to do that job!"

"You *do*." I'm definitive. "First, you created the entire legal structure. Second, we adopted the operating infra-structure exactly the way you recommended. Third, you drafted all the documents. But, most importantly, you really believe in what I want to do *and* you have the passion for it. You're the only person for the job."

"Never in a million years did I consider this, Ty." She fumbles in her purse for something, pulls out a Chapstick and slathers it on. "I have enough money saved to take a year off to figure out my next move."

"*Will* you consider it?" I can't help but hold my breath.

"I mean, well. Working in a non-profit like yours is what I envisioned doing when I quit, but I don't think it solves our issues." Zoey peers over at me. "Plus, what will people say?"

"I don't care what they say, I care that kids get access to play music. That's it." I reach over to take her hand.

"I'm just not sure I'm comfortable at this stage of my career. Are we even together right now?" Zoey looks at me like the weight of the world rests on her shoulders.

"Z, I have a lot of issues. I'm not going to deny it, and I can't promise I won't fuck up." I squeeze her hand. "The only thing I'm sure of in this life is that I love you and I want to be with you. I want you with me all of the time. I want to show you off. Shout it from the rooftops. I also need to take your feelings into consideration. It would kill me if our relationship ever caused you pain or fucked with your reputation, I'll do whatever it takes to prevent that. I promise."

"I want to be with you too, I just need to get comfortable with people knowing about me." Zoey finally squeezes my hand back.

"I've got to do a better job of looking out for you, butter-fly. So, will you think about working for the foundation?" I ease onto the West Seattle bridge. "We can work out the details if you want the job."

"You're dead serious." Zoey's still shocked.

"I *am* dead serious. Don't say no outright. Let the hamster wheel spin for a bit." I pull into my driveway and push the fob to open the gate. "For now, I have a lot of apologizing to do to convince you about the other part of my plan."

Once we're inside I get Zoey settled on the couch with an episode of *Vanderpump Rules*. My next step is plying my girl with food, she loves it when I cook for her, probably because her own culinary skills are nonexistent.

"There's nothing hotter than a rock star who cooks, that smells amazing!" Zoey calls from the living room, about an hour later.

"Roast chicken and potatoes. I'm auditioning to be your house-husband." I stroll into the living room and place my hands, still encased in shark-shaped hot pad gloves, on my hips, arms akimbo.

Zoey jumps up and kisses me. "You're hands-down the sexiest house-husband slash chef in the world."

Together, we take out plates and silverware to set up our places at the counter. I dish up the food and we sit down to eat, and launch into my official apology. "I want to formally apologize for how I treated you in LA. I shouldn't have just left you like that. I should have called, but all I could think about was finishing my vocals and getting back to you. You also need to know I met with Lisa and will continue to meet with her so I can deal with my shit and not put it on you."

"Thank you for saying that." Zoey puts her fork down and looks at her plate. "I mean, I need to apologize too. I'm used to solving my own problems, I'm clearly terrible at talking things over with you. Maybe if I could have just filled you in on the gerbils in my head—"

"Well, here's the thing." I tap my finger against my chin. "If our separation has taught me anything it's that I don't want to waste more time. In my mind, you and I are permanent, so when it felt like you were pulling away I reacted badly." I clasp my hands in front of me. "Despite our time apart, we've been desperately in love with each other for over eight years. In many ways we're moving as slow as icebergs. We've danced around it, but maybe we need the official full-blown commitment so we can put the past in the past."

She puts her fork down. "Ohmygod, I've been feeling the same way."

"I want you with me, and I want to be with you." I encircle her wrist. "I know that we still have things to work out, but would you be freaked out if I wanted to speed everything up?"

"What do you mean?" Zoey nervously fiddles with her silverware.

I decide to lay it all out there. "Move in with me."

"Ty." Zoey glances at me then looks away.

"Oh, shit. We're *not* on the same page." I can't believe how disappointed I am. "I'm sorry, I just thought—"

"Ty, you left me in an angry huff and shoved money at me for a cab to the airport when I was freaking out about losing my license. I *needed* you." Zoey swallows, but catches my gaze. Today, I quit my job to be with you. You just asked me to be the CEO of your foundation. It's already a lot. Now you want to add living together on top of it?"

"We spend every night together anyway," I reason, but when I see the shadow cross Zoey's face it's clear we aren't aligned. "*Fuck*. I really let you down in LA."

She simply nods. "Yes. But, do you know *why?*"

"Because I was careless? Because I didn't protect you from being outed?" I stand and pace the kitchen. "Look, all I can say is I've been trying to force myself to take things slow from the minute I saw you again, butterfly. I just can't. I want it all with you. I don't want to lose one more day together."

Zoey approaches me and places her hand on my chest to stop my frantic movement. "Stop. *Stop*. Why I'm upset about LA has nothing to do with us being together, because I don't want to lose any more days either." She entwines her fingers with mine. "At the same time, you've stormed off twice over a misunderstanding. I didn't hear from you for nearly three days. You were never like this before. It isn't the way to start our new normal."

"I guess it's PTSD from finding that note," I spit out and pull away from her, instantly regretting my reaction, let alone revealing something I need to talk to her about at some point.

"You know what? I've apologized for that multiple times." Zoey's voice rises in anger, an emotion I'm still not used to from her. "No one knows more than me that I'm far from perfect. But I've already paid a big price for a foolish decision made when I was eighteen. If you react poorly and think that you can justify your reactions because of that one incident, we don't stand a chance. The odds are already stacked against us when your fanbase realizes you're back with 'Z,' the woman you villainized on the album."

I cross my arms petulantly. "I can't change that *now*."

"Exactly, but do I bring it up every time we have a disagreement? *No*. No I don't." She takes her dishes to the sink. "If you can't stop throwing what I did in my face, how will your fans get behind you being with me? We can accept what our reality is today and try to move forward. Or we can call it quits."

"You're right." I'm such a complete asshole. "I *have* been doing that. I'm sorry."

"I never wanted to break it off, Ty," Zoey roars. "I *suffered* all of those years too, and yet you've forgiven Carter but not me?"

Is that true?

Fuck.

It is.

We've only had two disagreements since we've been back together, and each time I've thrown old shit in her face and stormed off like a toddler. I'm damn lucky she's still here. I don't deserve her, but I'm going to turn things around. I have to. "Can I show you something?"

"Sure, why not?" Zoey shuts the water off and crosses her arms protectively around herself.

I cross over to the small wood desk by the fireplace. Opening a tiny drawer, I grab a key and move the multi-platinum record for *Butterfly* off the wall, revealing a deep compartment. Unlocking the safe inside it first with the key then the combination, I retrieve my binder of financial statements and bring it back with me to the counter. Placing it in front of Zoey, I open the binder to a ledger of my financial assets.

"I hope you don't think it's weird that I'm letting you see this. I don't want to freak you out." I study her expression, which remains impassive.

Zoey looks at me quizzically, without even glancing at the statement. "Okay, but this stuff is none of my business."

"Well, I disagree. This is entirely your business." I tap the paper. "My schedule is about to get busy again until the end of this year. I just thought that before we go to New York, we could really make a commitment to each other."

She tilts her head. "Wait, what's this about me going to New York?"

"Well, I just assumed you'd be with me for the premiere." I'm such an idiot. I haven't even asked her.

She stares at me for a long moment. "Are you asking me or telling me?"

"Asking. Will you come with me? We'll get an entire PR plan put together to control the press as much as possible." I move toward her.

Zoey doesn't respond, but she finally scans the spreadsheet. "Holy shit, Ty. You're not just a millionaire, you're like a zillionaire!"

"I just want you to know that I'm secure. *We're* secure." I reach over and tentatively put my hand over hers.

Zoey shuts her eyes and sighs, looking up at me with a tight smile. "I haven't earned any of this."

"I beg to differ." I squeeze her hand. "The songs I wrote about you bring me royalties every year. This is as much your money as mine."

She's astounded. Her brow furrows as though she's deep in thought.

"Look, I wanted to show you my finances. Royalties from my songwriting and producing pay me as much as LTZ does. More even." I start babbling. "I'm investing wisely, aside from a couple crazily expensive cars. I'll never be able to spend what I have."

"Your money doesn't matter to me, Ty. Don't get me wrong, I'm proud of you." Zoey's eyes pool with tears. "You've come so far."

I shut the binder. "Well, Carter set us all up with his financial manager, who's been brilliant."

"This is all so much." Zoey buries her head in her hands. "I'm not sure how to feel."

"I'm hoping it makes you feel safe. I mean, you really don't need to work at the firm or at the foundation or at any job if you don't want to, Zoey," I attempt to reassure her. "You can take the time to do whatever you want. I just want to be with you every step of the way. And, I don't want to hide you anymore. We need to reclaim our lives."

She sighs. "I get what you're saying, but—"

"I know, I'm being impatient. Making assumptions about what you want. Or when you want it." I've said my piece, now I just need her to decide what she wants. "At least now you know where I stand."

Zoey sits at the counter and rests her chin on her arms. "I'm just trying to process, it's a lot of big changes. I'm feeling overwhelmed."

Without saying another word, I put the ledger back in its place and clean up the kitchen. Part of me is afraid that I'll say something I'll regret because I'm ready to take the next step *now*. The other part knows not to push her after my behavior in LA.

"Ty?" Zoey's voice snaps me to attention.

"Butterfly, why don't you go change? Relax. Maybe take a bath. I'll finish cleaning up." I move toward her, smooth her hair and kiss her on the forehead.

She gazes up at me uncertainly. "But—"

"Look, the truth is I have a few more band commitments that are important. I'm also not going to apologize to you or anyone else that I want you to be with me as much as humanly possible now and later and forever. Once the band is on hiatus, there is no guarantee any of this will ever happen again for LTZ. Or, even that we will even make music together again." I take a deep breath and express my deepest fear. "We could very well be tanking our career for good. There may be no more hit songs. No more Grammys. No more private jets whisking us to movie premieres."

My calm delivery camouflages my desperate need for Zoey to understand where I'm coming from. I refuse to leave anything on the table anymore, especially with her. "While I hope that doesn't happen, the thing is, I'm okay with it. I've lived this life nonstop for nearly a decade. Now I'm financially secure and can branch out into exploring the other things that are important to me. The foundation, for instance. But mostly, while I never, in a million years, fathomed that you and I would find our way back to each other, now that we have, *you're* the most important thing in my life. Full stop."

Zoey stares up at me with her big, innocent hazel eyes, letting me have my say.

So, I continue, placing my hands on her shoulders. "The thing is, babe? I support your ambition and encourage it. I don't expect you to give up anything. Truthfully, there is nothing I'd rather do than marry you, retire and knock you up a bunch of times and stay home with our ten kids while you run the foundation or work somewhere else, or excel at whatever you want to do. I'd be content to go back to having music in my life as a passion not a career if it meant you were happy."

"Ty—" Zoey looks like she's caught in a trap, which only means I've overwhelmed her. I need to give her some space to catch up to me.

"It's okay, baby. The truth is, we're in a holding pattern about our future because you're still conflicted. I know what I want, but I want you to work out what *you* want in your own time. The moving in together, marriage and kids' thing we can chill about." I squeeze her gently. "For now, I'm up against a deadline for the band stuff. Give it some thought about whether you want to go to New York, rip the Band-Aid off and go public. I'll be okay either way. We can take it one step at a time."

Zoey says nothing. She just wraps her arms around my waist and leans into me, nestling her face into my chest. I cup her head and hold her to me. After a few minutes she extricates herself from our embrace and walks back to my bedroom, leaving me in the kitchen.

I let her go.

When I finish cleaning up from dinner about a half-hour later, I decide to check on her.

I enter the living room and call her name. She answers from the bathroom, "Ty?"

"I'm right here, butterfly." I open the door to find her soaking in the massive double-jetted bathtub, red-rimmed eyes peering at me through a mountain of bubbles. Her tear-streaked face is so tragically gorgeous, despite the mascara running down her cheeks. I could write a million songs about just this moment.

Quickly kneeling by the tub, I take

her face in my hands and caress her temples with my thumbs. "God, I'm such a fuckup. I'm so sorry for putting too much out there. I didn't mean to make you cry."

"Stop. Ty. It's not that. I—I want to move in with you, there's nothing I want more." Her anguished sobs rip me apart.

"I sure hope so, Z, because we belong together." I embrace my naked girl, rubbing her back to comfort her as she lets it all out.

I realize she's probably never had a way to release the eight years of sorrow she dealt with largely on her own. I wrote songs about it. Became addicted because of it. She's buried it all inside because she's strong and resilient. I want to take some of that burden off her.

"I get in my own way." Zoey's sobs settle into choking cries.

"We both do at times, babe. Just tell me what you want. What you really, *really* want." I regard at her earnestly. "*Please*—I'll make it happen."

"*Zig a zig ah?*" Zoey sings off-key and starts sob-laughing hysterically.

I'm baffled. Not sure what to do. Ummm?" I have no idea what's going on.

"Spice Girls?" She cocks her eyebrow, setting off another fit of laughter-sobs, although more on the laughter side this time.

"*Ohhhh—*" I start laughing too, finally getting it.

Soon we're both laughing in fits causing the bubbles and water to splash all around, soaking me. When we regain some semblance of control, I need to be skin-to-skin with my girl. I strip off my wet clothes and get into the bathtub behind her.

Zoey relaxes into me as I kiss her neck, then cup her face and angle her head back toward mine. Exploring her mouth gently at first, then hungrily, our tongues dance together. My dick hardens, though my original plan was just to comfort her. How could it not? Her splendid tits bob amongst the bubbles. I can't resist pinching her nipples, loving how they immediately harden into tight bullets at my touch.

"We've always done sex exceedingly well." Zoey sinks back against my chest and presses her ass against my erection.

"We have," I agree, as I inch one hand down her body to stroke the slight swell of her stomach then dip into her folds. I slip my middle finger inside her and flick her clit with my thumb.

"The relationship stuff is tougher," she eeks out breathlessly, squirming against me.

I circled her nub faster.

Zoey lolls back against me. "*Yes.* Ty, I want all of it."

"Mmm." I increase my pace, nuzzling her ear, biting it gently.

She moans, "Ohhh *God*, that feels so good."

"I *always* want to make you feel good, Z." I suckle on her earlobe, using my nose to dip into her neck.

Zoey hums and presses against me, her eyes closed. Her head slips farther back against my arm when I push my finger in and out of her. Watching her reaction, I know I've hit the mark when her lips open slightly, and she puffs out little breaths. Her knees fall open over my legs. Her hips have a mind of their own, grinding against my hand, seeking something more.

Still strumming her clit, I lift her over the side of the tub so her ass is just above the waterline. The bathwater splooshes around us. Kneeling behind her, I grip my cock, stroke it through her folds and thrust deep inside her. Her hums grow louder and louder with every cant of my hips.

Zoey uses the edge of the tub for leverage and pushes back against me, forcing me even deeper. My balls slap against her ass when we find our rhythm, which happens to create mini-tsunamis, soaking the bathroom floor.

"Ty, can we do this somewhere more comfortable?" Zoey looks around at me, the faint mascara streaks giving her a dangerous and sexy vibe. "I love having you so deep inside me, but my knees are killing me, and we've made an absolute mess."

"Your wish is my command." I pluck her out of the bath and carry her to the bed, hungrily slamming my mouth against hers on the way. I place her down and position her so she's on her hands and knees.

Waggling her shapely ass in the air, Zoey flashes me a saucy look over her shoulder. "Do you like what you see?"

I nearly blow my load when she leans down and spreads her knees wider, flashing her gorgeous pussy, so pink, swollen, and puffy from our bathtub activities. "God, what you do to me." My already engorged cock twitches when I kneel behind her to take up where we left off in the bathtub.

"Ty, please don't hold back, I need you so much," Zoey begs.

I've got to imprint her. Make her feel my love through her whole body. I also don't want to hurt her, so I clasp her hips to mine and slowly enter her inch by inch. "Oh, Z, you are so goddamn beautiful taking my cock like this."

There's no place I'd rather be than between her silken walls. Nudging her inner thighs with my knees, I spread her legs even wider and splay my hand across her upper back, pressing her torso down on the bed while keeping her ass high in the air. Surging in and out of her velvet tightness from behind, I grip her hips to control our pace until I know she's fully adjusted to me being so deep.

My thumbs circle the little indents right above her crease, and dip closer to her tight ring. I press my thumb inside her ass. The sensation is so incredible, I can't help but pick up the pace.

Zoey moans loudly when I hit her cervix, reaching up to clutch the sheets above her head, her head sideways against the comforter. "Yesssss, babe, *pleeease* I want to feel you all the way through me, don't you dare hold back."

Wild blonde hair fanned out over the sheets, she bucks her hips back at me and clenches her walls around me tightly. I unleash my inner beast. Moving like a blur, my body takes over in a way I've never allowed myself to do before. I pound into her over and over again, relentlessly, until I don't know where she begins and I end.

Needing to touch all of her, I lean over her body so my chest covers her back. Beads of water from my wet hair roll down both sides of her breasts, which are smashed against the mattress. My hands intertwine with hers above her head as I continue to piston into my girl with the type of abandon I've only ever fantasized about all these years.

Zoey's moans intensify when I devour the side of her neck with opened-mouth kisses. Our grunts and cries are uncensored, our passion morphs into unabashed wanton fucking, relentless and feral.

Owning each other.

Branding each other.

Zoey's thighs shake uncontrollably. Banding my arm around her waist to support her, I reach for her clit to find her fingering herself. Together we circle her sweet spot until her juices soak me. Wet slaps of our connected bodies fill the room. Her inner walls flutter and she clamps around my cock until neither of us can hold on any longer.

Zoey screams through her spectacular release, which rips something loose deep inside me. Almost as if from a distance, I can hear myself shouting at the top of my lungs when I empty inside her, endlessly coming in bursts of pleasure I never dreamed existed.

When I have no more to give, lightheaded and panting, I kiss the side of her face as I cradle her from behind, my cock still pulsing. Breathing rapidly but shallowly, Zoey dissolves into the bed. Unable to hold myself up either, I collapse against her back and hold her to me until we're somewhat coherent.

"That was—beyond words," Zoey is finally able to murmur into the comforter.

"I don't think I can breathe." I shift slightly so my arm doesn't fall asleep and slip out of her, leaving streams of our beautiful release trickling in rivulets out of her pussy down her thighs. "Oh jeez, I need to clean you up, I've flooded you."

"No, don't leave me. I like feeling you dripping out of me." Zoey takes my arm and tucks herself under me, tipping her head up for a kiss.

Tenderly, our lips graze, and we sip from each other while moving under the covers. "I'll get hard again if you talk dirty like that, butterfly." I kiss her deeply then stare into her eyes. "How did you know?"

"Know what? That you needed it that way?" Zoey blinks up at me as she hooks her leg over mine so we're as close together as possible. "Maybe because I did too." She searches my eyes. "I love you, Ty. *So* much."

I kiss her softly. "I love you so much too."

Zoey traces my lips with her fingers. "You've always been my person, and I wasn't living fully without you. I'd never have lived fully without you."

I close my eyes at the words I've needed to hear. "*Z*—"

"I want to work for your foundation. It's my dream job, I'd be an idiot not to do it." Zoey strokes my chest. "I also want to live with you and commit to us. I don't want to miss one more second together."

"Really?" I prop my head up on my hand.

"Yes. Ty, I want to be with you. It's always been you. Only you." Zoey gently kisses my forehead, my eyes, and lips, then pulls my arm around her as she nestles back against me. "Remember that whenever you get worried. When we fight. *Trust* it."

I tighten my arms around her. "I'm so happy, God. Z—"

"Let's take it one step at a time. I'll go to New York, but we need a plan so I can get used to the public scrutiny and see how the LTZ fans react. I'm no PR expert, but it's probably best that we don't make any announcements about my role in the foundation until we get through that hurdle." She's nearly mumbling from exhaustion.

"Why?" I'm genuinely curious.

She blinks up at me sleepily. "I need time to adjust to our new normal, even if it's just for a couple of months. It's also best for the foundation. See? I'm already thinking like a CEO."

"Ahh. Of course." I don't want to wait to get kids the music education they need, but Zoey has a fair point.

"Only for a little bit, babe." Zoey melts into me.

I rub her back. "Okay, that's fair."

"For the record, I'm not conflicted at all." Zoey's voice is strong. Clear. She places her hand on my heart. "It's the first time in a long time that I haven't been. I'll be with you wherever you want me, nothing will keep us apart again."

Gulping, with tears in my eyes, I crush her to me and breathe her in. "Ah, butterfly."

It's powerful stuff.

Knowing we're in this together.

Knowing we're one.

My strong, feisty girl deserves my patience and faith, and I vow to show her that I believe in her unconditionally the way she's always believed in me. I vow never to do anything to hurt her again. After all, she's the best thing that's ever happened to me.

I just hope that the LTZ fans will feel the same way.

Chapter Forty-One

The Next Day

WATCHING TY'S STRONG HANDS shift the gears on his Porsche, I look up at his full lips peeking out from under his ever-present stubble as he scans the road. The skull cap barely contains his long waves which frame his sexy jawline.

Sensing my gaze, he glances over at me, and his lips quirk up in a knowing smile as he navigates us to a mystery location. Last night was emotional, but also a turning point in our relationship.

It feels like a *real* new beginning.

Like we're not immature adults still emotionally frozen in the darkest time of both of our lives.

Like we can forget the past and move on.

I reach over and trace his lip with my finger, and he draws it into his mouth, sucks and waggles his eyebrows at me. I'm instantly wet. The things Ty does to me are *definitely* very grown-up activities. I have visions of going down on him when I notice we've stopped at a familiar location.

He opens the door for me, slings his arm around my shoulder and, together, Ty and I walk up the stone steps to the ginormous old-growth wood door and ring the door-bell. Carter opens it a few minutes later wearing an old green Limelight T-shirt and black cut-off sweats, his gray-ish hair falls loose around his shoulders under a black bandana.

"Ty, Zoey! What the hell's going on? I didn't expect to see you two." Carter holds the door open so we can walk inside.

"Hey, Carter, hope we aren't interrupting anything," Ty side hugs him and leads me through the entryway down into the sunken living room. It's been so many years since I've seen the view from the big picture windows looking out over Lake Washington, nostalgia washes over me.

Ty sinks down into a cushy, oversized, navy-blue cor-duroy chair and tugs me onto his lap, snaking his long arms around my waist. I clasp my arms over his.

Carter takes a seat on the adjacent matching chair and gestures between us. "Good to see you finally back togeth-er." He focuses on Ty. "Did you just get home? How did recording go?"

"It went well enough that I'm home early." Ty hooks his index finger with mine. "The movie premiere is a couple of weeks before Thanksgiving."

Carter winks at me. "Awesome. Good news. Zoey, did you enjoy your visit?"

"I did, have you seen that car?" I'm not about to air our dirty laundry about our fight to Carter. Not when we've righted the ship.

"Nope, but I've heard all about it." He scrubs his jaw with his hand. "So, what's up, you so rarely stop by anymore."

Ty's arms tighten around me. "We came to share some news, Carter." Ty tenses just a bit. "Zoey and I are moving in together, and we'd like your blessing."

"Uh-huh. Well that's great and all but you certainly don't need any blessings from me." Carter stares at us quizzically.

"No, that's not true." Ty's voice is strong and clear. "You're like a father to me, and well—I just want to make sure there won't be any more misunderstandings or interference with us. You're too important to me, but—so we're clear—Zoey's the *most* important to me."

Carter palms his forehead then rubs his eyebrows nervously. A slight dampness shines in his eyes. "Tyson, I consider you my second son."

"You're the only father I've ever known." Ty's voice breaks slightly. I squeeze his finger with mine. "I don't have any role models of how to be a stand-up man in a relationship and I've already made some big mistakes."

Carter sheepishly shakes his head. "Well, uh. All of us here know that I'm no good at relationships." He furrows his brow. "Don't ask me for advice, you'll both figure it out."

"I'm *not* asking for advice. We both know this whole foundation setup with Zoey's law firm was your way of making amends, so *thank you*, but now that we're back together—for good this time—you need to stay out of our shit going forward." Ty waves his hand in the air in front of us.

Carter leans way back in his chair. "You're a very wealthy and successful man now, Ty. You're not that insecure, poor young musician who saw Zoey as your lifeline back when you first started dating."

"*No*! The band was *always* my lifeline, Carter. It was all I had for a very long time." Ty's voice raises defensively. "Zoey was my girlfriend not—"

"Don't rewrite history, Ty," Carter interrupts and wags his finger. "You would have given up LTZ for her in an instant—you almost did, and you didn't have anything to fall back on."

Ty slumps back in the chair. "I'm not sure what you mean."

"Do you know I went to see your mom a couple weeks after you first met Zane? I also kept track of her for a while after LTZ first blew up." Carter tilts his head. "I knew more about your situation than you think I did."

Carter has dropped a bomb on both of us, and my heart clenches for Ty, considering he's made such an effort to keep his relationship with his mom under the radar.

Ty's blurts, "You *what?*"

"Dude, I was perpetually worried about your welfare. You were so secretive about your situation, which wasn't normal for a kid of fifteen." Carter clasps his hands in front of him in a giant fist. "Your drive to make it on your own terms was so fierce. I respected that, I admired you for it, but I had to look out for you."

"I'm—wow. I had no idea. I'm so embarrassed." Ty can barely speak.

Carter shakes his head. "Ty, I won't say a bad word about your mom. But, when I saw with my own eyes what was happening, I knew—without a shadow of doubt—I needed to do everything within my power to make sure you were set up for success. You deserved your shot. You *needed* it."

"Shit. I mean, I knew you helped us, but I thought it was because of Zane." Ty rests his chin on my shoulder.

Carter shrugs. "Well, of course. I'm his dad. And the other guys, too, but they have their own families. You?"

"My mom lost her way." Ty's voice grows soft, reflective. "I used to feel like I was responsible for her, that I was never worthy enough for her to get her shit together."

"Oh baby." I turn and kiss his cheek. "You didn't deserve to feel that way, *God*."

"Butterfly, I'm okay. Therapy saved me, and I know better now." Ty nuzzles me.

Carter squints, studying Ty. "Have you seen her recently?"

"Nope. I haven't spoken to her in years. She could be dead, I really don't know," Ty's voice is flat, emotionless.

Carter rests his elbows on his legs. "Fuck, dude. We can't pick our family."

"I can and I did," Ty says confidently. "And I pick Zoey, you and the band."

"That means the world to me." Carter's eyes wrinkle with such love for Ty.

"Do *I* meet with your approval this time Carter?" I can't help but ask, I don't want to get blindsided again.

"Zoey, you always loved Ty so unconditionally when he didn't have a lot of love in his life, you made the biggest sacrifice of all so he could have his chance." Carter gets up, takes the two steps over to me and kisses me on the head. "I'm *so* sorry for everything. I truly wish I hadn't interfered. I guess I let my own bullshit...*fuck*."

"Now that we're together again, I can honestly say the wait was worth it. I'm just glad all of it is behind us." I settle back against Ty. He's my comfort. My home. "I'm finally where I belong, again."

Ty moves me off his lap and stands. "We're going to go public soon after we meet with LTZ's PR team in New York a couple of days before the show." He looks back at me. "The first thing on the agenda is to retire any song I wrote that's hurt you."

"No, you can't do that." I pop up from my seat, gesturing frantically. "I'm not going anywhere. Those songs are an important part of LTZ's history."

We share a look of understanding and Ty nods.

"I've also asked her to be the CEO of the foundation." Ty directs this comment to Carter.

"Oh, that's perfect!" Carter affirms to me with a nod. "You'll be great at it."

"Depending on the strategy that Sienna and Andrew come up with, would you go on the record about everything?" Ty queries as if I'm not part of this conversation.

"Of course." Carter bobs his head up and down. "Of course."

I march over to Ty and poke him in the side. "Don't talk about me like I'm not here."

"Zoey's such a smart, strong woman who can do anything she wants, and can have anyone she wants." Ty good-naturedly ignores my comment but gestures at me. "She came back to *me*. Now we can finally build our lives together in a way that makes sense for both of us. We have a lot of years to make up for."

Carter chuckles. "Have you told her that?"

"He has and he did." I throw my arms around him. Ty cups my face in his hands and softly kisses me a few times on the lips.

"Get a fuckin' room." Carter chortles before pulling all of us into a group hug.

An hour later, we leave Carter's house, taking the scenic drive along Lake Washington. We zoom along the winding road through brilliant red-and-orange foliage in the Arboretum, the October breeze blows crisp through the rolled-down window where Ty rests his arm. The drive brings back so many memories of when Ty and I were dating, because we drove this route often.

Glancing over at my handsome rockstar, I love seeing the serenity on his face. Like the weight of the world has finally lifted and he and I can finally begin our life together.

Ten minutes later we pull up to my folks' house, which makes me a little nervous. Mainly because I haven't told them I quit my job. It seems a bit comical that I'm more nervous about dropping that bomb rather than the "I'm moving in with my boyfriend" news.

As always, they greet us warmly. We settle at the kitchen table with cups of tea and they look at me expectantly, as if they already know what's what.

I take Ty's hand. "Mom, Dad, as you know Ty and I have been seeing each other again for the past few weeks and—and, um—well, even though it's fast, we're still very much in love with each other and both feel like we've lost too much time together. I'm moving into his house in West Seattle effective immediately."

"I love your daughter, I have from the *minute* I met her." Ty looks them both in the eye. "We just can't be apart anymore."

"Zoey, Ty, you're both adults and can make your own decisions, your father and I were already married when we were your age." My mom sets a tray of cheese and prosciutto on the table.

I can't help but laugh nervously. I don't want to freak Ty out. "Jeez, we're not talking *marriage* yet, Mom."

"I'd marry you tomorrow, but I'm not pushing my luck until I get you moved in." Ty squeezes my hand reassuringly.

I smile at him gratefully but swallow hard when I tackle the next subject. "In, uh, other news...I quit the firm a couple of days ago." I wrinkle my nose. "Ty's offered me a job to run his foundation. I'm trying to wrap my mind around all of it, but I want to make sure it's the right thing for him and for me." I look over at Ty. "We're going to be going public soon and the LTZ fans may not accept me—"

Dad interrupts. "You don't need our permission, sweetheart. As long as you have trust, the two of you will find a way to work together through everything. Even when you're pissed or scared. That's how your mother and I feel. We're a team, above all else."

"We *are* a team." Mom nods. "There will always be opinions from your family, friends, coworkers—but they don't know *you*. Your best bet is to figure everything out as a couple. We're here to support you both. Just remember, it shouldn't matter what anyone thinks, only what you think."

"You're not going to kill me for quitting my job and shacking up with a rockstar?" I laugh, pointing between my folks.

Dad points at Ty, a stoic look on his face. "No, but I might kill *him*."

"Dad!" I swat him.

"What? You're my little girl!" Dad rolls his eyes and fixes them on Ty. "*You*. Promise me you'll cherish her. Do *not* let anyone hurt her. That's my only condition."

"I *promise*." Ty is deadly serious.

Having my parents' support is a huge relief. On the way home it becomes all too real. Ty and I are really and truly happening.

Talk about a 180-degree turn around. All my dreams are coming true, except for one thing. My anonymity will soon be a thing of the past once we get to New York. Ty strokes my knee, and I look over at him.

"Are you okay?" I can barely see his eyes in the dark. "You're quiet and broody which means the hamster wheel is spinning. Please talk to me."

My heart beats a million miles a minute. "I'm afraid of saying this to you, Ty. We're in such a good place —"

"But—" Ty's voice catches.

I put my hand on his thigh. "*Please* don't take what I'm about to say the wrong way."

"Just say it, counselor, rip the Band-Aid off," Ty wheezes, clearly expecting the worst.

"What if I get swallowed up by this—this—lifestyle?" I gesture around the car. "This sounds so stupid considering everything, but shit just got *real*.

Ty's face illuminates in the street light. One eyebrow is raised as he looks at me. "Shit *is* real. You're moving your stuff in this week."

I squeeze his thigh. "You have no idea how excited I am."

"Well then, what are you churning about?" Ty seems genuinely puzzled.

I suck in a breath. "I'm not trying to be a precious Pollyanna, but remember when I first met you it was important to me to have my own identity, not to be known as only a "girlfriend" of a rock star..."

"You *are* the girlfriend of a rock star. You're also a kick-ass lawyer. Soon you'll be my kick-ass CEO." Ty puts his hand over mine on his leg.

"Okay, but—"

"Z. Jump off the cliff with me," Ty orders.

I lean over on his shoulder and kiss his cheek. "Oh, I'm jumping. I just hope we know what we're doing."

Chapter Forty-Two

Two Weeks Later

AFTER RECEIVING BOTH CARTER'S and the Pearson's blessings about our future plans, it's taken nearly two weeks to fully move Zoey's stuff over to my house.

For so many years, I've been touring. My Seattle house is technically my home base, but I haven't spent much time here. Either because I've been on the road or working with other artists in my spare time.

Now that I have Zoey back and we're making a life together, I just want to nest with my girl.

I love every minute of having her with me. Each day, I'm stoked to see her clothes hanging in our expansive walk-in closet, her toothbrush next to mine on the sink, and our bathroom shelves full of all sorts of creams, lotions, and perfumes.

Her fragrant citrus-and-floral smell permeates our bedroom, and I can admit, sometimes I take a moment to breathe it in—just to make sure all of this isn't a dream.

Now that she's settled in, we're planning a lot of home improvement projects. A new office for her. A studio for me. Renovating our master bedroom. Stuff like that.

While I've been finishing up band business, Zoey's applied to a few online programs for a Master of Nonprofit Administration degree. She's convinced it will ensure no one questions her CEO status when we make the announcement.

We haven't settled on the timing for her taking the role. With LTZ's hiatus so close, I think both of us would love to relax and be together without the pressure of outside obligations. As far as the band's concerned, I'm in the home stretch. After the *Phantom Uprising* movie premiere, we only have our holiday show in LA, although it's possible we'll have to attend a few award shows if we're nominated.

Today, however, is the beginning of a huge transition—not just for me and the band, but for Zoey too.

Zane, Connor and I are sitting at the mini conference table on the private jet to NYC trying to pay attention to Jace, who's in the middle of showing us the algorithms and other doo-dads that track our online SEO and whatnot.

My distraction is my sexy, blonde dynamo who's currently curled up in a seat watching a movie while we meet. She's so fucking beautiful, wearing black leggings and an oversize LTZ T-shirt, giant Bose noise-canceling headphones. I love her more than life itself and vow this trip is going to be so much different than our LA fiasco.

This time, I'm well-prepared.

Startled by Jace's fingers snapping in front of my face, I refocus my attention on him. He looks pissed. "Fuck, Ty. I'm doing this for her own good, you could at least fucking pay attention," he snarls.

"Shit. I'm sorry, she's distracting." I shrug, opting for the "ah shucks" method to get me out of a tongue-lashing.

"Clearly." Jace morphs into his all-business mode. "Andrew and Sienna are meeting us at Katherine's office. I think it's best if we start with a couple of posts on the band pages before the paparazzi figures out where we're staying." He fixes me with a pointed glare. "If the media find out, she might get blindsided. We're lucky she hasn't been fully outed yet, considering the Sirius show and what happened in LA."

"I know, dude. I know." I've learned my lesson and want to contribute to our PR strategy, but I'm also still used to showing up and doing what I'm told. Remembering the promise I made to Zoey and her dad, I've got to step up. Taking care of her is my responsibility—and top priority.

Jace is now scrolling through his phone. "Her social media is shit. I mean, Zoey's last post is a picture of that other dude, Ty."

"She doesn't do social media, she doesn't even have Tik-Tok or Twitter." I know we have to anticipate everything. I made Zoey a villainess in some of our best-selling songs, so now the challenge is to make sure our fandom doesn't continue to hate her. Once her identity is revealed, she's fair game. If she leaves up that old post our fans will doubt her commitment to me. She'll be ripped apart as a cheater and our relationship will be toast in the court of public opinion.

Jace puts on his reading glasses and types into his tablet. "Well, she needs to delete that shit or turn it off."

"Okay, I'll talk to her." I look over at Zoey, who's now dozing in the plush, butter-leather seat, pink lips partially open with her hair cascading all around her face. I hate to disturb her, but it's important she has control of her own destiny. That much I've learned over the past couple of months.

"What's the security plan for Zoey?" Zane butts into the conversation. "We're gonna be tied up for hours with rehearsal, soundcheck, and press."

"Sergey and one of his staff will be with us the whole time. If we're apart, she'll have someone with her too." I look over at Zoey. "Not that I'm planning on leaving her alone. I'm keeping her close to ease her into this, guys, she doesn't know how crazy it can get."

Jace huffs out a breath, agitated. "I just got an email from Andrew with their proposed strategy. I'll reserve judgment until the meeting, but I'm over both him and Sienna. We need to be prepared to take over."

As usual, Jace is twenty steps ahead of me. Not for the first time since I became famous, I feel annoyed at the bull-shit. I'm also annoyed on Zoey's behalf that she's walking into *my* bullshit.

Longing for the perfect and happy bubble of our new daily routine, I sit on the arm of Zoey's seat and brush the hair out of her face. Her sleepy eyes open and her radiant smile lights up her face.

She leans into my hand. "Hi! So, did I tell you I'm on a private jet with my rock star boyfriend?"

"You like it?" I kiss her temple and then her lips.

She gestures around. "Off the chain."

"I hate to do this, but it's time to go over the plan for the weekend." I gather her into my arms for a minute to breathe her orangey body wash and flowery shampoo. "I don't want to make any decisions without your input."

"Good." Zoey unfurls herself from her chair and we walk arm in arm to sit with Jace. Zoey's cheerful considering the circumstances. "I really appreciate you helping me out, Jace. What do I need to know?"

"Zoey, I know you haven't personally been through the media ringer yet." He regards her carefully. "Rather than waiting for the media and fans to see pictures of you and Ty and do their own sleuthing, we want to get on top of things. Andrew and Sienna from our marketing team want to meet with us when we land."

Zoey deflates a little. "Okay. I'll get mentally prepared."

"Well, you need to realize that nothing we do will prevent the trolls from fucking with you." Jace holds her gaze. "It's a lot to handle at first. When people start to recognize you, it's weird."

"I'll be with you every step of the way." I grab her hand. "I want the world to know about us, but only on our terms."

"No, I get it. I'm going to be recognized now." Zoey gestures at herself. "What's the angle?"

Jace explains—thoroughly and in great detail—what he wants Zoey do with her social media, then starts in on his view of the PR plan. She's completely shell-shocked, so I keep my arm around her for comfort.

I get that Jace wants to prepare her for the reality—"Z" is already known worldwide and now the fans will have a face to match up to the name, but he seems unusually on edge. I'm not used to my friend, who's usually the calm voice of reason, getting so worked up.

Though I'm trying to remain calm, my stomach hurts with the stress of the unknown. If we go through with this, Zoey's life is going to change. Me and the guys have had years to get used to it, but being thrust into fame overnight is bound to be an even bigger mind-fuck.

I wonder if putting Zoey through all of this is worth it. *Will she think I'm worth it?*

Zoey reaches for her oversized tote. "So, I'm going to change and put on some makeup. If my photo's going to be everywhere, I want to have a fighting chance avoiding being called fat and ugly."

"Babe, you're the most beautiful woman in the world. And the sweetest. I wish I could protect you from the assholes who feel the need to hide behind a computer and trash people." Before she goes into the bathroom, I grab her and kiss her to a chorus of "woo hoos" from the peanut gallery.

"We'll protect you, Zoey," Zane calls after her as she swooshes away.

Zoey blows a kiss at him. "Thanks, Zane!"

"Well, are you ready for our bubble to burst?" I exaggerate a pout, pushing my lip out at her. "I promise, I won't let anything hurt you, Z."

Zoey smiles at me and reaches up to stroke the stubble on my face. "I *trust* you."

My heart clenches with love. She's so perfect and I'm...not. I can't allow anything from my past to ever touch her.

Zoey teasingly thunks Connor with her palm as she passes him. The big ginger snarls at her good-naturedly, but she leans down and kisses him on the forehead as she sashays by. God, I love her sass, she's really getting her mojo back. We both are.

"Wipe that cheesy fucking grin off your face, Rainier." Jace socks me in the arm, his green eyes pierce mine. "Can you attempt to play it cool for once? My God, you wear your heart on your sleeve."

"How can I help it? I love her." I pull my hair back into a knot and sit in Zoey's seat to check the flight path, noting we're touching down in thirty minutes. "I'm finally getting my happily ever after."

Ten minutes later, Zoey emerges from the bathroom as an absolute Instagram-worthy goddess wearing a simple black tube dress, fuzzy gray sweater with a faux-fur collar, black, knee-high boots and half a dozen silver chains. Her hair is tousled like she's just been properly fucked and she's put on sexy smoky black eyeliner and bright red lips. Simple, but stunning. All the guys stare at her open-mouthed.

"What?" She twirls around. "I have access to my own social media expert; don't you boys underestimate me."

"Fucking right." Zane laughs at Jace when he blushes.

"Get over here right now, butterfly, before I have to protect you from all of these asshats." I reach for her hand, which she grabs and promptly sits on my lap. Where she belongs.

My band brothers make various gagging and choking noises, which I ignore because I'm lost in Zoey.

Life is going to change forever when we land, so for now I'm nuzzling and kissing her and I don't care who sees us.

She seems to have thought this through, and while I'm grateful to Jace, I'm pretty sure Zoey could outsmart us all.

Chapter Forty-Three

Half-hour Later

TODAY IS OFFICIALLY MY induction into the full-blown LTZ rockstar machine, something I've dreaded since Ty and I have been back together.

Although, flying in a private jet isn't so bad. From the special airport to the gorgeous, opulent interior of the plane, I've never experienced anything so decadent. All the guys take it in stride, so I tried to act cool and fit in.

Until Jace explained everything, I hadn't realized how much planning went into their travel logistics to ensure the band's security and privacy. The digital itinerary even has two-finger authentication passwords to protect everyone's location, schedule, and even their email and phone. Now that I'm back with Ty, I'm also included in all this madness.

I was prepared because a few days ago, Alex and I hung out so she could give me a heads-up on how all of it worked.

Alex warned me that, no matter how much preparation we do, some LTZ fangirls will annihilate me. She showed me some of the brutal things people said about Ronni Miller. Awful, awful stuff, and Ronni is a very popular and well-liked actress. Trolls will be trolls, I guess. I'm mentally prepared for the slut-shaming and the "she's too ugly for him" comments that are bound to fill up my social media accounts.

The best advice Alex gave me was more personal, though. She feels while it's important for me to listen to Jace and the publicists about PR strategy, I can't allow anyone to manipulate me. In her opinion, I have my own brand as a lawyer and professional woman who's not only Ty's significant other but the executive who will head Ty's foundation.

On the girlie fun side of things, my BFF helped me pack the right clothes and accessories to be on the arm of one of the most photographed men in the world. We spent an entire afternoon putting together outfits and makeup looks, and admittedly she helped me a lot.

I feel somewhat ready for prime time.

When we disembark the plane, two black cars are waiting. Zane and Connor take the first one to the hotel. I ride with Jace, Ty and Sergey to LTZ's midtown management offices for the publicity meeting with Katherine Sauer, LTZ's manager, Andrew and Sienna.

It's funny. For as confident as I felt moments ago, my nerves start to frazzle as we wait in Katherine's office overlooking the hustle and bustle of Times Square. Ty and I are sitting on a gray, tweed couch, his arm is protectively curled around my shoulder.

Jace paces in front of the window, occasionally tapping into his phone.

Moments later, Andrew and Sienna burst through the floor-to-ceiling glass door, chatting animatedly. Andrew is slight with thinning brown hair. He wears a skinny, gray-plaid suit with pants that are pegged at the ankles, and Louboutin loafers without socks.

I recognize Sienna from the Space Needle show. She's as artificial as I remember, supermodel skinny with flawless skin, her nearly black hair is slicked back in a long, sleek, ponytail. She wears a beautifully tailored caramel jumpsuit with black Mary-Jane Valentino pumps.

"Andrew, this is Zoey. Sienna, you two met in Seattle." Ty keeps his arm around me and makes no effort to stand to greet them.

Sienna's gaze on Ty lasts a hair longer than I like, but I tamp down my feeling of ick and smile. I'm not going to fall into a trap of wanting to kill every woman that ogles Ty in front of me, or I'll be in jail within an hour.

Andrew and Sienna openly look me up and down, assessing. They seem to share a secret eyeball communication, which makes me uncomfortable. Which, I think, is their point.

"You're so *adorable.*" Sienna taps her finger on her lip, condescending as fuck.

I paste a fake smile on my face, wondering how I'll survive this whirlwind of smarm. "Um, *thanks?*"

"Katherine's still stuck in a meeting, but we can start without her." Andrew takes a seat.

Rather than sitting next to me, Sienna sits on the other side of Ty. She familiarly places her tablet on Ty's knee, leans over so her tits brush his arm and thumbs through some screens, showing him something I can't see.

My blood boils when she reaches up to brush a hair out of Ty's face, catching my gaze as she does it. Ty flinches, though, and scoots closer to me to get away from her. He gathers me to him and kisses the side of my head. I place my hand on his thigh possessively.

My hackles are up with this chick, though. I'm not a jealous person, but I trust my gut and it's telling me to pay close attention to her.

"We've decided to immediately get a cover story placement for Zoey, that way we can control the narrative." Sienna is undeterred by Ty's rebuff and my staked claim. She wastes no time trying to bulldoze her agenda into my reality as if I have no say. "Zoey, I'm taking over your social media, so I need your passwords."

"Hold on a second. I need to know more details, S. We've already been photographed in LA. This doesn't need to be a huge thing. My main objective is to make sure our fans know I love Zoey and I'm not going to stand for any hate toward her."

Ty's sentiments are on point, but I'm *shook* by his nickname for Sienna. He calls me Z. He calls her S. If he has a nickname like "ladybug" for her, he and I are going to have a serious conversation. I trust Ty, but every bone in my body knows Sienna is not my friend.

"*Tie*-son," Andrew drawls. "We've already set the wheels in motion. I mean, this is freakin' *Z* in the flesh. We have a real opportunity here for your fans to learn why she dumped you so horrifically."

Ty winces and clutches my hand to his, rubbing my palm with his thumb soothingly. Sienna looks back and forth at us and our clasped hands, her face a smooth mask of hidden agenda.

I *want* to speak up, but I don't know what to say. Don't know if it's my place.

"Uh, *no*. That's not what we're going to do. LTZ will not exploit Zoey for our own gain because she's part of the LTZ family. Understand *that*. She's a person with her own career and her own privacy." Jace holds up his tablet and shows us an admittingly cute picture of me curled up against Ty, which he obviously took on the plane ride. My hands cup Ty's face, his arms are draped around me. We're staring into each other's eyes with cheesy grins.

"Our strategy is to be honest. I'll handle Zoey's socials. We're going to post this picture, let it be, and adjust accordingly depending on what happens." Jace asserts definitively.

"For the record?" I hear myself say out loud, though softly. "There's so much more to our story than the songs on *Z*."

"*Ooh*, how interesting." Sienna rolls her eyes and dismisses me. "Ty. Let's be real. We've done wonders to rehab your image after the Ronni Miller fiasco. Your track record of handling your own PR is shit. For the sake of LTZ, let us do our jobs. We'll make sure you're always the good guy here."

Ty visibly tenses. I've only seen the look in his eye once—the day he ditched me in LA. "That was only after my image was deliberately *trashed*, Sienna. I've been a PR puppet for fucking *years*. I'm done. My fans need to accept that Zoey and I are a couple now."

"You know we can't fully control what your fans think. And don't get so pissy. *You're* the one who wrote the songs about her. Everyone already knows there's a real 'Z.'" Andrew glances over at me and raises his eyebrows. "It's a great opportunity to get your story out there, Zoey."

I don't bother answering. How they talk to Ty—and me—pisses me off. And scares me, frankly,

"Exactly." Sienna nods enthusiastically. "Ty, the empathy you'll get from reigniting a relationship with the girl who broke your heart will be *amazeballs*. With one phone call I can secure any covers we want. *People? US? Vanity Fair?* Full-features. *Ooooh!* Maybe we should pitch a reality show!"

"Listen to me clearly. I won't permit anyone from the LTZ team to do anything that remotely hurts or exploits Zoey." Ty pounds his fist in his hand. His voice is like ice. "Sienna, your PR plan for us is completely out of the question. After Ronni, I made it clear that I wouldn't participate in anything remotely contrived again. *Don't fuck with me.*"

Sienna narrows her eyes and reaches around Ty to touch my arm. The look I give her must be harsh because she immediately removes her hand. "Tyson, we would never do anything to hurt anyone in the LTZ family, how does telling the truth about Zoey hurt her?"

"I don't mind the *truth*." I get up and walk over to the window by Jace, leaving Sienna and Ty sitting side by side. "I'm not active on social media and I don't want to be. I know we can't control what the fans or trolls say, but I don't want to drag it out. Ty and I are together, it's really that simple."

"You *are* kidding, right?" Andrew scoffs.

"She's not. This is not a story to be managed. You two have put Ty through a million spin cycles." Jace looks up from his tablet, clearly furious. "He's partying and fucking someone new every night. Then he's breaking everyone's hearts. Now he's dating a famous actress, but it's all fake. It's an endless cycle of manufactured shit. I let it happen, and I'm pissed because it was wrong to do that to Ty."

"The press we generated made LTZ *famous*." I can practically see steam coming out of Andrew's ears.

"Ty's sexual escapades were not forced. The videos don't *lie*, Jace." Sienna sniffs, shooting me a slight, almost imperceptible, smirk.

I look over at Ty, who doesn't appear to have heard her. He stares out the window deep in thought with a weird look on his face, then looks directly at Sienna. "What did you say about videos?"

"*Dude.*" Jace's voice is sharp. He glares at Ty with his lips pressed tightly together. Ty nods and looks down at his hands.

Something unspoken just passed between them. Something secret.

"The music made LTZ famous," I state unequivocally, looking at Andrew and then Sienna. "Ask anyone."

Sienna turns toward me with the most murderous expression I've ever seen. She narrows her eyes and I know that I'm her enemy. Chills run down my spine. I try to catch Ty's eye, but unfortunately, he's still staring at the floor, unaware of what just transpired.

"Okay, *Zoey.*" Sienna's face morphs into a clownish expression. "Let's do it your way. How about a simple piece on how you met, what happened, and how you reunited? That would be very sweet and would make the stories of the songs even more relatable than they already are." Sienna's ability to slip into such a cooperative mode scares the shit out of me. "We can still do a cool photoshoot, maybe get some quotes from your families—"

Andrew snaps his fingers, "Yesssss, I love this! God, unraveling the Z mystery is a publicist's dream!"

"Ooh!" Sienna points at Andrew. "That's the title of the story."

"I'm *right* here, you can speak to me like a real person." Nothing about any of this feels right. The energy in the room is so *weird*, but I don't know why. The problem is, I don't have any context or experience. I'm woefully out of my element.

"You don't have to do anything you don't want to, Zoey." Jace stops tapping on his tablet. "Neither do you, Ty. When I was in charge, we made our own rules, we did just fine. I don't like the vibe of this room right now."

My body literally sags in relief.

"Jace, with all due respect, PR is not your profession," Sienna snarls. Glares.

Ty's deep voice permeates the room with authority. "So far, no one knows Zoey's name, which means no one can connect her to being Z. Only two things are important to me. One, as far as any public statement goes, Zoey is my one and only true love. Two, I will not fucking stand for anyone to say a word against her or to authorize any negative publicity."

"God, this is infuriating. Do you know how important it is for us to control the narrative?" Sienna stands and puts her arm around me, which I shrug off. She's undeterred. "Zoey. Trust me. If we get on top of it, people will believe what we put out there. We can't risk a trash piece that we don't control, can we?"

"Who in the fuck would do a trash piece on Zoey?" Ty demands.

"As of now, no one." Jace rubs his temples as if he's got a migraine. "Guys, stop bullshitting. You know perfectly well if you publish a big, puffy story on Ty and Zoey, you're opening them up to a world of media scrutiny. That will lead to a swarm of media we can't control. Which will lead to more work for you both—"

Both Sienna and Andrew exchange glances, however briefly.

Bingo.

"Look, guys—this isn't my thing. I don't mean to interfere. I'll do whatever you think is best." Remembering what Alex advised, I direct my comment to Jace and Ty. "Remember, when I take over as CEO of the foundation, as much as it pains me to say this, we have to make sure whatever strategy you decide won't hurt the kids he's trying to help."

"You're the CEO of his foundation?" Sienna's disdain for me is clear when she narrows her eyes at me.

"Yes, I offered Zoey the job, and she accepted." Ty stares Sienna down. "But we're not making that public just yet."

"And we're just learning this now?" Andrew chastises. "*Fuck*, Tyson."

Sienna snaps her fingers. "Well, this cements it, we need press."

"No," Ty bellows. "Sienna, I don't appreciate how you're talking to Zoey. You can stop with the aggressive mean-girl shit right now. If you have a beef with me, that's fine. But she doesn't deserve it. *Back* the fuck off her."

"God, you're such a *caveman.*" Sienna sits back down next to Ty and takes his elbow. "*Babe,* you need to let us do our jobs."

Babe?

"Nah, with all due, we're going to handle this." Jace hovers his finger over his tablet. "Ty and Zoey let me know if this is okay."

Jace shows us the post he's drafted to post with the picture he had taken earlier.

She's finally back in the family. Keep following to learn more. #z #moretothestory #tyloves-zoey #zoeylovesty #LTZfamily #LTZ #ulti-matelovestory @tysonrainier @zanerocksseat-tle @jacedeveraux @connormcloughlinseattle @officialzoeypearson

"Zoey, I deleted your Instagram and created a new one." Jace glances at me. "I'll work with you on it over the weekend."

"I like it," I said. "It's simple."

"I love it." Ty bends down to kiss me. "This feels like us."

Sienna and Andrew peer over Jace's shoulder and give each other more secret-squirrel looks.

Sienna scoffs, "This is a mistake, Jace."

"I'll take the risk. From this point on you guys stick only to the movie coverage. Stay out of Ty and Zoey's story, do you understand?" Jace dismisses them, tossing his dark-blond hair over his shoulder, his green eyes flashing. "Andrew, I'll be working directly with you. Can I get the updated movie press schedule for this weekend please?"

Sienna's mouth hangs open. Andrew is in shock, but he scrolls through his phone and Jace's tablet pings a minute later. "There you go, it's on Google Drive."

They leave and we wait for a few minutes before shuffling out. Sergey accompanies us to the elevator. Ty kisses my head, but doesn't say much.

Jace mutters under his breath, "Useless fucks."

I grab his arm, and his startling green eyes flick to mine. "You saved us in there, Jace. Thank you. I don't really want anything to do with that woman."

He just shrugs. "I can't promise that shit won't go down, but right now I just want to keep them out of your business."

The elevator opens to the lobby and about twenty million flashes go off. Sergey and three other burly security dudes shove them away from the elevator and shield us. It's an absolute mob scene. I can't believe how many people are there to catch a glimpse of Ty and Jace.

"Fuckity fuck fuck fuck." Jace shakes his head.

Ty's face is red with anger. "Someone called the paps."

"Looks like it." Jace fires up his tablet again. "Zoey, stick close. If we get caught in a shitstorm, paste a pleasant grin on your face like nothing bugs you. Don't say a word, no matter what horrible shit they yell at you. Ty won't let you go."

A few seconds later, the elevator door opens onto a stark industrial floor. Our security lead us through a long, sterile hallway into a small waiting area. A few minutes later, our black car squeals up, and Sergey ushers us into the vehicle.

The driver speeds down the loading dock and out into the street. Several more flashes go off when the car emerges, but the windows are blacked out. My heart races as we zoom through the streets of Manhattan to the hotel. I look around wildly, but it doesn't appear that anyone followed us.

I finally relax enough to settle back into Ty's arms, he looks down at me with concern etched into his features.

"I'm fine, babe," I assure him, resting my hand on his knee.

He covers my hand with his. "I know, Z. You're *very* fine." The smile on his gorgeous face doesn't quite reach his eyes, though. He turns and looks out the window, clearly troubled.

"Just be cool, guys. Looks like it's just going to be one of those weekends." Jace doesn't look up from his tablet. Contrasted with Ty's expression, he looks bored. Like someone who has seen it all before.

This entire day is shocking to me.

I never knew about all of this behind-the-scenes crap and now I wish I'd never found out.

All I can do is take a deep breath and prepare myself for the onslaught.

Chapter Forty-Four

Forty-five Mintes Later

I'M MORTIFIED AT HOW the meeting with Sienna and Andrew went. How they treated Zoey was unacceptable, but I knew if I reacted in front of them...

Fuck.

We manage to get to the hotel without detection and Sergey escorted us to our suite without incident. I was hoping for some alone time with Zoey, but Jace is showing her the new Instagram page.

He posted a different photo from the plane. It's a good one. My arms are wrapped around Zoey, my hair hides my face. She looks up at me, her hazel eyes filled with a cross between desire and mischief, as her hands grip my wrists. It's cropped tight, so our heads basically fill the entire screen. The text reads:

"I'm so happy we found each other again. #z #ty #moretothestory #tyloveszoey #zoeylovesty #family #LTZ #ultimatelovestory @tysonrainier @zanerocksseattle @jacedeveraux @connormcloughlinseattle @officialzoeypearson

"That's the only post I want you to have for now." Jace peers at us over his reading glasses. "Don't turn comments on, I'll manage your profile for you. At least for now."

"Fine by me." Zoey shrugs. "It's a cute picture."

Jace raises one eyebrow but doesn't say anything.

"I'm booting you out," I say to Jace and open the door.

"Yeah, yeah. I just texted you the schedule for tomorrow." Jace waves over his head and walks out.

Zoey watches me from her spot on the light-blue, velvet sofa, her expression unreadable. I cross the room to her. It's now well past 10 p.m., the day has been long and tomorrow we have an early start. She reaches her hand out to me as I get closer. I take it, sit down next to her and drape my arm around her shoulder.

"Is this a normal day for you?" She leans against me.

I kiss her head and breathe her in. "Meh. This is a light day."

"What's tomorrow's schedule? I'm not really in the loop. I didn't want to say anything or be a pain in the ass." She reaches up to twirl her finger around a lock of my hair. "It's making the control freak inside me lose my mind."

I pull up Jace's text on my phone and list out my obligations. "Photoshoot, a few hours of press, rehearsal, management meeting, food, shower, change, red carpet, movie premiere, show, appearance at a VIP event, possibly more press."

"Wow, that's a busy day." She looks up at me, a cloud in her eyes. "Today was a lot. I'm feeling super nervous, but I'm going to suck it up."

"Yeah. At first this stuff is hard to get used to." I rub my hand up and down her arm, hoping to soothe her. "Don't worry, I'll handle it with Jace. Most of the day you can just chill here, go shopping or go to the spa. Sergey will be at your disposal until it's time to leave for the premiere."

"I'm so glad Jace took things back over. It didn't seem like the publicists had our best interest in mind. I'm not sure what I did to Sienna, but she clearly has a problem with me." Zoey looks at me. Searches my eyes.

I try to keep my expression neutral, but her observation makes me internally cringe. Something about how Sienna was acting toward Zoey bothers me too. "I wish I'd paid more attention to this stuff. I've always allowed other people to handle my business. It sucks to realize how deep I buried my head in the sand. Look how well that's worked out. I've gotten so much bad press over the years."

Too late now.

"Well, I don't trust them." Zoey watches me. "I'm not going to interfere in your band business, don't worry. LTZ doesn't need a Yoko."

"You're not interfering in band business. It's *our* business. I'll talk to Jace, but it's probably time to find another company to do our PR."

Because I need to keep Sienna away from Zoey.

"Well, I'm not going to lie. It wasn't fun to see you in all those situations back then." Zoey sticks out her tongue and makes a gagging sound. "Deep down, I always knew that guy wasn't really you."

"Look, I appreciate you saying that. It's important for us to both have to acknowledge that it *was* me for a while." I frown. "I know this might be hurtful, but as I've learned in therapy, pretending my past doesn't exist won't help us move on together."

Zoey purses her lips, but doesn't say anything, though I'm pretty sure I know what she's thinking.

"I know, I know. I've been super defensive about my past with you, but let's face it. The press is going to dig all of that up again." I run my hands through my hair. "Wait and see. Those old sex and drug pictures will be thrown in your face, so I've got to suck it up. If possible, I'll take the brunt of whatever's thrown at us to protect you—*us*. I've been dealing with this shit for years so I'm better equipped to handle it and not take it so personally." I want to remove her from the situation, for so many reasons.

Zoey shuts her eyes and sighs as if deep in thought. We sit in silence for a few minutes before she speaks. "How this goes down is important to me, Ty. You shouldn't do this alone, I'll be by your side no matter what."

"I know, baby. Today was a shitshow. Should we table this for now?" I enfold her into my body. "Tomorrow is going to be a long day. We should get some sleep. Welcome to the glamorous world of LTZ."

Zoey pokes me playfully. "This suite and the private jet were pretty fucking spectacular."

"Come here." I caress her face and rest my forehead against hers.

"Am I going to be a problem, Ty?" Zoey strokes the hair at the nape of my neck. "Tell me the truth."

"Never. You're my *solution*." I lightly grip her head in both hands and pull her lips to mine, losing myself in the deliciousness of my tongue sliding against hers. It's time to get lost in each other and forget about the outside world for a while. When I'm making love with Zoey, everything bad in my life falls away.

"I'm exhausted." Zoey stands and holds her hand out to me. We move into the bedroom to get ready for bed. Side by side, in the big en-suite bathroom, we brush our teeth. I dig out a hairband from my shaving kit and hand it to her. She winds her hair in a top knot and rubs cream on her face and neck.

She catches me staring at her in the vanity mirror and flashes me a radiant smile. "What?"

"Ahh, butterfly. All of this is going to be okay." I lean over and kiss her. "I love you so, so much."

"Then show me." Zoey dances out of the room.

After I passionately demonstrate just how much I love her, we snuggle in a cocoon of luxurious hotel linens and fluffy pillows. Soon, she's fast asleep, her arm wound around my waist, her legs tangled together with mine. I feel safe, satiated, and content in our hotel bubble, believing nothing can tear us apart if we stick together.

—※—

It's mid-morning and the four of us just finished a quick band meeting focused on production. Now we're headed to the venue, where our photoshoot is scheduled. All morning, I've been so relieved the paparazzi shots from yesterday were duds. You can't see Zoey, it just looks like Jace and I are annoyed at being ambushed. Which is the truth, so no harm done.

The Instagram post? That's another story. The cat's out of the bag. Everyone knows who Zoey is. The LTZ post has gone viral, we have three million likes and counting. Jace turned off the comments, but since all of our individual accounts were tagged, we're getting an idea of how the LTZ universe is taking the news.

It's the usual mix of supportive fans and assholes. I'm not sure if Zoey knows about it yet so I decide to text her before I get sucked under with the photoshoot and interview chaos.

Me:

You up?

Zoey:

Yeah, just had breakfast

Me:

Nice. Heads up our pic is at 3 million hits

Zoey:

> I know I have almost a million fol-
> lowers holy shit

Me:

> Are you ok?

Zoey:

> Well, I think I'll stay inside today

Ty:

> I thought you were shopping

Zoey:

> Dunno

Me:

> It's up to you, just make sure Sergey
> is with you

Zoey:

> I keep forgetting about him

Me:

> Just enjoy your day, whatever you do.
> I'll be back as soon as I can

Zoey:

> Sounds good are you super busy

Me:

> Yeah have photoshoot now

Zoey:

> The camera loves you, so do I

God, she makes my day better just by being there.

The car pulls into the service entrance and since none of us have the patience for hair and makeup, we head straight to the studio. Jace claps his hand on my shoulder. I stop because he clearly wants to hold me back from Connor and Zane for a minute.

He's wearing shades, so I can't see his eyes but I feel the judgment emanating from every pore in his body. "Dude, level with me. Did you have something going with Sienna?"

"Fuck no." I scowl.

He scrolls through his tablet and hands it to me. "Ty, I mean it. You need to let me know if something ever happened." Jace gestures to a picture of me and Sienna on her Instagram that's a few years old. I'm clearly wasted. Her arm is slung over my shoulder and I'm licking her face.

So much ick.

"I don't remember seeing this." I hang my head. My skin crawls, and I feel like I'm about to be sick. Seeing evidence of myself drunk and stupid is traumatic.

"So, it's *possible* you fucked her at some point?" Jace glowers at me.

I don't answer and I don't look at him.

I can't.

"Ty, look, I'm not judging. We've all fucked around, but I'm trying to get on top of something that I have no idea how to fix." Jace sighs heavily. "If Sienna and Andrew go rogue, she's going to leak this. If that happens, what are you going to say to Zoey?"

My blood turns to ice. Fear seizes my heart. "Something happened once. I don't remember anything. All I know is I woke up with her naked in my hotel room. There were condom wrappers on the floor, so... It was the last day I ever drank. Or did drugs. There were too many nights like that, and I knew I had to get my shit together for good."

"Jesus. Fuck. Do you think there are more pics?" Jace squints and pinches the bridge of his nose. "Dude, I swear to you I have my own shit going on, and I'm really at the end of my rope."

"It's not your problem, my brother." I slump down to sit on a planter outside the studio door. I'm not sure if my legs will hold me up.

"Oh, I know you *think* it's not my problem." Jace closes his eyes, looking like the weight of the world rests on his shoulders. "I swear to *fuck* I'm so ready for our break from all of this."

I know the feeling. "Dude, it was so long ago. She swore she'd never say a word..." I stop to scrub my hand down my face. "Sienna set me up with most of those women—"

"Well it explains her weird reaction to Zoey," Jace interrupts.

"I need to tell her," I whisper, almost to myself. "Tonight after the show."

Jace looks at me with what seems to be absolute disdain. Then his expression softens and he sits next to me. Pats my shoulder.

"My dude, I've thought for years that I let you down when we hired those two." Jace shakes his head. "I'd tell you to confront her, but I'm truly afraid that her vindictiveness will ensure Zoey shows up on TMZ."

"I don't think she has feelings for me. I've never gotten that vibe from her. I mean, we haven't spoken about that night since the morning after." I feel like such a fuck-up. "But, I'm not the best at reading these things. As we're all aware."

"Look, we're late for the interview so let's get in there. Remember, you're going to get asked a lot about Zoey today, just be mentally prepared." Jace looks me in the eyes, like I'm a lost cause. The fact that he's lost faith in me stings. Makes me angry.

He's right, though. Secrets have a way of coming out. "Do you seriously think I'd risk anything with Zoey? I'd *never* deliberately hurt her, Jace. *Never*." I stand and move toward the door. "Let's get this shit over with."

The rest of the day I'm on autopilot, going through the motions. I've been doing this for so long, I nail my part of the interviews. Whenever anyone asked me about Zoey—and everyone does—I stick to a basic script like a pro:

Yes, Zoey is Z.

I grew up in an abusive, alcoholic home.

Zoey and I fell in love before LTZ was famous.

She broke up with me before our first tour.

I wasn't aware that Carter from Limelight asked her to break up with me so I could have my shot at success.

We lost touch.

I wrote the songs to try to get over her, but all of us at LTZ protected her identity.

Carter brought us together again.

We've both been in love with each other all of these years.

Zoey is my future.

Repeat.

By the time the driver drops me off at the hotel, I need to wind down before the rest of the evening unfolds. The Sienna incident has always been in the back of my mind because it was the catalyst for me turning around my life.

I've been an idiot to think that a calculating woman like Sienna would just forget it and move on. Sienna's behavior toward Zoey is unacceptable, and I brought Zoey into this bullshit without warning her.

It's time to man up and tell her. I'm just so worried that it's not worth the risk. What if she feels as disgusted with me as Jace does?

It'll be worse if she finds out some other way.

It's a no-win situation, and losing Zoey isn't an option.

Chapter Forty-Five

Half-hour Later

AFTER TY HEADED OUT this morning for their LTZ obligations, my plan was to stay offline for the entire day. Of course, curiosity got the better of me. The photo Jace took of me and Ty is everywhere.

As someone who doesn't understand the appeal of social media, I found myself obsessively checking every five minutes to see how many likes our pictures had. By noon, my new Instagram account climbed toa million followers, which made me nervous to leave the room.

Ty's encouragement to go out with Sergey gave me the boost I needed. Yesterday, my encounter with Sienna made me feel a bit, well, basic. He suggested I go shopping in the designer stores on 5th Avenue and left his Amex black card with strict instructions to buy whatever I wanted.

I know he loves me no matter what, but now that I've been outed everyone will be looking at me when we're photographed together. Wearing Alex's hand-me-downs won't cut it. Sergey just escorted me to the hotel after my shopping spree. I'm excited to look through my bounty and figure out what to wear tonight.

I settle on the soft, black-leather Prada miniskirt with a thick, built-in belt. It flares perfectly over my curvy behind. I'm pairing it with a stretchy, black V-neck cashmere sweater and black Valentino Rock stud ankle boots. The clothes are pretty epic, but my favorite purchase is an expensive bottle of Creed perfume called Spring Flowers, which smells so fresh. I want to bathe in it.

Ty should be back soon. We haven't spoken much today, only a few check-in texts. While I wait, I try to resist checking the social media accounts and entertainment gossip sites, but fail. I'm relieved to see that coverage hasn't been too bad. I'd even go so far as to say it's mostly positive.

I'm relieved.

Glancing at my phone, I realize it's time to shower and get ready. Zoning out under the spray, I picture Ty and me walking hand in hand at the premiere and smiling as the cameras flash. I feel so happy about how things are going. I've quit my big law job, moved in with the love of my life, we're renovating his house...

Lost in my daydream, I'm startled when Ty raps on the shower door.

"Butterfly? How's my gorgeous naked girl?" Ty's piercing blue eyes peer at me, his hair is tucked under the black skull cap he uses to hide his identity. He smiles at me but looks tired. Stressed.

"Thinking about the sexiest man I know." I hold my hand out to him. "Wanna join me?"

"God don't tempt me. I'm headed to Zane's suite for one more interview but thought I'd check on you." He leans against the wall. "Do you want to come with me to soundcheck? If you want to chill, I'll be back to change after so either way is fine with me."

"I'd rather hang out with you guys." I've missed him all day. I hope I won't annoy the guys by tagging along.

Ty's smile spreads across his face, the tension erased. He holds out a towel to me. "I was hoping you'd come with us."

Stepping out of the shower into his waiting towel, I squeal when Ty kisses me and cops a feel of my boobs. I shoo him away good-naturedly and he leaves to finish up his interview while I get ready.

Using a YouTube tutorial, I fluff and tease out my hair a bit and do my makeup with a neutral eye, black liner, and red lips. After spritzing on my new perfume, I'm waiting on the couch in the living area when Ty returns.

"Wow, babe. You're so beautiful!" He kneels down and examines my booted foot. "These are fucking rad!"

I hand Ty his Amex. "Thank you for my *Pretty Woman* moment."

"Well, you outdid yourself." Ty kisses me and gestures to the door. "Mmm. You smell fantastic. I want to eat you up but that'll have to wait 'cause we gotta go."

A few minutes later, we're ushered us through the staff elevator into two Escalades. Jace, Ty, and I ride in one with Sergey. Connor and Zane ride together with their own bodyguards. None of us speak on the way, everyone is lost in their screens for the twenty-minute ride to the venue. I'm stunned to find out I now have over two million followers and my DMs are filled with brands who want to "work" with me.

The cars pull into the loading area where several golf carts wait for us. Sergey escorts Ty and me to Ty's dressing room where a very chatty production assistant hands me an all-access pass. Once inside, Ty peruses the catering setup and makes himself a cup of tea. He glances at me to see if I want one. I shake my head and take a seat on a retro green pleather couch.

"I missed you today, did you have fun?" Ty sits next to me, tracing my thigh under my miniskirt with his index finger. He's been distant and distracted, but I've also never been with him before a show of this magnitude, so I try not to read too much into it.

"It was fun." I watch his finger move higher. "I'm not used to spending that kind of money on clothes."

Ty leans back on the couch and slips his arm around me. "I love spoiling you."

"Oh yeah?" I burrow into him.

"Yeah." Ty traces my lips with his finger. I tilt up, pressing my mouth to his for a luscious kiss.

"I'm a little nervous, Ty." I reach up and hook his index finger in mine. "I've never been backstage at a show like this."

"Sergey will be with you the whole time." He squeezes my finger. "How are you holding up? The press seems to be okay so far."

I take his hand in both of mine and massage it. Study his blunt-tipped nails and the calluses on the tips of his playing fingers. It occurs to me that everything about Ty is beautiful. Even his hands and fingers. I start to fantasize about his hands all over my body later and forget to answer.

Ty's baritone snaps me out of my thoughts. "Zoey?"

"Sorry, I was just thinking that maybe we don't need to be so worried about everything." I stroke his cheek.

A shadow passes over Ty's face as he considers what I said. "Let's hope not."

Confidently, I press my lips to his, and he returns my kiss, opening his mouth and our tongues dance a bit. Pulling away, he nuzzles my face, temples, eyes, and lips and gets up. "I'd rather be kissing you, but I should probably do soundcheck without a boner."

"Ha Ha. Can I watch?" Feeling emboldened, I deliberately flash my thigh-high stockings when I stand.

Ty's eyes nearly pop out of his head. "You are an evil, evil vixen."

"Just giving you something to think about." I do a little twirl.

"Mean. Really mean. Of course, you can watch, your pass lets you go anywhere you want, babe." He points to my All-Access laminate.

Arm in arm we walk out to the stage, where the rest of LTZ is already in the middle of soundcheck. Drums. Guitar. Bass. Ty struts out to the front and grabs his mic.

"Check. Check. Check." Ty's deep voice booms into the empty room.

Jace's cymbals chime in and he taps out the opening beat to *Down*, looking over at me and nodding slightly. I brace myself. Tonight might be trial by fire, I guess. Ty flicks his eyes to me and I give him a thumbs-up so he knows I'm okay with them playing the song that used to make me cry.

Not anymore. It's a revelation.

Ty's voice weaves, aches and articulates as he gets into it. When the first chorus approaches, Ty clutches the mic with both hands, his head thrown back, hair flying out behind him. The lights of the stage illuminate him like the rock god he is.

His mouth opens wide and he belts out the chorus with as much passion as I've ever seen, punctuating each lyric angrily. Belting the chorus in perfect pitch. My body breaks out in goosebumps.

I haven't seen him perform with the full band since I was eighteen. I've never seen him on this big of a stage, and now that I'm seeing them with my own eyes, it's clear why LTZ is the most popular band in the world. Not only is he an exquisite specimen of the male species, but his power, passion, and authenticity are unmatched.

The band immediately launches into the next song. My eyes are fixed only on my man. I'm mesmerized by Ty as he gets lost in his stage persona.

After the third song, Zane takes off his guitar and sets it down. Jace and Connor also stop playing. Ty doesn't move. He stands at the front of the stage, looking out into the nonexistent crowd, panting from the exertion.

"Are we good?" Buck, their soundman calls from the mixing board.

Zane holds up both thumbs. Ty remains fixed at the front of the stage. Crossing over to him, Zane socks him in the arm, causing Ty to snap out of his trance. Laughing, Zane claps him on the shoulder and shoves him in my direction. Jace whispers something as he passes by. Ty gives him a pointed look before crossing the stage, taking my hand, and leading me toward the dressing room.

Suddenly, Ty stops in his tracks and looks at me pensively. "Z, I'm sorry we did *Down*, I went into autopilot when Jace started the song."

"Don't be, it was fine." I shrug.

He looks shocked. "But—"

"That song isn't about me anymore, is it?" I smile up at him.

Relief spreads over Ty's features, and his face lights up. "No, it's not. I didn't want to upset you, but man that song is cathartic to perform."

"It really didn't bother me," I assure him. "I just loved watching you on stage."

Ty and I follow Sergey, who guides us to the car. "Oh yeah? Wait until the show. I'll be singing to you the whole time."

In the backseat, I nestle under his arm while Ty traces the elastic on my stockings with his finger. The minute we're inside our room, Ty pins me against the wall and envelopes my body, devouring my lips. I shudder when he reaches under my miniskirt to caress my ass.

"I'm telling you, these thigh-high stockings. I can't fucking resist you," Ty growls. Nibbling my earlobe, he moves my panties to the side and slips two fingers inside me.

"Holy shit!" I suck in a breath and grip the back of his head.

"I love everything about you, butterfly. *Everything.* Nothing else matters but you." Ty urgently kisses along my neck, latching on to the space behind my ear that drives me mad. "All I've thought about for the past hour is how much I want to taste you."

"Oh, yes. Babe, *please*," I breathe, writhing against his pumping fingers. I want him. *Now.* I need a connection before we face the public.

Ty crouches in front of me, leveraging the wall to keep me upright while his unoccupied hand hitches my left knee over his shoulder. I hold my skirt up around my waist so I can see what he's doing and moan when he takes a long lick along my wet slit.

Alternating between sucking on my clit and lapping at my pussy, his lips make me crazy as his fingers stroke inside me, curling against my inner walls. There's nothing in the world more arousing than looking into Ty's eyes when he goes down, or in this case up, on me.

It doesn't take long for my entire body to shudder and explode against his mouth. Satisfied, Ty removes his fingers and adjusts my panties while I breathe through my recovery.

He stands and fixes my skirt then kisses me. "That should take the edge off. Now I need to get showered or I'm going to be late."

Following him into the bathroom, I watch Ty strip and step into the shower, sporting an impressive woody. I want to return the favor and start to pull off my shirt to join him.

"Don't even think about it. We don't have time." Ty holds his hand up with his palm toward me. "We'll slip out early after the show and then I'm going to fuck you all night long."

"Fine," I sass, though his promise makes me clench my thighs together.

While Ty finishes showering and getting dressed, I text Alex to give her an update on the last couple of days. She's been reading the posts and confirms my opinion that they're skewing positive.

I sigh with relief. Then I begin to actually get excited. Tonight's going to be such a cool experience! So many firsts. My first movie premiere. My first time seeing LTZ play live in a big venue. First time in public as Ty's significant other.

First time fucking my rockstar after a show.

Ty emerges from the bathroom, looking scrumptious in black jeans, a white T-shirt, and black lace-up boots. His damp hair flows around his clean-shaven, chiseled jaw.

God, I love this man.

Life can't be any better. I've been worried for nothing.

Chapter Forty-Six

Half-hour Later

SERGEY ESCORTS US TO the theater where Ty is meeting his band brothers to walk the red carpet. When we pull around the back to the designated meeting place, Connor, Jace and Zane are huddling with an older woman I can only assume is Katherine, their manager.

She beams when we walk toward the group arm in arm, and she introduces herself and hands me a different VIP All-Access laminate pass, this one for the Phantom Uprising screening.

"Zoey, are you going to walk the red carpet with Ty or come inside with me and meet him after?" Katherine takes my elbow.

"What would you like me to do? "I glance up at Ty.

Ty encircles me tightly in his arms. "It's up to you. You look amazing, but I'd love to have you to myself tonight. Maybe we can postpone your red-carpet debut until the Christmas show. We can arrange for hair, makeup and a custom designer dress."

I mean, *c'mon*. For an introvert like me is there a choice?

"Christmas show, all the way. This is already a lot to get used to." I smooch him and wish him good luck. Then he's on his way with the rest of LTZ.

Sergey stays behind with me and Katherine and sticks close as we make our way inside where we're shown to the cordoned-off VIP area. Once seated, I promptly feel a little awkward because I hadn't met Katherine until minutes ago and now we're stuck together for a while.

"Zoey, I've heard so many wonderful things about you from all the guys and Carter, I'm happy that you and Ty have found your way back to each other again." Katherine's slight, bony hand lightly caresses my shoulder.

It settles me. She has a soothing, motherly way about her. "Thank you, Katherine. I'm hoping the LTZ fans feel the same way."

She reassures me. "So far so good. There seems to be a genuine interest in both of you, Ty was interviewed about it all day today."

Katherine's phone keeps buzzing, so our small talk is thankfully cut short. While waiting, I take a picture of the stage and text it to Alex and read some more of the Instagram posts. A few pretty heinous comments have now appeared, which makes me feel icky, so I put the phone away.

I distract myself by reading one of my non-profit class books on my Kindle app. Soon, the hum of the crowd gets louder and louder when the stars and red-carpet walkers pour into the theater for the screening.

At the sound of Ty's distinctive voice, I turn and can't help but ogle him as he graciously works the crowd, smiling, shaking hands, giving hugs to the movie producers and, holy hell, the stars of the movie, Idris Elba, Chris Pine, and Gal Gadot.

Overwhelmed, I quickly turn back around so I don't gawk like an idiot. Feeling his nimble fingers stroke my nape a couple of minutes later, I look up into Ty's gorgeous, smiling face. He holds his hand out and draws me to my feet, tucking me into his side. Proudly, he introduces me as his girlfriend to all the stars and a bunch of the movie executives, with his arm draped protectively around my shoulders.

Every one of them act like *I'm* the celebrity when they find out I'm Z.

My mind is blown.

I'm giddy from the friendly interactions with the famous actors when the lights dim. Ty wraps an arm around my shoulders and doesn't let me go throughout the very male-centric action film. It's not really my jam, but when *Strike*, the featured LTZ song is played during the final scene, I'm so proud of Ty. It's a big deal to have a song featured in a release this big.

He smiles bashfully and kisses my forehead, squeezing me tighter to his side as if he can't believe I'm here with him tonight. I stroke his bracelet, still finding it hard to fathom that Ty isas famous as all the people who are on the screen.

Before the lights turn on, Sergey takes us out the side exit through the winding hallway leading to the venue. With just over half an hour before the concert, we stop by the dressing room so Ty can do his pre-show ritual. During his warm-ups, goosebumps prickle up and down my body every time he hits the high, wailing notes that are his trademark.

When he's satisfied that his vocal cords are ready, Ty sits cross-legged on the couch, closes his eyes, and starts visualizations. I try to make myself as inconspicuous as possible. Meticulous in his preparation, Ty mouths the words and runs through the set in his mind, moving his arms and legs slightly as he plans his stage attack.

Suddenly, Ty springs from his chair and pumps himself up like an athlete by shadow boxing, running in place, and spinning one way and then the other. He jumps up and down about twenty times, shakes out his hair, and looks over at me sheepishly.

"Ummm, sorry. I kind of geek out when I get ready to go onstage." Ty throws me a lopsided grin.

I hold out a cup of tea, though I'm standing across the room leaning against the wall. "Well, geek-boy, I think you're fucking *hot*."

"Oh yeah?" Ty stalks over, taking my face in his hands to angle my head for a soft kiss before cocooning me against his chest, his head on top of mine.

The door bangs open and Zane bursts into the room. "Jesus, my brother! We're late, we gotta *go*."

"Yeah, well I'm here, warmed up and ready. Where were you?" Ty looks up nonchalantly, taking a sip of tea.

"Let's just say I got stuck in the crowd." Zane waggles his eyebrows and takes a bite of a strawberry from the fruit tray.

Ty rolls his eyes, knowing Zane got tied up talking to the movie stars. "Where are Jace and Connor?"

"They went right up to the stage. So, let's do this." Zane dashes into the bathroom where we can hear him taking care of business.

Ty laughs and crosses his arms across his chest, nonplussed.

"Come up with us, Z." Zane emerges, reaches in his back pocket and puts another All-Access Band laminate around my neck. "We're going out on stage right; all of the execs and actors are on stage left. We can set you up by my guitar tech, so you can watch the show with our crew."

I'm touched he noticed I'd left my pass at the hotel. If I'm not with Ty, security won't let me hang out with the LTZ entourage. Clearly, I'm out of my element navigating these professional concert productions.

I follow Zane, clutching tightly to Ty's hand as we make our way past the crew to the stage where Jace and Connor are waiting. From the sidelines, looking out at the sea of ten-thousand fans at this private concert, it still actually feels like an intimate setting for LTZ who regularly play festivals with hundreds of thousands of concertgoers.

The entire theater is chanting "L-T-Z." I see dozens of posters professing their love for the band. Everything is exciting. Incredible.

"Spike, this is Ty's girlfriend Zoey. She's going to hang by you, it's her first show in a long time so be cool," Zane introduces me to his tech.

"Nice to meet you, gorgeous." Spike, who's at least three-hundred-pounds, rocks a hipster beard, a plaid shirt, overalls, and yellow crocs. He pulls me in for a bear hug.

"Hey!" Ty jokingly lunges at the big lug.

"I'm stealing her." Spike slaps Ty's arm. "Get your ass on the stage."

The energy in the venue is so electric, I can't help but get caught up in the excitement. I'm so pumped to see my sexy rock god perform. After the guys do a quick pre-show huddle, Jace breakaway and takes his place behind his kit. Connor and Zane follow and the crowd loses their minds. Ty keeps his arm around my shoulders and watches with me from the shadows as Jace starts tapping out the beat to *Rise*.

My heart swells, remembering the time when they were creating the song in Carter's practice space right after Ty saw my boobs for the first time.

Connor picks up the bassline and Zane's talented fingers work through the complicated intro. Watching the crowd sway, scream, and chant in unison is so incredibly powerful, all love and positive energy for my guy and his band brothers. They deserve the accolades because they're all such good men. Using a secret cue, Zane nods at Ty to signal it's time to take the stage.

Before he makes a move, Ty bends down to kiss the side of my face and whispers, "I love you more than anything. You're my favorite person."

I feel like the luckiest girl in the world when Ty runs out to the front of the stage. The lights sweep all around the venue and crisscross in a brilliant pattern of blue, green, and purple, hitting each of the guys but camouflaging Ty. When he reaches his mike, the entire theater goes black and a single blue spotlight hits the exact spot Ty is standing on as he holds out the opening note for longer than was humanly possible.

Utter silence descends on the venue for approximately one second, which is followed by unabashed crowd ecstasy when the lights dance in a pattern that matches the beat.

It's incredibly easy to get lost in the music. Jace's relentless rhythm is punctuated by pulsing moonbeam-like lights illuminating his entire body. Zane's extraordinary virtuoso finger work is beyond what I remember, his boyish smile is joyful as he works the frets. The boom and thump of the bass is Connor's way of keeping the heart of the band beating, his intimidating stare unforgiving.

But nothing can touch Ty, astonishing in his domination as an entertainer. Whether it's witty banter during a song, whirling dervish moves through hard-driving beats, subtle flirting with the crowd, his sex-on-wheels command of the audience, or the flat-out mastery of his vocals, he's where he belongs. On stage. He's absolute magic.

What melts my heart is every few minutes, even for a moment, Ty looks to the sidelines to check on me. Each time

I reward him with an air kiss or wink. I'm so enraptured that I don't notice when someone joins me.

"Good show." Sienna towers over me in a black-and-white-patterned jumpsuit, five-inch black Louboutin heels and her dark hair slicked back in a tight ponytail.

"Back in the clubs they were amazing, but now—they're unbelievable," I agree, trying to engage and be friendly.

We both look out as Pokey, Ty's guitar tech, hands him his Gibson Montana Hummingbird. He strums, smiles and stares out at the crowd. The spotlight zeros in on his handsome face.

"We've only played this once, and it was a pretty small crowd." Ty looks around the venue then over at me, smiling up from under his sexy mane of hair which has grown unruly. An undecipherable look passes over his face when he sees Sienna standing next to me, but he's a consummate professional and strums the opening chords of *Heart*.

Immediately a sea of phones light up the crowd who are slowly swaying to the beat Jace taps out. Connor plucks a smooth bassline. Zane's haunting guitar layers over the top of Ty's acoustic melody. Ty gives the most emotional performance of the entire night, singing his newest love song about me to the crowd.

This version is so beautiful it brings tears to my eyes.

As the last chords end, the crowd goes absolutely bananas. The cheers don't die down for a few minutes, despite Ty good-naturedly trying to get them to stop.

Turning from the audience, he hands his guitar to Pokey and struts over to where I'm standing and winks at me. I can feel Sienna's gaze boring into me, but I remain focused on my man, giving him a thumbs-up and kissy-face. Ty swaggers back on stage to the drum riser, takes a long swig of water, and whispers something to Jace.

Jace glances over at where me and Sienna are standing as Ty saunters back up to his place at the front of the stage. Now that the crowd has calmed down a bit, he holds his finger to his lips to quiet them. This time the entire venue is silenced within seconds of his request.

"Are you ready for a song about a butterfly?" Ty purrs into his mic.

The crowd loses its collective mind when Zane's fingers strum the flamenco-inspired intro to *Butterfly*, and Ty sings about releasing me and letting me fly away. God, it's such a beautiful song. It's surreal that some of the biggest musical hits over the past few years are about me—*us*.

After the song ends, Ty addresses the audience. "Did you guys see the picture of my real butterfly on our Instagram?"

The crowd roars. Shouts from the audience permeated the venue. "We love you, Ty!!" "Marry me, Ty!!"

"Aww, I'm not on the market, my friends, but I love all of you!" Ty looks over at me and points.

Shrinking into myself, I cover my eyes with my hand, feeling very shy about being the focus of any attention. Sienna turns and stares at me, her contempt not hidden even a little bit. In that moment, I know without any doubt that my gut feeling is right about her. She certainly isn't my fan and does not have my best interest at heart.

Despite my misgivings, I pretend not to notice. After all, I'm not about to let this bitch get the upper hand. I'm certainly not going to let her ruin the show for me.

Thunk. Thunk. Thunk. The initial beats of *Down* begin with Jace's heavy beat of the bass drum and Connor's low bassline intro. Zane's melodic chorus punctuates Ty's low growls of sorrow.

I'm completely sucked in when I notice Sienna standing in front of me. Her cold stare sends shivers along the back of my neck.

Trying to keep my cool, I stare right back, narrow my eyes, and cock my head slightly.

Sienna bends down to my ear and through her glossy red lips whispers just loud enough so I can hear her. "Sucks that they found out about you on TMZ, I knew you'd be a fucking liability to Ty and the band. I'm going to have my work cut out for me to fix it."

Startled, I stare at her, trying like hell to keep my face impassive.

"See for yourself." Sienna hands me her tablet and returns her focus to the stage.

Looking out at my sweet Ty, who's finishing the song with such power and command and then back at the tablet, I don't know what to do. Curiosity gets the best of me and I skim the article, unable to prevent myself from recoiling in horror.

Devastation sets in.

One of the best nights of my life suddenly turns into a nightmare.

Chapter Forty-Seven

A Few Minutes Later

CATHARTIC.

This show is absofuckinglutely cathartic. I feel invincible. Zoey being here with me makes performing so much better. Catching glimpses of her on the side of the stage, smiling and encouraging me, swaying and dancing to the music—*gah*. Incredible.

I can hardly believe this is my new normal. She and I will be together like this forever.

When I bellow the final chords of *Down* and the crowd goes crazy, as expected, I glance over to see Sienna hugging Zoey. Almost like she's comforting her. The hairs on my neck tingle with fear. Something is wrong. My butterfly looks absolutely shell-shocked. Like she's going to faint.

Panic sets in. I've never let anything interfere with my performance yet suddenly my focus is only on my girl.

I quickly address the crowd and signal to Zane to cover for me and run to the side of the stage where Zoey and Sienna are standing.

"What's going on here?" I direct my question at Sienna.

"I'm fine, babe. Finish the show." Zoey gestures for me to go back on stage though she's clearly struggling to keep it together. "This can wait."

I whirl around toward the source of the trouble. "What the fuck, Sienna?"

"Look, Ty." Sienna glances down to examine a long, red nail. "Don't worry, I'll fix it. I'm pulling in all the favors I can. I'll try to get to the bottom of how it happened."

"I'm doing a goddamn show, Sienna," I snarl. "What are you talking about?"

A look of hurt passes over Sienna's eyes. She touches my arm. "Ty, I'm here to do damage control."

"For what?" I look at Zoey.

She regards me with her big hazel eyes and shakes her head, handing the tablet back to Sienna.

"I need to check on the after-party." Sienna grabs her device and saunters off to the exit. "It's nothing we can't fix. Zoey will fill you in after the show."

She gestures to where Jace is subtly waving me over, glaring at all three of us. Zoey motions for me to go back on stage, then slumps against the wall next to Zane's guitars. I reluctantly obey, but it takes every ounce of professionalism I have in me not to stop the show. I'm so freakin' worried but also somewhat relieved.

At least Sienna didn't say anything about our hook up.

When I take my position back at the mike, I glance at Zoey, but she's not paying attention anymore. The wind goes out of my sails, but I manage to finish to thunderous applause before running off stage. Unfortunately, my earlier mood of elation is now replaced with anxiety.

And guilt.

Somewhat oblivious of the drama, Zane and Connor run ahead toward the dressing room whooping it up and pumping fists. Sweat flies everywhere.

Jace falls into step behind me as I approach Zoey. "Z—"

"No." Her face is a stone mask. "We can't talk here."

I reach for her hand, which she ignores, instead directing a question at Jace. "Do you know about the article?"

"No, what article?" He looks genuinely perplexed.

Zoey fights back tears. "It's really bad."

"Fuck." Jace punches his hand.

"Zoey, what is going on?" I reach for her, but she shies away.

She gives me a look that leaves no doubt that she's upset. "Not *now*."

"Zoey, don't make it worse. You're going to have to get used to people saying a bunch of fucked-up lies about Ty, me, the guys, and now you. Unfortunately, it's part of all of this." Jace whispers loud enough so that only we can hear him. "I *can* and *will* handle the press so if you can try not to add to the fucking drama in front of our crew, that would be great."

Zoey and I stare after Jace when he stalks off without another look. Road crew are already busy breaking down the stage and loading out gear all around us, averting their eyes. After my initial few seconds of being stunned at the way Jace talked to Zoey, steam comes out of my ears.

"Hey, you asswipe." I chase after him. "Don't you fucking talk to her that way!"

"It's okay, Ty. He's right, please do not make a scene." Zoey grabs my arm to stop me.

I grumble, "He can't speak to you like that."

"Can we just get to somewhere private. *Please?*" Tears threaten to spill down her pretty cheeks. I need to get my shit together.

I nod. Silently we make our way through all the crew activity down the ramps and pass by a fan staging area. When we're spotted, they cheer and chant my name. They also start shouting Zoey's name. I take her hand and this time she lets me but we don't stop until we reach my dressing room.

Zoey falls apart.

"What happened." I kneel down in front of her, placing my hands on her outer thighs. "Talk to me."

"You should just read it." With tears streaming down her face, Zoey frantically digs out her reader and pulls up the *TMZ* website where her blurry picture is front and center with the headline *Zoey Uncovered: Ty's Crazy Stalker Bitch.*

I read the article, my blood simmers and boils over by the time I'm done.

According to *TMZ*, Zoey was an underage Lolita who seduced me. When I fell in love with her, she had an affair with Carter and dumped me, which led to the release of *Z*. Sources confirm she stalked me for years which sent me further into a downward spiral leading to abusing booze and sex just to cope. Just when I turned my life around and found happiness with Ronni, Zoey managed to worm her way back into my life and into an executive role at my non-profit. The band's hiatus is because I'm under her spell again. She wants me to quit LTZ and marry her but she refuses to sign a prenup.

Clearly, it's ridiculous and almost comical. But Zoey doesn't know that. I remember how bad it felt when the first negative stories about me came out. I get it. All she can focus on right now is the perceived assassination of her character.

I'm a seasoned veteran. I *know* this type of shit always blows over in a day or two.

I'm also jaded. I *know* when a fake story has been fed to a site like *TMZ*. This one was planned. It's a personal attack.

An attack by people within my inner circle. The only people outside of me, Zoey, Carter, her parents, and the band who know about her role in the foundation are Sienna and Andrew. The pictures are old, archived photos of Zoey and I making out at the recording studio. Photos Jace removed from our social years ago, which Andrew and Sienna have access to.

God, this is an infuriating betrayal and nothing about it surprises me, unfortunately. Sienna essentially outlined her plan at Katherine's office. This is textbook clickbait. Unflattering pictures of Zoey? *Check*. Requisite quotes and interviews with people who claimed to know her well? *Check*. Wholly made-up facts? *Check*. Snippets from women I don't know claiming to have slept with me? *Check*.

There's one piece that is wholeheartedly distressing though. My long-lost mother, whom Zoey has never met, seemingly confirms the fictionalized timeline of my early relationship with her. She's quoted as saying Zoey was always a crazy, stalker bitch and she never liked her. Jesus. So much bullshit. I haven't seen her since I left Seattle on tour for the first time.

I guess I shouldn't be surprised. I can't believe it's taken her so long to sell me out.

"Oh, butterfly. What the *fuck*." I collapse down next to her.

She leans against me. "So, it's as bad as I thought."

"No, it's all a crock of shit. I should be fucking used to this by now, but I'm so sorry." I put my arm around her and stroke her hair. "You don't deserve any of this."

Something is really off about the piece, and I need to get to the bottom of it.

Zoey's eyes well with fresh tears. "I think I want to go back to the hotel."

"I'll go with you." I kiss her temple.

She doesn't respond, just tucks up into a ball with her head on my shoulder.

"Let me take a shower, and then we'll get you out of here. We can skip the after-party." I give her a quick kiss. "Will you be okay for five minutes?"

She nods. "Yeah."

After cleaning up, I shakeout my wet hair and pull on jeans, an LTZ T-shirt, and my black Doc Marten boots. Quickly, I stuff my sweaty clothes into my tote and gather my phone and charger.

Remembering my promise to Zoey's dad that I'd take care of her, I'm realigning my priorities.

"Let's go, Z." I hold out my hand.

Zoey reaches up to squeeze it reassuringly. "No, Ty. I'll be okay for an hour or two. It'll give me time to process all of this. Go do the VIP meet-and-greet, I'll just wait here."

"Just don't shut me out," I say softly. "I'll go and get this over with and then we can hole up at the hotel until my team can sort it out—"

"Are you decent?" Sienna's voice rings out as she barges into my dressing room. Andrew, Katherine, and Jace follow close behind.

"Zoey, are you okay?" Katherine weaves around the publicists and crouches next to Zoey. "I know this is upsetting."

"I'm fine." Zoey fixes her deceptively neutral gaze on Sienna over Katherine's shoulder. "I have to wonder how *TMZ* obtained the material to make up such a colorful story."

My girl's so fucking smart. She already gets it.

"Who *knows*." Andrew gestures to the air. "We can't waste any time worrying about things we can't know when we need to do damage control."

"Andrew's right, we need to protect Zoey's image." Sienna smiles sickly sweet at me.

To her credit, Zoey remains deathly calm while our manager, publicists, and Jace argue about how and when to "handle" the situation. She's so calm that it unnerves me a bit. After a while, Katherine sends me and Jace to make a quick appearance at the party.

I don't want her alone with Sienna, but I have a job to complete. Reluctantly, I leave her but make sure I'm back in twenty minutes. When I open the door to my dressing room, Zoey hasn't moved a muscle. She's laser-focused on the conversation still going on between our publicists and manager.

"Guys." I try to get everyone's attention.

No one listens to me.

"Guys!" I clap my hands.

Everyone turns.

Channeling my stage persona, I command the room. "It's late, there's nothing we can do about this tonight. I'm taking Zoey back to the hotel so we can get some rest. Let's all meet there tomorrow morning, say around eight, and we'll go from there."

"That's a great idea." Katherine squeezes Zoey's hand. "We'll get this all cleared up by noon."

After they leave, Sergey sneaks us out of the venue and into the service entry of the hotel. By the time I finally swipe the key to our room, I'm exhausted and starving. When I hang up with room service, I find my beautiful butterfly dozing in the bedroom, curled up against the pillows with her blonde hair fanning out around her.

Sitting on the edge of the bed, I brush a lock of hair away from her face and stroke her cheek lightly with my thumb, careful not to wake her. After I undress, I crawl beside her under the covers and spoon her tightly.

"Hey, is that a banana in your pocket or are you just happy to see me?" Zoey mumbles sleepily.

I grin against her hair at the old joke. "I'm always happy to see you, and there's always a banana in my pocket when I do."

Zoey turns around to face me and grips my jaw, using her thumbs to stroke my stubbly chin. She closes her eyes and softly touches her lips to mine. My tongue darts along the seam of her full lips, tasting her and encouraging her to deepen our kiss. My heart swells with emotion. Being with her is always the only thing that matters.

We're going to be fine.

Reaching down between us, Zoey grips my stiff cock and guides me inside her. Clasping her ass I pull her thigh over my hip and rock into her. She winds one arm around my neck and the other around my waist and our movements become more urgent. Her pussy tightens around my cock sending me right over the edge in a haze of electric sparks down my spine. Zoey follows, gasping through her release.

As we recover, Zoey traces my lips with her shiny, black-tipped finger. "Please tell me that being together like this is what's real."

"Of course, this is real." I kiss her finger.

She blinks up at me. "Why do you think Sienna arranged that article?"

"What do you mean?" The words come out before I can stop them.

Zoey furrows her brow. "Ty, c'mon. I'm not stupid."

Well, now the lead balloon in my belly is real. It's time. *Tell her. Tell her. Tell her.*

I can't get the words out. Not when I've literally just been inside her. I just can't. So, I babble, "Please don't worry about Sienna, she shouldn't have showed you. It made the night shitty for you."

"*Uh-huh.*" Zoey considers me for a minute. "Can I ask you a question? Why is she still working for LTZ?"

I answer too fast. Too defensively. "To take the pressure off of Jace. They've been really effective to get us lots of press. Their work helped propel those songs to where they are today."

"Well, as I said yesterday, I think you sell yourself short, but whatever." Zoey scowls.

"Sienna and Andrew were the ones who concocted the idea of making me a bad boy, to annihilate my reclusive image. It worked." I reach out and stroke her cheek. "Of course, then I'd drink myself into a stupor, and soon there were photos and videos of me with women I could barely remember."

Zoey just watches me pensively.

I continue to babble. "Andrew and Sienna were just doing their jobs. The coverage of my descent into hell sold records, and merchandise, and basically the band."

"Why were you willing to endure all of this?" Zoey is clearly appalled. "I mean, they encouraged you to do things so they could write horrible shit about you."

"Pretty much." I shake my head. "It became who I was, but it wasn't true to who I am as a person. It just didn't feel like me."

"Because it's *not* you." Zoey covers my hand with hers. "It hurt me seeing you like that. Learning you were a willing participant in all of it? It's devastating that you didn't value yourself enough to stand up for yourself. That you'd allow them to manipulate you."

Tell her. Tell her. Tell her.

The words won't come. I'm a coward. I continue my justification ramblings. "I know, I was stupid. It took a while for me to come out of it because of all of my substance abuse, but one morning I stopped. I've never looked back."

Zoey sighs but remains silent, allowing me to finish my story.

"I'm the one who allowed it. I knew I needed help." I try to paint a nicer picture than the one that actually is true. "My therapist specializes in counseling musicians. I was able to come to grips with a lot about my childhood, my insecurities, and my tendency to let things happen to me rather than me having a say in my life. Please don't worry about this article. Jace cleaned up my shit. He'll clean this up too."

Yeah, I realize the hypocrisy as I speak the words.

Zoey isn't fooled. "But you let them do it all again when they set you up with Ronni."

Tell her. Tell her. Tell her.

My heart pounds so loudly I swear I can hear it like Jace's snare drum.

The door buzzes, room service has arrived. Relieved at the reprieve, I get up to answer and tip the guy a hundred dollars just he'll go away. I return to the bedroom with a tray of food. Zoey join me on the edge of the bed. I set the chicken tenders, club sandwich, French fries, cheese sticks, and tomato salad on the bench.

We delve in and devour the food in silence.

After we finish, I shove the tray into the hallway and click on the "do not disturb" light and return to Zoey. "Let's get some sleep. Tomorrow, I'm getting to the bottom of this bullshit, babe. I will protect you. I will protect us."

"Okay. I trust you." She crawls into bed. "For the record, the article really sucks. In the meantime, I'll try not to let some shit-stirring publicist or any article define me."

"That's good." I slip under the covers next to her.

"After tomorrow, that bitch better be fucking fired though," Zoey mumbles as she drifts back to sleep.

God, I love my feisty girl so much.

I still don't deserve her. Not when I keep secrets from her. One of which is likely the root of all of this bullshit.

Still, I sidestepped a landmine tonight. The right thing to do is to tell Zoey what happened with Sienna. I just don't know how to do it. The words won't come out. Zoey is absolutely right to be skeptical of Sienna's motives.

LTZ's publicist is doing what we've paid her hundreds of thousands of dollars to do. Create controversy just to solve it.

Will she be the one who tells Zoey what happened that night?

Something tells me if I don't confess by morning, I'm going to face an entire field full of landmines that will be hard to come back from.

If I lose Zoey over this...

I can't even fathom.

Chapter Forty-Eight

The Next Morning

MY ANXIETY ABOUT THE entire mess waned when Ty cuddled me and promised to fix things last night.

Not so much in the early morning light, waiting for yet another discussion about the goddamn media. With goddamn Sienna.

So much about her bothers me.

From outward appearances, I probably look calm. Freshly showered, dressed in leggings and a plain white T-shirt, I'm sitting on the couch, watching the bustling city below me.

It's been a few hours since I first read the *TMZ* article. The shock and panic of being labelled a "crazy, stalker bitch" has fully set in. This weird fictional account of me is out there for everyone to read and it's multiplied.

I'm the biggest news story in the world. The article has more hits than the sweet photos Jace posted, which feels like a year ago.

Hell, if I didn't know myself, after reading it I'd also think I was a crazy, evil, ugly, fat, skanky, lying, opportunistic slut who'd toyed with Ty's emotions for years. Such a nice way to describe a twenty-six-year-old woman who never got into any trouble whatsoever. Gotta love the misogyny.

It makes me want to crawl out from under my skin and disappear. I can't even cry. I can barely breathe. All I'm capable of is staring out the window while my mind whirls. Contemplate ways I could move to somewhere exotic where nobody knows me.

Zanzibar, maybe.

Which makes me inappropriately laugh out loud because, well, Tenacious D. Thank God for my dad's musical library.

Katherine, Sienna, and Andrew are coming to some understanding about strategy. Katherine and Jace are off to his suite to call the legal team. Sienna and Andrew sit in our living area, tapping away on their laptops. I don't like that they're still involved, but I also don't have much choice.

To my chagrin, I'm relinquishing control and trusting that Ty and his team will have my back. Even though I'm certain that Andrew and Sienna do *not*.

From what I can ascertain, Katherine managed to get the original article pulled at the publisher level, but other articles have spun off and gone viral. Now, entirely new articles and publications have their own versions up. Every celebrity magazine is now running stories about a love triangle between me, Ty, and Ronni, and offering up their own "journalistic" commentary.

It's like a diabolical game of whack-a-mole, and I can't escape it.

A loud knock at the door startles me. Ty answers it, even though he's on the phone with one of the band's lawyers. As if things couldn't get any worse, the most beautiful, chestnut-haired, buxom beauty I've ever seen in real life practically dances into the suite.

My mouth hangs open when none other than a cheery Ronni Miller saunters into the room and gives Ty a big squeeze. They speak softly, clearly very close, and I feel like my heart is going to jump out of my chest. When Ronni shoots me a sympathetic look and familiarly clutches Ty's arms right above his elbows, I feel my fear and panic turn into rage.

"Zoey, I'd like you to meet Ronni." They approach me with big, cheesy grins.

Sienna watches from where she's sitting, clearly amused, which infuriates me even more.

"Um, hi." My voice doesn't sound like my own.

Ronni embraces me like we're long-lost sisters. "It's so great to finally meet the famous Zoey!"

I can't take it. Angry tears fill my eyes, which pisses me off. I'm so sick of crying over this shit.

Unable to deal for another second, I pull away from the beautiful actress. The stress of the past twenty-four hours overwhelms me. All day I've stoically endured the hustle and bustle around me, knowing that I can't add anything to the crisis control unfolding around me. Being embraced by the woman who I've seen canoodling with *my* boyfriend in hundreds of photos finally does me in.

"Excuse me." I get up and dash into the bedroom. If I'm going to break down, it won't be in front of Ronni fucking Miller.

Sienna's annoying taunt trails me. "For fuck's sake, you're crying again?"

Bitch.

Predictably, Ty follows close behind. He envelopes me in his strong arms when I shut the door. I try to push him away, but he won't let me go. He curves his entire body around me so my deep cries are muffled against his chest.

"It'll be okay," Ty repeats over and over, his hand splayed across the back of my head. "I've got you."

"Wwwhyissssssshheeheeeree?" I stutter into his black Henley shirt.

"She's going to give an interview to refute the bullshit." Ty holds me tightly. "That's why I was talking to the lawyers."

"*Grreeaaat*," I sob. "More good news."

"Oh, *butterfly*." Ty cups my face as his eyes find mine. "It *is* good news. I'm sorry. I didn't get a lot of warning that she was here, but you'll like her. I promise."

"Yeah, it's so great to have more people I don't know share in my humiliation." I pull away from him.

"Zoey." Ty looks pained.

"I just want to go home." I cross my arms. "I don't want to be here. I can't handle this, it's too much."

"Oh, babe—" Ty catches my hand, holding it tightly so I can't pull away. "We're working on it. I *promise* it will blow over."

"You know what? I don't want to be around anyone right now." I slump down on the bed. "I need some time by myself."

Ty looks crushed. "I don't deserve you. Being with me is why we're going through this."

"No, that psycho publicist is why *I'm* going through this," I snarl. "Do you understand that because of her my credibility is probably fucked forever?"

"Zoey, no. It's not." Ty tries to comfort me helplessly.

I pick up my tablet where I have the latest story pulled up and read it out loud.

"After speaking with multiple sources close to the matter, Zoey Pearson is a controlling opportunist who has haunted Tyson Rainier for nearly a decade. She chewed him up and spit him out years ago, leaving him a shattered man. Some of our generation's most prolific songs were written by Ty about Zoey, and just when Ty had gotten over her and found a love worthy of his affection, she reappeared. Not content to let Ty be happy with Ronni Miller, Zoey wormed her way back into his life first with a position at his new foundation, and now back into his bed. All of the LTZ guys hate her guts."

"Zoey, can't you see it's just bullshit? Please trust me. People will move on after a day or two. Katherine, Sienna, Andrew, Jace, and the lawyers are getting everything pulled down and retracted." Ty grabs my hand and tries to be reassuring. "We're working on a follow-up rebuttal story."

"You *really* trust them?" I shake my head.

"I do." Ty squeezes my hand tightly. "They've never let me down."

Unbelievable. My rage boils over, and I can't play nice anymore. "Never let you *down*? Are you *serious*? Pardon me for distrusting the very people who preyed on your vulnerability and used you for years to line their pockets. Fuck them. They never had your best interest at heart and they don't have mine."

"Fuck, Zoey. What do you want me to say?" Ty roars, stricken by my words.

"Nothing, of course. I'm beginning to think you like being the victim. That's how you've justified everything. Mean, psycho Zoey left you and boo hoo, Ty got hurt and was sad for sooooo long," I yell, unable to stop. "Has your publicity team considered how this affected *me* all those years, ever? I stayed away because I was asked to by someone you trusted. I'm *not* the villain here. If you *really* wanted me so much, after Carter told you what he did, why didn't you make the effort to find me then? Or at least fucking correct the record?"

He's visibly shocked. "Babe—"

"*No*! Seriously, if Carter hadn't arranged for you to run into me at the law firm, would we be here today?" My voice cracks. "I don't think so. No, I *know* so."

"Butterfly." Ty's face is aghast. He knows I'm right.

Even worse, I don't feel safe. I don't feel protected.

"Leave me alone, Ty." I wrench my hand away. "We danced around this last night, but if you think for one goddamn minute that I don't *know* that Sienna is out there planting these stories so she can fix them—don't say one more word about protecting me. Fuck you. Fuck her. I'm not going to let her do this to me."

My emotions are all over the place. Mad, of course. Heartbroken. Scared beyond belief to lose Ty again. Scared to stay with him.

Embarrassed.

Defiant.

Resolved.

Devastated.

Yep, devastated. That sums it up.

"My mom and dad, and my law school classmates, my former coworkers at the firm? All of them have probably read—God." The tears flow again at the sheer shame of it all. "I've got to get used to what my life is going to be. I'm always going to be the evil bitch who broke your heart. The world already fucking hated me because of the songs. I've lived with that characterization for years. Now, apparently, I'm also a stalker slut who slept my way through law school, with my firm bosses and with Carter? It's too much! *Especially* if the publicists for LTZ were behind it. Don't you see that? Are you so blind?"

Ty's face drains, he looks like he's about to faint. "Zoey, baby. I need to tell you something."

"Excuse me—" Ronni softly knocks on the door and pokes her head in, interrupting my tirade.

"What?" I whirl around and screech then find my manners. "I'm sorry, it's just been—"

"I understand." She smiles warmly at me. "Believe me I've been there."

I'm not feeling friendly, though. This entire situation is giving me a migraine. "Oh, that's right. You also think it's fine to have your publicists plant a bunch of fake shit."

Ronni's face freezes into a fake smile.

"We'll be right out, Ronni," Ty says, never taking his eyes off me.

"Katherine is trying to get ahold of you, she just called me. I'm only here to give you your phone." Ronni hands it to Ty. "Zoey, Sienna said she has something for you to approve before she sends it out. I'll leave you both alone, I'll be in Connor's suite across the hall."

I hang my head. "Ronni, I'm sorry. I've been rude to you, it's not personal. I just—"

"Don't worry about it. Everyone has the same reaction the first time something like this happens, then you get thicker skin." She smiles and pinches her arm before exiting the bedroom, and then the suite.

Well, shit. Ronni does seem nice.

"I need to call Katherine back," Ty implores. "Then I need to talk to you, It's important."

"Fine. I'll go see what Sienna wants to show me." I open the bedroom door.

Ty puts his hand on my shoulder. "No matter what happens, we're in this together, Z. If you want to go home and hibernate, say the word. You're the most valuable part of my life. Nothing is more important to me than making sure you're okay. I'm going to fire Sienna and Andrew as soon as I get off the phone."

I sigh and shuffle out to see the enemy, who's sitting on the window sill waiting for me. Her prey. Andrew is nowhere to be seen.

"What is it?" My voice is weary. Defeated.

"Ty never told you about us, did he?" Sienna's cold gaze narrows as I approach.

I thought I was at the bottom of the well.

Nope.

Sienna turns her tablet around to show me a video of her giving Ty a blowjob. Red lips stretched around the same magnificent cock that I've memorized every millimeter of. Despite the jerky motions of the camera, his face is slack with pleasure. I can't look away, which means I watch him jerk in ecstasy as she sucks him to completion.

My mind is a vortex of agony. A million icepicks pierce my body at the same time that a billion shards of glass cut me to shreds.

My stomach lurches. I turn and run for the door, knowing I'm going to throw up.

I have to get far away from this room and Ty or I'm going to implode. Bursting into the hallway, I bolt for the elevator. I can hear Sienna's laugh trail behind me when the door slams shut.

Sergey is surprised by my quickness, because I'm already inside the elevator, pressing the button for the lobby when he figures out that I'm leaving.

I turn and glare at him, hoping he doesn't dare follow.

To no avail. He manages to burst through the door before it closes. We ride down in uncomfortable silence. The second the door opens, before he can grab me, I sprint into the lobby where I'm besieged by a swarm of camera flashes. My head throbs.

Desperate to get away, I whirl around, spot a side exit, and make a beeline for it.

I know Sergey is close behind, but I manage to escape to the street where I hope to blend into the crowd and disappear.

Even I should have known it was a terrible plan. More paparazzi accost me, close in and scream my name. Fighting my way through the crowd like a panicked mustang, I find an opening and burst through.

My momentum carries me into oncoming traffic. The last thing I remember is a taxi barreling toward me.

Then everything goes black.

Chapter Forty-Nine

Late the Next Morning

A COUPLE OF HOURS out of surgery, my fragile butterfly lies in her hospital bed in the private wing of the hospital, sedated and sleeping. Sergey is in the room down the hall. He took the brunt of the impact of the taxi and fractured his hip, but saved her life. LTZ's security team is keeping prying eyes far, far away from us, which is the only saving grace in this fucked-up situation.

From what I've been told, Zoey tore a ligament in her shoulder, broke her arm and three ribs, and has some pretty gnarly road rash. Thank God they expect she'll fully recover, but the nurses and doctor won't tell me much more about her condition.

They also won't let me in to see her. According to the hospital, I'm technically nothing to Zoey. The doctors and nurses recognize me from the band but, apparently, my insistence that she's my live-in girlfriend needs third-party verification.

Destroyed and helpless, I have to make do by pacing the waiting room and peering into the glass panel of her door.

While she was in the operating room, I made the horrific phone call to her parents letting them know she'd been injured and I'd chartered a plane to fly them here. I played the celebrity card and Seattle's best orthopedic specialist is also on the flight, which is landing soon.

It's the least I can do. Zoey and Sergey were both injured because of me. It's my responsibility to make sure they have the very best medical care both here and back at home.

Zoey's outburst at the hotel shocked me with some cold-hard truth and snapped me out of my pattern of abdicating responsibility for my life, yet again, to people other than myself. I don't need to call Lisa to figure out it's just one more of my mommy issues. I'm an adult, for fuck's sake. I should know better.

The memory of yesterday is so fucking painful, but it's on a loop in my mind.

After I took the call from our lawyer and Zoey left to speak to Sienna, my plan was to take a stand and fire both publicists. Except, Zoey wasn't there. Before I even got a word out, Sienna handed me a handwritten note claiming it was from Zoey.

Ty, I can't take it. Don't try to call me. Don't try to find me this time. It's really over.

Furious, I crumpled it up and threw Sienna out. I was thoroughly repulsed by this disgusting woman who I'd let manipulate me for years. She crossed the line when she deliberately placed stories to hurt the love of my life. Disgusting.

Even worse, I defended my publicity team instead of having Zoey's back.

Nothing would keep me from making things right.

Raging, I called for Sergey to ensure Sienna and Andrew were thrown out and kept out, but he wasn't at his post. In the hallway, all I saw was chaos. LTZ's security guards were flat-out running out from the guys' rooms for the stairwell. Right then, I knew deep in my heart something had happened to Zoey.

I had to get to her. To find out where she went.

I flew down thirty flights of stairs and burst through the door to an unnervingly empty lobby, which shocked me because the press had been camped out all night. The situation became clearer when I saw and heard the commotion outside. Multiple sirens. Pandemonium.

There was no time to process anything. Instinctively I knew I had to get to my girl.

Immediately.

I managed to fight my way through the crowd only to catch a glimpse of Zoey crumpled on the pavement, her arm at a terrifying angle. Her screams of agony were like torture. The ghastly paparazzi swarmed and challenged the band and hotel security, who were doing everything they could to hold them back from her. Luckily, police officers approached from all directions to help contain the madness.

Once I was recognized, the pap fuckers lost their minds in an attempt to get me to engage. It worked, I screamed and swore. It took every ounce of strength I had to fight my way to her. I didn't care one iota about the millions of flashes capturing my reaction.

Ever dutiful, Sergey shielded Zoey as much as possible, despite the obvious pain he was in. I managed to break through and shelter her from the other side, clutching her good hand and soothing her until the ambulance came.

Zoey was suffering so much that she was barely coherent. She wouldn't look at me and kept trying to roll away. I was terrified for her to move because I didn't know if she hit her head or had a neck or spinal injury. I begged her to keep still. Instead she just passed out. I nearly lost my mind and sobbed and begged for her to wake up.

When a sleazy photographer stuck his camera in my face to get the money shot of me weeping over her limp body, I whirled around to grab his camera like a wild, untamed lion determined to protect his lioness. By this time more police arrived in full riot gear.

Within minutes, they formed a circle around us and used riot shields to thwart the swarm until the ambulance could get through. When the EMTs finally had a clear path, Zoey was still unconscious as they expertly loaded her into the ambulance. They allowed me to ride with her to the hospital.

Now it's 11 p.m. I'm sitting on a chair outside her room, alone in the eerily silent hallway. I hate the sterile hospital smell, it makes feel sick. All I can do is replay last night on a loop. Think about how many times I've failed Zoey and how I've failed myself. Not just today, but every day for the past eight and a half years.

From the day and hour I met her, it should have been my duty and privilege to cherish and protect her. She was right, I've made our separation all about me. My pain. My loss. I've been so selfish. Now, I may have lost her for good.

You didn't deserve her.

You never deserved her.

At some point, I doze off because the next thing I know Mike Pearson is roughly shaking me awake. "What the fuck did you do to my daughter?"

Olivia Pearson pulls him back. "Mike, stop it. I know you're upset but let him talk."

I stand and relay the days' events as I know them and apologize profusely. Mike wraps a weeping Olivia into his arms while they listen, his face set in stern indignation. He's not happy. Not impressed with me. He has every right to feel this way.

"Have you seen what they're calling her?" he seethes.

There's nothing to say. All I can do is hang my head in shame. It isn't the time or place to reassure them that a new scandal will take the place of ours. How can I when Zoey's accident is worldwide breaking news? Because of me. Hundreds of new photos and articles filled with speculation are now circulating. Sensational, fabricated stories.

If I were her parents, I'd try to keep her away from me too. Not that it's going to work. Nothing is ever going to separate me from Zoey again.

Zoey's doctor joins us and asks the Pearsons to sign a couple of forms and they are led into her room.

I try to follow, but Mike won't have it. "Tyson, we'll take it from here. Go and get some sleep."

"Mr. Pearson, with all due respect, Zoey is my *everything*. We may not be engaged yet, but we're committed to each other. I need to be with her. I love her more than life itself." I practically beg him on hand and knee.

Olivia strokes my back. "Ty, honey. Let us talk to her, we don't know why she was running. In the photos she looked so scared. You have to understand—as her parents, we need to make sure she *wants* you to be with her."

Oh, God. They think I did something to her.

"Olivia, I swear. I don't know why she was running. I've been focused on Zoey's health and haven't had the chance to get to the bottom of it." I'm frantic. Desperate.

Mike dismisses me with a wave of his hand. "We're going to see for ourselves. Until then, you should go."

"I'm not leaving her." I stand my ground. "After what we've been through you've got to know that I'll *never* leave her. Aren't you the ones who told us to disregard outside opinions and figure things out as a couple? Didn't you say you'd support us? How is this supporting us?"

The door shuts in my face without a reply. I peer through the window, broken hearted. Zoey is still sleeping. Her parents sit on either side of her, both look shattered. Like they've aged ten years since I saw them a week ago.

It's not surprising. She's their only child.

The anguish I feel knowing the woman I plan to spend my life with is on the other side of a hospital door that I don't have the right to enter is indescribable.

I *have* to be with her, she's my air.

I'm seconds away from barging into her room when Mike sees me staring at them through the door. He shakes his head, stands and pulls the privacy curtain around her bed, motioning for me to leave.

The curtain closes around her so she's blocked completely from my view.

Leaving me shut out of her life. *Again*.

Chapter Fifty

Later That Day

MY MIND IS FLOATING. My arm hurts so bad. Where am I? I can hear someone saying my name. Is that Mom?

"Mommmm?" My voice doesn't sound right. How funny. I can hear myself crying but it seems like the sound is above me.

More voices. I don't recognize them. Where is Ty?

"Tyyyy." My voice doesn't work. How can I ask for him?

My dad's voice mumbles above me.

"Dadddyyy." I see a shadow hovering above me, but he's so blurry. My arm feels like it's going to fall off and I can feel tears dripping down my face, but I can't move.

Where is Ty?

Why does my brain feel so funny?

People are hovering over me and now the pain is disappearing and I'm *soooo* tired...

Chapter Fifty-One

Later the Next Day

It's been nearly forty-eight hours since Zoey's operation.

Forty-seven hours, twenty-two minutes, and thirty seconds to be precise.

I haven't left the hospital. Mike and Olivia haven't let me in to see her yet. All I know is she's on some serious pain medication, so she isn't coherent. Until they are able to talk to her, I'm still banned.

So, I'm going out of my mind. Literally.

Well, maybe figuratively. Not literally. I don't want to be one of those douchebags who starts saying "literally" literally all the time.

Who the fuck knows, as I mentioned, I'm losing my mind.

I haven't slept since the night before the concert. I haven't showered. I'm a mess.

I'm also incredibly pissed that Zoey's parents are interfering in our relationship. I should be in with my future wife. The love of my life. My best friend. My lover.

Two fucking days of being relegated to the waiting room. I'm living with a silent rage. The only thing that keeps me from knocking the shit out of Mike Pearson is Zoey. She's already been through so much, and I'm not about to add to her pain.

So I try to put myself in his shoes.

I keep coming back to the same thing. If it were my daughter, I'd do exactly what Mr. Pearson is doing. Protecting his baby. Luckily, Olivia throws me a few crumbs and sits with me every now and then to give me updates. Zoey's currently being weaned off the heavy painkillers and should be able to have a more coherent conversation by tomorrow morning.

I'm counting down the minutes because I know Zoey wants me with her. I feel it in my bones.

***

It's five in the morning. I'm stretched out on the sectional couch in the waiting area trying to get some sleep. Zane brought me some fresh clothes on the way to the jet strip before my band brothers fly back home to Seattle. A nurse took pity on me and let me have a shower.

I'm clean and so ready to see Zoey. At this point, I'm just biding my time.

"Ty, honey." Olivia's gentle voice startles me.

I pop up, adrenaline pulsing through my veins. "Olivia, is she awake?"

"Yes, she's asking for you," she confirms.

I spring up and race toward her room.

"Ty, wait!" Olivia calls after me.

I whirl around, my voice too loud for the early hour. "You both have kept me from her for days, I'm not waiting a minute longer. I need to be with her."

"I just want to tell you what to expect." She crosses the room and takes my elbow. "She's still pretty loopy, the pain meds are strong. She doesn't remember the accident."

"Okay." I cross my arms in front of me.

She glances around the room then back at me. "Ty, it's pretty apparent that something really upset her."

"*Okay*." Dread fills my gut.

"Mike wants us to stay in the room, but I think you both need some privacy." Olivia squints, assessing my reaction.

"I'd appreciate that, Olivia." I try to keep my voice calm.

She nods. "We'll be right outside."

When I push the door open, my heart's beating ten thousand miles per hour. Zoey's sweet face tilts up at the sound. When she sees me, it's not the reaction I expect. Tears well up in her eyes. She has a hard time looking at me. I take a deep breath and pull up a chair.

God, there's nothing that matters more than Zoey. She's my everything. I take her good hand, bring it to my lips, and kiss it. With my other hand, I smooth her hair and stroke her soft cheek.

"I've been going out of my mind to get to you. No one would let me in." My tears spill down my cheeks. "Your parents thought you were running from me."

She just cries.

"Why did you run, butterfly?" I sob, I can't help it. "What happened?"

"I saw." Her eyes are squeezed shut. Tears flow like rivers now.

I'm confused. "What did you see?"

"You and her." She pulls her hand away.

"Who?" My spine prickles with fear.

She shakes her head slightly. "Sienna."

I'm still confused. "Did Sienna show you something?" There is that one picture, but it's just me licking her face. That wouldn't be upsetting, would it? "Whatever you saw was so long ago. I was probably high. It's not me anymore," I babble.

"I saw a video of her sucking your cock." Her voice slurs because of medication and sorrow.

The room begins to spin.

What the actual fuck.

"*What?*" I choke out.

"I need to go home." She bites her lip, her eyes still brimming with tears.

Seeing her in anguish kills me.

"Okay." I grab my phone. "Yes. I'll make it happen. You can heal at our house. We'll get a private nurse—"

She grabs my wrist. "No, Ty. I want to be with my parents. All of this is too much. Too fast."

"We're building our life together, we're finally—" I look at her, astonished.

Zoey shakes her head. "No, Ty."

"No, what?" I stare at her.

She closes her eyes. "We aren't."

"We are," I insist.

"No. My life is ruined. I just can't—" Her eyes flutter and then close. The pain killer dose is kicking in. Soon her breathing evens out.

Her words break my heart a new. She thinks I've ruined her life.

I should leave. But I can't. I'm going to sit here for as long as I can. Until someone kicks me out.

It's the first time I can really take in the extent of her injuries. Her shoulder is bound, her arm in a cast. Her ribs are broken. I can't see, but I know her knees are covered in road rash.

Zoey's hurt because of *me*. Because of Sienna, a person who, with deliberate calculation, set out to crush the only woman who I'll ever love. I let it happen with complacency and laziness. To add insult to injury, my band paid her for the privilege.

I can't wrap my mind around the fact that Sienna filmed herself giving me a blowjob and kept the video for years. It's triggering. Brings back memories of times when I had no control. When I was helpless. Times I'll never speak about. Ever.

Fuck. All this time she's held onto that video like collateral. Waiting for the perfect time to use it. Zoey was her target.

And it worked. She freaked the fuck out and ran. If I'd seen some guy going down on her?

Murder. I'd be in jail right now.

I have no idea what motivates people like Sienna. I've lived through some seriously fucked-up shit and there is nothing inside me that wants to hurt someone else. I inflict my demons on myself. Always have. Probably always will.

Sienna not only deliberately fucked with my band. She destroyed Zoey. Obliterated me. Now, I'm going to return the favor. If it's the last thing I do.

I know Zoey won't ever trust me again. She's made it clear I'm not the man for her. I know what I need to do, but it takes me over two hours of sitting with her before I can force myself to leave. It's my last time I'll ever breathe her in. Gaze at her beautiful body. I memorize each detail of her perfect face.

Finally, I lean over and kiss her eyes, nose, and lips. "I love you, Z. I'll never stop loving you."

When I close the door behind me, the Pearsons are waiting. I motion for them to join me and we cross the hallway to the waiting area where we are alone.

Then I confess. Almost everything. My upbringing. The band. What Zoey means to me. How I'd spun out of control for years and lost myself in the rockstar lifestyle. How I let our publicists use me to promote the band. Finally, I fill them in on what Sienna did and how I failed Zoey.

I also propose how I can make things right. Zoey's life means more to me than mine. I'm covering all of her rehab and medical costs. I won't stop until I clear her name. I'm setting her up financially for life so she can do whatever makes her happy.

My greatest gift is leaving her alone. Ever since I met her, all I've done is cause her pain. She deserves someone who is so much better than me.

She deserves everything.

And I am nothing.

Chapter Fifty-Two

Three Weeks Later

I'VE BEEN IN A drug-induced cloud for what seems like forever.

I hate it. I'm determined not to take any more pain killers. Or at least to get off the ones that are fucking with my head. My memories of the time since my accident are floaty, at best. Vague snippets of the hospital. Flashes of Ty sitting by my bedside. Flittering memories of the private jet that transported us back to Seattle.

The one thing I'm confused about is why am I in my childhood bedroom and not at Ty's house. Where I live. No one will tell me anything.

One memory that's clear as day always comes raging back, though. Visuals of Ty and Sienna I never want to see again.

Followed by me running out of the hotel like a lunatic. Then nothing.

I have virtually no recollection of the accident that fucked up my shoulder. No decent memory of anything that happened since, only the bits and pieces that seem more like movie clips of someone else's life. It's so fucking frustrating.

On the positive side of things, due to some crazy sports-medicine sorcery, my shoulder feels much better already. My rehab is intense. The team tells me with consistent, hard work I'll be as good as new when my cast comes off in another two weeks. The scabs on my knees are still a bit gnarly in places, but the itching has stopped. All in all, even though I have a ways to go, I can't believe my luck at having such a great medical team.

"Hey, sweet girl." Mom stands in the doorway to my bedroom with a cup of coffee.

I wave with my good arm. "Hi."

"Time to get up." Mom moves toward my bed.

Yawning, I fling the covers off and sit up. It's not easy, but I want to do things for myself. I'm so exhausted, though. The drugs really do a number on me. Swinging my feet over the edge of the bed, I tentatively inch my toes to the floor and use my good hand to support myself to a standing position.

"I'm up!" I smooth my long T-shirt down.

"Good job, honey. How's your head, feeling a little clearer?" Mom pulls out some leggings and a fresh T-shirt from my dresser. "Ready for a shower?"

"Actually, I do feel more like myself today, and yes I need a shower stat." I shuffle over to my mom, each step feeling like a challenge.

She helps me wash myself, which is slightly mortifying. Once my body is clean, though, I feel better. Mom leaves me to dress myself at my insistence. It takes a long time, but it's worth it. As each minute passes, my mind clears up. Thankfully.

It's time to get answers. For instance, where is Ty? My folks have been very vague about providing me with information. Each time I bring it up, they divert my attention, which hadn't been hard to do with all of the pain killers I've been on.

I've not only been in a drug-induced bubble but a knowledge bubble too. I couldn't tell you what day or month it is. Other than it's late in the year. I overheard my dad saying we'd missed Thanksgiving.

When I finally make it to the living room, I find my parents hovering over mom's laptop. She shuts it immediately when they realize I've joined them.

I ask, "What were you watching?"

"Nothing," my folks say unison, scared-rabbit expressions on their faces.

Nothing makes me crazier than being kept in the dark. "Tell me the truth. Did something happen to Ty?"

"What do you mean?" My dad takes my arm to help me to the couch.

I lean on him and sink down into the soft cushions. "I feel clear headed now. I'm grateful for both of you, but I don't understand where Ty is."

My folks exchange glances; an entire silent conversation passes between them. "Ty is in Los Angeles." My dad sits next to me on the couch.

I'm even more confused. "Why?"

More glances. More looks.

"Just tell me what's going on." I punch the seat next to me. "He hasn't been here with me and I'm freaking out. What the fuck is going on. Are you keeping me prisoner here?

"Zoey!" Dad is stricken.

"Where's my phone?" I frantically beg, feeling more agitated. "I know you're keeping things from me, but you have to understand not knowing is making it worse. Did something happen to him? Is he okay?"

"Calm down, honey." Mom rushes to my side.

My dad's voice is barely over a whisper. "Ty's been here with you every day, but he didn't want you to know. He had to leave for LA for some meetings this morning."

"What? Why didn't he want me to know?" My heart hurts so bad I feel like it's going to explode.

"When you were in the hospital in New York, you told him there was no future together. He wanted to bring you to his house, but you wouldn't go. And, well, we wouldn't let him. Not until you had time to heal a bit." Mom strokes my hair like a little girl. "He blames himself for all that happened to you."

"I don't remember saying anything like that." My mind races, trying to find some memory of the conversation. "I'd *never* want to be away from him. *Never.*"

Mom and Dad exchange glances. He winces. "Well, you were very upset by a video—"

"Yes, I remember the video." It's clear they know about what sent me running.

"Honey, you've been very out of it," Mom soothes. "You haven't been capable of retaining much information because of your surgery. The pain killers made you discombobulated."

"I'm not upset at *him*. I'm upset at what she *did* to him. We can't go through another separation because of miscommunication again. *We can't.*" I'm anguished. "Help me remember what happened that day."

"That woman showed you a video. No one knows what she said to you, but you fled. Tried to leave the hotel but there were too many photographers and fans so you ran out into the street. Sergey stopped you from being hit by a taxi and was hurt." Mom grips my hand. "When Ty called and told us you were hurt, he flew us to New York. You were in the hospital for three days until he arranged for all of us to come home on a private jet. He arranged for the Seattle Mariners' orthopedic specialists to oversee your care."

Of course he did. Ty is the most loving, thoughtful man on this planet. "I want to see him." My heart races. "It wasn't his fault about Sienna. Ohmygod. I must have hurt him badly for him to leave me like this. What have I done?"

"Zoey, please take a minute to relax." Mom squeezes my hand and eases me back against the cushion. "That *woman* set up horrible press articles about you. Whenever you'd wake up, you'd be agitated and crying about what happened.

We couldn't really get a clear picture, and at first, we didn't know if Ty had hurt you."

Hearing that my parents believed Ty might have harmed me is unbearable. "I was really mad at the situation, but he'd *never* hurt me, Mom. I'm the one who always hurts him."

"That's not true, Zoey. Your accident made headlines around the world. We've had news cameras and photographers outside this house around the clock. Thousands of LTZ fans waited outside the hospital for news of your condition. It was shocking. Unacceptable. I'm the one who was furious at Ty." Dad sits on the other side of me.

"*Dad*," I sigh.

"Blame me. I'm the one who kept him away from you because I can't bear to see my baby hurt." His eyes well up with tears. "Ty's never left you. He's made sure you have everything. We have some crazy secret-service paramilitary security posted outside to keep you safe. Our entire street is blocked off."

I squeeze my eyes shut. This is all too much. "How long has it been?"

"Three weeks ago, yesterday." Mom leans over and strokes my hair.

"Seriously. Get me my phone, please, Dad," I implore.

"Zoey, you need to be prepared." Mom cradles me gently. "Ty's managed to get a lot of the terrible stuff pulled off the internet, but I can't be sure there aren't things out there that will hurt you."

"You mean *Jace* got the stuff pulled down." I take my phone from him.

"No, it was *Ty*." Dad hands me a charger. "He's been on the press circuit this entire time. Giving interviews and all sorts of stuff. He hired his own crisis management team to help change the narrative. It's beginning to work."

"Are you sure you're feeling up to this?" Mom's concern permeates her face when I power up my phone.

It's hard to figure out how I feel.

All I know is that I need information so I can analyze it and try to put my life back together. For the next few hours, my parents leave me alone while I pour over every article, every interview, every video. I find some of the salacious stuff that's been printed. There are websites devoted to Ty and me as a couple and websites devoted to breaking us up. After an intense download of material, my head feels like it's going to explode. I'm getting very, very sleepy.

But I have what I need.

I put down my phone just as my dad comes into the living room with a sandwich. He sits across from me but remains silent. A look of understanding passes between us.

He leans forward. "He's flying back today. When he visits, it's usually around eleven."

"I *did* hurt him, didn't I?" I sigh. "Again."

My dad leans back and crosses his arms. Thoughtfully considers his words. "Zoey, in every relationship there will be times when you hurt each other without meaning to. Some people work through it and some don't. I'll admit that I've always had my reservations about Ty. He comes from a difficult background and no dad wants his little girl to give her heart to a rockstar."

Dad pauses, a lawyerly trait that I emulate often.

I wait patiently for him to continue.

"Throughout this nightmare, he's shown your mom and me who he really is." Dad has tears in his eyes. "I don't want to influence you, honey. Neither does he. He's willing to step aside. I'd say he's almost resigned to it. His only wish is for you to be okay. Happy."

"He *always* makes me happy." I smile. "I'm the best version of myself when we're together."

He nods. "That's all a dad can ask for."

"Why is he coming over so late?" It's the last piece of the puzzle.

As if on cue, Mom brings me my newer, less-potent painkillers and a cup of tea. "Ty wants to make sure you're sound asleep when he sits with you. He didn't want to be here when you were coherent in case he upset you or interfered with your healing and ability to process everything in your own time."

All I can do is swallow. And try to breathe normally. He hasn't freaked out. He's stayed the course and been there for me, even when I wasn't capable of comprehending it.

"We've spent a lot of time with him over the past three weeks." Mom kisses me on the head. "We approve. He's a very special man."

I've always known that. While it's comforting to know that my mom and dad accept him even after what happened, it won't matter if he doesn't believe in us anymore. "How do you know when he'll be here?"

"Ty just texted me." Mom holds up her phone. "He'll be here like usual. You have about an hour."

425

Chapter Fifty-Three

One Hour Later

IT'S HARD TO BELIEVE I've been doing this for three weeks already.

I'd do it forever, though, if it kept me close to Zoey.

After she returned to Seattle safely, I knew it was time for me to grow the fuck up. Katherine helped me find a good team and I got to work.

First, my insanely competent civil litigation team filed a lawsuit against Sienna and Andrew that will keep them in court for easily five years if they don't acquiesce to my demands, which includes a full admission of their misdeeds, a retraction of everything they've released about Zoey, the return of every photo and video of me, and cooperation with my crisis management team to put our *true* story out there.

Either way, I'll make sure they never work as publicists for any legitimate entertainer ever again.

Next, I hired my own crisis publicist to help me repair the damage Sienna had done to both me and Zoey. Banafee Partners has been on fire, setting up dozens of interviews with legitimate news outlets allowing me to clear everything up. It's taken a couple of weeks, but things are *really* turning around.

Today, I finally dealt with my mother once and for all. Evidence from my fucked-up childhood—police reports, child protective reports, and some of my journals documenting my abuse have been provided in conjunction with an exclusive interview I gave to *Rolling Stone*. The truth is coming out, I can only hope it will help another child like me have hope.

All these efforts don't erase the fact that Zoey's reputation has been smeared mercilessly, but it's certainly cushioned the long-term impact. As I promised Zoey's folks, my business manager set up a trust for her. She'll never have to work another day in her life.

It wasn't how I'd hoped our story would end, but money is nothing to me. If it's the only thing I can do, she can have it all.

When I gave the paperwork to Mike for safekeeping, his reaction surprised me. He told me that I was their son as sure as Zoey was their daughter. After his reaction to me in New York, I know it's not exactly true, but it makes me feel better all the same.

After all, his approval doesn't change my reality with Zoey, but at least I know that I've done the best I can to make things right.

Even though I'm exhausted, I live for the moment when I walk up the steps to the Pearson's front door. The very best part of my day is when I see Zoey, and I know our time is coming to an end. She's nearly healed. Last night she nearly woke up and found me sitting next to her, which can't happen.

I promised her parents I won't ever let anyone hurt her again and I mean it.

The front door opens a crack. I look up anticipating her dad and am blown away when Zoey steps through the door.

Wearing black leggings and an oversize University of Washington sweatshirt, my butterfly is stunning. Upright. Alert.

Breathtaking.

"Ty—" Zoey's eyes brim with tears.

I stop in my tracks. "*Z.*"

We stare at each other for who knows how long.

"Come in." Zoey holds open the door.

I shake my head. My voice comes out in shards. "I shouldn't."

"Ty—" She tilts her head and gestures for me to join her with the arm that's not in a cast.

I can't resist her. Ever. "Okay."

I follow Zoey into the kitchen, where she motions for me to sit before putting on the electric kettle. Silently she makes two cups of tea. My heart thuds. For weeks I've been resolved that I'll be alone. That my life will go on without the love of my life.

In my mind, at this moment, the next few minutes will only confirm my agony.

"Here you go." Zoey sets my tea in front of me and sits down across the table.

"Thanks." I can't look her in the eye.

The dead-quiet of the late hour is unbearable. The heater kicks on in the old Craftsman house, and I jump at the sound. Scrubbing my hands through my hair, I can't help fidgeting. And waiting. How long must I wait for her to cast me out?

Finally, Zoey breaks the ice. "I know I said some really horrible things to you. You didn't deserve it and I'm very sorry. I never want to hurt you. You have to know that."

I look up from under the curtain of my hair, barely glancing at her. "I deserved *everything* you said to me."

"Our reunion hasn't really gone the way we hoped, has it?" Zoey's voice is but a whisper.

"It's my fault." I clasp my hands around the hot cup. "Everything is my fault."

Zoey reaches over and places her good hand on my wrist. "Can I show you something?"

"I should really go." I don't move, though.

"Please?" Zoey calmly pleads. "It won't take long."

I nod, then shut my eyes. Zoey leaves the room for a couple of minutes and returns with a laptop. She sits beside me and powers it on. Clicks on a video, which makes my heart thunder in my chest. She wouldn't...

I hear my own voice.

"What is this?" I peek at her.

She strokes my arm. "Just listen. Watch."

So I do. You can barely make out it's me, but I recognize the video as a feed from a nanny cam in Zoey's bedroom. I can hear myself talking to her softly, professing my love, filling her in on my day, and assuring her that I'll respect her wishes to stay out of her life. Sometimes I sing her songs. Other times I just hold her hand. Or stroke her hair.

I shut it off after a few minutes. Bile roils in my stomach, I thought I'd come to an understanding with Mike and Olivia. All I want is to protect Zoey and make sure she's okay, and yet they've still kept me on surveillance. After what happened with *Sienna?*

Hurt pierces my soul. "I get it. Your parents don't trust me with you so they filmed me."

"No. They've never seen this video." Zoey rests her cheek on her hand and studies me.

I feel like I'm going to cry. Really and truly cry. "I don't understand."

"I can't remember much about my time in the hospital. As you know, I was really drugged up on pain meds. Apparently, I told you we had no future." She lets out a huge breath. Squinches her nose in pain.

My throat knots. Tears threaten to burst free. Knowing my time with Zoey would come to an end has been an inevitability for the past few weeks. Having this conversation with her is pure and utter torture. My hands clench into fists and I push them against my eyes.

"Look at me, Ty." Zoey's soft hand touches my forearm.

An uncontrollable sob bursts out. I can't look at her. I'm too ashamed.

"Ty. Look at me." Zoey grips one of my fists and moves it away.

I peer at her through a veil of tears.

"You're my *everything*. You *are* everything." Zoey's fingers interlock with mine. "My mom set up the video feed just for me. For us. So I'd have memories that would not have otherwise been impossible."

I shake my head. "I should have told you everything, I planned to. I didn't—"

"It's okay. Really." She squeezes.

"No." I shake my head. "It's *not*."

Zoey pierces me with a stern look and tightens her hand around my fingers. "Stop. Listen to me. I know about everything you've done since the accident. It's enough. You don't need to do penance for something that wasn't your fault. Neither do I. We've suffered enough at the hands of fate. At the hands of other people. *You* are the love of my life. *My family*. My *future*. You're the future father of my kids."

I look deeply into the eyes of the only woman I've ever loved and will ever love. A sense of peace washes over me. Can we really find our way out of this?

"Say something," Zoey pleads.

"God, I love you." Before the words are out of my mouth my lips claim hers, a final and definitive declaration that she's mine. Zoey wipes the tears from my cheeks and our tongues meet, tasting each other. We melt together as one.

"I love you so much," Zoey speaks against my mouth without missing a beat. "Come upstairs with me."

"Your parents?" I mumble, still sprinkling kisses all over her lips.

She gets up from her chair and motions me to follow. I know that once I take her hand I'm never letting her go. For *real* this time.

She wiggles her fingers. "They'll understand, believe me."

Without any further reservations, I enclose her hand with mine and follow her to my destiny.

Chapter Fifty-Four

Three Weeks Later

IT FEELS SO GOOD to wake up to sunshine. I'm so glad LTZ didn't cancel the LA holiday show. It's the last one before a blessed year-long hiatus. The fans deserve a blow-out and the guys are going to deliver.

We're having my folks and the entire band over for a barbeque later and I can't wait to see Alex. She's been a bit MIA lately and it's killed me not to be there for her when she's going through her own shit.

I guess I have an excuse because I'm still technically healing, but my sling is gone and the cast is off. Getting back to normal feels good.

Stretching, I look up into the deep-blue eyes of my love. Ty stands before me in only his boxer briefs, offering me a cup of tea.

I want something else. "Come here."

"Me?" He cheekily looks to the left and to the right as if there's someone else in our bedroom. When he catches my eye again, his smile is off the charts. We are so friggin' happy.

Our reunion was immediate the night he came over to my folks' house. I moved back into our Seattle home the next day. We're solid. Inseparable. *Permanent.*

Only one thing is missing. Today, I have the all-clear to resume physical activity.

Ty approaches me and climbs into bed next to me after he sets the tea on the nightstand. I roll toward him and tug his briefs down, taking great delight in watching his hard cock spring free, thick and gorgeous. *All mine.*

Wrapping my hand around his base, I angle his crown toward my lips and lick and swirl my tongue in a sweet tease before guiding his cock deep into my mouth. Groaning, he fists my hair and bucks against my mouth helplessly when I suck him hard.

Just when I think he's going to fall over the edge, his big palms caress my face and he pulls out. 'Not like this, butterfly. Today, I want to come inside you."

Ty kneels next to me and tenderly grips my calves, placing them on either side of his legs. His savage gaze focuses on my panties as he pulls them down to my knees and then all the way off. The anticipation of his mouth on me makes me liquid with desire. Ty laughs when I arch up to meet him.

"Impatient, are we?" Without missing a beat, he plunges his tongue into my pussy and laps through my folds. The vibrations of his deep voice send shivers through my core when he growls against me, "I love how you taste. God I missed this."

From between my legs, Ty's blue eyes blaze up at me. He watches my reaction when he sucks my pulsing clit between his lips and inserts two fingers inside me, curling them against my G-spot. My thighs tremble in time to his stroking. Good God, I missed his oral mastery.

My body needs him, needs this release. I shove a fist into my mouth to keep from screaming and alerting our houseguests to our activities. Ty doesn't let up until I come, limp and panting and floaty.

"Are you feeling okay?" Ty whispers, kissing his way up my body before stretching out beside me.

That's an understatement. "*Mmm.*"

"Did that feel good?" His hand strokes my stomach, caressing lightly.

I smile, feeling like I'm half in a dream. Ty continues to trace his fingers all over, my arms, hands, ribs, breasts, neck. His mouth follows, peppering me with gentle kisses. Laving my nipples into puckered points. I've never felt so worshipped. My guy *adores* me. Loves me unconditionally. I'm the luckiest girl in the world.

He eases down over me, careful not to put his weight against my still-tender ribs, but close enough to nuzzle my jaw then press his lips against mine.

Kneeling between my legs, he clutches my hips and pulls me to him. His cock nudges against my slick pussy. Gripping himself, he flicks the tip through my folds before pressing inside with one strong, slow thrust. My eyes fly open, the sensation of having Ty inside me again is so much more than physical.

It's *everything*.

"Zoey, oh God." Ty's voice cracks.

Ty picks up a steady rhythm, keeping a grip on my hips to ensure my own motions are limited. Steadily, he rocks me back and forth against him, careful not to drive too hard or too fast, even as he picks up the pace. I can't help but bite my lip, all of my inner muscles coil and tighten against his cock. He grits his teeth, holding back his own release until I come helplessly in a long, enduring tidal wave of bliss.

"I can't believe how fucking good you feel." Ty's eyes practically roll back into his head. "I can't last much longer."

"Then don't." I lift my hips so Ty can grab my ass and drive more deeply inside me. He watches himself thrust into me, mesmerized as his thumb circles my clit. I'm already on the brink of another orgasm when his cock hit my inner spot at just the right angle.

"Oh my God, I'm coming again," I wheeze.

Ty's eyes squeeze shut and the muscles cord in his neck when he empties inside me. His guttural, rough moans are so incredibly sexy, I yank him down to me. Without breaking contact, he shifts so he's lying by my side, shrouding my body with his. Only then does he press his lips to mine, trailing kisses across my mouth and neck. Wound together, our bodies touch wherever we can keep contact.

"I've missed making love to you," Ty whispers into my ear.

I circle his nipple with my nail. "Should we go again?"

Ty cocks his eyebrow. "I've just gotten you healed, that will have to carry you over for a few hours."

An hour later, I'm showered and dressed, sipping a cup of tea at the breakfast bar. Ty stands behind me, massaging my shoulder the way my therapist showed him, sneaking kisses. After all we've been through over the past few weeks, something has shifted between us. We're settled into a deep sense of trust. Unity. Something unbreakable.

A knock on the front door startles me, and Ty darts over to answer, saluting my folks who are approaching from the guest room as he cruises past. A few minutes later, a middle-aged woman with styled silver hair rolls two racks of high-fashion clothing into the living room. Close behind, a slight, dark-haired man follows with another rack of beautiful gowns

I recognize him as Christian Siriano, the famous designer.

"What's going on, Ty?" My eyes are as wide as saucers.

"You need some things to wear for the press interview and our holiday show. Ronni arranged for her stylist friend, Lily, to make sure you, your mom, and Alex are well taken care of." Ty wraps his arms around me. "Oh, and Zoey, Olivia, please meet Christian, he's graciously agreed to create Zoey's red-carpet look."

My mom is starstruck at first, as am I, but the designer is so gracious soon we're both at ease. Alex joins us a half-hour later and the three of us spend the next few hours trying on clothes and joking with Lily and Christian as they measure and pin the different outfits we pick out. After they leave, I'm not-so-surprisingly exhausted but psyched about the outfits I'll have when I face the public again.

While the three of us ladies were immersed in being fashionistas, Ty and Dad took off to grab lunch. When they return, we're out lounging by the pool.

"Hey, beautiful." Ty sits on my lounge chair wearing a loose T-shirt, baseball cap, mirrored aviators, and flip-flops. "Did you have fun?"

"It was *so* good, especially because Mom didn't embarrass me." I lower my Prada sunglasses, squinting against the sun.

"Zoey!" Mom chastises, still rocking a black bikini at age fifty-nine.

Alex pipes up from her lounger. "You're going to lose it when you see her dress."

"I always lose it when I see Zoey." Ty bends down to kiss me.

Dad joins us and sits on mom's lounger. "We're all set."

"For what?" When I sit up, my hot-pink-and-black bikini top shifts slightly, causing Ty's eyebrows to rise above his sunglasses.

"We picked up some groceries for a barbeque." Ty kisses my head. "We're cooking some dinner. The guys are on their way."

"I can help, babe." I start to get up, only to have Ty shake his head and motion for me to lie back down before he heads to the sliding glass door. My mom and dad follow.

Alex smirks, "Z, let your man take care of you, he's so good at it."

"You have a wise best friend, butterfly," Ty calls over his shoulder before disappearing into the house.

"Duh!" Alex calls back.

"Are you ever going to tell me what's going on with you and Jace?" I say quietly so only Alex can hear me.

She winces. "Zoey, the truth is I probably fucked it up."

"C'mon, you've been doing this dance for years." I lower my sunglasses. "He's a great guy."

"He's hot, he's funny, he's sexy, and we can't seem to figure it out. Especially—" Alex stops herself.

I crinkle my brow. "Especially what?"

"Nothing. It's not my place to say." Alex flips over onto her stomach. "Let's just say after everything you've been through, I'm hoping we'll work out. We're both tired of hiding, but I'm not sure where we stand."

"I'm sorry. I know that our situation hasn't helped over the years." I turn over too and rest the side of my face on my folded arms.

Alex swats a fly away from her face. "No offense, but it doesn't have anything to do with you guys. I'm just facing it head-on."

Through the sliding glass door, we can hear the telltale commotion that Ty's band brothers have arrived. We look up at the same time to see shirtless Jace standing in the doorway wearing board shorts and flip-flops, his long, blond hair blowing in the slight breeze. Mirrored shades cover his eyes, but it's clear he's appreciating Alex in her full bikini glory.

"I need a minute." Alex gets up, wraps a towel around her waist and heads to the guest cottage where she's staying.

Jace goes back inside. I can see him perched at the breakfast bar through the window. I get up and pad into the kitchen where Ty and my dad are preparing trays of steaks for the BBQ, a bunch of corn on the cob, and a big bowl of potato salad. I wave to Ronni, who's sitting at the counter next to Connor and Jace. Zane lounges on the couch in the living room, talking on the phone.

"If you don't cover yourself up, I'm liable to pop a boner and embarrass both of us." Ty comes up behind me and whispers into my ear, "You're so fucking hot I want a repeat of this morning as soon as possible."

Swatting him and giggling, I head to our bedroom and throw on a white caftan. When I check myself in the mirror, for the first time since the accident, I look normal. Except for some lingering headaches, I actually *feel* normal.

A lot of it can be chalked up to deliberately avoiding all social media and gossip sites, which has been great for my mental health and recovery. I glance over at Ty's tablet on the nightstand. Unable to resist, I pick it up, wondering if I should see what was happening.

"Put it down, baby." Ty stands in the doorway before crossing the room toward me.

I set it down. "You're right."

"You have press training before the interview tomorrow." Ty's cheek rests on the top of my head as he cuddles me. "Everything has leveled out. Don't go down the rabbit hole. Let's enjoy everyone in the safety of our house tonight."

"Yes. We can do that." I tighten my grip on him as we hold each other.

"I'll go grill the steaks." Ty pulls away but keeps a grip on my waist. "And then I'm sending everyone away so we can get a good night's sleep."

I waggle my eyebrows. "Sleep?"

"Well, at some point." Ty laughs and heads back to the kitchen.

Everyone has a great time eating, drinking and swimming until the early evening. Alex and I hang out with Ronni. Getting to know her is fantastic. She shares the funniest stories of when she and Ty were in their fauxmance and all the mischief they'd get up to.

I can't help but notice how Connor doesn't take his eyes off Ronni and Jace doesn't take his eyes off Alex, but both rockers sit stoically, listening to the three of us giggle and gossip. Ty, Zane and Carter seem to be in a deep and compelling conversation about music with my folks. My dad is a thousand-percent starstruck.

As I look around at the group, it feels like a million years since New York.

Ty catches my eye and winks. Everything is behind us, now. It doesn't matter what anyone says or writes about us.

We know the truth.

Together, we're invincible.

Chapter Fifty-Five

Two Days Later

THE TOWN CAR WHISKS us through Hollywood on our way to the television studio. I play with Zoey's fingers while she looks out the window. Feeling confident, I'm actually looking forward to the interviews we have lined up.

Zoey is beautiful in a simple black-and-white, color-blocked jumpsuit with black Prada boots. Her hair is styled in beachy waves and her understated makeup is perfect. I wear dark jeans, a white T-shirt, and green Valentino sneakers, which Zoey picked out for me during her meeting with Lucy.

"Are you nervous?" I bring her pink-tipped fingers to my lips.

She gazes at me, her eyes flickering green and gold in the sunlight. "Yeah, actually. I'm a little out of my element."

"You're going to be so great, don't worry about a thing," I reassure her.

Zoey leans her head on my shoulder. "It's intimidating."

"You'll be fine, just remember to think through your answer and be authentic. You can't go wrong." I snuggle her into my side. I'm never letting her forget that I have her back.

She strokes my thigh, causing my dick to perk up. "Do you know how good you are at this? You're so unbelievably poised and professional. It's very sexy."

"Knock it off, butterfly." I jokingly swat at her. "You're getting me all riled up on purpose."

"Fine, okay." She crosses her arms and slumps into the seat, giving me a sly grin from the side. "I think my idea is better than an interview though."

Once we arrive, after a whirlwind of activity from producers, makeup and lighting, we sit in two bar-height director's chairs facing Diane Kennedy, the network host of the segment. My team ensured me this will be a soft-ball interview, to re-establish focus on the foundation.

While I take the lead for most of the interview, Zoey kills it when she's asked questions. Not only does she look radiant and serene, her confidence and passion about the foundation and its mission comes through loud and clear.

She easily deflects Diane's query about the accident and our relationship in a way that is satisfying yet not over-revealing. When we finish a few hours later, we take some pictures with various staff at the studio and get into the car to head home.

With our media commitments behind us and the negative press mostly turned around, I can finally focus on the holiday show tomorrow, which is sold out. We're playing in front of nearly sixty thousand people. Because it's the last live show LTZ will play before our hiatus, we all want it to be extraordinary. Zane and Connor have taken the lead with our lighting and technical team, and when they share their plans it makes me giddy with anticipation.

The next day while me and my band brothers handle soundcheck and more media interviews. Zoey spends the day with Ronni getting beautified for the red carpet courtesy of Ronni's glam-squad. I arrive back home in the nick of time to change, and we're off for Zoey's first big Hollywood event night.

My beautiful girl clutches my hand as we walk the red carpet, looking stunning in a pink fluttery dress with silver straps and silver sandals. Her shiny, blonde hair is loose but held up by a myriad of small braids. I felt a bit showy in a Dolce & Gabbana black suit patterned with gold and silver stars, but Zoey and her mom gush over the outfit, so I wear it.

As the lights of the photographers flash and we pose on the step-and-repeat, I ignore all requests for my picture without Zoey. Making sure she's tightly by my side, we give the press ample opportunity to capture us as a couple from all angles.

On the other hand, when the paps request a photograph of Zoey on her own, I happily step away to let them capture my stunning girl in all her glory.

Both of us are in great moods. Last night, our interview aired. The response has been overwhelmingly positive, and the requests for more interviews, reality TV shows, and other appearances are being fielded by my new team. As far as I'm concerned, until it's time to promote the foundation and Zoey's role as CEO next year, my days of media-pandering are now done.

After the red carpet, we head straight to the venue to get ready for the show. Led in by a recovered Sergey, Alex and Zoey's mom and dad meet us in our dressing room. Zoey changes into more comfortable concert clothes and emerges wearing black, distressed jeans laced together at the sides and her vintage Van Halen shirt, cut out in all the right places.

"Holy shit! Is that—" I run to her.

Zoey twirls. "Yep, Mom found it in my closet."

"I'm still not too thrilled about it." Olivia raises an eyebrow. "Too much skin."

"Well I am! I love it, it's so perfect!" I run my hands along Zoey's sides, caressing the bits of soft skin through the tears in the shirt. "I'm having a flashback to the first time seeing you. My heart has never been the same."

Zoey stands on her tip-toes to kiss me, which I eagerly return tenfold.

I strip off my dress shirt and blazer and throw on an LTZ T-shirt and change into my combat boots, opting to keep the starry, shiny pants from the suit on. The rest of the guys filter in and change and we settle into our pre-show routine of vocal warm-ups, visualizations and, for Connor and Zane, shots of whisky.

Out of the corner of my eye I see Alex tentatively walk toward Jace, who's leaning on the edge of the sofa with his arms crossed and his head down. He looks up at her and shakes his head sadly. Her expression crumples and she tenderly brushes his dirty-blond hair from his eyes. He manages a weak smile, and she whispers something into his ear before returning to Zoey's side where they speak in hushed tones.

Jace has been there for me without question for nearly a decade. Maybe I can return the favor. "Can I help?"

He shakes his head. "Nope."

"Wanna talk about it?" I place my hand on his shoulder

He glares at me. "Nope."

"You've been there for me, dude." I catch his eye. "I'm here for you, too."

Jace exhales a breath that he seems to have been holding for a week. "Let's just get this show under our belt, once I take care of a few things I'll fill you in."

Just as I'm about to reply, we get the signal it's time for the show. All of us follow the venue manager, Spinal Tap style, through the labyrinth of hallways to the side of the stage, where Zoey, Alex, Ronni, and Zoey's parents take seats on a short bleacher area.

I can tell it's going to be one of those rare, perfect-energy shows. When the lights dim and the crowd begins screaming and chanting "L-T-Z," the familiar rush of adrenaline flows through my body as Jace taps out the drumbeat to *Rise*.

Fueled by the love in the room, I throw myself fully into the performance and savor every minute. Whether interacting with my bandmates or the audience, we're electric and everyone is going nuts. On the sidelines, Zoey, Alex and Ronni laugh and dance and seem to be having a great time.

I can't help but think that just a year ago, I couldn't have imagined this would be my life today.

We play nearly two hours. It's the most energized, fun, charged show that I can remember. In preparation for the first encore, the four of us wait in the wings to perform the one song we'll never leave out of our set. Before we take the stage again, Zoey hops down from her seat on the bleachers and flings her arms around me.

"That's the best show I've ever seen you play, rock star!" She's radiant.

"Well, we haven't played your song, yet." I kiss her fully on the lips and see Zane take his position out of the corner of my eye. "I have a surprise so don't miss it!"

Magically, at that exact moment the light show begins. A spotlight pinpoints Zane who sits under a single blue light playing an extended flamenco guitar solo that meshes perfectly against a backing track of a bubbling river. It's mesmerizing, even for me. The huge crowd is so entranced, the venue is nearly silent except for Zane's guitar.

As he builds up the melody, the river sound fades and the lights flicker in blues, greens, and purples, mimicking the look of the sun shining on the top of water. Zane's talented fingers moved up and down the frets, as the beautiful unaccompanied melody morphs slowly into the opening notes of

Butterfly. As he draws it out, the crowd starts to recognize the notes and loses their collective minds.

Dramatically, Zane strums the last flamenco note and holds his hand up high above his head, pick in hand, and throws it into the audience. He flutters his hand all around and stops, poised on the neck of his guitar. Timing it perfectly, he launches into the actual intro to the song at the exact same time the lights go black.

A single white, hazy light beams out into the crowd, pulling back quickly to reveal the most beautiful light show of 3-D colorful butterflies, which appear to be fluttering and flying around the entire stadium.

Gasping at the beauty of the display, Zoey grabs my hand and looks at me with wide eyes.

I give her a sweet kiss before taking my position on stage to sing my butterfly her song.

Chapter Fifty-Six

Minutes Later

As Ty sings the final notes to *Butterfly*, I'm actually sad. I don't want the splendor of the performance to end. It feels like living in a fairy tale, all the digital butterflies are so delightful fluttering all over the venue, sometimes landing on the guys as they play. LTZ's fans are enthralled, not only at the amazing light effects but at the emotional performance. It is, after all, probably the last time they'll be on stage for at least a year.

When the final notes end, Ty steps up to the mic.

"All of us at LTZ thank you so much for coming out tonight. Give a hand to Jace Deveraux on drums!" Jace obliges with a quick drum solo to the delight of the crowd.

"Connor McLoughlin on bass!" Connor thumps his thumb on the strings, popping out a funky beat.

"My brother Zane Rocks on lead guitar!" Zane jumps up and down in place, bopping his head while launching into the song *Eruption* by Van Halen to whoops and hollers from the audience.

"I'm Ty but I think it's finally time for you to officially meet my better half." Ty looks over at me on the sidelines and holds his hand out. A white spotlight finds its way to me and suddenly my face is plastered on every screen in the venue. My shocked and embarrassed expression causes the crowd to laugh and then everyone at the venue starts cheering.

I shake my head and try to escape, but Ty has other plans.

"Don't let my girl be so shy, do you want to meet Zoey?" Ty smiles at me from the front of the stage and motions for me to join him.

"Get out there!" Alex appears by my side and pushes me forward toward Ty.

"Fine!" I walk out to Ty, who clasps me to his side and plants a massive kiss right on my lips.

"This is Z, everyone. This is my butterfly, *the* butterfly," Ty says proudly.

If I'm honest, I equally want to crawl under a rock and jump into his arms, neither of which is appropriate, so I stand there like an idiot. A *touched* idiot.

As I brace for the boos and jeers, the lights shine in my face. I realize you can't see anyone past the first couple of rows. A thunderous round of cheers and whoops take over the entire place. It keeps going. And going.

Laughing, Ty reaches for my hand and the rest of the band surrounds us. They swoop down in a dramatic bow, taking me with them.

I finally manage to run off stage as Ty addresses the audience. "You ready for a few more tunes?"

The entire venue goes ballistic. The rest of LTZ resumes their places and look at Ty.

"We feel like jammin' and playing a few covers from our favorite bands, does that sound alright?" Ty holds the mic out to a rousing chorus of approval.

For the next hour, the band show off their chops by playing everything from rock classics *Whole Lotta Love, Sweet Child O'Mine, and Runnin' with the Devil* to a Seattle tribute of *Jesus Christ Pose, River of Deceit, Man in the Box, In Bloom,* and *Black.* To round out the segment, Carter joins them for a trio of Limelight songs.

It's a party scene. Everyone sings along. All of us on the sidelines are right there with them. It's seriously the most fun I've had in such a long time. My mom and dad are over the moon. Alex, Ronni, and I dance until our feet hurt. As the clock nears midnight, LTZ can't extend the fun anymore and they end with a throwback Beatles song *The End.*

"Good night, Los Angeles." Ty salutes the roaring crowd and waves. "See you guys later!"

Beaming at my gorgeous man as he steps offstage, it occurs to me that with this performance behind the band, Ty and I are now, officially, on vacation.

With the exception of the after party, of course. All of us stay until the bitter end because my parents are enjoying hobnobbing with all the celebrities who attended the show. Ronni and Alex work the room with Jace and Connor tracking their every move. Ty and I stay secluded in a corner and hang out with whoever comes to us.

It's crazy that this room full of A-listers not only knows who I am, but they're empathetic and enraged at what happened to me. To *us*.

When we finally make it home around 4 a.m. and are alone in our room, I wrap my arms around Ty's waist, nestling my head against his neck. Ty rests his chin on my head and enfolds me against his chest.

"What an unreal few days," I murmur. "I'm a little dazed."

"Well, we took charge of our own destiny, and now we're free." Ty presses a kiss to my temple and tips my chin up to look at him with his finger.

I feel so calm and at peace. "We've come a long way these past nine months."

"I was thinking that when I saw you with your parents, Alex, and Ronni backstage." Ty's eyes are bright.

"By the way, Ronni's really nice, you were right." I burrow deeper into his embrace. "I've had so much fun with her the past couple of days."

"Well, I'm sure you'll be seeing her around every now and then." Ty strokes my hair and begins the tedious task of unwinding a million braids. "I loved these, what a cool hairstyle."

I reach up to help him. "I had to step up my game for my gorgeous man."

"It's the other way around, always." Ty's lips sip from mine. "I'm excited to head home so we can kick back and enjoy the holidays. We have an entire year to make up for all of those other years we missed. I think a tropical destination should be our goal."

"Heaven." He smells so good, always grapefruit and leather. It's the scent that instantly makes me feel like I'm exactly where I need to be. I can't help kissing down his throat.

"You're my heaven, Z." He reaches down to the hem of my old Van Halen T-shirt and lifts it over my head, and then unclasps my black bra and pulls it off my shoulders.

I wind my hands around his neck and tilt my mouth toward his. Our kisses are passionate, but so much more. Like we're promising each other that no one will ever come between us again. When Ty rolls my nipple into a taut peak, I moan. His lips move downward, grazing my neck before he swipes his tongue over my other nipple.

Weeks of stress and recuperation have created a lot of pent-up sexual energy. The past few mornings of sweet, careful lovemaking have only scratched an itch. I need him.

I tug his shirt off and he sheds the rest of his clothes. Taking Ty by the hand, I lead him to our big bed and drag him on top of me. He's being careful, which is fine. I know he doesn't want to hurt my ribs. Sweetly, he braces his upper torso on his strong arms, hovering just enough so my beaded nipples brush against his chest. He rubs his scruffy day-old stubble along my chin, teasing me before seeking my lips for more kisses.

Reaching between us, I take Ty's cock and stroke the tip against my wet pussy before arching up to receive him. He sinks into me fully, sighing, and resting his forehead against mine.

"This is where I belong." Ty's voice is like a prayer.

Moving together in our perfect rhythm, I thread my fingers through his long hair and caress his face. Over and over he slowly and deliberately plunges inside me, taking me to places I can only ever go with him.

To places, we can only ever go together.

Where our hearts, minds and bodies are endless.

Epilogue - Two Weeks Later

I'VE GONE BACK AND forth about how I want to do it, but I ultimately thought that a quiet, private evening at home for Christmas Eve dinner with Zoey and our closest friends and family would be the perfect setting.

Zoey's mom and I spent the day preparing a beautiful beef roast, mashed potatoes, gravy, asparagus, and chocolate-peanut butter cake for dessert. While I wait for Zoey to get showered and changed, Alex and her mom help me string up a bunch of twinkly lights in the living room. Zoey's mom arranges dozens of poinsettias and white roses around the room.

The table is set with a gold tablecloth, silver plates and goblets, and dozens of candles. A roaring fire blazes in the fireplace. I take a deep breath and survey the scene. I thought I'd feel more nervous, but everything is just right, the room is perfect.

Zoey's dad opens the front door and the guys and Carter pile into the house, not knowing what they're about to witness. They immediately tease me while I frantically try to shush them and get them settled down. Alex joins us a few minutes later. After what Zoey told me earlier, I can't help but notice that she's deliberately staying clear from Jace.

I care, of course, but tonight their situation is not my problem.

Now that everything is ready, I go find Zoey. Through the door to our bedroom, I see her sitting at the vanity in the bathroom spritzing her favorite Creed perfume on her neck. She wears a gauzy, green off-the-shoulder blouse with black satin pants. The front of her hair is pulled back while the rest is long and curled.

My heart stops. She literally takes my breath away.

Catching my eye in the mirror, her whole face lights up when she sees me ogling her. Hi, sexy!"

"My god, you're perfect." I walk over to her, place my hands on her shoulders and look at us through the mirror. I'm wearing a simple black Prada sweater with black slacks and black boots, nice but understated so she won't be suspicious.

Zoey turns around and reaches for my hand. "Is everyone here?"

"Yep. Everyone's here." I lead her out to the dining room.

When we step through the bedroom door into the living room, Zane and Connor begin to strum the Beatles song

And I Love Her. Zoey's eyes widen when she sees the living room has been transformed with the twinkly lights, candles, flowers, and our favorite people standing around with glasses of sparkly cider.

"What's going on? *Ty?*" Zoey's gorgeous hazel eyes dart everywhere.

I lead her over to the fireplace, look around at all our friends and family, and clasp Zoey's hands in mine. When I drop to one knee in front of her, Zoey immediately bursts into tears, which I hope are happy tears, so I forge ahead.

"Butterfly, you're the love of my life. From the moment I met you, through all of the years we were apart, and even more so now that we found each other again, it's been you. I want us to spend all of our days together whether we are traveling the world, running the foundation, raising beautiful babies, or just hanging out, growing old. There is nothing in the world that is more important to me than you, and I am asking you in front of our friends; well, really our family, will you be my wife?"

I pop open the black box revealing a gorgeous custom ten-carat diamond ring, with smaller diamonds hugging the bigger one.

"Oh, Ty." Zoey weeps openly as she throws her arms around me. "Yes, yes, yes, *yes!*"

Sliding the ring on her red-tipped finger, Zoey holds it up as everyone gathers around to see. For easily a good twenty minutes, we're embraced and surrounded by our family and my band.

Looking around, I catch Mike's and Olivia's eyes, both are emotional but happy. Alex hugs both of us and kisses Zoey on the cheek. Carter beams, happy and proud. Zane and Connor look like they're ready to eat.

Jace stands apart with a weird expression on his face that's supposed to be a smile, but looks more like a grimace. He keeps fiddling with something in his pocket.

My surveillance is interrupted by my beautiful butterfly looking up at me with love and adoration. Unable to resist, I bend to kiss her sweet lips and cling to her like a lifeline. Today is our day and even though I sense a bit of drama in the air with the rest of LTZ, everyone I love is in the room.

I'll be damned if anyone's going to interfere with our love story ever again.

"I love you, Ty," Zoey purrs against my lips. "I've been waiting for this moment since the moment I saw you at The Mission."

"Me too, butterfly." I cradle her in my arms. "My love for you is endless. You've made me the happiest man in the world."

Want more Ty & Zoey, here is a bonus scene.

"I wondered if it was normal to feel like I was physically addicted to Alex" ...for Jace & Alex's story read Limitless.

For all things Kaylene, sign up for her mailing list.

Behind the Scenes

Endless Edition

At the end of each book, I like to take you behind the scenes and share a few ramblings from my journey to publish.

Nothing in this section is edited or proofread, there will probably be typos (especially if I don't have my reading glasses on – don't judge, I just am in denial that I need them).

Since you're at the end of the book, you know that END-LESS is the story of Ty and Zoey. This entire book was a labor of love, and also a love letter to my hometown of Seattle.

Their story originated many years ago, Ty was the man I conjured up as my "dream man" at age fifteen. He is special to me because he is sweet, gorgeous, and sensitive, but he has inner strength and finds a way to truly take control over his life. A life that could have ended up so much differently. Zoey is the beautiful, strong woman who sees Ty for who he is deep inside, his perfect muse.

There are many ways to be strong. There are many ways to be alpha. At least, that's how I see it. To me, the sexiest type of guy is a man who learns to take care of his partner, and puts her needs above his own. Where he's able to overcome his own insecurities and realize that being strong isn't fighting. It isn't dominance. It isn't even being rich and successful.

It's putting your loved ones needs above yours.

In ENDLESS, I wanted to explore the journey of this concept from both Zoey's perspective as a young, impressionable woman and then Ty's later on, when he must do the same for Zoey. In both cases, they let each other go – with the risk that they won't actually make it as a couple. In Zoey's case, it's based on a misunderstanding and an immaturity that most of us have when we're barely eighteen. Later on, we see Ty making the same sacrifice – but with the maturity of someone who is a young adult.

Anyway!!!

Next up we have LIMITLESS, which explores the worldwide, whirlwind adventures of free-spirited Alex and laid-back Jace. It is a sex-ay little journey to say the least.

Words cannot express how much it means to me that you've read this book. As a new author, I would LOVE and APPRECIATE any feedback you have about the Less Than Zero world.

You can write me at kaylene@kaylenewinter.com and find out all about LTZ on my website .

One final note – it is super important it is for authors to receive as many reviews of their book as possible. I'd love it if you could leave me a review or rating. Here's a link to my author page.

If you haven't received your free book, please make sure to sign up for my mailing list and get RESTLESS here, it is the LTZ prequel starring Carter.

Love,

Dedication

G—you are my biggest supporter and push me to be better in everything that I do. Thank you for encouraging me to follow my dream and publish my first book. To Sheila and Kris, the inspirations for Alex and Ronni—before digital, before Kindle, back when we still typed on real typewriters—who knew that the book I wrote about all of our rock star "boyfriends" would lead us here.

About the Author

KAYLENE WINTER IS AN best-selling author of steamy, contemporary romance.

Each character-driven novel is filled with snappy dialogue, pop-culture references and enough steam to make you fan yourself. Kaylene weaves authenticity, emotion and angst into a turbulent rollercoaster ride of love, passion and soul-searing romance always ending with a delicious HEA.

Kaylene lives in Seattle with her amazing Irish husband and her Pomsky, Phalen. She loves creating art of all kinds.

Acknowledgments

This book was an absolute labor of love, and I couldn't have done it without the help and support of the following awesome rock stars:

Cover/Graphic Designer/Finder of Hotties: Regina Wamba

Editor: Grace Bradley

Formatting: Willow Yanarella

PR: Dani Sanchez, Wildfire Marketing

Agent: Stephanie, Phillips, SBR Media

Website Maven: Sherri Kiarsis, Ruby Moon Designs

My Right Hand: Willow Yanarella

YAY to KAYLENE'S KREW !!!

Beta Readers: Anna Theurer & Beth Carbutt

My Inspirations: Gareth, Sheila, Kris

OMG! To the ARC readers, bloggers, bookstagrammers & my Street Team – **I can't do this without you.**

Thank you thank you thank you for helping spread the word—I'm overwhelmed by your love, support, kindness, etc. Thank you for making my dream come true!

Other Titles